NOBLE
HORIZONS

CHURCH HOMES, INC.

Ex Libris

Noble Horizons

A gift from

Mt Washington Public Library

BUCKING
the SUN

Also by Ivan Doig
in Large Print:

Ride with Me, Mariah Montana
Dancing at the Rascal Fair

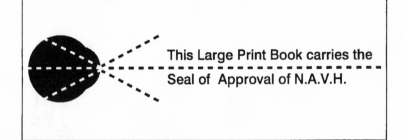

This Large Print Book carries the
Seal of Approval of N.A.V.H.

BUCKING
the SUN

Ivan Doig

Thorndike Press • Thorndike, Maine

Published in 1996 by arrangement with Simon & Schuster, Inc.

Thorndike Large Print ® Americana Series.

The tree indicium is a trademark of Thorndike Press.

The text of this Large Print edition is unabridged.
Other aspects of the book may vary from the original edition.

Set in 16 pt. Bookman Old Style.

Printed in the United States on permanent paper.

Library of Congress Cataloging in Publication Data

Doig, Ivan.
  Bucking the sun : a novel / Ivan Doig.
    p.   cm.
  ISBN 0-7862-0814-7 (lg. print : hc)
  1. Large type books. I. Title.
[PS3554.O415B83 1996b]
813′.54—dc20   96-20867

To novelists who deliver the
eloquence of the edge of the world
rather than stammers
from the psychiatrist's bin.

Roddy Doyle
Nadine Gordimer
Ismail Kadare
Thomas Keneally
Maurice Shadbolt
Tim Winton

Part One

THE SHERIFF

1938

Selfmade men always do a lopsided job of it, and the sheriff had come out conspicuously short on the capacity to sympathize with anyone but himself. No doubt ears still were burning at the Fort Peck end of the telephone connection; he'd had to tell that overgrown sap of an undersheriff he didn't give a good goddamn what the night foreman said about dangerous, get the thing fished out of the river if it meant using every last piece of equipment at the dam site. This was what he was up against all the time, the sheriff commiserated with himself during the drive from Glasgow now, toward dawn. People never behaving one bit better than they could get away with.

Die of eyelids, you could on this monotonous stretch of highway down to the dam, he reminded himself, and cranked open the window for night air to help keep him awake. He'd been up until all hours, sheriffing the town of Glasgow through the boisterous end of another week, and had barely hit bed when the telephone jangled. Catch up on sleep, the stupid saying went, but in five years as sheriff he had yet to see any evidence that the world worked that way, ever made it up to you for postponement of shuteye and all the other —

The cat-yellow shapes of bulldozers sprang huge into his headlights, causing him to blink and brake hard as he steered onto the approach to the dam. Past the bulks of earthmoving equipment parked for the night, on the rail spur stood a waiting parade of even more mammoth silhouettes, flatcars loaded high with boulders to be tumbled into place on the dam face. Then, like a dike as told by a massive liar, Fort Peck Dam itself.

The sheriff hated the sight of the ungodly pyramid of raw dirt that the dambuilders were piling across the throat of the Missouri River. He hated Franklin Delano Roosevelt for this project and its swarm of construction towns, if that's what you wanted to call such collections of shacks, and the whole shovelhead bunch down here who had to cut loose like orangutangs every Saturday night. Damn this New Deal crap. Wasn't there any better way to run a country than to make jobs out of thin air, handing out wage money like it was cigarette papers? The sheriff hated having to call himself a Democrat, though he knew that a person couldn't even get elected to town idiot these days without that tag.

By now he was nearing the floodlights, could see the workbarge with its crane arm poised and the cluster of men at the truck ramp where it must have happened. He crept the patrol car along the crest of the dam and when he parked made it a point not only to leave the car in gear but set the emergency brake, hard as he could yank it. Before heading down to the group at the water's edge, though, the sheriff stopped and took a long look east across the river, past last month's trouble here, to the bankside promontories of bluffs and badland ravines emerging in dawn outline like scissored shadows.

One thing Sheriff Carl Kinnick loved was his jurisdiction, his piece of the earth to tend justice on. The upper Missouri River country, or anyway the seventy-five-mile series of bends of the river that Valley County extended north from, like a castle footed into a seacoast. Kinnick's own climb up through life began beside this river, familyless boy mucking out barns and calcimining chickenhouses, working up to the haying jobs, the alfalfa-seed harvest jobs, up and up, squirreling every loose cent away until he had enough to make his start in Glasgow, the county seat. After that there was no stopping him, of course, but he'd always felt — still did feel — somehow that first lift into career, into politics (or as he preferred to think of it, law enforcement) had come from the spell of the river. As far as Carl Kinnick was concerned, the Missouri with its broad fast flow and its royal-green cottonwood groves and the deep bottomland that made the best farming in eastern Montana, the Missouri had been next thing to perfect the way it was. Until this Fort Peck project. Until this giant federal dike to put people to work with the excuse (*benefit*, the Roosevelters were always calling it) of stopping floods in the states downriver all the way to St. Louis. The sheriff believed it would be fitting justice if everything and everybody downriver dried up and blew away.

Duty. He picked his way from boulder to boulder down the riprap face of the dam to the cluster of men waiting for him. He nodded only to the night foreman. The owl-shift workers all had turned to watch him arrive, the bibs of their overalls fencing him in. The sheriff was the shortest by half a head in any group, and how he felt about that can be guessed.

Singling out his undersheriff, without preamble he asked what was delaying matters.

"We've about got it up, Carl, honest. The diver had a hell of a time with it in the dark down there."

The sheriff bit back an impulse to tell the big scissorbill that excuses are like buttholes, everybody's got one. Instead he folded his arms and rocked back and forth on the small heels of his boots while watching the crane at work. Its cable into the water was being reeled in by the operator on the barge, the steel strand making a steady low hum through the intricate pulleys of the boom arm, until suddenly — a lot quicker than the sheriff expected, actually — a wallowing sound came and then the splash of water falling away as the surface was broken upward by a Ford truck.

I've seen some lulus since I got myself elected to this badge, Kinnick thought as the vehicle dangled from the cable hooked around its front axle, water pouring from the wide cab and box as if a metal trough had been yanked straight up by one end. *But I never had to put up with them wrecking themselves on the bottom of the river before.*

11

For a moment he hoped the Ford's cab would be empty, then canceled that at the prospect of having to drag this river, lake, whatever this stretch of the Missouri amounted to anymore, for a body. Maybe, just maybe there hadn't even been anybody in the truck when the thing rolled down the ramp and plunged into the water about an hour after midnight. The section watchman swore he hadn't heard a motor running, only the splash; then when he raced over, he'd seen only what appeared to him in the lack of light to be the cab and boxboards of a truck going under. Maybe this was only a case of a poorly parked rig that coasted loose somehow. But if there wasn't some brand of human misbehavior involved in a truck visiting the bottom of the Missouri on a Saturday night at Fort Peck, Sheriff Kinnick was going to be plentifully surprised.

The Ford ton-and-a-half twisted slowly in the air like cargo coming ashore. When the crane operator lowered the load as far up the face of the dam as the boom arm would reach, the men clambered to it and the undersheriff, at Kinnick's impatient nod, wrenched the driver's-side door open.

The body question was settled instantly. Plural.

The woman lay stretched behind the steering wheel but turned sideways, facing down toward where the man had slid lengthwise off the seat, headfirst under the dashboard. Both were naked.

Without taking his eyes off the dead pair, the sheriff put out an arm and, even though he knew the gesture was useless, waved back the gawking damworkers behind him. This was the moment he always searched for in a case. The instant of discovery. Any witness's first view of what had happened, right there was where you wanted to start. Now that he himself was essentially the first onto the scene of whatever this was, though, the sheriff was more than a bit uncomfortable at the lack of exactitude here. An entire circus of circumstance, here before his eyes, yet somehow not as substantial as he would have liked. As if the bunch behind him with their necks out like an ostrich farm were sopping up, siphoning away what ought to be clearer to him than it was proving to be.

Kinnick got a grip on himself and tried to fix in mind every detail of how the couple lay in the truck cab, although the woman's bare white hip, the whole pale line of her body and the half-hidden side of her face, kept dominating his attention. No blood, no wounds, at least. He forced himself to balance on the running board and stick his head and shoulders just enough into the cab to reach across the woman to the gearshift. It proved to be in neutral, which made him uneasy; with these two people occupied with each other as they'd been, how the hell had something like that happened? He knew what he was going to find next, when he tried the emergency brake lever and it of course didn't hold at all; there wasn't a truck in Montana with any wear on it that didn't have the emergency brake burned out. Which made the damned gearshift situation even more —

A cloud of colors at the corner of his right eye startled him, making him jerk his head that direction. The wet wads of their clothing, plastered to the truck's rear window. The lighter wads must be their underwear.

"You know them or don't you?" the sheriff demanded over his shoulder, annoyed that he had to drag it out of the undersheriff.

Even then the undersheriff didn't say the names of the drowned two until Kinnick backed out of the cab and wheeled on him with a hot stare. The last name, Duff, the sheriff recognized from some trouble report or another — quite a family of them on the dam crew, a tribe of brothers and their wives, and a father, was it, into the bargain? — but the first names meant

14

nothing to him. That was what an under-sheriff was for.

Thankful isn't the word in circum-stances such as this, but Kinnick at least felt relieved that the undersheriff had named them off as a couple and that these river deaths shaped up as an accident, pure and plain. Terrible thing, but people were asking for it with behavior of the kind these two were up to out here in the middle of the —

The undersheriff still was staring into the truck, rubbing a corner of his mouth with a fist the size of a sledgehammer head, as if trying to make up his mind about something. The damworkers were overly quiet, too.

"What's the matter now?" Kinnick burst out. The little sheriff prided himself on always staying a few steps ahead in the mental department, but somehow he wasn't up with the expressions on all the rest of the men around the truck. *What's got them spooked?* It wasn't as if this dam had never killed anybody before. Naked and dead out in public wasn't good, no-body could say that. But you'd think it would take more than that to scandalize damworkers. Funny for a husband and wife to be out here going at it in a truck when they had a home of any kind, that was true. But Saturday night and all, who

15

knew what these Fort Peckers were apt to get up to. So what could be out of kilter, if this couple was — "They're married people, right? You said their names are both Duff."

The undersheriff hesitated. He hated dealing with this fierce doll of a man his job depended on.

"That's the thing about this, Carl," the undersheriff said at last. "Married, you bet. Only not to each other."

Part Two

THE MISSOURI
1933–1934

Siderius always kept to the same spiel, had it down slick by now: "Here on official business . . . kind of a hard thing, I know, but there's no getting around it . . . at least make you a fair offer." Saying it the same helped him, whether or not it did any good for these bottomland honyockers. But he hadn't come up against one like this before. The skinny man in worst workclothes was traipsing out of his riverside field of alfalfa toward Siderius's car in a zigzag route, taking his sweet time about it. With each step he put his foot down in firm aim, the way a kid playing hopscotch does. Then plotch down the other foot some other direction. As he crazy-gaited closer, it dawned on Siderius that the man was being sure to step on a grasshopper with every stride. The unmiti-

17

gated gall of the guy in figuring that he could stomp on enough grasshoppers to make any difference made Siderius mad, and when the hay farmer didn't so much as offer a handshake, just stood off at the fenceline to his precious field and looked him up and down, that did it: caused Siderius to jab the nasty part right out.

"Don't know if you'd've heard yet, but they're going to be putting up a big dam over by Glasgow."

"What's that to you and me and this fencepost?"

"This, this'll be under the lake."

"That's daft," the lofty man by the fence dismissed Siderius's assertion. "The Glasgow country," Hugh Duff spoke it a way Siderius had never heard, *Glazgeh,* "is a full hundred miles from here."

"More like a hundred and a quarter," Siderius let him know. "I just drove it."

"There you are, then." Still wearing his standoff expression, thin-faced, thin in every part of him, Hugh draped an arm on the fencepost, glanced back at his field of alfalfa and said as if in private amusement, "The blessed damn nature of farming is that we can always do with a dab more moisture than what we get. But we don't need it over our heads."

Siderius imitated Hugh Duff's measuring gaze across the field, pulled to the sight in spite of himself. The month of June was proving hard in this job, the early green height of summer and the work that went into these farms, the river-rich fields at their most promising: this time of year's habitual feel of crop and reward impended all along the bottom land. Add on that this brisk section of the river, so far upstream here where the Missouri forgot its wandering and fed through timbered bluffs in a straightforward course, this tucked-away cleft stretch of the river was an undeniable beauty, olive in hue and jeweled with sparkles from the sun at every ripple. Here and there stood pale attendant cliffs, the foundations of rock and time showing through, while the river trailed fertile sleeves along its steady channel. And put on top of the natural basis here that although this farmer was a lank specimen, his farm was not skin-and-bones. You could practically count like tree rings the year-by-year progress since this piece of land was homesteaded by these Duffs. That fence was taut as piano wire, the house and outbuildings which Siderius had driven down past to reach this bottomslope field showed every sign of decent care, and the field itself, a quarter-mile-long porch of luscious soil cupped right up against the sunny side of the river, was contour-sown in a way that ought to yield a junior fortune in seed alfalfa. Ought to. By now Siderius was staring with dread, past the fenceline figure, on across the green baize field to the rattletrap Model A pickup there and the trio of people at the job, the —

Siderius made himself not think any further in that direction and go back to work on the snippy farmer instead.

"Mister, I'm here to tell you, the dam is going to back up water this goddamn far. And it's my job to make you a price for your land."

Hugh went up and down Siderius with his eyes again, his expression saying he didn't care for any of what he saw. He cocked his head ever so slightly to the left. "That's a refrain we haven't heard, recent years. What, now that the banks have been on holiday, they can sneak you the backing to buy us out?"

"If you'd had your ears on, you'd know I already told you —" Halfway into his hot retort Siderius remembered he hadn't started this off as usual: *Backtrack, Chick,* he warned himself. *Sometimes to get ahead in this you need to.* Resorting to the recitation, he started in: "First off, I'm here on official —"

The dreaded smell was coming up strong from the field now on a shift of the wind: Siderius had to stop and gulp. The gulp was not a good idea. He had wondered how long his stomach could hold out, and the banana-oil odor, sweetly rotten, of what the people at the pickup were working at was finally too much. As he went sick he saw that the farmer was regarding him with more of that private amusement. Siderius put up the palm of his right hand toward the man, as if in a *halt* motion or the taking of an oath, marched behind his car and threw up. When he was thoroughly done retching and then spitting out as much of the taste as he could, he stayed hunched there with his hands on his knees, the only sound now the hail-like ping of grasshoppers hitting against all sides of the car. *This is your last one, Chick,* he had to rally himself, *the farthest up on their damn map of everything they're going to drown. Finish this one and you're done with these poor eaten-out bastards.* He straightened, mopped his mouth with his handkerchief, then went back to the waiting business at the fenceline.

"I'm not out here landhawking," Siderius this time told Hugh Duff, as if deathly tired of it all. "The government, the U.S. of A. government hired me on to do this."

From the far end of the field, the other three Duffs watched. The two of them who were mixing the next fifty-gallon batch of

21

grasshopper poison wondered out loud.

"That's a government Chevy," Neil pronounced, and Bruce nodded as if he'd known so. They were brothers, you could practically see that in the crimp of their hats. "Must be quite the job, whatever it is," Neil pondered. "Suppose they actually pay that guy to drive around in that?"

"Who it is," came Bruce's rendition, "is Herbert Heifer Hoover, out selling the cure for grasshoppers, and the Old Man's trying to jimmy the price down a little." Inch-long hoppers batted against the pantlegs of both young men as Bruce bucketed riverwater into the mixture of sawdust, poison, and attractant while Neil stirred with a long-handled shovel. "And he better hurry up," Bruce concluded.

"Whoa, the stuff feels ready," Neil called off Bruce's bucket-trips to the river. "Careful how we pour, okay?"

Bruce asked with a bit of a smirk: "Speaking of careful, how's your love bite?"

"Smarts a little, is all," Neil replied shortly. A burn the size of a dime was eating at his shin where the top of his sock would normally reach. Yesterday the grasshopper bait somehow had splashed once and soaked through his pantleg, the poison inflicting itself there overnight. Nothing serious, Neil figured, although you probably would not want to make a habit of spilling arsenic on yourself.

"You want to know what I really like about this?" Bruce provided as they poured the mushlike mix into the spreading machine. "All this free banana-oil cologne. Women'll be able to smell us a mile off."

As soon as the words were out of his mouth, he knew he'd laid himself open. All Neil would have to put in on him was something like *In your case, what's new about that much stinkum?* Nothing came, though. Bruce checked across the barrel of mix, saw the little grin on Neil, and realized with a flush that the silence had been the retort. It was as good as said, and that was good enough for Neil.

There. This is what it takes, the woman waiting behind the steering wheel of the pickup, watching the fenceline tableau of Hugh and the government man, told herself fixedly. There were times, and this was one, when Hugh had to be absolutely hit between the eyes with a fact. For a moment, seeing the car come, she had wished the news could deliver itself some more gentle way; then decided no, she didn't either. Let it get over with all at once, bango.

For waging war against grasshoppers, Meg Duff wore one of Hugh's old workshirts, bib overalls, and a scarf tightly tied, despite the heat in the pickup cab, to keep stray hoppers from flying into her hair. Under each edge of the bib of her overalls a neat roundness showed, as if she had an apple in each shirt pocket. With her hair tucked up under the scarf only the little vee of origin at the back of her neck showed the interesting color of honeyed brunette. Her skin was not the sort that sun and wind are kind to. Her eyes, though, were the memorable blue of a Wedgwood piece (the sons produced by her and Hugh were copies of his tall spare Duff build, but their eyes and hair color fetchingly took after her side) and she had a little nock in her chin, a tiny divided place like a mark of character. Long years of practice at holding herself together, otherwise known as marriage to Hugh, had made Meg her own best judge, and this minute of back and forth in herself bothered her, even scared her some. *Don't be afraid of being scared,* she bolstered herself. *This is a family that can use some sense scared into it just now.*

"Ready again, Mother," Neil came up to the cab of the pickup and told her. "Let's murder some more bugs."

"We're becoming all too practiced at it," she took the moment to tell him, "but still, Neil, be careful how you go." Her edge-of-the-bed voice, more deep and dramatic than a woman's generally reached, had the assumption that it could steer these sons of hers past casual poison as handily as it had carried them through every childhood ailment.

She put the pickup in low gear and began driving at as much speed as possible along the outside edge of the alfalfa. As she did, Bruce piled into the back of the pickup to mind the five-gallon cans of extra water, and Neil stood virtually beside her on the running board of the driver's side, an arm up inside the cab to hold him in place, and watched behind to see that the spreader was working. In sporadic sweeps, the bait spewed out the way grain falls when scattered by the panful: the watered sawdust mush, the amyl acetate "banana oil" mixed in to act as attractant, the adhering arsenic.

In the field of alfalfa beside the swath of poison, the grasshoppers amounted to a creeping acid. When the pickup wasn't running, they could be heard making a meal of everything that grew; that undersound of millions of minuscule mouths each biting through a leaf a stem, a stalk.

Every year the same surprise, Meg silently cried the thought across the infested field to Hugh. This had been a wet year until spring seemed fully launched, no hint of the hot dry previous turns of weather that made grasshopper eggs hatch in profusion. But then came rainless days for the last of April and then May and then on into June, and the clouds of grasshoppers rose from the ground one more time. Stubborn against the evidence as usual, Hugh still maintained that the grasshoppers could not keep on being annual, just as he'd kept saying the price for a coveted seed crop such as alfalfa could not continue going down and down. *Out we climbed, and found ourselves in deeper.* The ragged chant of riddle from their schooldays in Inverley pertained exactly to this situation of them and the place, Meg was convinced, although Hugh would never admit so. Nor let himself see ahead in the family, for that matter. Of these two sons of theirs here working themselves blue in the face against grasshoppers, Neil might have stayed with the place, but Bruce already was as good as gone. What seemed to be coming over him were runaway impulses, in more ways than one. Men never pay attention to how their voices carry, so Meg had heard the news through her open kitchen window one haul day. Bruce had taken a pickup load all the way over to the seed warehouse in Glasgow — the offer price was pennies better there — and when he drove back into the yard just before supper, there came the slam of the pickup door, Neil's offhand asking of "How was town?" and Bruce's proud report, "Got laid and everything."

In certain circumstances you would just as soon not know the behavior of your offspring, Meg reflected at the time, if for no other reason than it sets up unwelcome comparisons. For all her surge of motherly shock at Bruce, part of her already could not help but be amused by that *everything.* It played in her mind, stayed with her like a teasing tune as she contemplated Hugh and herself and their long tug-of-war over what was love and what was lure and where lay the confusing ground between. Did the everything of her and Hugh have to forever include the portion she would sometimes like to bat out of him with a broom, as well as the share of him that she would not have traded for all the silk in China?

By now not only was the afternoon boiling, so was the engine of the pickup. Roaring along in low gear was necessary for spreading the grasshopper bait as thoroughly as possible, but it meant she had to stop often for Bruce and Neil to hop down and put water in the radiator. This was everybody's least favorite chore, unscrewing the cap of a hot radiator. All they could do, though, was for one or the other to wrap his right arm in a coat and with a gloved hand cautiously loosen that cap a little at a time until the pressure, and the chance of being scalded, went down. Watching, Meg always held her breath a little.

Not today. She never even looked as Bruce fought the radiator cap and compared it to the temperature of the doorknob of Hell. Across the field, she saw Hugh drop his arm from that affectionate rest on the fencepost, saw him stand differently.

"Let me get my feet under me, a minute," Hugh was saying slowly, there at the fenceline. "Land like this, taken for a dam halfway across Montana from here? You're sure you're on the reach of the river that you think you are, are you?"

Siderius compressed his lips and simply nodded yes.

"I can't believe you," Hugh spoke as if telling him the time of day. "A dam that'd — why would they do such a thing?"

"It's kind of beyond me," Siderius was forced to admit, "but they're about gonna do it." In spite of himself he shook his head at what was even harder to swallow. "With dirt, no less."

Hugh Duff's face changed radically.

Watching the man, Siderius warily got back to the part he knew by heart, "appraisal involved . . . so-much per acre . . . fair deal as possible but . . ." But none of it made a dent in the stricken look that had come over the farmer. The growl of the pickup from the far side of the field, the yelps of the two young men whenever the spreader clogged or the radiator spewed, all seemed as lost on this man Duff as Siderius's spiel.

Perplexed, Siderius decided to jump ahead of himself again and offer:

"You'll get preference."

"What's that supposed to mean, preference."

"In getting hired. At the dam project."

Hugh let out an alarming chuckle, a sound of mirth gone dry and bitter. "Man, do I look anything like a skilled hand at that sort of work?"

You look about like any other sad sonofabitch of a honyocker who needs a job, of whatever the hell kind, Siderius thought. *About like me.*

"Listen," he told the other. "I don't know if this helps any at all, but I been through this myself. The dam's going in right on top of me. I had a hundred and sixty acres of the best seed alfalfa you ever saw, just this side of Fort Peck."

29

Duff didn't even blink at him.

Siderius shrugged. "At least there's jobs with the dam, we anyway ought to be thankful for that."

Hugh studied him bleakly. "And you're right there at the head of the sugar-tit line. No wonder you puke at the sight of yourself."

"I'm at least doing something besides the grasshopper quickstep," Siderius shot back. "How many summers now you been walking that way? Three? Four?"

"I'm stepping on my own ground," Hugh said in the coldest tone Siderius had ever heard, "not on the necks of my neighbors."

Afterward, in the years of the Fort Peck Dam project, Chick Siderius stayed leery of the Duffs. By then he couldn't see that they had any gripe coming, they'd been paid the exact damn same for their land as everybody else. And they did end up with jobs, the whole slew of them, didn't they? But even when Siderius spotted one of their women — good God, their women — he would cross the street to stay out of their way. He never forgot how treacherous the exchange with that old bearcat Hugh suddenly turned, there at the fenceline, and the final flub he'd made in trying to calm things down. All Siderius had said was:

"At least you and the wife aren't up against this alone. If I know family resemblance when I see it, you've got a couple of sons helping you out, right?"

"We've three," Hugh Duff had given the government hiree that terrible corroded chuckle again, then swung around as if to hurl the next sentence across the field. *Haven't we, Meg.* When it came, the words practically spat from him. "But one's a dirt dam engineer."

The sheriff later dug up the fact that, back there in '33 when the alfalfa farmers were being cleared out of the Missouri River bottomland and in turn hired to clear the dam site of brush and cottonwoods, the name *Duff* was already part of the Fort Peck vocabulary. It gave Sheriff Kinnick something more to think about, that this dogfight bunch amounted to, what would you have to say, the first family of the dam? As well as being the authors of that truck in the river. Where the Duff record was concerned, the sheriff spent immense time trying to get his mind around the size of all the contradiction. But then, he would remind himself bitterly, that was always the thing about the cockeyed dam. From day one, everything about Fort Peck was going to set a record.

W. abutment: layer cake —
  glac'l till
    on
  alluv'l silt etc.
    on
  Bearpaw shale

The Eversharp pencil paused on the pocket notebook, then rapidly jotted down:

E. abutment: badlands —
  B'paw shale up the gigi

"So what do you think of her, Duff? You ready to make mudpies with Miz Missouri?"

Day one at Fort Peck for Owen Duff had come in early May of 1933, in company with a handful of other first hires specked across a bald knob on the bluff overlooking one particular crimp of the river.

The wind was up, naturally, and Owen could have kicked himself for not wearing his wool-collared short mackinaw instead of trying to appear climateproof for the Army Corps of Engineers big shots. The other civilian engineers looked equally chilblained, but Owen alone had grown up in this northern Montana wind, was so habited to it that even in the High Line Hotel in Glasgow he would catch himself slanting ahead into a braced position when he felt the start of a breeze through an opened window.

Never mind with the weather, he instructed himself. *This is the damnedest chance anybody ever dreamed of. Charlene will see. This is something we'll be able to hang our hats on for the rest of our lives.* Tucking his notebook and mechanical pencil into their accustomed pocket of his garbardine jacket, he turned and answered Sangster:

"I'm ready for any sonofabitching thing that constitutes construction."

"Uh huh," the shorter man agreed. "If the railroad cut back any more, I'd have had to figure out how to teach trains to jump creeks."

From Owen's own line of engineering there was a similar stock of standard wisecracks he could have chosen from, about trying to underbid gophers on tunnelwork, or the difficulty Montana dogs were having in burying their bones with so many unemployed dirt engineers eager to do it for them, and so on; but he didn't trouble to. Not now, not here, not worth interrupting this chance at absolutely kicking aside the Depression and its lame jokes. Instead, arms crossed and hands tucked in his armpits for warmth's sake, he walked the same few strides back and forth as he kept studying the course of the Missouri below. Owen was an even six feet tall, and thin except in the head. There, a strong forehead and brunette eyebrows and china-blue eyes oversaw a surprisingly wide-cut mouth where the usual expression was partly quizzical, partly provocative. When that mouth was set seriously, as now, he looked a lot like a bothered Will Rogers.

"Enjoying the sights of Fort Peck?" he abstractedly asked Sangster. There was no fort to Fort Peck anymore, or for that matter, anything except the matching benches of land and the flat floor of the river valley that had beckoned up from the Corps of Engineers map as a dam site. A stockaded trading post briefly propped up by sternwheel steamboat traffic, the last of Fort Peck had been swept off its ledge at the base of this bluff by high water sometime in the 1890s; the name, though, had the lives of a cat, attaching itself to the nearby Indian reservation and now to the dam notion that had these engineers by the eyes. In this first hundred days of the New Deal, as the Roosevelt administration wheeled laws, funds, money, and projects into being, the senior senator from Montana — fortuitously named Wheeler — had been right at the head of the line for a dam and ten thousand jobs here.

Owen and Sangster and the other fresh civvie engineers had been briefed half to death about this project already, but a good long stare at this remote stretch of the Missouri had things to tell them, too. The first of which was, on this river that scrawled from west to east for hundreds of miles across upper Montana, the axis of the dam was not going to be crosswise to that, north-south as every fiber of logic said it had to be. The river hadn't heard the logic, and as if bored with the oxbow bends it had been scrolling all the way across Valley County, here it shot out of its writhings with a notion to keep going north. It was the midpoint of this north-ward veer, the Fort Peck speck of geography, that presented the dam site, a narrower and higher set of benchlands than where the lazy curves were.

A west-east dam on a west-east river; you just had to adjust. Owen Duff thought ahead to more than a thousand days of sunrise at one end of the dam, sunset at the other, sun in the eyes of his dredgeline crews; it would make a difference in where he laid those lines.

"Bastardish big open country out here, isn't it," Sangster said. "Anything between here and the North Pole, come winter?"

"What," Owen now grinned fully and joined the formula of weather complaint,

35

"you want the wind cut with something besides a barbwire fence?"

"Any more of a breeze than this," Sangster squinted against the persistent blast of air, "and this is one sissybritches engineer you'll find hunkered down behind those cottonwoods."

"That's all going to go, first thing."

"The whole works?" Sangster glanced at him, then back to the winding thicket of cottonwood trees and diamond willows that hedged the west riverbank of the Missouri as far as could be seen.

"Mmhmm. Clearing out the bottomland will help with the dredging, the idea is. Besides causing gobs of jobs." Owen was thinking out loud now. "If I was you, I'd make sure that cottonwood doesn't get consigned toward your bridging. These Corps guys — they know how to push a project until it squeals, but we don't want them doing it through shortcuts in procurement."

"Jesus no," said Sangster, realizing that Owen was seeing around bends besides the river's. "I'll goose up my specifications on all bridge timbering."

"Wouldn't hurt," Owen approved, but was already back to gazing at the bluff across the river, the distant shoulder that his dam would rest against. His own tall order of engineering, so big that it needed imagining in segments.

Think of a mile, and pile its entire length with a pyramid of earth as high as a twenty-five-story building.

Think of another mile, do the fill again.

Think of a third such distance, same.

A fourth and final mile, equally level.

The mountainous amount of gravel needed for the downstream toe of a dam that size? Bring it in from the big pit at Cole, eighty miles. That wasn't so hot, Owen thought. The glacier-size quantity of rock for the upstream face? Bring it in from the Snake Butte quarry, one hundred and fifty miles. That definitely wasn't so hot. But hauling the staggering tonnages of gravel and stone into here from Hell and gone was not Owen Duff's given job. Heaping those materials correctly once they got here, along with more than a hundred million cubic yards of material dredged from these riverbanks down there, into a firm gentle berm across those four miles, pervious edges married onto impervious core; handling the Fort Peck earthfill, the biggest earthen dam ever tried: that was going to be his.

Soon came a shout from the top of the knob, time to be briefed by the colonel. The Corps seemed to be big on briefing, all right. "Guess we better get used to it," Sangster said, "or marry money."

37

He stopped, embarrassed. He had let that out before remembering that Owen Duff was a married man.

Owen threw him a look, but with it a fleeting expression that Sangster didn't know how to construe.

"Sometimes it can be worth it," Owen told him, "even if only small change is involved."

Charlene Duff wondered how it had come to this, that she all of a sudden was jealous of a mound of dirt.

The Fort Peck Dam occupied Owen from the minute he heard the rumor of it. The next thing Charlene knew, the job there had plucked him away and left her rattling around the apartment in Bozeman. Housing would be flung up at Fort Peck as soon as possible, Owen kept telling her, but meanwhile he and the other engineering whizzes were hoteling it in Glasgow and she had to make do here alone. She no longer liked the notion of alone. Not that she liked the sound of Fort Peck much better.

My dearest, she began this night's letter to him, and thought, I should probably quit right there. Just write that over and over fifty or a hundred times, like a kid who has to stay after school.

So glad to recv yours of last wk, she

jotted in store hand, and hurried the ink on through disposal of the weather and Bozeman's onslaught of collegians again, now that September was here. Then she and the fountain pen took their time, careful with the next:

It is just about more than I can stand, being apart from you this way, sweet one. You know the song — the "Miss" in "Missouri," that's me missing you. Oh Owen, I wish you were here right now and — well, you know. But next to that, what I wanted to tell you is that I met up with Prof Z downtown today, and he told me there is going to be a "Bozeman bunch" hired for the 2 Columbia River dams, Grand Coulee and I forget the other one. I wonder, darling? If you could latch on at one of those, maybe we wouldn't have to wait and wait for Fort Peck to ever put a roof over our heads. . . .

The Missouri River had maundered through enough of Charlene's life already. Her father had been the barber in the little riverside town of Toston, a place with none too many male heads to start with, and those there were in the habit of a haircut only about every sixth Saturday night. Her mother passed her days trying to pretend there was enough clientele among Toston's females, even fewer and more set in their hairdo habits, to justify her beauty parlor in a partitioned-off area of the barber shop. Both of these scissor merchants devoted their spare time, a nearly unlimited amount, to trying to catch every fish in the Missouri River. In short, with these parents who had about as much enterprise as pigeons, Charlene Tebbet spent her Missouri River girlhood sweeping up hair and raising herself and her younger sister, Rosellen.

The Missouri was only twenty miles old at Toston but already five hundred feet wide and so implacably smooth you knew it had to be deep, drownable deep. When the Tebbet sisters played along the riverbank, beneath the flight paths of fish hawks and just above the swim zones of muskrats, Charlene simply assumed that the responsibility for not falling in was hers, for both of them. Not that Rosellen was a careless or reckless child, but she could be mischievous enough that Charlene felt obliged to order her around for her own good. Rosellen took the bossing without open warfare over it, but by the time Charlene packed up for a store job in Bozeman and Rosellen was about to start high school, they both knew that the older-sister superintendence had run its course.

   . . . *I haven't had a line from Rosellen since Christmas, the little rip. Will write her anyway as soon as I finish this to you. . . .*

Bozeman put Toston so far into the shade as to constitute total eclipse. The stimulation of city traffic, two movie-houses, the Big Dipper ice cream parlor, a room to herself at the Gallatin Riverview boardinghouse, the freshness of working as a counter clerk in Cunningham's Department Store, the other young women on the staff full of jokes and pranks and sass and gossip, all this and an actual salary, too — Charlene giggled more her first month in Bozeman than she had in all her previous life.

And all of a sudden, Owen.

Always after, Owen maintained that if he had been content to count on his fingers instead of replacing the slide rule he had lost, he would still be a free man. He was on his way across town from campus to another of his odd jobs, night minder in a chick hatchery, when he swerved by Cunningham's for a new slide rule. He found the one he wanted and kept fiddling with it, to get used to how the middle tabular part slid, on his way to the counter. When he looked up, he saw that the clerk had coal-black hair and dark, dark eyes and carried herself like one of those hieroglyphic princesses, head tautly up, shoulders just so. Charlene, in turn, saw a strong-featured face with an engaging quizzical underline to it in the wide cut of the mouth.

While she wrote up a sales slip for the slide rule, Owen dug a couple of silver dollars out of his pocket. Charlene took the dollars and dropped them clinking into the canister. She yanked the dispatch cord and the canister whizzed up to the balcony office where Priscilla or Janie would make change.

This was the part that gave her the fidgets, the waiting. She always saved to now to ask, "Would you like that wrapped?"

Owen considered. "No sense to. I'll be using it right away."

"Oh." Charlene fussed with the sales slip pad. What was keeping the change canister? She managed to glance over the customer's shoulder to the balcony. Pandemonium up there in honor of the tall goodlooking man. Priscilla was out from behind her desk and doing a little Charleston shimmy while biting her lip suggestively. Janie, worse, was not even counting out the change yet but just leaning over the rail lapping him up with her eyes. If the customer turned around . . .

"What does a slide rule do?"

He looked at her in surprise. "Just about anything. Multiplication. Long division.

Logarithms."

"You're at the college, then."

"You bet. Engineering."

"That sounds ambitious," Charlene said, trying to stare the pair on the balcony into civil behavior. "I can't imagine what's holding up your change."

Owen laughed, an interesting grin staying on after. "Could be they're testing the silver in those dollars."

Could be they're going to get their hair roots pulled out when I get hold of them, too, Charlene thought to herself, just as she heard a descending *zing.* "Oh, here it comes. At last."

When Charlene opened the canister she saw a scrap of memo paper along with the sales slip and the change. Shielding it with her body, she peeked down and read:

He's a dish! Don't let him get away!

Charlene crumpled the note, turned and placed the change in the man's broad palm. Then she took a breath, uncrumpled the note and pushed it across the counter to him.

What compels love?

Cross-examine the Charlene of 1933 and she would never tell you that Owen's blue blaze of drive, there in his eyes and on

43

inward to his brain and gut and backbone, had singly been enough to make him compulsory for her, five years back; wasn't that the likelihood, though?

Try the question on the Owen of then and he would swallow his tongue rather than count off such small attractions as the way Charlene's hair topped out perfectly for his cheekbone to rest against when they danced and so on; but add up enough of those and don't they become compulsion?

Sharing a close call can clinch the matter, too, as on the long-since night when the pair of them were in the college's hydraulics laboratory where sometimes Owen worked late on his thesis research and sometimes they necked. The night watchman could be heard on his way, so Charlene, her dress mildly askew, hid down behind the nozzle cupboard. Flinging open the lab door, an aroma of moonshine brew emanating in with him, the watchman appraised Owen at his flow sink and recited:

The heights by great men
  reached and kept
were not attained by sudden flight;
but they while their companions slept
were toiling upward in the night.

Then slammed the door and went away.

Charlene and Owen laughed into their hands until they were sure the watchman was out of range, then really broke loose. They stayed in this silly spasm to the point of hiccups, until Owen managed to catch his breath, straighten up soberly, and say to her:

"What if?"

Her heart dropped. What if they'd been caught, he could only mean; what if he'd faced expulsion for — what did they even call something like this, violating college premises by . . .

But she saw he was smiling, not at all resembling someone about to announce that they must never neck in the hydraulics lab again.

"Charlalene, what if that guy is right, hmm?" Owen said urgently as he reached both arms around her waist and a little below; reached and kept. "That this beats sleeping."

They stayed a steady couple on through Owen's years of college, each of his weeks dizzy with classwork and the desperate odd jobs and the details of Charlene, hers crammed with him and the ever longer hours at Cunningham's (but for gradually less pay, a personal impingement by the Depression which started her thinking about the order of things). 1928, 1929,

1930; those years sped and yet seemed endless, the waiting, waiting, waiting until Owen graduated and latched onto a job and they could get married.

Making love helped. It scared the daylights out of them, too, every time. Whenever the kissing and embracing and fondling led to more, separately and mutually they would vow afterward that they had better quit this. (Charlene did not know so, but Owen had been keeping a diary ever since he came to college, one of those five-year ones with a quintet of spaces down each page, and it was when he found himself jotting *Ch. & I again* below the previous year's identical entry that he gave up the diary.) Bleary watchman aside, there was really no one to catch them sinning away like burglars of each other's bodies, yet everything teetered when they did: if Owen made Charlene pregnant, here came premature marriage and there went her paycheck, his college trajectory, and their chance of climbing, any at all, up life's splintery rungs. They (mostly Charlene) learned just enough precaution so they could keep scaring themselves that delicious way.

She wondered even yet, pen to the page, at the risk built into love. She could remember how daring she felt when she shed Toston and tried on Bozeman, seven years ago. New to herself. Once before, some spring and early summer of her girlhood, rain for once came to Montana at perfect times and amounts, and the ranchers from the Big Belt Mountains when they swung into town for groceries and haircuts kept saying of the unbelievable grass, "It's like Africa." That's the sort of thing she first thought about herself in Bozeman, how much taller and more lush and rare and therefore chancy her life suddenly was. Then she met Owen, and learned what a dare really meant. The geography of another person, that was where you went blindfolded and raw and in over your head. The magnitude of being apart had come into it now, too. Out the window of the apartment, down the Gallatin River to the Missouri's headwaters at Three Forks, on past Toston, the distance to Fort Peck was 625 miles.

Resentfully she eyed the hour on the clock, which somehow seemed both too early and too late to suit her. Nights now, she hated to go to bed, with no future there except sleep. She supposed bed blues like these were no more than right a first time apart in three married years, but knowing so didn't take any of the edge off the feeling. Of course, according to his hurried letters Owen had his own rankles, but of a different sort. Dispatches from a stampede, his account of life in Glasgow sounded like. Glasgow woke up at 2:30 one morning and realized that its fortune was piling into town. What unfolded first was a hotelier's dream: so many men of the Fort Peck project suddenly coming and going that rooms could be rented out twice in the same night, first to those who wanted to catch some sleep until time for the "through train" at half past two, and then to those who tumbled off the Pullman cars. When either shift climbed out of bed they wanted a meal, so the cafe owners hit it rich five and six times a day. Reasonably often the food was washed down with a few drinks, and the bars along the south side of the railroad tracks lit up. Among the swarm of Fort Peck comers and goers were quantity buyers, for either the government or the construction contractors, who would snap up all the axes in Glasgow one day and, the next, hire every fry cook and washerwoman. Amid this frenzy, Owen and the other engineers had to contrive the dam plans, which his most recent letter had likened to trying to sort pie tins in a hailstorm.

So, Owen had his own load, Charlene didn't deny that in the least. But there still was this of hers; with Owen gone these months on the Fort Peck job, this was like being married to herself.

Dear one, about the other dams, she finished off the night's letter to him. *I hope you don't mind what I had to say. I only want the world to really see how Goin' Owen can go.*

The next-to-last Monday in October, ordinarily a time of year when not much is underway in northern Montana except the weather sharpening its teeth, the money began at Fort Peck.

The hiring in Glasgow that morning had a carnival spirit to it. Men milled into lines, expectant, not wanting to hope too much but buoyant with the prospect of a paying job, a steady half-dollar-an-hour after the cashless bafflement the Depression had brought. Preference, Hugh Duff noted, seemed to be wholesale. From the talk of them, here were other bottomland farmers and backpocket ranchers from along the river, yes, but the streets of Glasgow had been swept to come up with some of these other specimens. He and Neil and Bruce stayed together in the crowd, for what that was worth. They had filled out employment forms, been given a brass button with an employment number *(9* for Hugh, Neil *10,* and Bruce inexplicably *57)* to pin on a shirt pocket, and stood around waiting for the transportation which the government men told them every five minutes

49

would be here in five minutes; the first day of anything has some wobble to it. At last they climbed up into one of the crew trucks for the jouncing ride of seventeen miles to the river. So far, Hugh thoroughly despised everything about government relief work.

The Duffs knew enough about riding in the back of a truck on rutted sectionline roads to stand up behind the cab, hanging on to the boxboards, and so while the Glasgow street denizens tried to sit and were getting their spines pounded from the base up, Hugh, Neil, and Bruce met the Fort Peck country face-on.

When their truck, in the lead, topped into the view of sprawling river plain, Neil's and Bruce's first thought was the same: that the makeshift little convoy of trucks and pickups and a couple of touring cars would turn one way or the other from this overlook and head off toward tighter terrain where the dam site must be. But there was nothing to head off toward.

Upstream and down, across and beyond, the valley of the Missouri boomed away to horizons of its own making, wide-open country split down its middle by a muscular tan channel — no, on closer inspection, two channels; the river here divided around a massive wedge of silt called Cow Island — where century in and century out these twin flows — no, honestly three flows; the third a river of timber and brush, in and of itself substantial, miles of diamond willows and stands of leafless cottonwoods along the near bank — had ebbed and swelled with the methodical might of the seasons.

Everyone aboard the truck now stood and peered, calculating madly on how many man-years of wagework it was going to take to throw a dam across this, and a voice from the back put all their incredulity into:

"Keep a light in the window, Mother, I'm coming home to die!"

As their truck lurched down the bluff, Neil pointed.

There where the river plain met the base of the benchlands, perhaps a mile yet below the truck route, sat a farm with a stepped-roof barn, so much like the one on the Duff place that Hugh felt stabbed by the sight.

Neil's gesture, though, pinpointed the helpers working behind a survey party, spreading sacks of lime in a white line across the ground from stake to stake. The straight streak of white narrowly missed the back of the barn, and it could be extended with the eye across the middle of Cow Island, and then across the stubble of the alfalfa fields on the opposite side of the river, and at last up out of the bottomland to where the axis of the dam would meet the far bluff.

Downstream from the white line, the trucks cut their engines and men piled out and stood looking around skeptically at the underbrush and big wrinkled cottonwoods that cloaked the river. During the hiring sign-up in Glasgow, the war veterans among them had been freely saying this was reminiscent of army life, all right, much commotion but little motion, so now everyone became impressed at how briskly an Army Engineer lieutenant dealt them into three groups, one crew to saw down cottonwoods, another to clear brush, and the third to build a toolhouse. When the lieutenant strode by the Duffs, he designated Bruce to the sawyers, Neil to brushwhacking, and Hugh for the toolhouse crew, which infuriated Hugh. Who was this Army shavetail anyway, to decree that Hugh Duff was too old to do axework? He stepped out after the lieutenant and said in a stung tone, "I've fought brush all my blessed damn life and can fight it some more."

"If you'd really rather," the lieutenant said brusquely. He darted his attention back to Bruce and Neil. "One of you to the toolhouse detail, then."

Neil spoke up. "I wouldn't mind."

Owen didn't strictly have to be there, this first day of the manual labor force descending on Fort Peck, but only death or disablement could have kept him away.

That morning, he stuck his head in the temporary Corps office in Glasgow only long enough to make the excuse of needing to run another porosity test on weathered shale, then caught a ride to the river on the tool truck. There he went through the motions of sending the rock docs across to auger out more samples from what would be the dam's shaley east abutment, but mainly he wanted to view this next day one.

His brothers had already crossed paths with him, while his father deliberately did the opposite, at the community hall breakfast thrown by the Glasgow Chamber of Commerce a few hours ago. He had only seen them, what, half a dozen times in the years since he took himself to Bozeman. Pair of unfolding kids, they'd been then, and while in a sense he knew each of them from the ground up — Neil who always watched his way as if he were on stilts, Bruce built on springs — Owen worried a bit that they were not ready for Glasgow and Fort Peck. In the community hall's thronged atmosphere, wild with passed plateloads of breakfast, they especially looked short of adjusted. Young men who knew plenty, but maybe not this particular verse. But who's to say who is out of place at a time like this, Owen told himself as he went over to instigate handshakes and the quizzical grins that were a Duff trademark.

Bruce couldn't help but be first into brother-talk:

"Got yourself a dam to build, Ownie, huh?"

"Not quite by myself. There'll be stuff that needs some main strength and ignorance, Bruce."

That hadn't come out as lightly as Owen wanted, but Bruce seemed to take it as teasing. "You're the expert. We're just here to fill in around the edges, aren't we, Neil?"

"Four bits an hour, up from nothing." Neil smiled around his words. "That'll be different."

"Yeah, helluva deal," Bruce backed that with an even bigger smile. "When did somebody come up with this wage idea, anyway? The Old Man never told us it existed."

"Uncle Sam is here now. You're going to see a lot that didn't exist before five minutes ago." Owen checked his wristwatch as if that had reminded him. "Speaking of which. I better say hello to Mother, then go try make something happen." He looked dubiously at Bruce, then Neil, then Bruce again. He felt oddly responsible, and half perturbed along with it, that these yearling brothers of his were going to be at the tail of his eye here, from now on. "You guys —" What, though, advicewise. *Keep your pecker in your pocket, lest the new horde of whores on Glasgow's south side of the tracks flirt you into something stupid? Save your pennies for a rainy day, the Depression isn't over just because a federal paper-shuffler is handing you a job? Don't kiss a bear when you have honey on your lips?* What could be said that would stay heard, when they were at that age? Nothing much, Owen decided. "You guys let me know what you're up to, once in a while."

Before Owen could turn to go, Neil with a sweep of his head and his eyes open mock wide indicated out beyond the jam-packed breakfast function to the dam project that had brought it all here, and expressed in wonder:

"As the Old Man would say, how does this thing do?"

Well might he ask, Owen thought now, traipsing in exhilaration along the base of the west bluff, past where the makeshift truck convoy had spilled out its little army of brushwhackers. Look it over casually, or even several degrees closer than that, and Fort Peck appeared to be taking place all ways simultaneously. Here they were, starting clearance of the biggest dam site in the world, and test holes still were being drilled. People — well, like the Duffs — were barely out of these bottomland houses, and the white lime outline of the dam was cutting across their tracks. Even Owen had to keep systematically bringing to mind the overlaps of how it all fit together. That the thicket off ahead of him along the riverbank where the first brush and trees were being whacked down was precisely where the fleet of dredges and barges and pontoons for his dredging setup would be built. That a trellis of railroad track would emerge, straight on in from the vee of the valley ahead of him, soon next spring. That on the apron of the bluff up to his left, after the spring thaw the Corps would unroll an entire townplan onto the prairie, where he and Charlene would be able to set up housekeeping.

Thinking about it all — hell, *seeing* it, on the flip-pages of his mind — he didn't quite slap his sides in enthusiasm but could have. Complicated didn't even begin to say it about this showcase project of the New Deal, this fevertime of history. And he absolutely damn loved it, the jigsaw excitement that had swept in with Roosevelt's inauguration. The alphabet agencies, the economic pump priming — it was already legend that the Chief Engineer of the Corps had not even signed off on the Fort Peck Dam plan before the Public Works Administration had started funding it.

He hadn't yet gained sight of his father and Bruce, somewhere in the bottom-land thicket at their work of clearing-away but he could easily make out Neil across there in the open where the tool-house was being constructed, and threw him an exultant armwave. Then Owen stayed still a minute, listening, savoring. He knew the Fort Peck plan in its every inch and angle, yet even he almost could not believe that the dam was now under-way, *this* way, with the echoes of axes and the timber yells of men who yester-day were farmers or worse. Blueprints showed none of this.

Meg had presented herself at the kitchen in the community hall at five minutes to five that morning. Through the serving window, she saw that the volunteers were coming along nicely at setting the tables, and soon would be ready to be fed before everybody else descended. Tim Jaarala, the cook, had a baggy face of red, ruined skin. With bachelor indirectness, he spoke toward the vicinity of Meg:

"This first day you better just watch,

lady. See how I need things set up for the cookin'."

His pronunciation of it as if it were the German word for cake, *Küchen,* momentarily threw her. But then the just-watch part sank in. Owen had seen to it that, with this breakfast shindig and a Great Northern Railroad delegation to be fed at noon and then the facilities becoming an emergency cookhouse for the swelling Fort Peck workforce, she could start right in earning her own paycheck as cookhouse help. But she hadn't come here to be insulted. Meg's maiden name was Margaret Milne; Milnes had died in Prince Charlie's kilted ranks when English cannon raked the battlefield of Culloden in 1746, and Meg held the attitude that 187 years was about enough of superior forces walking over her and hers. She drew herself up and told the cook's turned back:

"I have seen a kitchen before, Mr. Jaarala, I'll have you know. I am someone who has cooked for harvest crews."

"That ain't cookin'," Jaarala said forlornly in her direction and set to work.

He started hand over hand on a flat of eggs, ambidextrously breaking each one with a soft tap on the bowl edge, seeming to squeeze the contents out and consign the eggshell halves into the garbage in the same motion. When he immediately had a few dozen yolks and whites in the bowl, he whisked them together, poured them on the grill in six identical amounts, and with quick pokes of a spatula created rectangles of omelet. Without looking he reached to his left to gather a stack of cheese and flipped the slices into the frying omelets as if dealing cards. He watched the fleet of omelets briefly, whistling to himself almost soundlessly — the stately tromp of *O Tannenbaum*, it seemed like to Meg — then flicked his spatula to crimp a seam into each end of each frying egg-cheese mass, folded those tabs over, then flipped them all, luscious packets of golden texture. Somewhere amid this, Jaarala had babied a mound of hashbrowns into perfect sizzle at the edge of the grill, and now he was manipulating another flat of eggs into his mixing bowl.

Meg felt slightly faint. The one thing she knew to do was to stay out of the way of this virtuoso, until she could figure out how to be any dab of help.

When Owen poked around the corner of the kitchen on his way out, she manufactured a frantically pleased smile and rattled a few plates as if in extreme industry.

After municipal quantities of omelets and hashbrown potatoes and summer sausage had been dished and dispatched to the dining tables and the hall was clearing out, the cook moved some more air around with that barely hearable set of whistling, and seemed to be thinking. At length, Jaarala provided over his shoulder:

"You could open some cans of vegetables for me if you want."

Meg glanced around trying to recognize canned goods and finally realized they were the gallon cans stacked like kegs beneath the serving shelf. "What kind?" she asked eagerly.

"Mixed."

"But what with what?"

In what seemed vast surprise, Jaarala looked over his shoulder almost at her. "Carrots go with peas, corn goes with lima beans, string beans don't go with anything. That's what 'mixed' means," he said in an injured tone.

Neil could hear, even over the loudest of the toolhouse carpentry, the nearby racket of men tearing at clumps of willows, hoeing out the lesser brush with the half-axe half-pick implements called pulaskis, sawing down cottonwood trees bigger around than themselves. After the crash of a tree, the next minutes would fill with the stillness of anticipation, until the *ba-BOOM* of a dynamite stick splitting the stump, and soon the roar of a D-6 Caterpillar dragging away the big rootball.

He waited until noon to ask the point of it all.

The foreman recited that the engineers wanted the river basin cleared, it would make the eventual dredging easier, less debris and so on.

Neil still didn't get it. "The alfalfa fields on the other side of the river are already clear — why don't they just dredge those?"

The foreman grinned and didn't answer.

"Kid, what we're doing here is making frogskins," one of the Glasgow street bunch told Neil after the foreman left. "Money. Have you ever heard of it?" The Glasgow man jerked his head toward the stands of willows and groves of cotton-woods. "Bucking this stuff out of here — who the Christ knows if they really need it done or not? But it gives them a way to get us some pay. Don't jinx us by asking half-assed questions about it."

And if they don't hand out some moolah somehow, the sheriff was mulling with a hot towel over his face, reclining in the barber chair in Glasgow as on every Monday noon since he had been elected, *if Roosevelt and his brainbust bunch don't put people on these so-called public work jobs* — well, that was moot, they surely to Christ *were* signing every man who could stagger to a crew truck onto the Fort Peck payroll. How to make wages flow: pump them out of the government treasury. The idea on high was from some fruitcake Englishman professor named John Maynard Keynes, compensatory-sending-by-the-government-to-set-the-economy-in-motion, by way of Roosevelt's alphabet-soup agencies. Make the American eagle lay dollars into hands that had forgotten the feel of a nickel. The sheriff uneasily crossed his feet, one neat little boot of handtooled leather atop the other. He couldn't argue with the need to do something about the economic side of things, although he sorely would have liked to. Out there in the street this morning while the hiring was going on, the sheriff had kept an obvious eye on the crowd and even contributed a couple of minor offenders to it, telling them he'd bounce their butts right back into jail if they didn't hang on to these jobs on a platter, and he'd managed to stay impassive at the sight of Corps officers and civvie bureaucrats busy as bees; but the Fort Peck project rankled him. Some New Dealer's finger had come down on Valley County, Montana, on a place where the Missouri River seemed a little skinnier than elsewhere, and now there was going to be five years of dam building commotion. Yet the sheriff had to look only a couple of counties away, over by the North Dakota line, for the example of how things could go if something wasn't done about the Depression. When there was enough rain, the soil of the northeastern corner of Montana grew hard red wheat. When drought came, politics of that same coloration sprouted instead. In '28, Sheridan County had elected as its sheriff a Bolshevik, no less. Calling himself a Fusion candidate but amounting to Communist and proud of it, Lawrence Mott had lost office in the Roosevelt sweep of '32 but pretty damned narrowly. (As someone who prided himself on enough gray matter to run as a Democrat if that's what it took to reach office, Sheriff Kinnick could not savvy why Mott hadn't at least called himself a Roosevelt Communist.) Mott and his — what do you call a nest of Reds — cadre still had a Communist newspaper going, over there in the Sheridan County seat of Plentywood. *The Producers News*; you bet, they knew how to produce trouble, whenever they had half a chance. At least he, Carl Kinnick, did not have to put up with that kind of Red ruckus in his county, nor would he, not even if it took —

"Ready to get skinned, Carl?" Shorty the barber asked as he always did while he stropped his straight razor. Sheriff Carl Kinnick didn't strictly need a haircut every Monday and even less a barber shave, but somehow it got the week off to a decent start for him, marked a change from his heavy weekend duties. Besides, how often did a person get a chance to put his feet up and contemplate the state of things?

As Shorty's steel scraped away at the sheriff's cheeks and neck and Shorty jabbered about the haircut heaven ahead when all the Fort Peck hirees were going to need a trimming up at once, some soon Saturday night, the sheriff only barely listened, his mind still stuck on the question of this Fort Peck Dam. Depression, drought, grasshoppers, you name it, the past several years had dumped them all on northern Montana. So the sheriff had to admit that this part of the country could stand something done for it. But to it?

Hugh was clobbering away at a jungle of diamond willows. Beating with his axe at each thumb-thick willow as if it were his personal enemy. He had gone off on his own, a little away from the rest of the brushwhacking crew, as there didn't seem to be any boundaries on the amount of brush along the Missouri River. He was already tired. He had *started* tired, dragged down with a feeling which he had only been able to describe to Meg, when she kept urging him to snap out of it, as the weight of circumstances. She, of all people, ought to understand the load of everything he'd been hit with. Not simply the news of the dam, the day of Siderius. The silence that said something, too. He had tangled with Meg about it as soon as he could get her alone, that day when the farm went from them.

"You knew about this, did you."

"Owen wrote, yes. That there might be a dam, but there was no telling when. It was up to politics, he said."

"And you couldn't have said anything to me?"

"A time ago," she had reminded him, *"you went deaf where Owen is concerned."*

"I said," a voice came in on him again between axe strokes, "what're you now, mute?"

"Eh?" Hugh, startled, realized that Owen had come up behind him in the brush patch. Hugh barely glanced around at him and threw aside the willow strands he had just cut.

This never goes right, Owen thought impatiently. *But we've got to sort ourselves out somehow, now that he's here.* In genuine curiosity he asked:

"How's it feel to be on a regular payroll?"

Hugh looked at him full-bore now. "Putrid," he said, and turned and gave the next willow a savage hack.

"Hey, give it a quit," Owen said with command sharpness.

Confused, Hugh held up with his axe and checked the particular clump of diamond willow he'd intended to attack next, then the prodigious thicket of brush to the right and left of him. "What'm I to leave off doing?"

"This happy horseshit of pretending each other doesn't exist."

Hugh took the chance to catch his breath. Panting a little, he said: "Engineers talk that way, do they. Wouldn't you think all those books between their ears would make a bigger difference."

"I figure the sooner we get this over with, the better," Owen went right on. "You're going to have to, you know. Put up with the fact that I'm here, and that I have some say in this project."

"Owen, I know you're next thing to almighty, but I wasn't told you're the one who signs my famous paycheck."

"I don't personally, but I tell Eleanor and she tells Franklin Delano, and he's liable to dock you for being snotty if you don't watch out."

The whippet mind of Owen. Once again

Hugh Duff was amazed at his quick son, and immediately peeved at being caught amazed, just as much as when

the boy was eight, at his side from day-break to dark those summer days, the younger sons little yet and Meg forever needing to be on hand for them at the house. But Hugh couldn't have asked for better help than bladesteel Owen, who could go from one waiting chore to the next without waning. Whenever a characteristic cloud to the west warned them to head inside to wait for the rain to make its way down the canyon, father and son retreated to harness work in the barn, Hugh hammering in the gleaming new copper rivets as Owen held the leather straps steady on the anvil. This day, as the first heavy drops drummed the roof, a flock of chickadees went in to feeding acrobatics in the serviceberry bush outside the barn window.

Hugh kept at the rivetwork, but his son's holding of the harness hamestrap was drifty.

"What're you doing, Owen lad," Hugh finally said, more sharply than he'd intended. "Counting the raindrops?"

"Dad, why doesn't the rain hurt the birds?"

"Eh?" Hugh's look shot not toward the chickadees in question but to his son. "Whyever should it? A dab of moisture?"

"No, the size of it compared to them, I mean. When it hits them."

In a flash he saw what the boy meant. The globular raindrops, the thumb-size birds cavorting unbothered by such barrage. *Christ on a crutch. Here I've been seeing that all my life and never thought anything of it.*

"Don't know, Ownie," he admitted. And much more: "Wish I did."

The grown Owen he studied now wore sharply creased tan khaki pants, short sheepskin coat with a thick wool collar, sand-colored Stetson with a divvy crimp the same as on Bruce and on Neil. Hugh himself had taught them that; train the brim in at the front to show that you have enough sense to let the rain run off you, and let it go at that. Sweatstains of that hat aside, Owen now was quite the picture of dam engineer swank, Hugh thought, and felt more tired than ever.

"Ownie, surely you have engineery things to go be at. What is it you want with me?"

"Just about anything short of civil war, while we're all on this project, will do nicely."

"Then let's try something like smoke signals. At a good distance. I know your mother will want you to be on hand to her, and I can't stop that. Your brothers, either

— they can consort with you or not, it doesn't matter a browncolored whit to me. But what's between us is still between us. And this drowner of yours" — Hugh indicated the dam site — "doesn't help matters any, does it."

"It's not just mine," Owen said tightly. *To hell with this noise.* "I'll take you up on that idea of smoke signals."

After the first hour or so, when the teams of sawyers and powder monkeys were starting to make a dent in the cottonwood grove, Bruce gravitated to where the D-6 Caterpillar was about to start skidding out the split stumps. Each time, a cable with a logchain hook had to be noosed around the protruding trunk remnant — called setting the choker — and then the Cat would clank away with the stump uprooted and dragging behind. The foreman here, Grimwade, was also keeping an eye on the brushcutting gang and so was on horseback to commute between the two. Bruce brazened right up beside Grimwade's stirrups and asked if he could have a crack at choker setting; helping the Old Man yank out brush year after year to make way for more alfalfa finally might pay off, he figured. Skeptical of him at first, Grimwade made Bruce show he knew his stuff as choker setter on several stumps, then nodded and rode off.

This fast vote of confidence made Bruce strut a little, acting as if it was mostly his own doing when the hefty stumps erupted from the ground. The only drawback to the job was trudging after the stump to the burn pile, in order to unhitch the choker. Then, though, inspiration came again: he began catching hold of the roots and jumping on to ride the upended stump like a bucking plough as it was being towed. The ride was rough, as each crooked comet of wood bounced across the ground, but that was the major part of the fun. Hopping off when the stump reached the pile to be burned, Bruce would undo the choker and climb up behind the cat-skinner for a lift back to the next stump. The other guys on the crew were laughing and calling out about Bruce not even needing a saddle, busting those stumps bareback, which confirmed to him that he had a pretty slick system going.

Until he bounded down from a stump ride and there was Grimwade frowning from his horse perch.

"What's your button number?"

"A-1," joked Bruce, still jaunty.

Grimwade leaned down in his saddle and inspected Bruce numerically. "The point of this whole shitaree is to give you guys jobs, not for you to figure out ways to break your neck. Any more antics like riding stumps, Little Mister 57 Different Varieties, and you're going to draw your walking papers instead."

Off rode Grimwade, and now the rest of the crew razzed Bruce unmercifully, offering to lay bets with him on how quick he was going to make history as the first man fired from Fort Peck. Bruce's face burned as he marched behind the skidding stumps. He watched his chance. At noon, when Grimwade tied the reins of his horse to the bumper of a crew truck and ducked into the cook tent for lunch, Bruce slipped over, took the lariat off the saddle and slung it on his shoulder, then quickly uncinched the saddle and lifted it off the horse. He had singled out an especially tall young sapling, poking out of a thick tangle of willows, and ploughed his way through the brush carrying the saddle. When he reached it, he formed a dab loop in the lariat and on his fifth upward toss caught the top of the sapling. Drawing the tree over in a bowlike bend as far as he could, Bruce knelt on the saddle while he knotted the taut lariat in through the hole beneath the saddlehorn. He carefully got off the saddle while holding down the rope and tree, then jumped back and let them all fly, the sapling springing back into place and catapulting the saddle up with it, like a fish on a line. Grimwade's saddle swayed there a satisfying twenty feet in the air amid the jungle of brush.

After being fired, Bruce barely had his half-day's wages in his pocket before Owen collared him.

"I hear you treed Grimwade's saddle for him."

Bruce couldn't help grinning, but changed his face when he saw Owen's. "He had it coming, Ownie. He jumped on me for no real reason at all, so I —"

Owen hit him above his left ear, an openhanded swat but enough of a clout to rattle Bruce's brainbox.

"Hey! What! —" Bruce's impulse to hit back wrinkled away under Owen's forth-right grab and twist of the throat of his shirt. In theory Bruce knew he was too grown-up to be cuffed around like an errant bear cub, but Owen was doing just that.

"This isn't tiddlywinks," Owen ground out. "What the hell do you think you're going to do if you can't hang on to a job here? *Hmmh?*" He tightened the twist atop his brother's Adam's apple in reiteration. *"What?"*

"I —" Bruce realized he had not thought quite that far ahead yet.

"That's right, duckbutt, you don't have any least idea, do you. Yet you figure you can toss away a paying job for the sake of some joke? There's unemployed guys every damn inch of this country right now, and it's about five minutes until winter will be here — what'd you think you'd do then, hunt with the snow snakes? You better get yourself going here, kid."

He abruptly released the shirtfront and Bruce coughed for air.

"This once," Owen told him, "I'm going to save your hide. I had to talk like a good fellow to do it, but I landed you on the hammer gang with Neil. If you mess that up —"

Owen left the *if* dangling, which he hoped would leave Bruce at the mercy of his own imagination.

At the end of that day, Hugh stiffly eased himself down the cellar steps in Glasgow. He sat down heavily. Next, Meg knew, he was going to sigh like a punctured philosopher, and he did.

"My hip pockets are dragging out my tracks. By God, Meg, if I never meet up with an axe again in my life, that'll be soon enough."

"You'll toughen in," she said, although she had started wondering whether he would. No, never mind *whether*. Hugh *had* to.

He stared around the basement, the coal bin and furnace at one end and the shelves of garden canning at the other. The muddle of sagging bed and rickety chairs, in between, which amounted to their "rented room."

"I almost can't believe —" he murmured, then blinked as if coming to. He turned toward Meg. "Enough about my day at the races. Did you show that cook how to cook?"

Suggest tell him POGOP, Owen scrawled in the margin of a contractor's letter which cited innumerable reasons why a delay was unavoidable in that particular contracted-for portion of the dam project, and routed it back to the glass-paneled corner office they called "the cage."

Owen did not really expect squishy little Major Santee, also known as "the marshmallow in the cage," to tell the contractor, Piss or Get Off the Pot. But as chief of operations under Colonel Parmenter, who had never seen a schedule that was not sacred, the major was sooner or later going to have to tell the foot-dragging contractor something along that line, Owen figured.

Or was that, as the major periodically accused Owen and Sangster and the other non-Corps engineers of "civilian logic."

Owen stretched at his desk. Atop his heaped IN box the next sheet of paper began:

FROM: DIVISION ENGINEER, MISSOURI RIVER
DIVISION, KANSAS CITY, MISSOURI.

SUBJECT: CONSTRUCTION OF FORT PECK
DAM ON THE MISSOURI RIVER.

1. UNDER SEPARATE COVER ARE BEING FOR-
WARDED TEN COPIES OF OPERATION PLANS
PURSUANT TO THIS TOPIC.

Owen puffed out his cheeks and tried to
uncross his eyes from the Corps-ese.

2. DREDGING OPERATIONS WILL BE EXE-
CUTED WITH A VIEW OF MAKING THE CLO-
SURE OF THE DAM BEGINNING 1 AUGUST,
1937.

*Yeah, well. No kidding. Here we thought
we were supposed to drop FDR's hundred
million dollars directly into the river.*

3. DREDGING OPERATIONS IN THE INTERIM
WILL ENTAIL A GROSS YARDAGE OF SUIT-
ABLE MATERIAL IN THE UPSTREAM BORROW
PITS TOTALING 84,900,000 CU. YARDS AND IN
THE DOWNSTREAM BORROW PITS 38,800,000
YARDS; OR A GRAND TOTAL OF 123,700,000
CU. YARDS.

*Jesus fiddling Christ. Look at that! Actual
numbers! What's got into them back there*

in Kay Cee? They aren't just woofing, now.

Owen did some rapid figuring, working out the monthly average of dredging it would take to add up to that total, allowing for 20 percent shrinkage of the fill material, winter shutdowns, and so on. He looked for a while at his result. It was a lot. It was more than plenty. But he let himself dream ahead to his dredges and their output of fill, flying through the air like mucky magic.

First, though, Duff, back to the heavy lifting.

He picked up the next piece of paperwork.

Hugh had waited as long as he could stand to, a total week. By now he utterly had to drop by the cookhouse and make sure this Jaarala was as much of an old maid as Meg advertised him to be.

The cook (big bruiser; damn near an axehandle across, there in back of those shoulders, Hugh uneasily estimated) loomed at a kitchen counter fussing with whatever cooks fuss with, meanwhile semiwhistling a set of sounds which registered on Hugh as *yoo hoo hoohoo . . . YOOHOO HOO HOO.* Meg, though, was nowhere in sight.

"Hello then," Hugh announced in through the doorway. He went as if to put a foot in the kitchen. Jaarala stared down at it, and Hugh withdrew the foot.

"Help you?" Jaarala husked.

"I'm, eh — Margaret Duff's my better half. Came by to, uhm, walk her home."

"The mister, are you." Jaarala gave him an inch of nod, as if he had been expecting this misfortune, then reached behind himself to the counter and with a lightning move was thrusting something at Hugh's midsection.

Hugh was glad he had stood his ground when he realized what was aimed at his middle was a platter of deviled eggs. He reached and took one between his thumb and forefinger, Jaarala's baggy flaming face hanging over him.

"Goohb," Hugh mumbled as he ate the filled egg. It was actually leagues better than good, it was mouthwateringly delectable, it was supreme art in deviled-egg form.

Jaarala nodded two inches this time.

Hugh gawked around the kitchen as if Meg might be on top of one of the cupboards. "Guess I missed her?"

"That's what you did," Jaarala concluded, presenting that expanse of back and shoulders again.

The Fort Peck Dam project kept growing so fast that its myths couldn't keep up with it. The original seventy-five men, the Octoberists who had set to work with axes and pulaskis and saws, peeked around in the brush at the end of two weeks and thought, *Holy Pete, there must be three or four times as many of us in here whaling away at this stuff;* there actually were five hundred in the bottomland workforce by then. By the end of November when they went around boasting that several hundred of them were letting daylight into the Fort Peck thicket, the thousandth man was being handed a job brass.

By then, the farms were being burned.

On each of the brush-clearing crews you could pick out the bottomland honyockers, the alfalfa-seed farmers and those who had held small riverbank ranches, by their stance — a petrified minute of staring upward as the black geyser of smoke rose from the kerosene-soaked houses, barns, and sheds. Each time, Hugh hoped that it was the farm of that hired-out mouthpiece Siderius.

The forenoon when the stepped-roof barn next to the white line of the dam axis went up in crisp flames, Bruce poked into sight at Hugh's patch of brush and gave him a single rueful shake of the head. A moment later, Neil appeared and did the same.

Hugh attacked his work again as the

boys each went back to theirs. *"If we keep at it, the wages will pile up,"* Meg had maintained to him in their latest go-round. *"It's a chance."*

"So was the damned farm," Hugh had retorted. And he'd had it on the tip of his tongue to add: *So was English Creek before that. So was Inverley, back before that.* Anciently fought and lost, by all concerned. Wouldn't you think, Hugh brooded, that a man and a woman could at least agree on the ground under their feet?

"Margaret, I'll do this. I'd paint the private parts of monkeys if it meant a wage. But don't ask me to blind myself to what we're at, here. This piddly work-by-the-hour, this coal bin we have to live in, this is all forced on us by —"

"— the weight of circumstances," Meg clipped in. *"Hugh, I don't even care what is to blame, anymore. I only want some-thing promising for us from here on. If that has to start with an axe and a spoon, then let's."*

Disgusted that he had let her have that last word, Hugh kept to himself and smashed away at the thicket which might keep him chopping for eternity.

A new man, scrawny everywhere except for a notable hawknose, and whose clothes didn't look even warm enough to work in, sidled over to him. "Don't take this wrong, but it tuckers me out to watch you."

"Eh?" Hugh needed a moment to fathom the first Oklahoma accent he had ever heard. He stood up as erect as his complaining back would allow him, his axe still in hand. "We're being paid to work. Consequently, I'm working."

"You go at it the long way around," the other man maintained in that high drawl.

"Mister, I have chopped more ungodly damn wood than you have ever laid eyes on, so don't be giving me —"

The scrawny visitor reached over to the sapling next to Hugh and with one hand bent the small tree until it was taut and with a lazy swipe of the axe in his other hand, severed the trunk. He gave Hugh a glance, shrugged, and started to turn away.

"*Wait*," Hugh called. "Wait, wait."

He considered the cleanly sliced shaft of sapling. By comparison his array of stumps looked like an assault by beavers.

"Maybe," Hugh suggested, "you could show me the doing of that?"

Thereafter Hugh worked devastation on his area of thicket, once Birdie Hinch had taught him the knack of bending a sapling into tension and then giving it a clip with the axe. The gossip mill promptly provided the derivation of Hinch's nickname: arrest and conviction for stealing chickens. ("Buggers think they're funny," Birdie drawled without rancor. "Just because a man draws a little hoosegow time for trying to feed himself.") Hugh also discerned that, aside from Birdie's knack with an axe and possibly with poultry, he was an absolute flub at anything requiring manual dexterity. Birdie could barely work the cork in and out of the waterbag. Hugh wondered about Birdie Hinch's prospects at Fort Peck once they were done slaughtering timber. For that matter, Hugh wondered about Hugh Duff's.

At quitting time, he and Birdie trudged together to the crew truck. They met up with Neil and Bruce, both full of bounce.

When Hugh introduced Birdie, the hawknosed man peered at the younger Duffs inquisitively.

"Be you twins, or brothers?"

The pair wrinkled their noses at each other as if making faces in a mirror, then laughed.

Neil was the one who said, "We're guilty on both counts."

Two more sons at once, before noon on a bright September day in 1914, had multi-

plied Hugh Duff beyond any prior estimate of himself.

Giddy with pride, he carried the twin bundles around the kitchen table as if he couldn't wait to start these dazzlers going on the world. Father of three, just like that. His own father, blusterbox though he was, had only managed two; and Hugh's younger brother Darius back in Scotland had none to show. (At least his total had better be none — the scamp never had married.) No, this was family-founding with no doubt about it, Hugh Duff–style, Missouri River–style, he and his would fill this valley before they were done, work this fresh Nile to a perfection. It dizzied him, the complete turnaround from only a few years ago: this alfalfa-seed farm, sons in triplicate now and Meg there in the bedroom having come through the birthings fine, a bit peaked but fine.

One of the babies began to squall, and that set off the other one. Hugh hooted with pleasure at the duet. Out of the bedroom swooped the midwife Mrs. Austin, chiding him with a scowl. Before yielding the treasures over to her, he asked, "Who's the older of these opera singers?"

"Can't say." This was the point of the September baby season where she always got digusted, blaming men and December when they didn't have enough to do outdoors. "I lost track, which one came first."

"But that's frightful, Mrs. Austin," Hugh half pulled away from her in mock reproach, bundle of noise still held in the crook of each arm. "How will we ever know, then," he peeked from one to the other with delicious exaggeration, "which to call Pete and which Repeat?"

For something else to do, he started toward the bedroom to look in on Meg again, then remembered. He swung around, out onto the porch, and called:

"Owen! Come see! Something in here for you!"

After a moment the boy materialized from the mouth of the coulee west of the house. Honey-haired, alert. Even across this distance, however, Hugh could see he was pinched with worry. Motioning urgently for the boy to come to the house, he hurried back in to pluck the twins away from Mrs. Austin again. He did not know quite everything about this multiple fathering yet, but he was determined to be the one to show Owen the amazing little brothers.

Mrs. Austin was clattering at the cookstove and his father was sitting in the armchair gently bouncing a wrapped-up baby in each arm when Owen slipped in from outside. Two! Nobody had warned him there would be this many!

"Brothers for you, Ownie. A pair for the

cost of one, what do you think of that?"

The boy considered the newcomers. He drew enough breath for honesty, then told it out:

"They look like mice."

"Eh?" With Mrs. Austin in the same room, Hugh chose to mishear. "Yes, they do look nice, don't they. Best babies ever. Why don't you trot on in and tell your mother you think so."

In the bed, his mother looked tired, tireder even than after washday, and she turned her head toward him as if even that was a lot of work. "Ownie, did you see your brothers?"

His worried "Yes, Mama" was barely above a whisper.

She whispered back as if it was just their secret: "Aren't they funny little monkey-bunnies?"

Owen's heart raced with relief. She knew! Now he wouldn't need to point out to her, as he'd tried to with his father, these babies' pink all over, squinchy, general balled-up helpless kind of look. His mother knew they were an awful disappointment, why had he ever been afraid she wouldn't?

"Ownie, they'll take some getting used to," his mother kept in a whisper.

He certainly didn't doubt that. "Uh huh."

"Sometimes they'll be a real handful for

me," she whispered on. "You know there are times when your daddy has to be gone. That's when I'll need you to — to be my help, with your brothers. Will you do that for me?"

In the kitchen, Mrs. Austin walloped some food onto a plate for Hugh, to try to get him fed and out from underfoot in the house so that she could pat the situation of the new mother and twin babies into place. To look at him, you would think Hugh Duff had just invented parenthood. Yet she had seen this man in town drunk as a skunk not a month ago. Which meant that his pregnant wife and the little boy Owen were here home by themselves while he was getting himself soused. True, at the time he had been at his wagon loading his groceries with the concentration of a clockmaker — no one is as overly serious as a drunkard — but Mrs. Austin gave him no marks for heading home while it was still daylight; if he hadn't he would be a brute on top of being a spree hound.

Her civility was in short supply, then, when she observed to Hugh that twins were no simple newcomers to a household. "The mother can't help but feel done in, for a while. I can send our girl Cora to help mind the babies and their brother some afternoons. I'd think your wife would like that."

85

Hugh rounded on her so quickly it scared her.

"You're a doubly adequate midwife, Mrs. Austin," he told her softly. "But you don't know thing one about Margaret Duff."

Neither of them was ever able to pass up a mirror. And neither wanted to see any twin exactness reflected back.

Hugh and Meg Duff's double helping of sons were not identicals, that was never the question. Naturally they'd had all the mysterious pacts that twins start out with. As toddlers, Bruce and Neil, Neil and Bruce, prattled away in their private language for everything from the spoon in their mush to petting the dog. As growing boys, they were possessed of that spooky knack of always knowing what the other one was up to, even when out of sight. (Owen sometimes speculated whether they navigated off each other like bats in the dark.) But by something like instantaneous mutual decision, at about thirteen they'd had enough of being a matched set. (Their father, they already knew, was eternally going to see them that way, as two halves of the one thing — his prize workhorse team. Their mother, they equally sensed, could always catch them at their differences before they themselves could.) Bruce let the world know so by his war paint. Neil came out of the wallpaper at you.

The truth of the looking glass, though: there was no total cure for being twins. At Fort Peck they still habitually tagged around with each other after-hours, to see what that might provoke; while at the same time you could not have paid them enough of a wage to make them work side by side. By keeping some distance between them on the job, they at least could avoid the name mix-ups. Neil and Bruce, Bruce and Neil, grudgingly accepted that they shared a resemblance, but for the life of them they didn't see how anyone could think either of them was the other.

Winter came early to Fort Peck that year — there were those who claimed it did every year — and, at least to the Duffs, felt oddly welcome.

Birdie Hinch and other out-of-staters for whom this was the first Montana winter thought it was cold when the temperature sank to zero or so, and the Montanans laughed at them and maintained that this was an open winter, no three-day blizzards, next thing to shirtsleeve weather. Maybe so, but the route from Glasgow to the dam site, dim excuse for a road in any season, now had ample windshield-high snowdrifts to create work for squadrons of shovelers (Bruce among them, although Neil had been picked as a carpenter's helper in the setting up of the boatyard). Teams of horses were called into use to pull out stuck trucks (briefly giving Hugh something he could handle the reins of) and to draw haysleds carrying massive construction timbers, apparitions in harness trudging their load across snowy prairie to this most modern of dam sites. In Glasgow, though, winter was simply the white calendar outside the windows while officework kept on furiously as ever (Owen, closeted with blueprints and specifications, would have told you it blizzarded inside all that winter), as did the round-the-clock feeding (Jaarala, Meg was pretty sure, had actually smacked his lips after tasting one of her dozens of batches of dough for cookhouse Christmas cookies) and other necessities to keep up with the Fort Peck project's constant spasms of growth.

Eight-thirty, Saturday morning, December 23rd, Charlene worked the pair of nightlock keys to let herself in the big double doors of Cunningham's. A nice fresh inch of damp doughy snow squelked beneath her overshoes; on that entire block of Main, about a good snowball fight's worth. Just enough to pretty the street, put a holiday cap of white on down-town Bozeman. She hoped, though, that the man sleeping it off behind the steering wheel of the muddy Ford coupe (doubtless one of the hick bachelor ranchers from the gumbo country around Maudlow, her Toston prejudice said) parked at the curb hadn't frozen to death during the night. Probably not; the coupe's windows were merely fogged up, not iced over; serve him right if he had, though.

She went on into the department store and turned on a side-aisle bank of lights, so she could see her way up to the cloak-room. While she still had her coat and scarf and overshoes on, she really ought to go back out and wake up the swacked-out sleeper in the car, she knew. She considered leaving him for one of the younger salesgirls, Aggie or Wilma, when they came in at nine. Tell them there was a ready-made boyfriend waiting for them outside, just needed a little thawing out. Oh sure, and if the snoozehound froze stiff in the meantime . . . Charlene giggled; or in any other part of himself . . .

As she opened the store door and stepped back out onto the snowy side-walk, the window of the coupe rolled down and Charlene Duff realized she was look-ing at another Duff.

"Bru— Neil! Isn't it?!" She crossed the

sidewalk while the breath of her words still hung in the air.

"Yeah, hi, Charlene." He accomplished the feat of yawning and smiling at the same time. "Didn't know just where you lived, so I —"

Owen! The world fell around her. Owen had drawn Christmas duty, but was coming down next weekend to spend New Year's with her. Something had happened — Something so awful they couldn't resort to a telegram, had to send a member of the immediate — Charlene stared, glared, at Neil. She understood why olden peoples killed messengers who showed up with bad news.

"Owen's good," Neil recited, still a little sleepily. "Or was, when I left yesterday forenoon."

"Then what — why're you —" Charlene knew that her mouth was hanging open, and when other people did that she asked them if they were catching flies. "Neil, tell me what your being here — what this is about."

"Came to see if I could take you up north."

Charlene's silence seemed to fill the street. Neil fidgeted behind the steering wheel.

"I figured I'd give Ownie a kind of a Christmas present," he said, suddenly shy. "That's if you like the idea, too."

She saw immediately what Neil had put into this. Talking somebody into working a double shift to cover for him at the dam, having to pay it back later. Borrowing somebody else's car; probably that would need to be paid off, too, with extra work. Then coming all this way, presenting himself on her doorstep. Even wackier, on the department store's doorstep.

"There's one thing, though." Neil seemed reluctant to say it. "I drove all of yesterday and most of last night getting here. If I play out, can you drive some?"

This was dopey. To the utmost. Owen's kid brother needed his head examined, breezing in here to cart her off to Glasgow and Fort Peck as if —

Charlene heard herself saying, "I can drive lots."

"So, do you mind?" she whispered, her fingertip playing at his earlobe.

"I sure as hell do," he murmured. "This having to keep the noise down cramps a person's style. Hotel rooms might as well not even have walls."

"I meant my showing up. Out of nowhere."

"Out from under Neil's hat, more like. That goddamn milk-calf kid anyway." Owen laughed, Charlene joining in, the bed shaking. "What did you think, when he hung his face out that car window at you?"

"I thought he was crazy. Sweet, but crazy —"

"Huh uh. You want crazy, that's Bruce."

"— and then I thought, maybe he has something there."

"Sweet, huh? That the kind of guy you go for?"

"I go for Bozemaniacs, you may have noticed."

"I did notice something of that sort." In the semidark, Owen's hand had started up again, doing one of the things she liked done. "But that was way last night, and this's this morn—"

A storm of coughing announced that the occupant of the room next door had come awake.

They went still, trying to hold in their laughter. Owen nudged Charlene's bare hip with his own. "Go sell that guy a box of cough drops, why don't you."

"Oh, sure, *me.* And what if he wants a slide rule, Mister Smartie Ownie, where would that leave you?"

"Never mind on the cough drops. I'll go next door and pay him not to cough."

They talked on in low tones, catching up on having each other so near, so available. Charlene felt as though she had somehow kidnapped herself, dared to take herself away into another custody, Owen's, Owen's *and* her own. The car trip had been more than cutting catercorner across Montana for a hurried Christmas with a husband. More like the world's longest free taxi ride, near endless but exhilarating. Neil had driven like a person newly back from blind. Like most farm kids, he could handle a steering wheel and still be seeing off in a dozen directions. She would have bet that his gaze had registered every butte, mountain, coulee, fencepost, and jackrabbit between Bozeman and Glasgow. While she conjured the only direction that interested her one whit, ahead, and sneaked peeks at Neil to make sure his eyelids were still up. In profile he looked startlingly like Owen at the age when she had met him and fallen for him like nobody's business, but in the next moment Neil would gawk one way or another and all she could read on him was w-e-t behind the e-a-r-s. But so what, if he had had no notion of how thoroughly he was fetching her to Owen, to Glasgow such as it was. Every minute that Neil's borrowed coupe had scooted north, she had been that much farther along in abandoning lonely. For Christmas, Charlene was giving herself Owen.

"Nobody has any real place to be," he

was laying out the Duffs' holiday situation to her, "right now." *Including us,* he thought. Sangster had nobly vacated his share of this hotel room and moved in down the hall with Cody, but Cody's room partner would be back from Kansas City a few days after Christmas — Owen had half his mind going, all the time now, on where to put Charlene and himself. Did he mind that Neil had deposited her practically like a bedwarmer on Christmas Eve? No. Did he mind that he was going to have to scramble to come up with lodging for them in chockful Glasgow? He sure as hell did. Charlene's unwrapping-us-for-Christmas-Eve announcement that she had handed in her job at the department store back in Bozeman threw him for a minute. Here she was, for permanent, way ahead of schedule. In the desperate matter of housing, the only shortcut he could think of was to ask the Corps officers to use their influence. He supposed that's what colonels and majors were for.

"As far as Christmas dinner, the cookhouse is about it," he went on now. Charlene watched him from horizontal inches away. "We'll grab a table for the six of us, and Mother can get off long enough to eat with us all."

"We're on our own for Christmas Day," Charlene asked, trying not to sound relieved, "until then?"

"I have plans," Owen said. "Some of them may even take place out of this bed."

The day was cloudless, the snow brightly silken in the fields along the road to the river. They both were a little woozy and smug from their start-of-day lovemaking, and Owen honked the horn and gave a languid two-fingered wave to every truck they met, while Charlene sat over next to him so close you couldn't have put the edge of a dime between them. Wearing a capacious pair of his wool pants and one of his flannel shirts and her own heaviest coat, she felt wonderfully swaddled in clothes. Owen was spiffy all the way down, even in winter getup; she had always liked his habit of fully buckling his overshoes with his pants legs neatly bloused into them, so that he looked like something instead of flapping along buckleless like most men.

At the Fort Peck bluff, he pulled into a turnaround banked high with plowed snow, parked the government pickup, and with a straight face told her this was it, Mrs. Nanook, they had to mush on foot the rest of the way.

Charlene could tell he was kidding but not how much. The snow stood as high as her head, everywhere around. *Oh, Owen, don't do this to me, not when I'm trying, really I am.* Before knotting the headscarf she was putting on, she swallowed and asked: "How far?"

"As far as you can see," he said but grinning now. "Right there, the top of that biggest snowbank, is all. Come on, I'll give you a hand up."

They clambered onto the firm pile of snow, and the site where the dam-to-be had risen to Owen's eyes that spring and the bottomland farms and fields put their pattern into view for Hugh and Bruce and Neil that autumn, now stunned Charlene with stark winter river.

The first snow, more than a month ago, had done away with the chalked outline of the dam, but the cutting by brush and timber crews had incised the boatyard into the landscape. Work was scheduled to begin on the hull of his first dredge only two weeks from now, so the boatyard was automatically the first place Owen looked. The immense hull timbers could be seen waiting, asking to be envisioned into his 170-foot-long vessels, the white fleet of the Missouri River.

Beside him Charlene peered just as hard, but she could not have told you at specifically what. Ruts ran everywhere, gray muddy tracks of trucks and heavy equipment darkly streaking the snow of the bottomland. There were giant muddy gashes along the riverbanks where timber had been torn out. War, fought with mud, this mainly looked like. What appeared to be a cross between a lumberyard and a junkyard held all of Owen's attention, she saw, in fact had him smiling wide with satisfaction. Yet if he were to turn to her right now and say, "Surprise! We're in a dream," or in Siberia or somewhere, she would not have been surprised. The Missouri, which she had been picturing as a bigger version of the stretch of the river past Toston, looked nothing whatsoever like its younger self there; this was an eternity of river, something beyond vast, winter-ugly even in the rare December sun. The split channels around Cow Island were edged with ice. The color of the water, even, said *colder than you can imagine.*

Charlene moved around to warm up, and Owen came and put his arms around her from behind to help out. He rocked from side to side a little, her enclasped body swaying with his, as they both gazed out over the valley and the start of the damwork. Then he asked:

"So what do you think, prettypants?"

"It's lots of river."

"The bigger the better, for making people some work." He might have been commending the room capacity of paradise to her. "The PWA guys about wet their pants when they hear we can put five hundred men onto the boatyard down there, and near a thousand on the spur railroad, and on and on. This is going to be one of the population centers of Montana before we're done, know that?"

She felt him stop the gentle swaying, as if having come to what he needed to say next.

"You maybe can't tell from the looks of it yet, but it's on its way to being one sweet hell of a dam, Charlalene." He laughed, close above her ear. "I know what you're about to say — what's the sense in hanging around to build it if I've already got the thing built in my head, hmm?"

"Owen, now, I was not," she maintained. "It's just that for somebody who isn't you, it's so — so hard to put together."

"The devil is in the details, you bet. But the big thing here is pretty simple when you think about it. This is an even-steven process, really that's all in hell it is. Using the river's own water and riverbed to regulate it. Dredge the fill, pipe it to where you want to make your dam. That's the trick. You don't need to pile concrete a mile high to have a dam, or have you heard me say that before?"

He laughed once more, while she wished

again she had gone to Panama and Pennsylvania with him the summer of his thesis research. Not simply because she had missed him like everything, the long days and slower nights — the half-sick flu-ey feeling that told her definitely there was no mistake, she loved Owen Duff to the base of her being — but so she might have seen with him, all along the way, the earthfill history that entranced him. From here on out, she told herself as she leaned back against him with determination, at least she could join him in his Fort Peck vision. She could begin by swallowing the fact that what looked to her like the most haggard country in the world looked to Owen like dirt engineers' heaven.

Charlene had vowed to herself she would pull her tongue out by the roots rather than tussle him about the domicile topic on the very day of Christmas, but Owen thought of it himself, glancing at her a little guiltily.

"Oops, the townsite. It'll be right down over there, on that apron of land just up from the base of the bluff, see it?" She thought she more or less did. "When they get rolling on the construction next spring," Owen was assuring her, "the town'll go up so fast it'll make your head swim."

"They're going to name it Owentown,

aren't they?" she teased to reward him.

"Hnn nn, no such luck. The Corps boys came up with something real original — 'the Fort Peck townsite.' But tell you what, we'll do better than that, right now."

Owen struck a pose, one overshoe puttee out in front of the other. "I claim this territory in the sovereign name of Charlene, the — what rank do you want? —"

"Empress, why not."

"— the Princess —"

"Queen!"

"— the Duchess of the Big Muddy prairie."

"Oh, swell, just what I've sat up nights wanting to be," she gave him with a poke toward his ribs. He dodged, then grabbed her in a roundhouse hug. They laughed at each other at extremely close quarters.

When they had to break their clinch or risk freezing together into nose-to-nose statuary, Owen glanced at the sun and said they'd better be heading back to Glasgow. As Charlene turned to find her footing down the snowbank, she heard him make another pronouncement:

"That's the family dam. Now for the damn family."

So, Charalene, no matter how we set our faces for it, this is how a Duff gathering goes. Bruce won't give me the time of day, which suits me fine. The Old Man and I agree we're going to disagree without quite taking an axe handle to each other. And as you already noticed about Neil, he's got his own set of tracks he follows. Sometimes it's a pretty close call, isn't it, whether enough of us are speaking to the rest of us to get the salt and pepper passed. With a dozenth sideways glance Owen checked to see how she was doing. From the look of her, Charlene was taking it like an ace. Determined to dress up for Christmas dinner even if it did mean squooshing in at a cookhouse table where the plank bench and oilcloth supported forty-two other fannies and sets of elbows besides those of the six Duffs, she had put on her green velvet outfit. It definitely paid off, Owen thought; with her hair gleaming dark and her arms and just enough neckline gleaming white, he could not remember when he had last seen her this snazzy.

Glossy as a magpie, thought Hugh, giving one more regard to Charlene's combination of ever so black hair and snowy complexion. " *'Under my plumage everything prospers,' sang the checkered bird."* *Better get used to marital prosperity again, eh, Owen?*

Fawncy came to mind in Meg, the old Inverley term for those who took their tea in thin cups, although she told herself she did not like to think that of Owen's choice of a wife, really she didn't.

"— knows his stuff when it comes to Christmas presents, don't you, Neil," Charlene felt forced to carry more than her share of the dinner conversation. "Delivered me for this right on time. Now all you've got to do is go shopping for yourself. Something that comes in redhead, maybe?" She could tell that Neil, poor kid, had a crush on her, and figured the sooner she razzed him out of it the better.

One moment was going to stay with Bruce from this Christmas, which otherwise seemed to him pretty much a sad soup-kitchen affair; with the cookhouse horde for involuntary holiday company, he missed the homestead in a sizable way for the first time.

Neil was sitting next to him, more than a little unsettled from Owen's roughing his hair and asking him if he had a patent yet on coaxing women to ride in a car with him all weekend. Next to Neil, the Old Man automatically performed his "We'll come to the table as long as we're able and eat everything this side of the stable," which all but Charlene had heard him do any number of times before, and she did not seem overly impressed. Across from the Old Man, their mother seemed to be trying to make Charlene welcome for Owen's sake, but not necessarily for Charlene's own.

Here she was, then, Bruce suddenly saw — highly attractive Charlene with that black hair any man would want to bury his face in, midnight jewel among the worktanned Duffs — and yet Owen seemed a bit elsewhere. Bruce tucked that away, this first glimmer that Owen could have more on his mind than he knew what to do with.

No one in all the planning at Fort Peck had foreseen the town without limits, Wheeler.

The town that picked up the name of Montana's senior senator and dam-wangler sifted to the dam site on tradewinds as old as enterprise and lust. On a day that was neither quite the end of the winter of 1933 nor the start of the spring of 1934, one lone trailer house suddenly was parked on the prairie near the official Fort Peck townsite ("the cookie cutter town," as that Corps version of municipality already was being called), brought in by some arithmetician who had torn out the modest double bed and installed eight bunks for workmen weary of the drive back and forth from Glasgow. Not much sooner was that trailer house unhitched than here came a tavern or two or was it three; they replicated so fast it was hard to keep track. In a dead heat, housing and houses that were not to be confused with housing started mushrooming. Happy Hollow, snug in a little dip at the back end of Wheeler, was the distinct area where the houses of prostitution proliferated, under nicknames such as the Riding Academy and the League of Nations. Some of that particular trade also freelanced in the dancehalls that kept springing up until downtown Wheeler was rife with them.

As to housing in a more domestic sense, everything was built on the principle that temporary was good enough. When the dam was done, Wheeler's population would pick up and move anyway. So, tumbleweed structures built up and built up along streets that drew themselves onto the prairie. Into your shack, shanty, lean-to, or dugout you could barely fit such basics as bedsprings and kitchen table — all over Wheeler, family trunks sat outside the door under a drape of canvas tarp — and for decoration, a framed famous picture such as that wolf gazing down at a ranch house on a midwinter night, his breath smoking, would suffice.

Squalid, flirty, hopeless, hopeful, nocturnal and red-eyed, Wheeler almost immediately grew to three thousand strong (fifteen hundred damworkers and fifteen hundred camp followers, the demography was usually given as) and still burgeoning. In the midst of this, across a couple of weekends the Duffs whacked together sets of Wheeler lodging, a rough lumber cabin of two rooms for Hugh and Meg, and a one-room beaverboard special for the enthusiastic new bachelor householders, Neil and Bruce.

Sheriff Carl Kinnick took up the implications of the Wheeler frontier with the county commissioners in Glasgow.

"I'm about to have a Klondike on my hands. What do you want done about it?"

What they wanted, when translated, was for blood not to flow openly in the Wheeler streets but the gush of damworkers' wages toward cash registers to stay unobstructed in any way.

The sheriff at least shamed them into granting him another undersheriff. He would have told you it was coincidental that the one he hired and assigned to Wheeler stood six feet three inches tall and looked bigger.

Owen swung by to see his parents' new place of residence.

He sat in the government pickup a minute, determined to swallow the lump in his throat. Every day now he had been driving past Wheeler and its alley-cat aspects, but it never fully registered on him until seeing this particular clapped-together shack. Worse, he felt obscurely guilty, although it was none of his doing that the cookie cutter town of Fort Peck was being built for the Corps personnel and the civvie engineers and a big swatch of barracks for manual laborers who weren't married, while those with families were left to fend out here on the prairie — what the hell, the Corps would build anything you pointed it toward, and in this particular instance it simply had not been told to house people universally. And it wasn't as if he and Charlene were having such a swell time of it in Glasgow either, making do in one of the breadbox trailer houses out back of the temporary Corps offices.

But no two ways about this, Meg and Hugh Duff's new home was a tough looker. Rough raw boards and a couple of small windows and, as the Old Man doubtless had already said, not enough room to cuss a cat without getting fur in your mouth. Oh, Owen knew the place was still in process, his father and the twins would bank dirt around the base of the house before winter and his mother would coax out flowers, even if it was only morning glories. But he still felt burdened by what he was seeing, as he opened the door of the pickup and headed for the house.

"Owen! Welcome to the holy city."

The sight of his mother didn't help. She had just come off her morning shift at the cookhouse newly installed near the boat-yard and while she had all the usual smile for Owen, the rooms around her resembled a rummage sale. He recognized household items from the homestead, stacked and piled into corners, with no particular order nor apparent prospect of any.

Meg gestured as if she would take care of it in a moment. "We're in, and a roof over us. That's at least something."

"I'll get Charlene to come down and give you a hand."

"Oh, that's not —" Meg said, too swiftly, then did a major repeal. "Of course, that'd be appreciated."

"She can come down with me Monday, stay the day here with you. Do her good." He grinned broadly at his mother. "Do you both good. Maybe do the metropolis of Wheeler some good, even. How's the cookin'?"

"Adventurous. Those dredgebuilders of yours are on an onion-sandwich kick. One of them started it, and now Mr. Jaarala and I spend half our time in tears, slicing

— Owen, whatever are you looking at?"

"What I'm afraid it is, is daylight."

He went to the back wall and felt at the join of the uneven lumber. Sure enough, he could put the end of his little finger in some of the cracks between the boards.

"Your father hasn't come around to accepting tarpaper quite yet," her words barely reached him. "There's time, luckily, before next winter."

Owen blew out a depressurizing breath to keep from saying anything.

Meg busied herself at pouring coffee, as though that would put etiquette between them and the matter of Hugh. When she handed Owen his cup, though, his expression said they weren't done with their oldest topic. They knew each other too well. He took one sip and asked her outright:

"How's his behavior?"

"Predictable, at least." Meg laughed her laugh that played with what she had just said. Then she looked over at her prize son. "Not what you think. He hasn't gone on one of his tears since — well, it's been some little while, honestly, it has, Owen."

Which means he's overdue. He felt it traveling around and around in him again, why it had to be this way with his father, whether it might have come out differently when

Hugh and the eighteen-year-old Owen

were finishing the seed harvest, the late-summer glorious time of the year, there on the homestead. Financial daylight at last, Hugh was sure with a crop like this. An absolute shortcut to the bank: with alfalfa seed you needn't even build haystacks nor run the hay through sheep or cattle nor be at the mercy of livestock buyers in gabardine suits. You merely harvested the hay, sacked up its rich little seeds and sold the sackfuls. Infinitely easier than flax, which was slippery stuff to make cooperate with a binder reel, and a better payoff, much better, than oats or barley. By now, a decade and a half into the homestead, he had the touch for alfalfa seed if he did say so himself. It takes anyone ten years to learn how to farm a particular piece of land. But when you got it right, learning to live with one year's rainfall and the next year's lack of it, figuring out the pattern of yield hidden in the soil, and the splendid alfalfa sprang into gallant green and bursting purple, which led at last to this harvest of the valuable buckshot-size seeds: this was as close as Hugh Duff could come to prayer.

And there would be more such fields. He and Owen simply had to keep at it. "We're very nearly there, Ownie. That lowlying acreage will set us up, something wonderful. The two of us can clear it and break it out yet this fall, eh?" — Owen gave a short uninflected response — "then next spring we can work it . . . What'd you just say?"

"Not me."

Hugh peered at him, trying to comprehend.

"More schooling, is what I've got in mind," Owen answered the question unspoken. Then he swallowed, and said it entirely: "College, at Bozeman."

Here again how life could change in the space of a word or two; Hugh had always hated that and forever would. Just when a person thought he had found his footing, that's when something like this caved it out from under him again.

He controlled himself to the extent necessary to say:

"I need to ask you . . . to hold off on that, a year."

Owen was ready for that one. "Then there'll be another year. Something else you need me for. No, this is quits. This year."

Hugh did not want to ask further, but had to. "Just when is it you're taking yourself off to such great things?"

"Not for a week yet." Owen had this readiest of all. "I can take care of the place while you go to town."

While you go on your bender. While you fall off the water wagon as you so regularly do. While you hide in a bottle. Owen might

as well have spoken the charges every conceivable way, it would not have mattered more. What hit Hugh was his son's
basic calculation, Owen's calm allow-
ance of time for his father to behave in
the expected unreliable manner.

"Throw salt on it and walk away, eh,
Ownie?" Hugh spoke with fury. "That's
going to be your notion of life, is it? Don't
trouble yourself any here. Your mother and
the twins will get by while I'm in town.
Those of us who can take a knock for each
other's sake will get by."

"Has he said — will he stick with the
work here, do you think?" Owen asked his
mother now, past his original intentions.
*What the hell else can I do, when she's
sitting here in a shack the wind will pour
through? Damn him anyway, why is it
always so rough —*

"There is no other choice whatsoever,"
Meg willed away his question just as she
had done all the times it rose up in her.

"That hasn't always stopped him, has
it?" His mother and he had always been
natural allies. *Yes, go,* she had told him
the summer of his break from home. *Have
it better for yourself than we've been able
to. You are special to me, Owen, and I want
to see you make your way to fine things.*
"Hanging on to the homestead practically
forever," Owen cited as if prosecuting in

absentia, "the way he did. You saw he was throwing good money after bad, I saw it — how did he get to be the only Scotchman who doesn't know how to keep his hand around a dollar?"

"He's Hugh Duff," Meg said. "He takes slowly to persuasion."

"He'd better take the chance here," Owen said reflectively, eyes on the chinks of daylight through that back wall, "or he'll find himself sweeping out whorehouses, the damned old —"

"Don't!"

She was giving him a look that peeled him back to boy, the scold that seemed to hurt her twice as much as him. He felt his face flush. Then his mother seemed to come to herself, and smiled the apology. "I'm never going to like hearing you take on against your father, even when I feel like knocking his ears down myself."

"All right, I guess we better keep our priorities straight," Owen resorted to. "Nailing his hide to the wall isn't nearly enough to help this place any." He figured he knew just the thing that would, though.

The Blue Room, it came to be called, after Owen snuck back the next day with an armful of discarded blueprints and a pot of wallpaper paste. Paperhanging was not his strong point and the room's corners ran every way but square, but the heavy plan paper covered over the cracks and knotholes.

When Hugh came home that night, he stood for a long minute looking at the white-on-blue lines of the cross section of the dam, the elevations and dimensions of Owen's engineering world.

Watching him, Meg bit her lip, wondering which way this would go.

It somehow went more than one. Hugh first of all said with savage satisfaction, "Have him perform a few more hundred domestic miracles around here, and we'll almost be living like people again." But then he passed a hand over his face, a downcast expression following it.

"Hugh, wash for supper," Meg quickly urged.

He shook his head. "I'm going downtown. I may be a while."

"I wish you wouldn't." They both paused, and when he made no answer, she said with familiar anger, "But don't let that stop you, I suppose."

"It never yet has," he dropped over his shoulder as he went out the door.

Two days later.

Neil and Bruce were in their cinematic period. A Wheeler entrepreneur had deduced that people could not drink and dance 100 percent of the time, and opened a moviehouse; the two Duff brothers became instant addicts. For days after seeing George Arliss and Reed Beddow in *Squadron from the Clouds*, they piled into the crew truck with the cry, "Pilots, to your machines!" They yowled for a week after Charlotta Hoving, playing the advertising agency secretary in *Stupendous*, attained the halibut magnate's hand by thinking up the winning slogan "Lutefisk, the hominy of the sea." Night after night the pair of them goggled in the dark of the movie theater, in the congregation of hundreds like them, and swaggered out as if they'd been to harems and casinos. When they piled into their parents' house on their way home and retold that night's movie, Hugh and Meg had something to agree on — that their twin sons had not behaved this way since they were five-year-olds.

This particular end of an afternoon, Bruce and Neil were a bit ahead of themselves, as they generally were in trying to burn up their leisure time, and so decided to sample the latest sights along the main street of Wheeler until the sacred moviehouse opened. As usual the town reeked of newly cut lumber and fresh pitch, as if the community perfume were turpentine. Construction would flare up in one spot, then seem to change its mind and hop across town. This was one of the things about Wheeler, it built and built and changed and changed but wasn't nearly all in working order yet. Directly in front of them down the block, a top-heavy man in a suit and vest shot out from a vacant slapboard building, turned, and gave the fresh construction a kick. He seemed to think it over briefly, then kicked the structure twice as hard.

"I felt that from here," Bruce said aside to Neil. "If that guy keeps on, he'll be in the market for assistant kickers."

"Wait a minute," Neil said. "Let's just see." He went over to the edifice assailant. "You putting up this building, mister?"

"No," the man said with supreme disgust, "I'm just throwing money at the goddamn place for exercise."

"What's left to do?" Neil peeked into the walled-in shell of building, atop bluish Fort Peck clay. "Only the flooring? My brother and I can handle a hammer."

"Look, junior, the last jackleg sonofabitch of a carpenter left me in the lurch here. I need the real item. Every minute this place isn't making me money it's costing me money. Fort Peck's got carpenters up the gigi, and they're all out there" — he waved toward the dam site — "on Franklin D.'s payroll, God bless him."

By now Bruce had his head in the

115

structure beside Neil's. Off behind the stack of floorboards stood a pile of cardboard boxes that advertised Mighty Mac bib overalls and Peerless work-socks and so on. "Opening a line of dry goods, huh?"

"Wet," came the sarcastic correction. "Buddyboy, you're looking at the Blue Eagle Tavern. Or would be, if it had a sonofabitching floor in it."

"We can lay your floor for you," Neil asserted. "Give us a crack at it, Mr. — ?"

"Harry. Tom Harry." The man in the suit looked at the pair of them as skeptically as if checking the sex on new puppies. "This'd need to be done on a strict contract basis. Meet the deadline, or no pay — I can't be forking out to jacklegs who don't come through on the job. You two ever worked that way before?"

"All our lives," Bruce tried to testify, Neil cutting him off with:

"Say we do contract it, what'd be the pay?"

Tom Harry named his price.

"You're on!" Neil and Bruce told him in chorus.

It was Neil who cast a second look at the stack of floorboards and thought to ask:

"How long have we got to do this floor-ing?"

"Tonight," said Tom Harry.

Neil and Bruce hammered while Hugh hefted lengths of floorboards and Tom Harry sat and smoked cigarettes.

The hammer sounds racketed into the Wheeler night. *Wham wham wham,* Neil's was a steady three-beat delivery onto each nailhead; Bruce's tended to surround the matter, *WHAM wham-am WHAM-am. While the hammers hit those higher notes, a pile driver gave bass whumps* beside the river. The bluffs of the Missouri here had heard din before — the bawling rumble of buffalo herds, the last-stand discourse of Sitting Bull's winter camp before the summer of the Little Big Horn, the axes of steamboat woodhawks — but there had been half a century of comparative silence since any of those. Now and for years to come, a river of sound waited to drown down onto the site of Fort Peck — the opera shrieks of shale saws, the incessant comings and goings of locomotives and bulldozers and trucks, the falsetto of steam whistles, the attacks of jackhammers. Tonight the Duffs began their accompaniment of that full clamor of work. Tonight the true first pinions of the Fort Peck project were being driven: the pilings of the railroad trestle, the nails of the Blue Eagle's floor.

To the great surprise of the Duffs, the

flooring proved to be hardwood, high-grade. Nice seasoned tightgrained tongue-and-groove oak; lovely, really, if you weren't trying to drive nails into it or lugging twelve-foot boards of it all night long. Hugh, at the lumber pile, had a bit of perspective that Bruce and Neil, kneeling in arm-earnest exertion on the fresh flooring, lacked. "You could dance on this stuff."

Tom Harry blew a cumulus of blue smoke and said, "What the hell did you think the point of this is? Civic beautification?"

"Taxi dancing," Hugh identified, as if he knew the boulevards of the world. "Hate to be the one to tell you, but the Wheeler Inn has beat you to it. Half the women west of Chicago are already working that dive."

"Check out the arithmetic," Tom Harry said, unperturbed. "Soon as this dam project really gets geared up, there'll be three shifts a day — one gang working, one sleeping, and that will still leave about thirty-five hundred men off shift, any hour of the day or night. Not going to be any shortage of guys hanging around hot to trot, don't worry."

Neil tried to take the floor-laying task in little seasons. He would fit his end of a board into place, immediately drive the nails to snug it, catch his breath while

Bruce whaled away at the far end, then start down the length of the wood, nailing it at every joist while Bruce similarly worked toward the middle.

Before tonight, Neil was exulting to himself he wouldn't have said his prospect of becoming a contractor at Fort Peck was anything to write home about. He still wondered whether a handshake with Tom Harry constituted the full basis of a contract. But only as long ago as this morning, he hadn't known enough about it to even wonder, had he. One major fact stood out clearly to him: this flooring deal wasn't any so-much-per-hour as decided by somebody else, it was going to be a lump-sum payoff for Duffs working like Duffs. And wasn't that something?

Either his hammer or Bruce's consistently drowned out parts of the conversation between Hugh and Tom Harry, so that they seemed to be carrying on a grave discussion in addled shorthand:

"You really — *blam* — *there'll be* — *bang* — thousand people in this — *whamblam* — excuse for a town?"

"Twice that. Simple arithmetic — *blam* — thousand making a living from the dam and — *bang* — thousand making a — *whammedy-blam* — living off them."

"Where's — *bang* — good in that?"

"I didn't say a — *blam* — thing about

good, I'm just — *whang* — you it's going to happen."

By midnight, Bruce was convinced that his future was going to die out in nail-heads. He had a vision of himself: his right arm drooping down eighteen inches longer than his left, the entire right side of his body from his cramped foot to his raw knee to his aching shoulder swollen up irreparably from all this hammering. He would come out of this night looking like half a gorilla, he was convinced.

He nearly keeled onto his face in relief when Tom Harry announced he always ate a bite at this time of night and if the Duffs were interested, he supposed they could chow down with him.

The saloon owner resorted to his stack of cardboard boxes, pulling one out with a grunt, then began handing around to Hugh and Neil and Bruce tin cans that had no labels.

One of them asked, "What've we got here?"

"How would I know?" Tom Harry answered. "The labels came off at some forest fire camp, that's how I was able to buy the stuff cheap."

The men ate, plums preceding beans. Then the three Duffs were back at the flooring.

It was Bruce, head down, who hammered his way to the footings at the back of the building and, still on his knees, reared back with a grateful sigh to rest. He immediately found that he was looking not at the footings of the back wall, but the supports of a platform of considerable size.

"Bandstand," Tom Harry identified it for him.

Even in his stupefied state, Bruce gave it a try:

"Now, the floor of a bandstand wasn't brought up in our deal."

"Floor is floor," stated Tom Harry.

Around 3:00 A.M., Tom Harry said: "There's an outside chance you knotheads might get this done." The tavern impresario stepped over to his cardboard boxes again. Out of the top one he lifted a mounted deer head, lugged it over to the wall along the floored section, stood on a sawhorse and hung the piece of taxidermy as high as he could reach. Back to his next box, which produced the snarling head of a grizzly bear.

Tom Harry cradled the tremendous head, he and it glowering back at the bleary stares of the Duffs.

"Deecor," he explained, and went off to affix

the baleful grizzly above the front door.

An entire safari of stuffed heads gradually aligned the four walls of the Blue Eagle saloon, until Tom Harry came at last to a flat box. Reverently he plucked out the wadded-up newspapers protecting the picture frame, and, just above where his cash register would be, hung the campaign portrait and its bold print:

A GALLANT LEADER—
FRANKLIN D. ROOSEVELT

By dawn, Hugh and Neil looked done in and Bruce could barely creep, but you could have skated figure eights across the fresh floor of the Blue Eagle Tavern.

With a practiced thumb, Tom Harry riffled out the green bills of the contract price and held the money out to Neil.

"Tell you what," the saloonkeeper gruffly invited the numb trio, "come back in half an hour when I get the bar set up and a bottle opened, and I'll let you buy the first round of drinks ever served in the Blue Eagle."

"You can jitney down with me," Owen had said, reasonable as pie, "and come back on your own after you help get Mother's place kicked into shape." Here then they and the Monday morning of it were. Outside the Downtowner Cafe in

Glasgow, Charlene and Owen and two dozen damworkers trooped into the first jitney bus of the day. The workers were quiet, in honor of a wife, and she could feel the generalized envy, which made her even a little more proud of Owen and herself than usual.

When the jitney drove down over the Fort Peck bluff, miles of muck and machinery sprawled across the bottomland — twice as much of everything, it seemed, since Charlene had last seen the dam site. Other jitney buses and crew trucks were disgorging workmen by the hundreds, a human chaos pouring out on top of the mechanical one. Owen again pointed out to her the preparations at the Fort Peck townsite, but she couldn't tell if there had been any real progress yet. The one sure measurement she knew how to make here was that she could see more of the river each time, the channel edge sharper as new sections of the riverbank were denuded of timber. The bus made a stop in the inexact middle of Wheeler, and Owen and she stepped off. If the Fort Peck dam site was becoming a jungle of mud and grotesque equipment, the so-called town of Wheeler was running amok like an overgrown Hooverville. Everything looked like a back alley. And from all the bottomland clearance effort, everyone had woodpiles the size of haystacks. (Cottonwood was about the worst firewood there was, but free wood was free wood.) It crossed her mind that a lot of Wheeler's so-called houses would be better burned in the stove and the firewood stacked up for shelter. But she kept that to herself as she and Owen picked their way to his parents' shanty.

"Here you go, Mother," Owen announced. "Brought you the other love of my life." Then Owen Duff strode off to engineer his dam, and Meg Milne Duff and Charlene Tebbet Duff were left to fend with each other and the long day ahead.

"Charlene." Meg had a way of saying the name as if it was a sentence unto itself. She keenly asked, pretty sure she knew: "How are you liking Glasgow?"

Charlene restrained herself to saying Glasgow was quite a place, different, going night and day.

"Funny that they put that name to it, I still think," Meg seemed to muse to herself, the Scottish burr very much in her throaty voice. Charlene was apprehensive that this was going to lead into some kind of Old Country story — old countries were part of the territory Charlene was determined to climb away from in life — and so she rapidly changed the topic to the surefire:

"How's everyone doing?"

Meg brightened right up at that, and although Charlene mainly still thought of Neil as a skim-milker and Bruce as a wild jackass and Hugh as she wasn't quite sure what, she found herself a little intrigued by Meg's blends of tart pride in each of the Duffs of the dam.

The first dredge, the *Gallatin*, was aswarm with timberers and caulkers and shipwrights at other tasks Bruce realized he was going to have to figure out in a hurry, as he reported aboard. He knew this was a break, being shifted up onto the dredge-outfitting crew, and he couldn't help looking pleased with himself as the boatyard foreman, Medwick, had him sign onto the roster.

Bruce cocked his head and asked, "Say, are you any relation to —"

"No," the stocky foreman said by rote, heartily sick of having to tell the world he was no kin to Ducky Medwick, the St. Louis Cardinals outfielder. He wished Ducky Medwick had gone into the priesthood.

He took a look at Bruce and wished, too, that he had been sent somebody besides yet another drylander to help build this dredge. But Cecil Medwick said only, "Draw your tools at the ransack shack and we'll see what we can do with you."

Now that he had been picked for the trestle crew, Neil had risen spectacularly. He had become brace monkey.

It fatigued any normal human being to watch him. Using telephone poleman's climbing spikes, he would scale a trestle piling, dragging up with him the pneumatic drill and the length of air hose that powered it. In place up there, twice as high as a house, he had to bring the hefty drill and its twenty-inch-long bit above his head, position the apparatus so that it would bore through the piling at the desired angle, and hold it there while the air pressure fed the drill into the wood. Whenever they could, Bruce and Hugh and Meg and Owen sneaked glances at Neil up there, the ribbons of drilled wood festooning down from him, the drill held overhead as if he were making a matador's stiff-armed plunge into the bull. The other Duffs knew this was out-of-this-world work, but they didn't know the half of it either, the tricks of the trade he was picking up. In the climbing, he had needed to unlearn the natural tendency to shinny and instead climb with one side of his body at a time, right leg and arm up and clamped into place, then left leg and arm up in the same clamp-step, then both right limbs again, on and on. That was the first trick, and the next, once he was up there thirty feet, was to lean back into thin air, absolutely trusting the climber's harness around his waist while he put all his strength to the pneumatic drill.

"Takes a little getting used to," was all Neil said of this.

Hugh, though. Hugh was having none of the spurious notion that there was such a thing as advancement, in make-work such as this. He would do as he was doing. Go each day in a bone-rattling crew truck a little farther into the bottomland. Hop down and head with his axe into the reachable enemy, the Missouri's army of brush. Work himself numb.

Under her report on the men's jobs, Meg was wondering about Charlene. How much time she spent on keeping her hair so perfect, and the extent to which she was kicking herself for having tossed her job in Bozeman over her shoulder, and why she and Owen were waiting so long to have children. *I wonder why I even bother to wonder, though.* Meg was not alone among the Duffs in thinking the answers were on the surface of Charlene; everything about her seemed a bit self-elevated. But, Meg had to remind herself again, if Owen —

127

Owen's mother seemed to have a mood a minute, as far as Charlene could see. Meanwhile, Charlene was fairly itching to do something about the housekeeping in this shack, which somehow seemed gauntly unlived-in and wildly cluttered at the same time. *Wouldn't you just know, the only thing in here that looks like anything is Owen's blueprints.* "Well, better put me to work," she more than volunteered.

They spent considerable time deploying boxes and shuffling furniture around before either of them realized they were putting together two opposite households. Charlene would clear a boxful ("These are all knickknacks — it's a shame you don't have space for them here") out of sight under the bed only to have Meg shortly resurrect it ("I need these where I can get at them"). They sparred through half the morning with packings and unpackings.

"Let's say," Meg at last said carefully, "this will do, for now."

"If you think so," Charlene replied with determined neutrality.

She couldn't manage, though, to stop glancing around the two rooms of shambles, still not sure what she was seeing here in the house of Meg. A craving for disorder? Some loco brand of order that was all Meg's own? Whichever, Charlene

128

could have done without it in a mother-in-law.

Out came cups and coffee, a ritual either woman could have performed under ether. But instead of plain cookies, Meg produced a plateful of golden ring-shaped ones with a delicate dusting of sugar crystals. Charlene disliked sugary dustings, but went through the obligation of picking up one of the things. It was so light it almost flew up out of her hand. She took a bite. The most delicious item she had ever tasted.

"*Mmm.* What do you call these?"

"I call them booty from the cookhouse," Meg said with a wry expression, "but Mr. Jaarala calls them ballenacrunchers." Jaarala took considerable explaining, as did his cooking wizardry, both women glad to have something definite to fill the air with.

But when that topic ran dry, they simultaneously knew that Charlene herself was going to be their next.

Meg did manage to put most of a smile on it as she asked:

"What do you find to do with yourself?"

Good question. See the sights of Glasgow, by walking to the post office and back. Correspond with her salesgirl chums at Cunningham's, but that had been dropping off lately, at the Bozeman end. Cook three meals a day on the trailer house's tiny sheepherder stove, at least there was some challenge to that. Read. Sit. Breathe. Yawn.

"Crosswords, a lot," Charlene found to reply.

"Those puzzle thingies?" Meg could not help looking surprised, if not shocked.

"Mmhmm. You can learn a lot. New words. It kind of turns a person into a dictionary." Owen was already one, or something beyond. *"Ownie, I've looked up everything on water there is — what can they possibly mean, 'shortest name for a river,' two letters?" He thought for two seconds and said, "Po." And naturally it fit.*

"Well," said Meg, letting it stand as a full sentence. Then resorted to: "When they build that Fort Peck town and you're right here —"

"— it should be better then, yes," Charlene filled in before she could. It was bound to be better, in an actual house in a real neighborhood with all the other wives of engineers and Corps officers, close at hand to Owen's work. These days, this Glasgow captivity, the problem with watching Owen engineer the Fort Peck Dam was that she never saw Owen. *Her* Owen. The one who kept being a surprise, always putting some fresh tickle into life for her. Here and now in this session with

Meg, though, she kept to "Everybody is pretty much on the run until then," loyally saving him out of it.

To her great surprise, Meg said it for her. "He can be devilishly solitary, our Owen."

Charlene nibbled at another ballenacruncher, thinking hard. Was Owen's own mother taking *her* side? If so, how far? Lord, the ins and outs of these Duffs.

"He's up to his ears in what he's doing, I imagine," Meg went on. She laughed a little, as if inviting Charlene into her rueful view of men named Duff. "They're all that sort. From Hugh on down, they don't know any other way about it but to beat a job to death with work."

"Owen maybe needs — other work," Charlene produced. She watched her startled mother-in-law and decided she might as well put the next card on the table, too. "Away, maybe."

Meg looked worse than startled. If Owen went, before the rest of them could find their footing here at Fort Peck . . .

"I just mean," Charlene brushed the sugar from the pastry off her fingers, "he can go so far, he knows such a lot, if he gets the right thing to work on."

And you get to swish yourself someplace where you needn't to look at mud and shacks. Meg tried, though, to be hearty with this next: "You can't mean that,

Charlene — don't they keep saying this is the biggest dam of its kind, ever?"

"Could be it'll be the only of its kind, too. Then what, for Owen? There's only so much you can build with earthfill. When he has to move to concrete, the engineers at Grand Coulee and Boulder Dam and so on will be years up on him."

"Owen has always made a way for himself," Meg's voice stepped out to his defense. "I'm surprised his own wife would hold him back from what he most wants to do."

"Hold him — ? Just a cockeyed minute here. I only ever pointed out —" Wedding band instinct took over in Charlene, and she said flatly enough to set any mother-in-law straight: "That's between Owen and me, wouldn't you have to say?"

"No, actually, Charlene, I'd say it's a matter for Owen," Meg gave back to her at least as instructively. "I've never known him to put a foot wrong" — except, her tiniest pause suggested, in who he walked to the altar with — "and if he thinks this dam is the work for him, he should see it through."

"It's not that simple a proposition, it really isn't. Owen himself says that if Fort Peck works the way it's supposed to, it'll be a feather in his cap, yes. But if something goes wrong, it'll stick to the engineers here. Back we'll all go to cow pasture dams, he says so himsel—"

"Charlene. I am for Owen. I can't help that, and I won't even try."

"He's not just yours to be *for* anymore, though, is he. He went out and added a wife."

"I'm not trying to take him back from you. That's silly to even think." *(Oh, is it?)* "But he doesn't *stop* being my son just because —"

"Nobody *said* he has to stop being your —"

"*Well,* then?"

"Well then, *what?*"

"How'd it go?"

Owen was perfectly cheery, chirping that out, when he got home to Glasgow after work. He could afford to be, Charlene figured, before she started on answering him; he didn't have any in-laws around.

"We didn't see eye to eye."

"On what?"

"You name it. Anything."

She saw he was going to wait her out, with not the best expression in the world on his face, so she confessed the specific.

"You. She and I got into it, a little, over —"

"Me? Goddamn it, you two. Couldn't you just unpack boxes and pat that shack into place a bit without getting into a battle royal about — what'd I have to do with it, anyway?"

"What you and I have talked about, is all. Where Fort Peck is going to lead to, as against the other dams."

"I thought you and I agreed we'd look at that a little farther down the line," Owen said in the dead-level tone he employed against surprises. "Like when we have an actual house to live in and I have an actual dredging operation to size up — the actual factual to judge by, on how things are going, then decide from there."

"I know we did. It just came up some-how, with your mother." Back at the department store in Bozeman, the first one to see Mr. Cunningham slip out of his office on one of his inspection prowls would always scribble a note and zing it down in the change canister, *Have you seen the big scissors?* Charlene right now felt as if the big scissors of life had sneaked up on her unannounced. Here she was in the second fight of the day and all she'd been trying to do was to cache some damn boxes.

"All right, then, those things happen," Owen said as if he didn't at all see why they had to. "Let's just get back to maintaining some peace."

"And what is it you think I'm supposed

to do about that?"

"Maybe tone things down a bit, where the rest of the family is concerned."

"Owen, it was only a spat. It was not as if your mother and I threw furniture at each other."

"Listen one damn minute, Charlene, okay? I'm trying to help the members of my family, and my mother is the main one we've — I've got to team up with. The Old Man will pay attention to her, some, and Neil will pay attention to me, some, and among us we can maybe hogtie Bruce. But if you're going to be fighting with my mother, that kills it all. The whole bunch of them will turn their backs on you. On us. And that's something I can't have happen."

"You know, Owen, I only remember marrying one Duff."

"The rest get thrown in free. Charlene, this is only until they can get themselves squared away here. I have enough say, here and there on the project, that I've managed for Neil and Bruce to come up with pretty good jobs. I can probably even send something the Old Man's way, whenever he comes to his senses enough to take it. They all of them can keep on up the ladder, if they don't decide they'd rather put a foot in my face. So, all I'm saying is it'd help everybody's situation by not having my mother on the outs with us." Owen put a hand into her hair, stroking ever so lightly. "How about giving that a try for me, think you can?"

What Charlene deeply thought was that the circumstances had not yet been invented, in human annals, under which Meg would ever let herself be on the outs with her perfect Owen, and that this was always going to pose a problem for a daughter-in-law of Meg Duff. But what she confined herself to saying was:

"Ownie, I'll make every try. But you're letting yourself in for some real refereeing."

The dam's first principle was to build not from the bottom up, but from the bottom down. To give a dirt dam builder a nightmare, merely whisper "seepage": water eating its way beneath, undercutting the dam's mass of earthfill.

Owen had worked the topic to death in his degree work at Bozeman, evaluating the performance of earthen embankment dams. Rode the rails to the West Coast, his last college summer, and signed on as a coal stoker on a freighter in ore to reach Panama and explore the Gatun Dam there, which made use of the material moved in the cutting of the Panama Canal — Gatun was the biggest earthfill dam ever tried, before Fort Peck. Then the rest of his freighter voyage, on around to an East Coast port, and Pennsylvania to be hitch-hiked across, so he could look back on the one that spooked everybody — the South Fork Dam, which had been above Johnstown.

Fort Peck's shield against seepage had to be steel, thirty-four million pounds of it in girder form, driven side by side straight down through riverbed's sediment and clay into bedrock. Amid all the other fever spots of site preparation here in 1934, pile drivers were beginning to mo-notonously peg the girders into the earth, to an average depth of one hundred feet. Day by week by month, the cutoff wall, as this was called, would rise and extend as a metal palisade across the Fort Peck valley. On top of this cutoff wall would come the pyramid core of earthfill dredged from the river's bottoms and banks, and on either side of the core the more gradual slopes of fill, all engineered with Fort Peck's singularities in mind.

"Any earth dam, to be built to perma-nence, must be tailor-made to fit its indi-vidual location," Owen phrased it in the thesis that tipped the balance for him when the hiring was done for Fort Peck.

Taken together, then, the watertight cut-off wall and the impervious core and the vast pervious buttresses of fill would form the heavy lid to hold back the river water, permanently.

Two thousand two hundred and eighty people died at Johnstown, when that less than permanent dam went out in 1889.

Colonel Parmenter's decision to name Owen Duff as the fillmaster, overseeing the dredging and mounding of a world-record quantity of earthfill, was the kind of jump a career needed only once.

"He's young for it," Major Santee objected.

"He'll get over that quick enough," the colonel said.

It was not even Saturday night yet, mere Thursday, when Hugh dragged himself home from fighting brush and found himself invited right back out. By Meg, who was telling him:

"I thought we might both go downtown tonight."

"You don't want to do that, Meggedy," he said uneasily. "Just a lot of drinking and carrying on, there."

"Hugh, I do too want to."

That tone let him know she meant it, and it threw him. For one thing, he was much less than sure that Bruce and Neil, who were in their bowling period now, were actually at the bowling alley this very night rather than draped over a taxi dancer apiece. For another, Hugh couldn't think where his and Meg's next move could possibly be, if she took a look at Wheeler in full howl and vetoed staying here.

"I'll go alone," she was declaring, "if I have to."

There is no alone in Wheeler, Hugh thought, *that's the point of this place.* Aloud, though:

"Put on your madhouse clothes, then, and let's go."

They could hear the downtown activities long before they were there, the din of the big Wheeler Inn the loudest of all, and so Hugh steered Meg into the Blue Eagle instead. It too was packed with drinkers and dancers, but Hugh had in the back of his mind that Tom Harry did not seem the kind to tolerate total riot. Indeed, the interior of the Blue Eagle hummed and jangled — a solo piano was providing the taxi dance music this night — but there were none of the bloodcurdling shrieks the Wheeler Inn seemed prone to.

Hugh with his effective elbows managed their way to the bar, Meg as close as possible behind him with a fixed expression of gameness. She had Charlene to thank, or not, for this excursion. Determination had been building up in Meg, ever since their set-to over standing by Owen, to sally out with Hugh to his nether side of life; show him she stood by him, even here, even in this deepest precinct of the *everything,* if that's what it took. Such was Wheeler. People, Margaret Duff to name one, who would have sworn they hated the roistering side of life now found themselves practically aswim in it, just from residence in this town.

Tom Harry was presiding beside the cash register while the hectic squad of part-time bartenders manned the bar. The nearest one stopped in front of Hugh and Meg and gawked.

The familiar nose like a sail set in the wind made Hugh laugh. "Birdie, my man," he said feeling suddenly and unaccountably ritzy. "Couple of Shellacs, if you please."

Meg herself half-smiled. "You almost sound as if you know your way around."

Hugh handed her one of the two bottles of Great Falls Select Beer that Birdie Hinch thrust at him. "Three times for luck," he recited and clicked his bottle against hers once, twice, and again. "Don't forget, love, it was Duffs who laid the foundation of this place," he grandly indicated the vicinity of the floor. "We know its every cubit, do Bruce and Neil and I."

A moment or two later, he felt further ratified in his choice of venue when a massive undersheriff appeared in the doorway, took the temperature of the place by craning a look to Tom Harry, then went back out. Hugh ever so carefully sipped his beer instead of swigging. Meg couldn't have swigged if her life depended on it. Around them the business of pleasure tuned up.

People's life stories were pouring out on both sides, a gaunt Dakotan recounting the five hundred miles of mud he and his wife and three kids had inched through to reach Fort Peck, and a big-shouldered man with a chomping accent telling another about his misadventures in Butte's mines and, if Meg was hearing right, brothels.

Rumor and gossip were spreading with barracks alacrity. President Roosevelt was coming to Fort Peck to commend them all in person, she overheard, and hourly wages were going to be put higher because the foremen were reporting that they had never seen human beings who worked like these. No, she heard a moment later, a wage cut was on its way, because never had so many managed to do so little; and it was Eleanor Roosevelt who was on her way to Fort Peck. The town of Wheeler was going to stay so wide open, she took in on her left, that they were going to take the doors off these saloons; no, it was said on her right, Wheeler was about to be patrolled by Army troops.

Above all the talk the piano was going like a house afire, played by a pouter-breasted woman who looked like a church organist. Distinctly unchurchly, however, was the procession of amber drinks lined up along the top of her piano. Amid her music making, men eyed the taxi dancers, the taxi dancers smoothed the fabric down their thighs. Meg studied these actions. *So this is how they do it.* Each woman, some pretty and some desperately homely and the majority in between, sat waiting on a bar stool until a male paid the fare by buying her a beer or a mixed drink — the mix, naturally, being water and cake coloring — and entitling himself to a dance. Watching this commerce, Meg knew she had to disapprove. The question was, how much. Quite a lot of the dancing, she was surprised to note, was decorous. But the night was young yet in Wheeler.

When it came to bowling, Bruce was something terrific and he knew it. His style had sweep and power without quite overdoing the speed of the ball, and his strikes had a resonance nobody else in the bowling alley could match — a sound-of-doom *KWONK* that mowed down all ten pins at once.

"Fun to see them fly," he announced after his third strike in a row.

"You'd use a double-barreled shotgun on them if you could," Neil observed. He wasn't nearly as good a strike maker but could pick off spares, where Bruce seemed to rely on the windforce of the ball passing the pin.

"Suppose there's a living in this?" Bruce joked.

"Sure. Right down at the other end of the alley." Neil inclined his head to the lame boy working as pinsetter.

Knowing there was no limit on the number of times Bruce could stand to win, Neil simply went along with the bowling for what he thought was long enough and then called it off.

"Still early," Bruce said. "Buy you a beer. Buy you a tootsie roll! Buy you a roll with a tootsie!"

"Big talk," said Neil, heart hammering.

"Well, we could start with the beer," Bruce maintained.

Down the bar from Hugh and Meg, a pair of Corps of Engineers officers forged in. "Bourbon on the rocks," one ordered.

Birdie Hinch goggled at the bottles of mixers under the bar. "What's rocks?"

Next in the parade of arrivals was a

group of men not in uniform but dressed so alike that they might as well have been. With them, Owen.

He came over at once, his eyebrows up.

"Meg, it's our firstborn!" Hugh announced, as though this were a miraculous conjunction. To Owen, he delivered: "Your mother expressed a wish to see the night-life of Wheeler, which seems to include you, Ownie."

"Came in to have one before we head back to Glasgow," Owen indicated with his head toward the other engineers, but still trying to size up the latest unexpected family situation. The Old Man at least looked sober, and his mother appeared determined to get an education about Wheeler, all right. "I'll have it with you, if I'm invited."

"What do you think, Meg, are we picky about our company?" asked Hugh. Nonetheless he high-signed to Birdie to bring a beer for Owen.

"This pleases me," Meg smiled around the words at Owen, "my men paying court to me, with all the competition there is around."

"Married men don't go in for that kind of behavior, do they, Dad." The taxi dancing revved up as the piano player produced a sultry waltz. *Holy Christ, I wish they'd get the cookie cutter town built. If*

Charlene ever lays eyes on this . . . Owen pulled his attention back to the immediate issue, his father's behavior around anything bottled. Hugh, though, seemed to have turned into a saloon statesman, sip by sip at his beer instead of guzzling it, staying attentive to Meg's every word, and benignly scanning the Blue Eagle throng as if he were an operagoer.

All the years. That first and last fight, Owen tearing himself away, the road to Bozeman and now to here. Owen felt a surge of reinforcement, the world had brought the matter out in his favor instead of his father's. They could finally talk truce, he figured, it was the only thing left for Hugh Duff to talk, wasn't it?

If Owen had had it to do over again, though, he would not have begun with:

"Dad, you look like dambuilding is starting to agree with you."

"Do I? That surprises me no little bit, Ownie. My end of this dambuilding is strangely like tedium," Hugh Duff informed his eldest son. "Not to mention blisters, sore back, and general debilitation."

Now you see why I went into engineering, the thought rushed in Owen. "The brushwhacking won't last forever. When we reach the point of using big equipment, jobs'll be better."

"I can look forward to advancement all the way to wheelbarrow pilot, can I."

"Shush, Hugh, you'll be fine," Meg told him as if to convince all three of them. "Don't listen to him, Owen, he's only saying that to hear his head rattle."

Hugh, though, was looking a new question at Owen, asking it as if in all reasonableness.

"How can this ever work?"

With a start, Owen comprehended that Hugh must have spent evening after evening gazing at the shack's walls of lateral blueprint, the dam in its unprecedented width. "It'll work, don't worry yourself about that," he maintained stoutly. "What we'll be doing is using the flow of the dredge material to sort —"

"No," Hugh cut him off, "not your engineer sermonry, Ownie. I mean the nature of the idea itself. Fiddling with the river — what's the point of that?"

"First off, flood control —" Owen began and realized his father had been lying in wait for those words.

"Eh, ignorant me. Here I had the notion from somewhere that there's going to be a permanent flood, out of this," Hugh pronounced. "A hundred and twenty-five miles or so of it, in back of your whackety great dam."

"Hugh, drop this right now," Meg warned.

"No, let him, Mother." Owen drew a fortifying breath and looked at his father. *Get it out of his system. Out of all our systems.* "There's a lot of politics behind this dam, I don't kid myself about that. All down the Missouri, and then the Mississippi Valley on from there, people get flooded out in any wet year, and then they're after somebody to do something about it. Partly this dam is on account of that, partly it's Roosevelt having to put people to work somehow."

"But I *had* work!" Hugh blurted.

Beside him, Meg had her eyes closed and wished she could do the same with her ears. Yet and again, here it came, Hugh's refusal to see the homestead as it had become, these last years. When there weren't too many grasshoppers, there was too little rain. When the crop was good, the price wasn't. When the price was good, the crop wasn't. For the life of her, Meg could not understand how he could stay so fixed to all that.

"*We* had work!" Hugh was exclaiming. "Bruce and Neil and" — he gazed at Owen, then away — "myself. The place —"

"It was blind work," Meg told him tensely. "There was no seeing a living, these past summers."

"Other summers would have come, Meg," he said back to her, then targeted Owen again. "Your precious people downstream, who get their socks wet when it floods — why can't they be told to put their enterprises on higher ground?"

"You can't *un*do that much of things, that's why," Owen answered in ready exasperation. Meg glanced around apprehensively to see if the entire Blue Eagle by now was watching her husband and her son go at each other, but realized that even their raised voices didn't make a dent in the din level.

"People are established there," Owen was going on, "they're determined to live where they want and —"

"And those of us who chose best higher up the river get drowned out because we're fewer," Hugh put in.

"Now that's malarkey, and you know it."

"I don't know that, Owen. I don't know that at all."

"Then maybe it's time you did. What is it you think, that Fort Peck Dam looked around for the person to inconvenience the most and chose exactly you? Dad, for crying out loud, there are dams being built right now on the Columbia, the Colorado, the Tennessee, the Sacramento, the you-name-it. It's too bad we can't build any of those without putting water over somebody. People have to contend with that, a little. But there's no —"

"A *little?*"

"More than a little, then. Some. *A lot!* Is that better?"

"Bothers you, does it." Hugh looked at Owen in cold satisfaction. "It fucking aye should. Margaret, I'm sorry about the language."

"And I'm sorry about you," Meg gave him, her voice up there with theirs now. "I thought there was more to you, Hugh Duff, than this mooncalf notion that we've been put out of a paradise that would send Eden to shame. That wasn't the only place on the face of the earth where you can grow a stalk of alfalfa. The wages here, if we" — her look said *you* — "keep at it, can get us onto our feet, wherever we want. Hugh, the place, these years — the place made us a start but it never made us much else."

"At least it was greatly more than a shack and an axe and a spoon," Hugh hammered those words.

Owen made a last try. "You want to go back to basics, here's one for you." With the moisture condensed on the bottom of his beer bottle, he drew a damp straight line on the polished wood of the bar. "This is the Missouri, our place to here, right this minute." Above that, he sketched a wet arc. "But the original river went like this, all the way up north of Havre and around, in the bed of what's now the Milk River — you maybe didn't know that, I bet, but until glacial times royally rearranged things, the Missouri River didn't flow anywhere near our place." *Hydraulics 330, the course at Montana State College that made Owen sit up straighter and straighter; Professor Zell, by way of illustration, intoning to him and the other students about the incomparable forces of the glacial process, which Zell pronounced as if it rhymed with "no less."*

Tutor to his parents, Owen glanced up earnestly to make sure they, particularly the male one, were following this revelation of the Missouri River's past. "So, see, what a river does, any river, is geologically temporary. Rivers are *always* changing, so here we're just —"

"These are not glacier times!" Hugh thundered.

"Christ Jesus," Bruce let out, as he and Neil halted at that voice and made the sighting at the bar of the Blue Eagle. "It's the Old Man and Mother and the Reverend Ownie."

Uncomfortably joining them, Neil proffered "How you doing, Ownie?" while Bruce said to nowhere, "Thought we'd get

150

out of the house for a change."

"A dire need of fresh air, no doubt," said Meg.

Neil cleared his throat. "Bruce owes me a beer for letting him beat me by a million pins tonight, don't you." Bruce grunted and started trying to flag down Birdie Hinch.

"So," Neil said next. He decided the dam would probably be the most popular topic. "Ownie, when's the bigger work start?"

"Any day now."

"Ask him how much more whacking down brush his dear old father can look forward to, why don't you?" Hugh prompted loudly and took a tilt of his beer.

"A hundred and twenty-five miles or so." Owen stared Hugh in the eye to be sure there'd be no mistaking his meaning.

Hugh choked on his beer. "All the way to our — ?"

"All of it," Owen vouched, "the whole lake bottom, if we can."

"But you're going to put water over all that anyway! What's the point —"

"More frogskins," Neil contributed.

"That's about it," Owen agreed. "Wages are the thing." He cocked his head as if to angle this into Hugh most effectively. "You cussed as loud as anybody when this country came to a stop, I seem to remember."

Hugh went right back at him. "This country will get going again, then, as long as everybody puts in enough hours on the woodpile?"

"You pair are going to wear your tongues out," Meg tried to turn them off. Neil and Bruce, dumbstruck, were watching as if they had just been adopted into a family of cutthroats. "Christ all mighty," Owen was saying in a gritted tone to Hugh's last point, "it's always more complicated than that."

"Simple it down for me, then," Hugh challenged. "Tell your old daftie of a father where this is going to lead to, this work that doesn't need doing except so people can be paid for doing it."

"Owen doesn't have all night," Meg put in.

"The loyalty of a loving Scotch wife," Hugh announced to the rafters of the Blue Eagle. "There's nothing like it except possibly ambush and slaughter."

Just then, at the end of the bar next to the bandstand, a ruckus broke out among the taxi dancers.

"That's my stool," stated the one with white-blonde hair and aviatrix slacks. "More to the point, snooks, that's my customer."

"This stool doesn't have your name on it anywhere I see," maintained the plumpish redhead.

"Probably it's got yours by now," said the peroxide blonde, "from the weight of that fanny."

"You're the one to know about fannies," the redhead retorted. "You peddle yours every chance you get."

"At least I get the chance," the blonde said coolly.

Owen, taking this in with the rest of the Duffs, reminded himself that he absolutely was going to have to start getting home earlier these evenings and do the night fantastic with Charlene. The platinum blonde — no, what was beyond platinum; chromium? — was starting to look pretty good to him. She clearly knew her business where her competition was concerned, keeping after the redhead: "Now, clear off of my stool and away from my customer."

"You can have the stool when Jimsie and I dance," cooed the redhead. "Isn't that right, Jimsie?"

The blonde abruptly turned away and marched up a little set of stairs to the bandstand. There she turned around again, took a quick running start, and sailed off the bandstand, her spread legs catching the redhead around the waist and her arms locked around the copper head of hair. Like a toppling totem pole, the entwined women hit the floor, the redhead underneath.

"Ow," Bruce commented feelingly. "Floorburn."

Meg astonished and Hugh and Neil and Bruce and Owen deeply interested, the Duffs spectated as the blonde, still astraddle the redhead with the breath knocked out of her, groped for her opponent's ears as handles to bang her head against the floor.

Before she could get fully underway at that, Tom Harry had vaulted the bar and swooped his arms around the blonde from behind, pulling her off the flattened redhead.

"For cripe's sake, Shannon," he complained, "you could of broken her neck. You could of broke both your necks, and then where the hell would I be?"

The blonde, now a tornado of elbows, tore free of her employer, caught hold of the customer Jimsie, and went out the back door with him in tow. Tom Harry shook his head and stooped to the redhead who was woozily attempting to sit up. "Music, Gert," he directed the piano player. When the first hesitant notes of *Roses of Picardy* did not dissolve the thick circle of onlookers, Tom Harry looked up.

"*Dance!*" he roared. "This one's on the house!"

The taxi dance women a little sulkily, the

men eagerly, pairs of partners again filled the floor of the Blue Eagle.

"I'm going to call it a night," Owen announced, "before the blood gets over our heads." He still had the drive back to Glasgow, the day's shale core samples to tabulate, and needed to assemble his thoughts for the morning's inevitable series of brieftngs. He gave his father a minimum goodbye, each of them still wanting to clout some sense into the other; his mother a gallant kiss; and Neil and Bruce a wry last look. *I'm the one who ought to be twins.*

Bruce and Neil evaporated off to somewhere. Hugh turned to Meg and asked drily, "Enough Wheeler for you?"

"No," she surprised him again, determinedly displaying her beer bottle with still a sip in it. Not quite yet."

The southern tip of Valley County, Montana, had become magnetized, Sheriff Kinnick grew convinced.

That spring and summer of 1934, besides Sangster weaving his railroad bridge up into the air above the channel and Owen's fleet of dredges and barges amassing along the riverbank, work commenced on the four giant diversion tunnels to carry the river beneath the dam and on stripping away the fifteen thousand years of silt the Missouri had deposited where the core of the dam needed to rest with absolute firmness. Pile drivers, which already had everybody at Fort Peck ear-weary from pounding down the wooden trestle pilings day and night, in July remorselessly resumed with steel, the girders of the cutoff wall. And to the sheriff's furious dismay, in August here came Franklin Delano Roosevelt, merrily dragging all the trappings of the presidency of the United States with him, to spend ten minutes giving his political benediction to the Fort Peck Dam. "Fort Peck is only a small percentage of the dream," the President said in the direction of downstream constituencies. "Before American men and women get through with the job, we are going to make every ounce and every gallon of water that flows from the heavens and the hills count before it makes its way down to the Gulf of Mexico." As far as Carl Kinnick was concerned, FDR could have simply jotted that onto White House stationery and dropped it in the mail, saving Valley County and its sheriff an immense amount of bother.

But bother kept coming, by the dozen. Just when the sheriff was getting used to the problem of Wheeler, would-be Wheelers sprang up everywhere around the dam site. Delano Heights, Lakeview, Midway,

Parkdale, Willow Bend, Valley, McCone City, Park Grove, Idlewile, New Deal, Square Deal, Free Deal . . . like urchins imitating higher society, the places built themselves, shack by shanty by flophouse by gin mill, a new "town" for every month of the year 1934. Wheeler still predominated at such levels as taxi dancing and drink consumption and emporiums of prostitution, but what law officer in his right mind wanted whole towns cropping up in his jurisdiction before he had properly even heard of them? So, as some brand-new rough arrangement of neighborhood followed onto each spate of jobs created at Fort Peck, the sheriff sucked in his breath and told himself that all this was temporary.

If a person could just stand "temporary" as including the next four years.

Owen and Charlene's trailer house now was parked on the official Fort Peck townsite, where the Corps had contractors simultaneously laying out curvaceous residential streets on the pattern of the Country Club suburb in Kansas City and erecting the mass of barracks that was going to make Fort Peck the biggest bunkhouse on the planet. There at the edge of the zone of construction, Charlene would not exactly have described herself as entertained, but at least the routine here was more diverting than Glasgow had been. Whenever he wasn't in a meeting Owen would come home for lunch, a nice bookmark in the middle of the day, they both thought. And after work, as now, he could practically be back at the trailer house and kissing Charlene before his head knew he had left the office.

"Owen."

He swung around, only a stone-skip from the trailer house. Neil was perched on a windowsill of a prefabricated barracks framework that hadn't been there at lunchtime.

"Catching some air?" Owen asked him. Then, wondering more than he wanted to: "Or did Charlene put the run on you for not knowing when to take your hat off?"

Neil shook his head, letting Owen try to decipher that and his quiet grin.

"I need to ask you to pitch in on something," Owen's no-longer-such-a-kid brother said. "A business proposition."

The next Saturday morning, they borrowed Tom Harry's big Packard and away the bunch of them cruised, propelled by Neil's idea. Meg vigilant between Owen and Hugh in the front seat, and Neil and Bruce spread all over the backseat as if practicing to be rich.

"Come on, Ownie, try this boat out," Bruce urged. The fresh paving of the new State Route 24 went north ahead like a gray slither between a hundred miles of prairie on either side.

Owen was tempted to point out that the Duffs already were shooting along at their greatest velocity in history. In spite of being told to by Bruce, he actually was romping on the accelerator a little in the highway's straighter stretches, the speedometer needle arcing over onto 60, more than enough to make Meg and Hugh purse up in apprehension, and he'd liked to have brought Bruce down a peg by telling him that the five of them were moving with the combined momentum of a person going 300 miles an hour, was that fast enough for him?

"Keep your shirt on, how about," Owen stayed determinedly amiable. "We all get thrown in the calaboose for speeding, it'd be the Fort Peck record for most arrests in one family."

"Not a good thought, eh, Bruce?" Hugh still was detouring his words around Owen, but at least they were words and not shouts. "How would they ever test the famous suction pumps without us?"

The whole carful laughed for a mile. The suction episode had come about because the boatyard boss, Medwick, was grousing over being shorthanded for a booster-pump test that needed to be run immediately and Bruce, helpful, cited his father and Birdie Hinch as willing temporaries. Medwick pulled the pair off the brushcutters' crew truck and the next thing they knew they were aboard a bargelike pump unit moored to the riverbank. All this was, Medwick stressed to Hugh and Birdie and Bruce and a few other boatyard hands he had conscripted, was a simple rev test, to see how the floating barge behaved when the 2,500-horsepower pump was revved up. When he gave the word they'd run a few minutes of muck through the intake pipe and the pump and the outlet line, and that would be that. Medwick looked dubiously at Hugh, a farmer if he had ever seen one, and stuck him out on deck to watch against clogs at the intake. He put Birdie Hinch, senatorial-faced and nodding, in charge of the pump's gate valve meant to prevent vacuum surges in the suction process. Bruce and the others took their posts in the pumphouse and Medwick started up the big pump. Things hummed and gushed nicely for a minute until Medwick yelled to Birdie to check on his gate valve. The Roman-nosed little man studied the wordage on the valve in professorial fashion, although as Hugh knew and Medwick didn't, Birdie Hinch could not have spelled squat if you spotted him the *k* and the *w*. Then, veteran incompetent that he was, Birdie managed to flip the valve setting the only wrong way possible, totally backward. At once the suction pump sucked much too enthusiastically as a vacuum surge shot through the intake line, blowing off the top seals of the pump, sudden tons of silt and water gushing into the panicked pumphouse. The avalanche of mud, grit, and water flushed Medwick and the two men nearest him and on top of them Birdie out of the pumphouse in a tumbling act featuring yelling and cussing. Bruce, the last man washed out the side door, managed to flip the emergency switch on his way past and shut down the fiasco.

"Medwick never even so much as told me 'thank you'," Bruce complained now with profound mock hurt.

"I just wish you had closed that pumphouse door," Owen chided him in similar tone. "You let a lot of good fill material get away."

Meg, monitoring her men, glanced over her shoulder to smile at Neil, who gave her a wordless grin back. Intricate, families are, she thought. If this expedition had been Owen's idea, Hugh would have scoffed it to death. If Hugh had proposed it, Owen would have been mortally dubious toward it. If Bruce had thought it up, everybody else would have written it off as a pipedream. Only Neil, quietly central as Switzerland, could have put this out on the table and not had it knocked off.

They were nearly there by now. Bruce took a last chance to razz his father about the shortest boatyard career in history. "Medwick told me, Dad, he'd have kept you and Birdie on if he had an unlimited supply of suction pumps and barges."

"Tears as big as horse turds rolled down his cheeks, I'm sure," Hugh said drily. "Margaret, I'm —"

"— sorry about the language, you every time are," Meg chanted to him. "Owen, Bruce, Neil, any of you," she lightly inquired, "do you know where I can send a man to have his tongue scraped?"

The Packard swept into Glasgow. Homely as it was, a town deposited onto bald nowhere by railroad iron, Glasgow nonetheless looked Parisian after Wheeler. Meg made mental note of a paint store.

Owen parked a block down the street from Moore Motors, Hugh having pointed out the fiscal suicide in pulling up to an automotive dealership in a swanky Packard.

At once the Duff sons fanned out through the lot of used trucks, Meg and Hugh sticking with Neil. Their show of support perhaps paid off. It was Neil who spotted the big Model AAA wide-body.

He approached the truck as if he could rub it and have three wishes granted.

The ton-and-a-half Ford had a distinctive cab, with a little cap peak of outside visor above the windshield, and out in front of that an impressively long hood atop fenders arched as judiciously as the shoulder-flaps of Roman armor. At the opposite end of the wheelbase, the rear wheels were duals, fourfold traction that appealed to anyone who had ever fought Montana mud. Besides that, the Triple A was a favorite in the High Line oilfields for its roomy cab, letting four roughnecks — if they weren't too brawny — ride abreast during pipe hauls. True, the cab, hood, fenders and the rest of *this* Triple A had seen better days, quite a number of them. The paint had to be guessed at as the original Ford "any color you want as long as it's black." From farm experience, though, the Duffs knew that when sun and other elements had blistered a piece of machinery down to blue metal, it was just getting nicely broken in.

"Not bad," Owen came over and praised.

"Mr. Jaarala says that although Henry Ford should be taken out and shot," Meg provided, "his trucks are sound."

"It does look like it's hell for stout,"

Hugh came up with.

"That's what we want," confirmed Bruce. Then generously deferred: "Don't we, Neil."

Neil was too stricken with truck-itis to answer. The Model Triple A seemed to stand there like a well-broken pack animal, in waiting agreement with him and what he had grasped about Fort Peck. That everything Fort Peck needed had to be hauled in from somewhere. The dam site itself was no more self-sufficient than a polar base camp. Right now Owen's fellow engineers were bending railroad iron down from the Great Northern in a spur line for construction supplies, and there'd eventually be another rail line from the quarry at Snake Butte just to bring in rock — *rock!* A place that didn't even have rocks of its own, that told you something.

No, Neil had it figured cold. That loads of whatever kind (heating stoves, workshoes, bulldozer attachments, angle iron, two-by-fours, kerosene, groceries — good grief, even drinking water) were going to have to be brought in to Fort Peck and the worker towns almost endlessly until the dam was completed, and he might as well be the trucker of some of those loads. With family backing, such as Bruce to occasionally spell him in the driving and the other Duffs giving a hand as needed, this could be an enterprise for them all, why not. Even Charlene, Neil had been proud to find out, was kicking in on this in her own way. She had outright volunteered to have the celebratory meal ready for them when they came home to Fort Peck as truck tycoons.

The four Duff men all but took the Triple A apart bolt by bolt, in assuring themselves the truck was in decent running condition.

They are something to see together, if I do say so myself. Meg, sitting in the driver's seat out of the sun, watched the quartet of long-boned forms bending over the engine in front of her in learned disputation about aluminum pistons. *Put a frame around them and the curious can line up for guesses.*

Aren't they a lot for the heart
*   to stand, Mrs. Duff?*
— The heart picks and chooses,
*   more than you might think.*
If you had it to do over, would you
*   put so much bright into*
*   your eldest son?*
—Ask him yourself, you need to on that.
*   Mothers and even wives do not dare*
answer everything.
And the dual set of sons — would
*   you have two at once, again?*
— A major question, there, whether it

165

has been fair to either.
Your sparring partner Hugh —
how do you account for him,
as your mate for a lifetime?
— I am still working on that,
to this moment.

"We can stouten up the springs," Hugh was chipping in, through the windshield in front of her. "Put in new leaves. I can tend to that." He was sure Birdie Hinch would know the whereabouts of heavy-duty spring-leaves in the dam site supply building. Neil and Bruce were vying with each other about how high to make the new boxboards. Owen, looking bemused, was writing out the check for a downpayment.

One of Neil's figurings about the Duff trucking enterprise could not have been more completely off. Bruce showed no interest whatsoever in driving any of the hauls. "Your set of wheels, Neilie, you get to use them. I'll pitch in on the loading and unloading."

It took precisely a week for Bruce's abstinence from the truck to be explained. That next Saturday, he bought a motorcycle.

The world looked different from behind the steering wheel of the Model Triple A.

Neil all but lived in the truck, taking on short runs after his trestle shift, mostly loads of firewood that he would deliver out of the bottomland, then on Saturdays and Sundays he would line up longer hauls, need-it consignments of equipment or spare parts that a contractor wanted in a hurry from Glasgow or Havre or even Great Falls. On the local stuff, evenings, Owen, or Hugh if he could drag enough energy out of himself after a day of bashing brush, or Meg — not Charlene yet, though — had been helping him out at tossing stovewood off the truck; and naturally Bruce was a windmill at this, able to empty a load while most people would still be standing around looking at it. But then away Bruce would scoot, round-goggled pilot on that motorcycle, burning up miles to no advantage that Neil could see. Why did people have any trouble at all telling the two of them apart?

About now Bruce would be whistling into his graveyard shift at the Missouri River boatyard while here Neil was on the other side of the Continental Divide, across the entire Rocky Mountains, at the lumber-mill town of Coram with a hard-driven four hundred miles behind him since he got off the early shift at Fort Peck that morning. He had managed to get the truck loaded with lumber before utter dark, and now he would sleep stretched out on the seat of the cab, then before daybreak start the drive east, back to Fort Peck. Wake up cold and stiff, but climb down and walk around the truck a dozen or so times to stir himself awake, then head onto the highway. By sunrise he would be on the plains out from Browning, and while the sun seared up through the highway, just as he had met it sinking molten through this same road at sunset yesterday, he would crimp his hatbrim lower, duck his head a little to one side, squint at the highway's edge and the borrow pit, and as a last resort slow down the truck. But he wouldn't ever stop. If he had to buck the sun, morning or evening, its trajectory and his stubbornly coinciding, so be it.

Almost a little scary, how undodging and powerful the view of things seemed to Neil now. Time spent in the truck brought him thought after thought about the routes of life. He went back and forth over the past year, the homestead to Fort Peck. The homestead had been — well, *home.* Neil was one who liked living by seasons, and the changing complexion of each year within the canyon had suited him fine, the overnight green when spring arrived and then the gradual tanning of summer; he could take almost a chameleon comfort in those surroundings. It required no leap of his imagination to have seen himself staying on there, working the home place, watching for a chance to marry a schoolteacher. And the Old Man was not wrong about the crop. Alfalfa seed was a kind of annual gold. If you could last out the bad years, farming that riverbank bar, the good ones would be heavenly.

But Fort Peck was a jillion times more interesting. Hectic, yes, scruffy, you bet, and somewhat dangerous into the bargain. Nor could he see the point of work shifts done strictly by the clock.

Yet Neil could not help but think, here in the last mindturnings before sleep, that the chance to be in on Fort Peck outweighed any of that, the lull of what he had known on the homestead or the bothers of being a timeclock worker.

He rolled over on the truck seat, his hip grazing the knob of the gearstick, as if it was nuzzling him for more hauling of the infinite bits and pieces needed at the boatyard, the trestle, the workers' towns, the diversion tunnels, the spillway . . . the only envy Neil would admit he had of Owen was that capacity to see how Fort Peck's scatteration of projects was all going to fit together into one gigantic functioning dam, presto, by some exact day.

The two of them were in the best kind of tangle, from his hand submerged in her hair, fingers spread there in a loving sift, restlessly making strands, cupping the curve of the back of her head, her arms fastened tight across his back and her legs locking the lower part of him to her, while his other hand stroked curves there; between, the touchings that happened without any guiding, the hard buds of her breasts and the hilt fullness of his erection; and everywhere else summer on their skin, at last out from under the bedcovers of autumn and winter and spring, this chance to wrap around each other on the white open of sheets an arousal in itself; now the coming-in, she understood why the word *come* was applied so many ways to this, Charlene could say it herself within the murmured chant of *darling, can you, there, yes, you can* and not even mean it as dirty, mean it as come *to* her without the, well, the *in* and all, the egg-puddle that was the male messy contribution to this, the girls at the department store used to laugh about how men were always spilling their tapioca, she giggled far down in her throat; so much better, this, than the beginner's moan which could pass for a groan, or vice versa — love tutored this, even though she'd had to learn the language of it herself, although that wasn't quite fair either, Owen had had some inspirations, whispers, *help me a little, as now, there, let me, now you,* the bed sound too, a sudden gallop to it, *what,* he thought, *what's she . . . Oh listen to us,* she thought, *noisy, we're so — the bed, it's never — that's not —*

The insistent knocking on the trailer house door froze them.

The urgent voice asking "Owen? Owen, are you there?" did worse, dissolving their coupled position.

Rolling off the bed, Owen lurched into pants, angrily threw on a shirt and started to tuck it in, then thought better of that and let it drape over his front. "Okay!" he yelled at the knocking. "Okay, okay! Coming!"

When he opened the door, his mother was there in the moonlight. She looked silvery, Owen needing a moment to realize she still was wearing her cookhouse uniform. "I hated to, Owen," she was saying. "At this hour. But —"

"That's okay," he lied. He cleared his throat and blinked hard a few times. "Come up, come in." He gave her a hand up into the trailer house. "What's wrong?"

Charlene whipped around the partition from the bedroom to where they were, the white chenille bedspread wrapped around her. Owen and Meg both stared at her apparel, nubbins and tassels everywhere on her.

"Your father," Meg resumed to Owen. "He hasn't come home at all. I didn't know where else to turn." She glanced at Charlene with what Charlene considered a characteristic mother-in-law hex expression of both *Sorry* and *Serves you right.* "Neil went off on a haul after work and Bruce is on shift until morning, so I —" Meg swallowed, then raggedly started up again: "Payday, this was, and we were going to go downtown together the way we've been doing, all orderly, but he —"

"Okay," Owen said with an expulsion of breath. "I'll go find him." He glanced back and forth at Charlene in her bedspread and Meg in her cookhouse uniform. "Can you two —"

"We'll be just ducky," Charlene said stiffly.

Not knowing what more to say except yet another "Okay," Owen headed out into the night.

It was a sweet soft summer night to be out in, Owen had to grant his father that. A full moon, silver as a new dollar. By now the day's heat had gentled down entirely and these hours across midnight and earliest morning had the crystal quality that brings on vows to practice more poetry or astronomy. (Best of all, though, Owen still thought, for what he and Charlene had been doing. He had already made up his mind to ask her, whenever he got back from this, if she had saved his place.) The new skeleton frames of buildings by the dozens were moonlit as he hightailed it through the Fort Peck townsite, walking as fast as he could. From the cutoff wall in the bottomland came the *buh-THUD buh-THUD* of pile drivers, incessant mating call that would go on until carpenters' hammers started again here in the morning. Immediately below Owen, along the river, the boatyard was lit up. The dredge *Gallatin* had been launched, first vessel on this stretch of the Missouri since God knew when, and now finishing-work was being done. Bruce and the other boatrats, caulking and painting the long white dredge, perfecting the first of Owen's earthfill fleet. *Get it done! Finish your goddamn finishing-work!* The dumb fury of that — the dredge couldn't be put to use anyway until the dam's cutoff wall was far enough along, weeks from now — told Owen he had better simmer down, tend to his task of truant officer.

He crossed into Wheeler, and hubbub. In the wide center strip of the main street a softball game was in full roar, enough illumination from the moon and the down-town beerjoints to play by, more or less. "Swat it, Ott!" the team at bat was howling. The batter with a foot-in-the-bucket stance was said to be the brother of Mel Ott of the New York Giants, and while who the hell knew whether there was any truth to that, he was a wicked pull hitter. Owen veered very wide around the first-base side while the guy ripped a grounder whose last bounce was off the first baseman's chest. Skirting the spectacle, Owen thought of also telling Charlene the two of them were going to have to take up soft-ball, it was something you could play at night.

Then he was utterly, coldly furious again.

Jesus Dudley Christ. This is all I need — any of us need. The Old Man out here somewhere on another one of his benders. I'd like to bend him, the old sap. What gets into him? Can't he stand prosperity? Try and try to pull this family one step ahead and there he goes, right back. I just don't savvy it. I do not savvy it, how he can —

Directly ahead of the figure of Owen, the main street of Wheeler pulsated in the prairie night, ogling back at the moon, winking suggestively at the constellations. Spit on your hands and hone your hooves, Centaurus, and we'll make you into a dambuilder. Cassiopeia, darling, you can find work in this town. Gemini, you twins eternally stuck with each other, we have some of those around, too. None of which registered on Owen Duff, neither Wheeler's summonings to the stars nor its narrower neon urgings for him to *Drink Budweiser* or *Choose Great Falls Select, as he set his mouth and started his search.*

"He stomped out of here a couple hours ago," Tom Harry reported, Owen knowing almost before he heard the words that his father getting tanked up here in the Duffs' home port, the Blue Eagle, would have been altogether too simple.

Before Owen spun to go, the barkeeper nodded a slightest nod of apology to him.

"Sorry, Duff" — he called all of them that — "I should've coldcocked him and slung him into the back room for you."

Owen trudged down the block toward the vividly audible Wheeler Inn. He was not sure he was employing logic, maybe more like going back into evolution, to try the Wheeler Inn next, the oldest and biggest of the downtown drink-and-dance places, Ruby Smith's place. Supposedly Ruby had been through all this before, in the Klondike gold rush, and wherever she had learned it, she did know how to draw a full house. Owen was hardly inside the door before one of Ruby's veterans, a hard blonde whom everyone called Snow White, strutted up as if welcoming him home from farthest foreign parts.

"You look like the right kind of dance would do you some good," she prescribed.

A lot of things would. "I'm taken, sis. You seen anything of a guy who looks like me, but older and ornerier?"

"Can't imagine that recipe, buster," Snow White gave him with a huff of dismissal.

I hardly can either, he thought, *but I damn well better. Hugh Duff, the Houdini of the Missouri. Where would the old coyote go?*

Charlene was making coffee, no small trick with one hand, the other keeping the bedspread from cascading off her. By all rules of civility she ought to go and put some clothes on, she knew, but the bare feeling under the bedspread shawled around her this way was a stimulating reminder of what she and Owen had been busy at.

"Charlene, really, you needn't."

Besides, if manners were the issue, what was her mother-in-law doing interloping here in the dead of night, strayed-off husband or no strayed-off husband? This can't have been the first time Meg ever had to face an empty side of the bed.

"Charlene. This is putting you out more than I ever intended, fixing coffee and all."

Payday, though, did add something a little more serious; Charlene could grant that. She'd gathered from one of Owen's steamings about his father that Hugh threw money into the wind when he went off on one of these toots.

"I'm not even sure I should stay for a cup, Charlene. I probably should just take myself —"

Charlene silently laid out two cups and both women concentrated on the coffeepot for a while, until it began to chug.

Charlene poured, then delivered a cup in front of Meg along with what she had worked herself up to asking:

"You had to have thought about leaving him, haven't you? — Meg, what's funny about it."

The hard laughter she had set Meg off into wasn't bad enough, Meg was shooting her an expression as though Charlene was complicit in tolerating these hopeless ways of men. Charlene did not see herself so at all, and her next tone said so.

"I can't loan you Ownie every payday night, you know."

"No, no, now." Meg rubbed a finger along the rim of her coffee cup as if testing it for sharpness. "It's not a matter of that." She glanced up and at Charlene's hair, which

Charlene all at once realized still had the runnels of fondling and other muss made, by Owen's fingers. "I know Owen and you have yourselves to do with."

"Maybe you'd be doing everyone a favor" — Charlene paused, then put everything into it — "Owen too, if you ditched Hugh."

Instantaneously Meg shook her head. "I am one who fights it through, I suppose." She stopped and thought. "It's a bad Scottish habit, really. Culloden and those places, it tends to leave us in shreds."

"Listen though, Meg. You've been married practically forever, compared to me. And it's not that I have anything against Hugh. But don't you have to ask yourself where the limit to all this is?"

"Draw a line, ought I, in the soil of Fort Peck. Declare, 'Hugh Duff, if you stray across that, you're a gone geezer.' " Meg had drawn herself up commandingly, flummoxing Charlene. "It has its appeal," Meg bobbed her head in agreement and smiled ever so slightly at the younger woman. "But Charlene — when we have our say, that way, it still only works if they give a listen, doesn't it."

Practically swimming through the tight-packed throng along the bar of the Wheeler Inn, Owen saw man after man he knew from the dam crews, Stetsoned-up or suited-up or still in muddied work-clothes, and drunk and sober and between. The squad of Great Northern gandy dancers, Montenegrins or some such, who had set a track-laying record on the final mile of Sangster's railroad spur line to the dam site. The flinty newcomer from the rim of the Rockies, powder monkey turned rancher turned powder monkey again courtesy of the Depression and its sunken livestock prices, who had a reputation as a magical handler of dynamite in the diversion tunnel excavations. Other tunnel muckers, the Butte gang and the ex-coalminers from Roundup, drinking separately. Montana Power linemen here to string the web for the dam project's insatiable draw of electricity. A few Ad Building staffers, conspicuous in lack of sunburns, who daily crossed paths with Owen. Grudgy construction foremen who knew him and his name from persnickety memos. Shoulder deep in all these, staying on the move, Owen kept asking *Seen my old man?* and the answers continually came *No, Naw, Nope, Sure haven't* or *Yeah, but it was some time ago,* with a stinger generally in the tail of that last: He *had quite a load on.* Working his way clockwise — what the hell, any method was better than none — through the horde, Owen at last arrived at the beefy young football player from the University of Texas who served as Ruby Smith's bouncer, but who produced no news of Hugh. Then Owen discovered Birdie Hinch perched in a back corner watching the activity at a poker table with his chickenhawk gaze, and Birdie yielded even less. Peering down at the clamping grasp Owen had on his arm, Birdie piped out: "If I do run acrost him, I'll sure-hell tell him to steer clear of you."

Outside again, Owen took the relief of fresh air into his lungs and against his eyes. He stood a minute in the street, under the sky frosted with stars, clear ice-glints. He saw that the moon had moved significantly while he had been winnowing the Wheeler Inn crowd. Down the street there still was the Buckhorn Club and the Dewdrop Inn and Ed's Place and the Bar X and doubtless some others since he had last paid any attention. He plunged on, into the first of them.

The story was the same in all such places: men ached at women, and the women considered the men and tried to single out those worth aching at in return. Owen, no prude, nonetheless was growing alarmed at how he could almost taste this wanting at the back of his mouth. So many of the damworkers and taxi dancers were young, or rejuvenated by a job here at Fort Peck, and wages had brought possibilities; a payday and a Wheeler Saturday night when the wallet could at last back up the longings, you did not have to be a major philosopher to define possibilities out of those. As he sifted the town, saloon by saloon and dancehall by dancehall, there were a number of situations where he was just as glad not to find his father then. But he kept at it and at it. The dam's workforce now totaled five thousand, and Owen would have sworn he already had sorted that many by hand tonight.

Wheeler was taking note of Owen Duff this night, too.

Max Sangster and the nurse he was going to marry emerged from the late show at the moviehouse as Owen cut across the street, half a block away, striding like a pair of scissors going. By now Sangster had seen several sides of Owen but not this nightflying one. When his date asked what was the matter, who it was that had him stopped and staring, he mused: "The guy I work with. He looked kind of wound up." In the saloons, the dime-a-dance joints, his marches in and out of them, early as his brush against the midnight softball game, others too had noticed Owen Duff, his searching presence passing into their eyes, up the brainstairs to memory. In wraiths and wisps that are the moments remembered, such existence as we have to others, Owen's excavating course through Wheeler became part of all the recalling about the Duffs in the time ahead, ferreted and unfolded by a fierce small sheriff. The seeds of memory this night were glimpses of Owen quizzing the town and murmurs that tagged after him.

That's the fillmaster. Yeah, him, there, he's the guy they say is going to pour the dirt for this dam. . . .

One of the engineers, Owen something. They say he's bright enough to read by at night. . . .

Duff, one of that Duff tribe. . . .

More women than men looked at Owen, some of them frankly commercial as the taxi dancer had been, others simply looking, wondering what he had so different on his mind on a Saturday night. All the way back at the Wheeler Inn a trimly built woman named Nan Hill, long married to the flinty rancher/dynamiter, had turned from beside her husband and watched Owen pass through the crowd, a ruffle of recognition in her but not quite able to put a name to it, as when we try to identify the most elusive flavor in a stew.

Owen meanwhile was dreading the conclusion apparent as he barged into Ed's Place, the final and most rinkydink bar along the street.

No Hugh, and no more downtown places. That left only Happy Hollow.

Owen wiped a hand across his mouth, said something fervent, and went out and hitched a ride with a pickup heading over the hill to the brothelopolis, the two men in it arguing the merits of the spirited Riding Academy against those of the more cosmopolitan League of Nations.

Owen hopped out into Happy Hollow almost before the pickup had stopped. The brothels sat sociably in a fence corner, plowed fields behind them, six enterprises down one fenceline and four along the other.

Great, just sonofabitching great, he thought about the prospect of having to ransack ten whorehouses in search of his father, and stomped into the closest one, whose sign after all announced it was The Trail.

The madam, with a nice pussycat bow adorning the top of her blouse, appraised Owen.

"You seen —" he said and moved his open hand almost under his chin, indicating to his face.

"In the kitchen," she did her own indicating, with an amused shift of her eyes in that direction.

Not quite able to believe it, Owen shouldered through the swinging door between the brothel's parlor and its capacious kitchen.

At the end of the long table, empty glasses arrayed in front of them, sat Hugh and an overly endowed woman with hair the color of a brand-new brick.

"Owen! By whatever's holy, it's Owen!" Hugh turned and drunkenly confided to the woman, "You don't see Owen out and about, much. He's domesticated."

"Pleased meetcha," Hugh's ample companion slurred out.

"This's —" Hugh peered at her in confusion.

"Celeste," she stated.

I'll bet, Owen told her by look and thought. "Dad, listen. It's time you went home."

"Been there before, Owen." His father simultaneously wrinkled up his nose and shook his head. "Long time, been there. Not all it's cracked up to be, home."

" 's nice here," Hugh's partner in glassware agreed. She picked up her drink and carefully aimed it at the mostly empty glass that stood in front of Hugh. "Here we go — 'Three times for luck!' " The *clink, clink, clink* sounded tuneful as the two men wordlessly watched. Right there handy, Owen noticed, stood her little bottle of nail polish for daubing her mark on the money Hugh tossed down for each round of drinks. Whatever the whore's cut of the booze take was in this establishment, Celeste plainly had been having a highly profitable evening out of this customer.

"Chase off to bed, why don't you," Owen instructed her. "Alone. Just this once."

"Oh, and aren't you purer than driven fucken snow," the woman flared. "What've you got against playing thread-the-needle in bed, sonny? You plopped into this world by way of what's down his pantleg, didn't you?"

"Bet you didn't bargain for that, Ownie." Hugh gave Celeste his solemn admiration.

"Onto your feet, Dad." Owen stepped gingerly around the table on the side away from the woman and dragged Hugh up out of his chair. Patting Hugh's money pocket while exchanging glowers with the prostitute, Owen was relieved to feel a semblance of silver dollars there, not many but some.

Hugh half struggled, half shrugged against Owen's grasp, saying over and over, "Show her."

"Neither one of us has anything to show Celeste. Now come on."

"Not her. Other her. Show her, her and her dam work. Damn dam work." Hugh paused, evidently in thrill of hearing what he had just said. Then his face soured. "I — she thinks she didn't decide right, none of it, back — that mother of yours thinks she can turn me into —"

"Never goddamn mind!" Owen cut him off savagely.

Grappling with Hugh, steering him and partly carrying him at the same time, he got his father out into the parking area of Happy Hollow. He propped Hugh against the fender of a sedan and waited, panting. In a minute a pair of customers emerged out of the League of Nations.

"— said she's a white Russian, but hell, ain't they all?" one was pondering as Owen called out, asking for a lift, saying he had somebody with him who was pretty badly out of commission. Sure, hop in, the other two said back, they'd drop them wherever they wanted in town. Hugh put up an incoherent protest as Owen fought him into the backseat of the car. But once in, Hugh simply sat, staring. Meeting himself on the long road, according to his expression. Owen's gaze was sideways at his father, full of *why?* Hugh was snoring against his shoulder by the time they were halfway home.

The stabs of pain centered at the back of his head, as if his brain was being bounced against the inside of his skull.

186

"Whuh," he let out to indicate he had life in him. Then an "uhhh" as each wicked jolt shot upward through his spine and hit home.

Hugh blearily realized his leg was in the air, tucked under the arm of a figure with his back turned but who possibly might be Neil, administering the bunkhouse wake-up cure by pounding Hugh's heel with the palm of his hand.

Sunlight was pouring into the shack. Wincing, Hugh could not see Meg any-where and gradually figured out that she must already have left for the cookhouse. When he at last quit *uhhh*ing and let out an angry *ow,* Neil turned around and gave him the awful news that it was time to go to work.

The day before the next payday, Hugh and Birdie were called out of their brush-cutting and told that a transfer to the trestle gang had been cut for Hugh Carlyle Duff and John Bell Hinch.

Birdie only said the bosses must think the two of them were joined like Siamese. Hugh knew whose hand was behind the switch in jobs, but he couldn't get why Owen had gone to the bother.

He did the next day, when the trestle workers filed into the pay line and right there alphabetically behind him was Neil, saying he'd give him a lift straight home in the truck.

A weekend in the middle of the week; what could be better if you were Bruce and on the loose? Fresh off the graveyard shift with the rest of July 3 ahead of him and then the Fourth as a holiday, all he had to do was to figure out where to point the motorcycle. The city of Great Falls was not out of the question, the city of Billings was not out of the question. The city of Calgary, *Canada,* was not out of the question, even.

Trying to decide, one delicious distance over another, breezing along on the motorcycle minding his own business at about fifty miles an hour in a twentyfive-mile-an-hour zone, Bruce all at once heard the Wheeler undersheriff's siren start up.

He had what he considered an inspiration. He veered the motorcycle onto the road to the Fort Peck townsite, zipping along Milk River Drive there toward Owen and Charlene's trailer house.

Just his current luck, though: Captain Brascoe, the Fort Peck town manager, was right there at the new Administration Building when Bruce *brapp-brapp-brapp*ed by.

Bruce screeched to a halt in front of

Owen and Charlene's, and had barely un-straddled the motorcycle when Brascoe's government car was there, with the un-dersheriff's car pulling up behind that.

The traffic pileup brought Charlene out of the trailer house. "Bruce, what?!" Even at this time of day, in a keepcool frock that showed her bare arms and more than a suggestion of shoulder and throat, she looked dressed up. "What's happened now?"

"Hi, Charlene, how you doing?" he started brassing it out. "I just came over to do some borrowing from Owen."

"Owen's never around at this time of day, you know that."

In the big silence that followed, she heard how that sounded. She crossed those bare arms over her breasts and gave Bruce a lethal glare.

"His . . . tire pump," Bruce fumbled onward. "Got a real soft, uh, tire. Needs a little . . ."

The Corps captain and the undersheriff were keeping their faces straight, too straight.

"We just seem to have a speeding case here, Mrs. Duff," Captain Brascoe im-parted. "If you'd like to get on with your day while we handle it —"

"Gladly," Charlene flung in the direction of Bruce and spun into the trailer house.

He flinched at Charlene's slam of the door, then put his mind back to that inspiration of his. "Wait a minute, here. How can you arrest me if I'm not one of your Corps guys?"

"Oh good," the captain said wearily, "a barracks lawyer." He turned to the under-sheriff. "Norm, you want him instead?"

Bruce could scarcely wait to triumphantly trump that, too. "But this is government whatchamacallit, jurisdiction, in here, isn't it? Got 'US of A property' on everything in sight."

The undersheriff and the captain both eyed Bruce.

"Nail him with 'pursuit'?" Brascoe suggested to the undersheriff.

"Could, although that always complicates things up. I think I know something swifter." The big undersheriff leaned down toward Brascoe's ear and murmured a few words' worth.

Brascoe nodded, took a parade-ground step forward toward Bruce and intoned: "You're free to go."

As Bruce climbed back on the motorcycle and delightedly lifted his foot to give the starter-kick, the captain continued:

"But I'm placing this motorcycle under arrest. It's going to serve thirty days' detention."

Some certain morning, August freshly onto the calendar and the sun-count ever so slightly farther from solstice and toward equinox, you step out into the day and the air carries the first minty trace of a turning season. Only a hint, cool and astringent and brief, then the summer sun asserts itself. But from then on, you can never quite put it out of your mind that autumn has been heard from.

Owen stretched backward in his chair and stared again at the twelve-month planning calendar on the Administration Building wall, where all months were crucial but they weren't nearly equal. October. The nine months before then existed only to gestate October. By October, things were going to have to fall into place, in a big way. The three-hundred-mile powerline from Great Falls was supposed to be finished by then, which would bring the juice for Owen's dredge motors. Gravel for the toe of the dam, the immense downstream retaining pile that all the other elements of the dam had to rest against, was supposed to start pouring in by the trainload then, too. And, Sangster's song to be sung, the railroad truss bridge was supposed to be in service by then. When all this supposed-to-be had definitely happened, then and only then the dredge

Gallatin could start placing the fill; Fort Peck Dam could actually start rising from the much worked over site. If those deadlines weren't met, winter could catch the project before the first of the earthfill was underway; same as last year, they'd be in snowdrifts up to their hind ends, having to plow and shovel and cuss to get the least little thing done, and meanwhile the river could freeze tight at any time, leaving Owen's dredges to sit useless in the winter harbor until spring breakup.

Owen rapped his pencil on the desk, wincing down at his dredge fleet-to-be. He sometimes wished he could trade places with Bruce, whistle through a shift of hammering on something instead of sitting in here Octobering his guts out.

MEALS 50¢
BIG FEED 75¢
HELL OF A GORGE $1

The eatery nearest the boatyard, the Rondola Cafe, was medium-busy all day long, interspersed with two frenzies of feeding when the dam crews changed shifts. One crew poured in to have big breakfasts before work, while the men coming off shift arrived famished for supper. (The owl-shift changeover at midnight was firmly ignored by the owners, Ron and

192

Dola, who claimed they needed sleep sometime.) Bruce came off shift this particular August morning, started for home, decided he didn't want only his own company at the shack, and so, for a change, popped into the Rondola. Half of Montana was in there already, but amid the swarm Bruce spotted Boudreau from the dredgebuilding crew at a place at the counter, and went over and goosed him in the ribs and stood behind him, making conversation until Boo was done eating. As soon as he got up to leave and Bruce slid onto the stool, the waitress appeared, simultaneously scooping away dirty dishes and asking, "What'll it be?"

She was lanky, poker-faced, with inspiring green eyes. Auburn hair, bobbed. Bruce took a little longer than necessary to enunciate what he ate for breakfast every morning of his life, hotcakes and fried eggs, up, if that wouldn't cause her too much troub—

"STACK OF JACKS AND A PAIR, SUNNYSIDE," she called over her shoulder while pouring him a brimming mug of coffee, then side-stepped along the teeming counter doing refills. There were three other waitresses constantly flying by to the ready-counter that opened off into the kitchen, but he sized up this one while she worked. Slender. Straight-backed. Tall, for a woman.

193

Not much balcony on her, there in the uniform blouse, but some, some.

The waitress behaved like one of those people who can do any number of things at once — here she was dealing out a tableful of plates while glancing from group to group to see who needed coffee or wanted dessert, and maintaining small talk along with it. Bruce wanted to be like that, a juggler of life. In his most preening moments, he figured he was getting there.

Business racketed in the cafe while he ate, dozens of conversations bouncing off the low greasy ceiling, the wall-top frieze of commercially printed clever signs adding a visual din to the spoken. He tried to figure out how to make time with the ever-busy waitress; his inventive requests for more coffee brought him just that, coffee.

Then on one of his eye-follows of her, as she stacked dirty dishes on her arm and carried them in to the continual kitchen calamity, he spotted the heap of dishes at the sink. Draining his coffee cup and plunking down his meal money and what he figured was a staggering tip, he headed into the kitchen.

Dola and another woman were so busy frying and grilling and buttering and gravying that they didn't even notice

Bruce's existence. He proceeded to the sink and rolled up his sleeves. Over at the meatblock, Ron was slicing an entire flitch of bacon as fast as he could make the butcher knife move.

"Stand some help on these dishes, can you?" Bruce called across and without waiting plunged into the chore.

"Absolute rescue, is what we need," Ron called back, gratefully. "Our pearldiver went on a bender. A world of thanks, mister."

Only the vicinity of it that involved the lanky waitress interested Bruce, and he made a point of turning and taking the dishes right out of her hands, saving her the scraping and stacking, whenever he saw her from the tail of his eye. He scrubbed, swabbed, rinsed, dried, piled up the clean plates; changed dishwater time and again as it turned gray and filmy; caught up on the logjam of silverware, even gained on the terrible pots and pans. Eventually he could just do the dishes as they arrived, which gave him more time to spectate the poker-faced waitress coming and going.

The Rondola's trade eased off at mid-morning, and the next time the waitress swished in and handed him a small stack of dirty dishes as she'd become accustomed to, Bruce didn't take them. Instead he stood looking at her and came straight out with:

"I know how to dance, too."

The waitress never even batted a cool green eye. "That makes two of us, then."

Kate Millay. Wasn't that just the peachiest name, Bruce asked himself sixty times an hour for the next several days.

He had squired Kate to the Blue Eagle the first night, not about to pass up that ace-in-the-hole boast of having nailed into place the very floor on which they were dancing, and whether it was that or the phase of the moon, the two of them seemed to click.

The sheriff was stepping out of his patrol car for a late bite of supper at the Downtowner Cafe in Glasgow when the motorcycle rocketed past him, not quite taking his car door with it.

About time I made an example out of one of these speed demons triggered in his mind, and he ducked back into the car and hit the starter and then the siren.

The motorcycle already had fogged into the night, out of town and down the road to Fort Peck, naturally. As with everything else to do with Fort Peck, Sheriff Kinnick wished the new highway had never happened. Word had reached him that the damworkers who lived in Glasgow were bragging about setting speed records, least minutes from the Glasgow city limits to the first shack of Wheeler. The county commissioners were climbing all over him about the speeding and the car wrecks, and as much as it graveled him to have to ask for help, Kinnick had put in a plea to the state for a highway patrolman. Although where was the state highway SOB right now, when he could have been some use in nailing this two-wheeled maniac.

The highway between Glasgow and Wheeler measured seventeen miles, and it took the sheriff a full dozen of those, pushing down hard on the accelerator, to draw within glimpse of the motorcycle. Or what, ahead as far as his headlights would reach, had to be the motorcycle, though it looked like a white flag whipping along at eighty miles an hour. His siren was not noticeably slowing the motorcycle miscreant, and the sheriff had started to wonder about the science of this situation: was the damnable motorcycle possibly traveling faster than the sound of his siren? The white whatever-it-was kept on billowing and flapping, cleaving the night up ahead. Carl Kinnick swallowed hard and trounced on the gas pedal just the little bit more that he dared to.

The patrol car gained enough that he could see her all: the white blouse, pulled untucked from her slacks by the wind of the ride as she hugged the back of the motorcyclist, the fabric tenting up and out from her shoulders like a cotton cape in a hurricane. Below, Kate's long bare back; and the blazing white brassiere strap across it.

The sheriff stared as long as he dared, at a speed like this, then slacked off sharply on the gas pedal, jammed a hand to the siren switch and killed the wail. Coming down the main drag of Wheeler, he coasted to a complete stop while he watched the taillight of the motorcycle ember away into one of the streets of shacks.

The sheriff shook his head. But instead of turning around on the highway, he revved the patrol car again and sped ahead. He slammed through Wheeler like a rock through chickenhouse sheeting, past the dirt street where the motorcyclist and passenger had turned in, past the saloons and dance joints and brothels, speedometer needle jumping and jumping as he floored the gas pedal. Then, at the far end of Wheeler, he braked, turned around, and drove decorously back to Glasgow.

Neil of course was the first to know that

Bruce was a goner. He had only to be around the two of them together for five minutes, Bruce going into the damnedest antic he could think of and Kate simply meeting it as if it was the time of day, before he figured *She's the brand for him* and mentally began moving out to the barracks.

For the rest of the family, Bruce spelled it out in sugar, scarcely able to let go of her hand long enough for Kate to shake any of their congratulating ones. Everyone had to agree with his proud point that he'd brought home one who fit in with the Duff altitude. Indeed, Kate was not only up there in height but had strikingly thrifty construction; you could look her in the face and tell she was long-legged. Bruce was not the first Rondola customer and possibly not the last to find her angles of attraction intriguing, just enough here, there, wherever it counted, to add up. In ancient Greece the foes of the region of Laconia demanded surrender with the ultimatum *If we conquer you at arms, we will kill you,* and back came the message, *If.* Both the nature and build of Kate were along the laconic line of that *if.*

As the lovey pair made their rounds, Meg tapped her fingernail on the edge of her cup and thought about how far off she had been in her expectation that Bruce was going to have caravans of girlfriends before settling down at about age thirty-four.

Hugh could have done without one more female eye of judgment on him. He felt he was perpetually up against Meg's medicinal scrutiny, and next had come Charlene with her attitude that the Duffs ought to puff themselves up like the duke's balloon, and now here this Kate, deadly in the way she could sort you into your bin without a word said. Were there no jolly, neutral, unsharpened women that the Duff men could ever find?

Charlene was simply relieved to have Bruce no longer on the loose.

Smart enough not to show what a kick she was getting out of a clan of men who were tall enough for her — Bruce, Neil, Owen and Hugh in a bunch reminded her of pencils sticking out of a cup — Kate more than held her own with all the Duffs until Owen. History was the culprit. Out of all the tortuous routes that were depositing thousands of people willy-nilly at Fort Peck, Kate Millay's story was the least expected: local. Her father, and his father before him, had been the ferryman on the Fort Peck cable-ferry, a glorified raft which had operated a little way upstream from the present dam site activity. ("About down the bluff from Happy Hollow, if you know where that is," Kate had slipped in on Hugh with a straight face.) Owen, though, heard a faint echo in one of the side-canyons of his mind. "Millay. Millay. Wasn't there somebody else by that name, in the Indian Agency when it was still here?"

"That was still us. My grandfather started out at that."

Owen cocked his head in curiosity. Government clerks usually stayed government clerks. "How'd he get from that to running a prairie ferry?"

Kate gave him a very long look, and then the summary: "My grandmother used to say, over her next-to-dead body."

High water everywhere when the original Millays, Kate's grandparents, came to Fort Peck, every creek tearing at its banks as their wagon and wiry team of horses struggled across fording places on the journey from Miles City. Where the route was not flooded or muddy, it was dusty and acrawl with rattlesnakes emerging from winter. Henriette Millay was white-eyed by the time they reached the Missouri River. She also had come down with a ripping cough. Philip Millay could see across, not far downstream from the ferry crossing, to the stockaded trading post. He was to be the assistant agent at the Indian Agency there, a chance upward in the world from the Land Office clerkship in Miles City, but also a heartstopping traverse across such water.

The ferryman grimaced as he eyed the wretched pair, and then the high-running river. "I ordinarily wouldn't, until this water lets up some," he let Philip know. "But that's a sick woman there."

"Come, Henriette, we have to."

"No," wildly. "The water is too —"

"We must get you across."

"No." The cough tore out of her. She shook her head incessantly, refusing to look at the river.

Philip went to the back of the wagon for one of the ropes he picketed the horses with at night. Then he climbed back up to the wagon seat. "Give me your hands Henriette." She watched listlessly as those were tied, then began to scream as he wrapped the rope around and around her waist, lashing her to the iron support of the wagon seat. After he had knotted the rope, Philip put a hand over her mouth. Henriette stopped her screaming and simply stared at him. Swallowing hard, he said: "So you won't . . . fall out."

Kate's grandmother told that on herself, when the distances of age lay between her and that crossing of terror, when at last the whispers connecting Philip Millay's pur-

202

chase of the Fort Peck ferry and missing funds at the Indian Agency had sufficiently abated. All families have stories, sometimes in what is not said in the outright telling. Kate knew as if by birthright that her grandmother had been brought hogtied into the Missouri River country not past falling but past jumping.

"Say again?" Owen followed up on Kate's "next-to-dead" remark, as if they were having this conversation over a field telephone and the connection was bad. "What, you mean his quitting the government job spooked her that much?" *Charlene ought to be over here hearing this, get a different slat on things.*

"It was just something between them," Kate said, looking him in the eye. "Some family matter."

"Examining her pedigree?" Bruce was back on the scene, slipping an arm a long way around her willowy waist. "Bet you never thought I'd have out-of-state in-laws, Ownie, even if it is only North Dakota."

To Owen's questioning expression, Kate reported that her parents had moved to Bismarck. "Hell, that's too bad," he interjected. "Suppose your father would come back for a job here? We could use somebody who knows the river currents."

Owen just asking for it from her this way — Bruce loved the moment.

As casually as if punching a meal ticket, Kate told Owen: "Probably shouldn't hold your breath. He left here cussing about being drowned out by the dam."

Their honeymoon was a half-hour flight in a Waco-10 biplane.

"Been up before?" the Fort Peck Air Excursions pilot asked as he strapped them in side by side in the cockpit behind him.

"Hell, no. We're a goodlooking pair, but we're not the Lindberghs," Bruce informed him.

The pilot dipsydoodled at the start, to see how they'd take it. When Kate, upside down, broke into a little grin and Bruce outright laughed, he decided they'd be no fun, so he flew along the river, downstream as far as the town of Frazer where he banked the airplane tight around the grain elevator, then back up the Missouri, bumblebeeing atop the twisty course of the water. From there in the air Fort Peck looked as if an insanely wide roadbed was being laid across the river valley, the base of the dam a mile-broad mud terrace, all of it crawling with machinery. Bruce dapperly pointed to the boatyard, the dredge he'd been slapping paint onto a little over an hour ago, and Kate craned over the lip of the cockpit to see. The moment they were upstream from the tractorized sprawl of the dam project, she touched the pilot's shoulder and motioned that she wanted him to fly lower. The plane lost more and more altitude, as she kept motioning downward with the flat of her hand, the flight path now below the rim of the bluffs, and Bruce was really beginning to notice how distinct the branches were in the tops of the cottonwoods reaching up for the plane's bottom wing.

Abruptly Kate pointed: the landing and abandoned cable rig of the Fort Peck ferry, almost alongside the airplane rather than below it. Thousands of crossings made here, back and forth by the Millays before her, and now she was flying the route of the river itself, magical as a dragonfly.

The dynamiter's wife watched, through clouds of laundry, as the newlyweds settled in next door. She did feel a bit sorry for the unattached brother, Neil, having to move out; on the other hand, the constant racket of truck or motorcycle roaring back and forth ought to calm down by half or more, now.

Nan Hill had had her eye on Duffs all her life and still couldn't entirely make up her mind about them; quite what they constituted, quite how their stubborn streaks and brainstorms weighed out, in those disturbing long-boned exclamation mark bodies. The first of the Duffs she knew anything about were from Scotch Heaven, as if that green cleft of valley into the footings of the Rocky Mountains had been set aside for exactly their thistly sort. Back then, back there, a full three hundred miles from Fort Peck, rumor about wrathy Ninian Duff had hardened into legend — how he underwent early trouble on his homestead with loss of cattle, until a pair of suspected rustlers went somewhere off the face of the earth. From that kind of start, Ninian and Flora Duff parented the homesteading community along the North Fork of English Creek, anchors of example and lighthouses of beckon to the Erskines and Findlaters and Frews and McCaskills and Barclays and other populators of Scotch Heaven. Nan as a girl growing up in the west end of Gros Ventre would see Ninian Duff come tornadoing into town on one or another of his self-appointed Scotch Heaven civic tasks, black cloud of beard above his breathtaking blood bay team of horses. Ninian Duff looked like the station agent for Judgment Day, but he never failed to boom out going past, "Ay, good day there, Miss Nan."

Ninian's letter had instructed them to

arrive in June, green advent of summer, but there were delays common with emigration, and the calendar of 1910 was on August when Hugh and Margaret Duff, young and edgy, stepped down from the train onto Montana ground. VALIER, the sign on the gable of the depot confidently heralded, as if the scatter of fresh wood-frame buildings across the prairie already amounted to a town for the ages.

While Illinoisans and Belgians and all others thronged off the train and tried to sort themselves out for the homestead life ahead, the young Scottish couple paused. A knobblier version of Hugh, with a somber beard down to its chest, made its way toward them.

"You're here and in one piece," Ninian Duff boomed. "Good for you, Hugh lad. And this will be Margaret." He noted the cool blue eyes, the face like any pretty girl's except for the slip of the Maker's chisel that gave her a pert mark there in the center of her chin. A bit combative by the look of her, but of good stock, at least according to report. Ninian gazed on down, to the tyke with a hand lost in each of theirs. "Ay, and the future, whose name I've forgot."

"This is our Owen," Meg supplied, with a cough at whatever was in the air. She saw that Hugh, with a fixed smile, was casting glances past his uncle to the hazy sky.

"We've a bit of a wagon journey ahead," Ninian was saying. "We ought to start." And in no time, their America trunk and suitcases and themselves aboard, they were rolling west into the pungent haze.

A copper sun smoldered in the murk. Meg held Owen in her lap and willed Hugh to ask what this universal smoke was about. Just when she was all but ready to put the question herself, Hugh licked his lips and asked: "Whatever is afire to this extent?"

"Forests," Ninian replied shortly.

Meg had not yet seen anything taller than bunchgrass on their route. "How near?"

Ninian slapped the reins on the backs of his fast-stepping horses before answering her. "Idaho. The big forest fire is across over there, a few hundred miles or so. And we've one now in our own mountains, in north of Jericho Reef. Don't worry any — even that one is a good distance from the North Fork."

The smoke persisted, ashy and eye-burning, as the wagon carried them through the town of Gros Ventre and up English Creek and then its fork toward where Ninian assured them Creation's noblest mountains somewhere lurked and at last into the yard at Ninian and Flora's homestead. Tired, flustered, apprehensive, the Duffs newly from Scotland went through the motions of meeting and being greeted and then went to their bed as if ready to hide under it. First impression is worst impression, *Meg always had to remind herself of that. But she could not put away the feeling that English Creek's introduction of itself to her and Hugh and Owen could be seasons long, perhaps years.*

"I have been holding land for you," Ninian announced at breakfast the next morning, after concluding a grace of such length that Hugh and Meg had begun to wonder if they might starve to death before it was over. "The old Spedderson place, up across the creek a bit. We will go to it first thing."

Flora Duff, broad-beamed from childbearing but otherwise formidably agile, said she would fix a bite of snack they could take with, to fortify themselves. Samuel, the oldest boy, a keen-minded eleven-year-old who pestered Hugh and Meg about any glimpse they'd had into the radio room of their ship across the Atlantic, was roundly instructed by Ninian in a day's chores of sheep and hay and horses and other homestead matters that Meg thought would challenge a grown man. Then Ninian had them in the wagon again, again facing into the forest fire smoke that clung like acrid fog.

Flora gave them a wave through the kitchen window as they started off, but then shook her head about Meg. The girl was standoffish, something always on her mind. Spent her time doting on the little boy, Owen; would spoil him rotten if she kept on. Flora Duff was going to be glad to have Meg out from under her roof.

On the wagon ride, thankfully not a long one, Meg alternately crooned solace to Owen — poor tiddler, the stinging smoke provoked him, he seemed to be indignantly trying to figure it out — and ran her tongue around the inside of her mouth against the air's taste of soot, while Ninian preached sheep to Hugh. They passed a flock of the creatures, gray soft fleecies like rolled balls of the smoke, on a dimmed sidehill which Ninian pronounced to be Breed Butte, then abruptly the wagon angled down the slope, down and down, Meg clutching Owen while bracing against the tilt, until water, a suprise fresh coolness of the creek, ex-ploded in glossy spray around them as Ninian plunged the team of horses through the crossing to the Spedderson place.

Willows. Wild hay. An old hay sled in rheumatic sag. Then house, lambing shed gone scabby from missing shingles, barn, caved-in root cellar. Little else. Not even, Meg instantly divined, a clothesline.

Ninian tromped them around the property as though it were a glen of Eden. Amid that, the smoke drifted into tatters briefly as a wind sprang down the valley from the west. Before the gust died down, Meg saw stone standing in the sky; columns of cliff nearly atop them, it very much seemed to her.

The creekside meadow of wild hay was being extolled by Ninian now, Hugh able to nod knowingly about something that grew from the ground. On the MacLaren estate just outside Inverley he'd had a good name as an oatfield hand, and when the right time came Hugh Duff would find a way to let this strutting Bible of an uncle know about that attainment.

Meg spoke up. "Who and where are the Speddersons?"

"They pulled up stakes, a few years since," Ninian said as if that amounted to explanation. He turned back to Hugh. "I stepped in and bought the relinquishment, so the price I'll make you can be carried across as many years as you need, Hugh lad." Ninian swept an arm toward the house as if uncobwebbing it. "We can fix the place up in no time. I'll put out a community shout and everyone will pitch in some Saturday on a new roof and — whatever. House, shed some sheep, or cattle if you must, this country" — he indicated off into the hazy mountains — "to run them on, and you're set."

Owen tugged at Meg's hand, wanting to explore everything all over again. As she let the boy lead her off in a toddling but *determined circle of the house, the two men watched. After a minute, Ninian said aside to Hugh, his voice for once soft:*

"I can see that you will need to resort to some suasion there."

Coax. Just give her a try, he encouraged himself. See if she'll put out. Even if it is broad daylight.

Kate was ironing her Rondola uniform when Bruce walked in. "Sweetheart! You're off early — something happen?"

"No. Lunchbreak, is all. And I figured I'd come home and see what we can cook up."

The unmistakable Duff frame went by while Nan Hill was clothes-pegging pants (25¢, washed and pressed) onto a line. Her sign out front, LAUNDRY DONE HERE, steadily kept all six clotheslines at full sail, her earnings actually more than J.L.'s paychecks for handling dynamite. Not that J.L. showed that he minded. He was the kind who simply had pushed back from supper at the ranch one night and said: "There're wages at Fort Peck. We better throw our tails in the air and go over there." Here they were, then, washed in from almost the most distant tributary of the Missouri, English Creek. The only farther branch of water, Nan had grown up knowing, was the North Fork, once the country of the Duffs.

He was going to burst if he couldn't put his craving where he wanted to. He tossed his hat in the direction of the nearest chair and went straight over to the ironing board and kissed Kate to the utmost, keeping the kiss going until she caught the idea.

"Br-r-r —" she gradually managed to clear her lips from his, "—uce, mmm, though —"

"Me, all right, doing this," he kissed her in further example and stroked down from her waist. "It better be me."

Like an intermittent show of comets across Nan Hill's field of vision, these Duffs were. To this day she could close her eyes and see not only patriarchal old Ninian but his bright and bold son, Samuel. Samuel had been only a few years older than Nan, and when he came to high school in Gros Ventre she developed a crush on him that lasted until Samuel Duff went off to the Great War and was killed in a trench in France.

Outside the window, glimpsed past everything Bruce was doing, Nan Hill still was hanging laundry, the flapping sounds of shirts flocked in the wind audible through the thin beaverboard wall. "Nan is right out there," Kate's whisper blew warm against Bruce's suddenly unshirted shoulder.

One of his hands let up on her long enough to pull down the windowshade. "We'll make it dark so she can't hear us."

J.L. Hill was a good man, earnest and not flighty. Nan knew that, couldn't escape such knowing. But Samuel Duff did come back to mind, here when his lookalike Bruce buzzed home for lunch and a minute later the unmistakable noises of lovemaking started to kick up behind those puny walls next door. Quite a luncher, this Bruce.

When they had eaten, Flora's version of sandwiches as substantial as planks, and Ninian began prescribing to Hugh precisely how many sheep the Spedderson place would carry, and Hugh still hadn't said boo to any of it, Meg was appalled.

She all but pried him away from Ninian, tugging him down to the springhouse where they could talk alone. Ninian's stare of astonishment and reproof followed them, particularly her.

Beside the springhouse, Meg stopped sharp and said: "We can't do this."

Hugh thought she meant the doing of

214

things the way these English Creek flock keepers did them, which had been on his mind too. "But I can see what they're at, in this valley. It's country for animals" — at her stare, he wished he had explicitly said "sheep and cattle" instead — "not entirely what we're used to, but if we put our minds to it —"

"We could put ourselves to it down to our toenails and this would still not be the place for us," Meg said flatly.

Hugh gaped at her. The thing that had impelled them from Inverley, was it between them again already? Hugh's hope had been that they left this behind them in Scotland. But he never quite knew, with Meg. That was the glory and the damnation in being wed to this woman. He loved her so much, how could hers for him possibly be equivalent? Back there in the Inverley life he had won her, then was afraid his victory might not hold, and that brought the turn to America. An ocean and most of the American continent seemed to Hugh about the right distance between them and the Inverley memory.

Brass tacks were in Meg's voice now.

"Hugh, to live here — I cannot and you ought not."

He felt a mix of terror and relief. What he heard himself saying was, "The smoke can't last. They say this is the worst fire

215

ever in these parts."

"*It's not simply the smoke. Here, we'll be under Ninian's thumb.*"

"*What, then. Where?*"

"*It can be almost anywhere,*" she provided, "*as long as it's away from here.*"

Ninian Duff looked off toward the mountains. "*We've a man up this valley with a wife who has never taken to this country. She says nothing, but the misery is there. Not good, that.*" He turned to Hugh. "*I do not wish to see kin of my own in that predicament. Land is being opened up*" — Ninian flapped a hand to indicate, without much enthusiasm, the horizon beyond his valley — "*all across Montana. I'll stake you to finding someplace other than this.*"

Hugh burned inside from his self-enforced drought as he and Meg and little Owen passed back through Gros Ventre, Meg looking better every inch away from Scotch Heaven and God's sergeant Ninian, and then south to Great Falls and a land locator there. Hugh in fact saved his binge until well after they were settled on the Missouri River place: miraculously, more than a homestead claim, a relinquishment with a good house and a strong barn, and the promise in that bottom-land soil. Ninian telegraphed him the

216

money for the downpayment, and with it the message MATTHEW X: 36. *Hugh had to look it up:* A man's foes shall be they of his own household.

Charlene did not particularly want to be caught at this — prowling around in Permanent Residence #1; the King's House, as everybody already called it — but if it came to that, she had her story ready.

The carpenters had pulled out and the painters hadn't yet pulled in and so this morning there the house of the commanding officer of Fort Peck just stood, empty and inviting, and a person could not help but exercise natural curiosity by poking her head in, could she? After all, she would lightly tell the colonel's wife or the colonel if either happened to show up (she hoped it wouldn't be the colonel), she was the only soul out of the thousands at Fort Peck who had seen this house go up nail by nail, totally. Which was pretty much true. Carpentry crews came and went (Owen claimed Fort Peck had crews to do nothing but evict other crews), and the townsite planners and Corps officers periodically dropped by and stood around looking wise, but only Charlene's view from the trailer house amounted to perfect attendance. If you wanted to know the absolute truth, now that the King's House was built she felt entitled to a tour.

So this fine brisk blue morning, September's usual early batch of bad weather gone by now and Indian summer turning up on a day-to-day basis, while Charlene ostensibly was out to stretch her legs with a stroll around the horseshoe of Kansas Street, actually she was counting bedrooms in the King's House. Thus far she had found five.

Holy Pete, as Owen would have put it; Colonel Parmenter and Mrs. Colonel Parmenter could about sleep somewhere different every night of the week without ever leaving home. Bonanza of bedrooms, full basement under the place, stonework around the front door, garage out back; the royal treatment, all right.

She kept touching the walls as she drifted through the house, as if satisfying herself that they honestly were of plaster instead of the rest of Fort Peck's chronic beaverboard. Her footsteps in amplification in the empty new rooms, she showed herself around as thoroughly as she wanted until she came to what she had been saving for last, the view from the picture window in the living room. By whatever military writ, a commanding officer's quarters always faced away from everyone else's, so this house put its back to the other eleven

Permanent Residences along this side of Kansas Street and addressed itself south to the Lab and the Ad Building as if keeping its eye on the office troops.

All at once she realized that out a smaller west window — the corner of the kingly eye, so to speak — her and Owen's house-to-be, the first in line of the Temporary Residences across the way there, which they rated because of Owen's rank as fillmaster, stood in plain sight from here. So far, so good, and possibly better to come. She and Owen at least were up here on the horseshoe with the Colonel and the Mrs. Colonel and the majors and the captains and their wives, and that in itself was a long way from Toston, in more than miles.

By now enterprise was the fever, the mental epidemic of Wheeler, New Deal, Square Deal, Free Deal, Delano Heights, McCone City, Park Grove, the prairie around and all roads in.

Now that people had a little money, ideas on how to generate more bubbled up overnight. The Duff and Hill households on Fifth Street awoke one morning to find that Tarpley, the neighbor across the alley behind them, had gone into the pet sideline with a yardful of frantic Chihuahua dogs. At suppertime, Bruce and Kate and

Nan and J.L. Hill conferred about whether to buy the whole yipping pack, sack them up and drop them in the river; but decided to hold off and see whether the first night of hard freeze might eliminate the Mexican hairless dog situation. It did.

Not as short-lived were the schemes of all-purpose salves, franchises of sewing machines, commission sales of gas irons (Bruce bought Kate one almost before the peddler could knock on the door), and sundry other household commodities that people hadn't known they could not live without. The Fort Peck project was producing new tangents daily, not to mention nightly.

She wished the date was over. And this was before it had even started.

She fussed with her dress and then with her lipstick, and ended up in brighter versions of both borrowed from Louise, the nurse she roomed with. Now for her next region. "Jeez, Louise, what am I going to do with my hair?"

"Throw it away and borrow mine, probably," she got told by Louise, who then left for night shift at the hospital.

At brushstroke thirteen of the hundred she was counting on to spruce up the hair situation, the buzzer outside the hotel room went off.

In a semipanic she dropped the hair-brush, squirmed this way and that in front of the dresser mirror, judging herself over one shoulder and then the other, then muttered, "Hair is hair. He can take it or leave it."

Downstairs in the lobby, he looked like a noodle in a sugar bowl. "Hi!" She went over to him. "You're really on time!" Ten minutes early, actually.

"How you doing," Neil said tightly.

They got out the doorway of the hotel without quite knocking into each other, and at the vehicle Neil, acting as though he'd memorized the maneuver, shadowed her to the passenger side and opened the door for her.

She negotiated the altitude of the running board in her high heels and vaulted up onto the seat, hearing herself ask like a fool kid, "Is this your truck?"

"Yeah. Well, no." Neil's Lincoln-coin face and shoulders hung in the windowframe of the door. "It's all of ours. Owen made the downpayment, and we all chip in on the rest."

The ways of the Duffs. Charlene had warned her they took some getting used to. But something of the same could be said about Charlene, Rosellen thought grimly, already wishing she could take back her "Why not, I guess," when that

221

sister of hers had announced "Owen's fixed you up with his brother, you're going out and have a little fun." Good grief, three weeks settling herself in here at her job and the hotel mishmash, that wasn't as if she'd locked herself in a nunnery, whatever Charlene thought. Meanwhile on his way around the truck, Neil wondered again what he'd been thinking of, agreeing to take out stuck-up Charlene's probably stuckup sister. Traipsing around with this leftover kid-sister-in-law while Owen and Charlene, and for that matter Bruce and Kate, doubtless were home in bed going at it like fury.

The truck trundled to the movie theater. Neil had to count out the admission for the two of them in small coins, including pennies, and wished he'd thought to trade the chickenfeed to Owen for a couple of silver dollars. Then there was the matter of the movie seats, Rosellen there close beside him but five hundred people around them, an awfully public situation even in the dark. Even the elbows of the two of them stayed shy of each other, as if the armrest between them was greased.

The movie itself was a dud, too. Some king of England fought some king of France, and everybody paraded around in yards of robes.

As they headed for the truck afterward,

Neil all of a sudden stopped in his tracks. He gazed elaborately upward and said, "The night's still young."

Rosellen was pretty sure a person couldn't tell time by the moon, but she peered up, too, and said, "Uh huh, well —"

"Could you stand to dance a little?"

She cast a glance at the rec hall, saw its windows were dark and started to say so. Then she caught his meaning. "Uhm. Little while, maybe?"

"You ever gone to the, ah, Blue Eagle?"

"No. No place. In Wheeler, I mean."

"Uh huh. Well, the Blue Eagle isn't too bad of a place. For Wheeler, I mean."

But neither was it Toston, nor any other environment Rosellen Tebbet had set foot into in her nineteen years. The drinkers were a customary three deep at the bar, the dance band (fiddle, accordion, cornet and inevitable piano) was playing loud enough to be heard in Canada, and the heads of stuffed wildlife stared eternally at one another through a ceiling fog of cigarette smoke. Immediately inside the door, Rosellen stopped cold and took a look at everything.

"Oh, hey!" She spotted the corps of taxi dancers at the far end of the bar and pointed with her index finger like a tiny pistol. "Are those the —"

"Those're them," said Neil tightly again,

and steered her off to a table by the wall.

He surprised her, when he set off to fetch their beers, by knowing enough to circle around the bar mob and make his transaction directly with the dour saloonkeeper at the cash register. Then she saw him fishing around in the palm of his hand. More chickenfeed.

"Here you go. Great Falls', finest, and onliest," Neil presented her a longnecked bottle of Select, and hoisted his own in a fractional toast.

"This sure saves on firewood, doesn't it," Rosellen heard herself rattling out. He was looking at her blankly. "Prohibition being gone, I mean. Out from Toston, we used to see bootleg smoke all the time." *I'm yapping on like a ninny. He doesn't even know where Toston is. No, wait, of course he does, on account of Charlene.* "People had stills up just about any coulee." *Why did I get on to this? I'm making myself sound like I'm from the bootlegger boondocks.* "One time" — *once upon a time, story of my life* — "Charlene and I went on the train to Loweth to visit our cousin there, and we counted seventeen of those little columns of smoke on our way. Just" — she had that index finger of hers out again, but this time in a sinuous little rising waver like smoke; you could almost catch the whiff — "every old where."

"No kidding." Neil noticed during this that she had a little nhn chuckle in her manner that reminded him of the first perk of a coffee pot. He decided he kind of liked that chuckle.

With the beer as prompter, they talked themselves into another round apiece and then he asked her if a dance sounded good.

Neil on a dancefloor, she rapidly discovered, was very smooth going indeed. Without managing to keep the surprise out of the question, she asked: "Where in the world did you learn to dance?"

"Grade school." He smiled for the first time all night.

"Grade school, come on. Really?"

"Sure thing. We had a teacher, Mrs. Baugh, who was an old rip otherwise. But she made all of us, little kids on up, know how to dance. She said that way we'd always be able to get acquainted in town, have something we could join in on." Rosellen had an interesting habit of keeping her eyes fastened on a person for longer than expected, as if trying to figure out whether he amounted to a bargain or not. Neil glanced down at her hair, same satin black as Charlene's, and nearly told her how nice he thought it was, but finished his recital instead. "Old lady Baugh always started us off, boys would dance

225

with boys and girls with girls, so we wouldn't die of embarrassment. Mostly it fell to Owen to teach Bruce and me. He was the oldest, he was supposed to be the expert."

Rosellen leaned back in his arms and contemplated him still further. "Seems to have worked."

Neil considered. "To some extent. Although I'm not sure this is the kind of town Mrs. Baugh had in mind."

There was another pair of beers involved, and closer dancing, and her telling him about having taken evening classes in typing and basic bookkeeping at the Lewis & Clark Business School in Helena while supporting herself with a day job as waitress in the Parrot Cafe and the complete surprise of the job opening at Fort Peck for a typist with a speed of sixty words a minute, minimum, and so now here she was, and even closer dancing, and him telling her the boundless future of haulage at Fort Peck, and closer dancing yet, before the two of them found themselves in the cab of the truck, trying out some kissing.

Rosellen's head cleared, however, when she regarded the clammy seat of the truck.

"Let's — go back," she said.

Neil straightened up from her as if snapping out of a trance. "Sure," was all he said.

Back at the hotel, though, she provided: "Louise — my roomie — works late."

"She does?" He swallowed. "That's good. How late?"

"Pretty late."

Neil looked at the hotel as if he'd never seen one before. "You mean, they'd just let me . . . kind of . . . come in with you?"

"Huh uh, they're strict as the dickens. There's a fire door, though."

"In case of emergency," he thought out loud, so solemnly it startled them both, then sent them into giggles.

Two minutes later, she entered her darkened room, and a minute after that, his tall thin form was there, too, in through the hallway fire door she'd released from the inside and wedged open for him with Louise's tube of lipstick.

"We're going to have to whisper," she whispered nervously.

"That's okay, it's worth it," he whispered back fervently.

Kissing resumed.

"This is crazy."

"More than likely."

Longer kissing.

"You're quite the date."

"Look who's talking."

"Nh*n*. Here, I'll . . . your fingers are big

for buttons like these."

"Maybe they're better . . . here?"

"Yes. They're doing fine there."

The next morning Bruce met him with a smirk. "So did you get anywhere with her?"

"Considerable."

Bruce's smirk went. "You did not."

"Doubt away," Neil told him and serenely put the truck in gear.

Within days, Neil and Rosellen had scooted in to the county courthouse in Glasgow for their license, looked up a Justice of the Peace, and spoke their marriage vows as if they couldn't wait to spurt the words out. Meg and Hugh and Owen and Charlene and Bruce and Kate met this variously with disbelief, awe, and amusement, but beyond that saw nothing to be done except stand back from this romance lest it knock them over.

"So, kiddo, here we are in the same family twice over." Charlene seemed a little haughty in her congratulations, Rosellen thought.

"It's your doing," Rosellen couldn't pass up the chance. "If you'd chaperoned me the way you always used to, Neil and I would still be shaking hands goodnight."

At the shivaree which was threatening

to become an almost monthly Duff family tradition, the bride and groom were celebrated in a fashion Rosellen had not even dared to dream of.

"Give us a song, Mother," Neil popped right out with.

"Oh, would you?" Rosellen chimed in. "I can't carry a tune in a bucket. I'd love for you to sing something for us."

Easy girl, thought Charlene. *Our ma-in-law takes her own sweet time about letting go of a son.*

Meg pulled a face, made ready to give out devastating reasons why her voice was not up to the occasion, and then took a good look at Neil, bright of eye, earnest as a month of Sundays. After a moment, she said:

"Hugh. First chair accompaniment, if you please."

With a mock formal bow, Hugh fetched a kitchen chair for her to stand on, then went to the wall of the shack and leaned back with his eyes closed to listen.

Facing the newly marrieds, with Owen and Charlene and Bruce and Kate camped around them like more veteran troops, Meg announced in a tone that Rosellen at first thought was a direct order: *"Waken, Thou."*

Swallowing delicately, Meg clasped one hand in the other at the exact distance in front of hers where a hymnal would be held, and began to let her sons and daughters-in-law know what singing is.

"Seven long years I served for thee . . ."

Her low rich contralto reached Hugh as if from another country, this voice of Margaret Milne of Inverley that could fill in if a tenor was missing in the choir. It all came back, the honey waterfall of her hair when she let it down, and this, the rich sound of the young in love.

"The glassy hill I clamb for thee,
The bloody shirt I wrang for thee —
Will thou no waken and turn to me?"

Clamb! Wrang! Rosellen was giddy with the glory of all this. This was like *Weir of Hermiston,* her favorite Robert Louis Stevenson book. The Scottish lingo, and the amazing part where the man character and the woman character keep eyeing each other in church. The woman wearing a frock cut low but *drawn up so as to mould the contour of both breasts, and in the nook between* — how did he write it? — *surely in a very enviable position, trembled the nosegay of primroses.* Not that she and Neil were being that open about it while his mother stood up there singing, she told herself, but couldn't help giving him another little look. Everyone else in the shack could have told her that she and Neil were sending glances hummingbirds could feed on.

After the applause and Meg shushing them, and the beer had been poured in Charlene's best glasses that she and Owen had brought for the occasion, Hugh made his way over to Rosellen, appraised her, and remarked:

"The Milne side of the family is a bit fierce in its ballads."

"No, no! I thought it was a doozy!"

Rosellen ended up thinking that about the entire shivaree night. In the course of the evening she managed to make fast friends with Kate, and Neil held up well under the kidding from Owen and Bruce, and Meg and Hugh clucked appropriately over the whole brood.

The first second thoughts came to Charlene.

She couldn't deny feeling some pride over Rosellen. The town of Toston had figured the Tebbet sisters were going to have to get by in the world on their slender ankles and promising chests, and though Rosellen was always going to be in the panther-beautiful shadow of Charlene, she was chesty and curvy enough in her own right to outdo Tosten's expectations.

But there was no denying either that Rosellen as a kid generally had the tip of her tongue against the roof of her mouth, as if life was all peanut butter. Watching her in action now, as shapely outside and in as a Shakespearean ampersand, and cute as a wink besides, she still showed signs of being chronically young, at least to Charlene. Neil wasn't more than knee-high in experience either, was he. Charlene knew he had just been starting to climb out moneywise with his trucking, and now look, here he was a family man with all that entailed. Charlene felt something like a pang about that hasty date she'd marshaled them into.

"How do you like that kid sister of mine?" she whispered to Owen when they were at the cake plate for second helpings of Jaarala's scrumptious angelfood. "Evidently when she puts her mind to it, a guy doesn't stand a chance."

The fact of the matter was that Owen had less than liked the idea of Rosellen from the minute she popped up at Fort Peck, adding one more flank to an already complicated family situation. And he had been a dab perplexed by the courtship whirlwind that had just been witnessed. What, were Charlene and him the last people ever to wait until they could afford it before getting married? On the other

232

hand, Neil right now looked so happy he might spontaneously combust, and Rosellen had not yet shown anything drastically wrong with herself except for being such a hopeless snip of a kid.

"Evidently," Owen left it at, and dug into the cake.

Bruce had got Neil to one side. They grinned at each other, and clinked glasses. "So," Bruce started in. "Where you going to spend your hornymoon?"

"In the truck," Neil replied.

Bruce blinked at him.

"Moving in," Neil explained with an even bigger grin, "up onto Broadway," which of course meant Wheeler.

If this gets any better," Sangster confessed, "I won't be able to and it." October, so far, had been like Christmas come early for the engineers.

"Some of us aren't there yet," Owen maintained, as nervous and happy as he had ever been in his life.

"Sure you are. All you have left to do is connect up the watchamadingus to the doohickey, then watch the mud poop out the other end."

On the first, the absolute maiden morning of the month, not one clockhair behind schedule, power sang down the wires from the generating station at Great Falls three hundred miles away. Owen, at the sub-station when the massive voltage feed was hooked up, alternated between ecstasy at having this torrent of electricity at his command and apprehension at now having the entire feeder system and dredging operation on his shoulders, with a breathing space of less than two weeks to work out all the catches. Then on the fourth, courtesy of Sangster and his elegant long truss bridge for the trains, here came gravel. At river level, with each bombs-away avalanche from a dumpcar straight overhead, one hundred thousand pounds of gravel came down in a solid noise that had splashes at its edges. For the past nine days, the rest of Fort Peck's construction noise had been punctuated by these barrages: forty successive enormous sounds like *KASHOOSH,* then the brief wait for the next trainload. And now, this very day, only the thirteenth of the month, dredging was about to commence.

"Mine will run quieter," Owen shouted to Sangster next to him. *If I can get this entire cobbled-together layout up and running at all.*

"Well, sure, plumbing is *SUPPOSED* to run *QUIETER* than real *MACHINERY,*" Sangster yelled back over the clatter of a dumpcar and the thunder of another satisfying discharge of gravel to the toe of the dam.

But if the *Gallatin*, a dredge 170 feet long and 40 wide, waddling in the river under the load of the largest dredging equipment ever made, wasn't real machinery, then Owen Duff did not want to know what was. The thing about dredging at Fort Peck, the aspect that had him simultaneously exhilarated and dry mouthed, was that his equipment as fillmaster amounted to miles of apparatus that had to run as one earth-eating dam-making machine. The *Gallatin*'s cutterhead, like a nightmarishly rough and gigantic dentist's drill — taller than a man — was going to have to dig into the riverbank, and the dredge's suction pumps were going to have to ingest the slurry of bank soil and river water, and the booster pumps along the dredge-line ashore were going to have to move this semi-liquid fill material through the big pipeline — the "plumbing" as Sangster called it — to where the slurry would gush out against the gravel barrier of the toe, the fill material mounding up and the water running off, creating the core of the dam.

What had to make it all go, and this was the Fort Peck dredging difference, was electricity. A hellish amount of electricity, to move this much earthfill and to loft it as high as this dam was going to rise. "Jesus Mercy Christ, Duff," the electrical engineers moaned in fights during briefings, over Owen's horsepower specifications to make his dredging system run. Moaning had never yet budged Owen Duff's arithmetic. On the Fort Peck scale of dredging, each suction pump had to be driven by an electric motor with horsepower equal to a fleet of sixty Model AAA trucks, and there were two such pumps, needing two of those voracious motors, on each dredge, and ultimately he was going to have four dredges operating and a flock of pipeline booster pumps besides. He had held to the argument that it was either meet his power specs or cut back on the dam schedule, and the colonel inveterately held to the sacredness of the schedule, and so the juice jockeys ended up having to feed power into Owen's dredges and dredgeline pumps by stringing big, stiff cable out across series of pontoons, electricity gone nautical. The *Gallatin*, here on start-up day, looked as if it was leading a pack of pontoons alongside it on leashes, each of which was a three-inch-thick conductor cable.

One side of Owen thought this was as nifty as the engineering process could possibly get, cycling the river's own force so beautifully through the generating dynamo at Great Falls and across the prairie on the march-step forest of power poles and down through the feeder web of cables, putting out watts to spin the dredge's cutterhead and the suction pumps' impellers; refining the energy of the river to change the river. The other side of him, which had been scurrying for the past dozen days to try to make the carnival array of dredging and power apparatus hum in unison, yearned for the steam-engine dredge days, shovel the coal in and it'd make this move that, forget about hydro-electro-hydraulic elegance.

Just digging a little ditch, that's all we're doing this fall, don't get antsy about it, Owen told himself again while he waited, antsy, for the dredgemaster to finish his last-minute crew check.

Any fill we can move now is a leg up on next year, is all this is, sure, you bet.

The *Gallatin's* task, before snow flew and the river iced over, was to cut a winter harbor for itself and the other dredges and barges; simply chew a nice docking channel, four hundred feet wide and a thousand feet long, at a right angle into the riverbank.

And not so incidentally, pump the dredged material most of a mile and spew it out as the very first earthfill onto the dam.

The dredgemaster at last sent down word that his crew was as ready as they'd ever be and Owen might as well come aboard.

Sangster wordlessly gave Owen the gesture they'd been trading since the previous autumn, a couple of yanks on an imaginary whistle cord the way a locomotive engineer would toot the highball signal, and headed up the bluff to the Ad Building to watch the dredge inaugurate itself.

The destination for Owen was the lever house on the dredge. Up there, where the captain would be presiding on an ordinary vessel, sat the operator with controls thumbing up around him like beer-spigot handles, and Calhoun the dredgemaster hovering behind him. On his way through the *Gallatin*'s labyrinth of cable drums and pump motors, Owen paused at the topside forward compartments. He tossed his work-gloves in onto the desk of the cabin that would serve as the fillmaster's quarters — *his* quarters — when he was aboard, and breathlessly climbed on up into the lever house.

He had his own checklist, but before it, he ran a lingering gaze around the entirety of Fort Peck from the perch there high on the dredge.

Out here in the middle of figless nowhere, all this had been forced into being.

Four-mile construction sprawl of incipient water barrier and diversion tunnels.

Dozen towns.

Whole railroad.

Midair bridges.

Cat's cradle lines of the electrical feeder system.

Pipeline on nearly a mile of strutting stanchions.

Boatyard teeming with fresh hulls.

The *Gallatin* herself.

Every detail colossal, and not a pore of it would ever have existed at Fort Peck if it were not for the idea of an earthfill dam.

Even after his site inventory and double-checking his checklist, Owen was taking his time. Actually, monumental what-ifs were taking his time. What if they blew out the pipeline's flexible steel ball joints when they ran the pumps up to the pressure of sixty pounds per square inch. What if they burned up one of these fancy sonofabitching super-expensive electric motors first thing. What if Owen Duff turned into a puddle of worrysweat right here and now.

Fillmaster, was he. Then he had better master the goddamn fill.

"Give it the soup, Cal."

Calhoun told the operator to put on the power but for Christ's sake easy, and the seven-foot-diameter cutterhead slowly, ponderously, began to whirl. When its revolutions per minute came up to speed, the operator hit the boom controls, the massive A-frame boom at the nose of the dredge lowered the cutter shaft into the lip of the riverbank. The entire dredge, the size of half a street of houses, shuddered. "Jesus Mercy Christ, Duff," indeed. The 700-horsepower motor driving the cutter shaft, the 2,500-horsepower motors running the suction pumps in tandem, all of the dredging force bucked against the huge steel spud posts anchoring the dredge into place at the stern. The *Gallatin* thrummed with working machinery, none of which blew out, burned up, or caused fatality in Owen Duff.

The thirteenth of October, and they had done it: less than one year since the first axebites into the Fort Peck bottomland, its earth was being moved onto the axis of the dam.

Then they saw him, all of them, Charlene and Rosellen side by side cheering along with the crowd on the bluff out back of the Ad Building, Meg tense with pride on the doorstep of the cookhouse, Kate on tiptoes in the whooping bunch outside the Rondola Cafe when the word passed that the dredge was being started up, Bruce grinning like mad on the roof of the lever house of the next dredge being built in the boatyard, Neil watching in fascination while propped in his climber's belt twenty feet up a piling, Hugh bleak but intent at the foot of another piling: saw Owen come leaping ashore. Owen running. Sprinting along the dredgeline, then loping to save breath, then running as hard as he could again. He stopped beneath the last stanchion before the carrypipe, as close to the gushing cascade of water and muck as it was safe to go.

Harvested wheat, when it pours out of the spout of a combine, spews down in an exalted golden rain. To Owen, the muck falling from the carrypipe was that golden.

Honestly. You'll be playing house out behind here between coffee refills, next."

"Igloo, that'd need to be."

"Nh*n*. Rubbing *noses*."

"For a start. Eskimo kindling."

"And then make mad pash."

"A girl can hope."

The two young women laughed back and forth across their window-side table in the Rondola Cafe. Rosellen was having the chicken and dumplings, Kate the ham steak, and winter was having Fort Peck for supper.

"So you're over yours?" Rosellen kept matters going. "I wish to gosh I was."

"Ran enough irrigation through myself,

241

I ought to be," Kate offhandedly answered. "Did I tell you Bruce right away wanted to know if he was going to come down with 'sisteritis or whatever it is,' too? I told him since I was out of commission, he might as well be."

The dry granular snow of a ground blizzard stung at the window beside them. Rosellen made a face out at the weather, and Kate warned her not to be teasing it that way. This time of day had become their own, shared, prized — dusk's bonus of traded confidences that had to be spent then and there. Rosellen coming off work at the personnel section in the nearby Ad Building and Kate about to go on shift here at waitressing, suppertime was the perfect crisscross where the two of them could compare newlywed life (Kate's extra few months of experience had immeasurably helped Rosellen when her own case of cystitis cropped up) and swap whatever else was on their minds. Right now, there *was* nothing else in Rosellen's mind besides Kate's confiding of lunchtime passion with Bruce. Kidding each other, leaning in to glean what the other one thought about this or that, not oblivious to the fact that they were the Rondola's main attraction, the two of them bobbed like corks, Kate the slim wine-bottle variety, Rosellen as robust as a brandy stopper.

"Oh, did I tell you? Neil has off Friday night, he traded shifts with somebody. Now we can go to the show with you and Bruce." Rosellen made another face in the weather's direction. "Probably be *The Call of the Wild.*"

"I have to hand it to Neil, driving in this," Kate drew a finger squiggle on the wintry window. Out in the early dark, whenever the snow-carrying wind stopped long enough to catch its breath, the lights of the diversion tunnel project constellated against the opposite bluff on the river valley. Determined to see what could be done under the nose of winter, the dam-builders were pouring concrete for the huge portals of the tunnels; so far, they had learned they could get away with pouring it at temperatures down to seventeen degrees below zero. Almost as audaciously, up beyond the diversion tunnels the spillway excavation had begun, a gouge a mile long into the winter-stiffened earth. Neil had latched on as a driver there; not of the beloved Ford Triple A but a drafty rattling beast of a dumptruck, on the four-to-midnight shift, colder than the inverse of Hell. Lifelong veteran of Fort Peck winters that she was, Kate shook her head at Rosellen over how miserable her hubby must be about now and said, "Not this kid. They'd have to tie me to the wagon."

"Where's that come from?" People, the thousand and one ways they talked, always intrigued Rosellen.

"It's a saying, is all. Didn't you hear me just say it?"

When spring came, Neil was vowing, he would go back to his own trucking with never a murmur no matter how tough any haul turned out to be. Better to be master of his own coracle than a mate in this polar dumptruck fleet. The constantly gnawing wind, the snow which either flew around insidiously in the spillway pit as dry as salt or so fat and flakey you could barely see the dumptruck ahead of you in line, the night always so black, hell, so *bleak*. Huh uh; no more winters of this. What he wished right now, if the truth were told, was that there was some way to bring into the freezing damned truck the warmth of being a newlywed in bed. He needed to wish beyond that, of course, for Rosellen to hurry up and be over with this whatever-itis in her plumbing. This on top of the monthly intermission which he'd known about, sort of. Women were surprisingly complicated.

"Maybe that'd be the way to keep him

on the wagon," Rosellen shifted to. "Our disreputable pa-in-law."

"You'd have to go some to find ropes thicker than he is thirsty," Kate evaluated.

"What do you suppose gets into a person, to go off and tie one on — see there, you've got me doing it. To go off on the crazy binges he does, I mean."

"Beats me. Meg would be about enough to keep me on my good behavior."

What Bruce termed their nightly sessions of "blahdy blah" and Charlene characterized as the pair of them being "as thick as thieves," the two young women viewed as necessary oracle sessions on the family they had married into. They raked patterns in the Duffs, and the next day, as if the night's wind had wiped everything fresh, they could start over again. Hugh, who was wintering as if alcohol was his personal antifreeze, perturbed them both.

When spring finally came, Hugh was vowing as he hoisted yet another drink in the Wheeler Inn just then, he would try out Meg on finding work for themselves, any work, on farms down along the Yellowstone River valley. Owen's ilk hadn't got around to damming up the Yellowstone yet.

"But maybe she's the other side of his

habit," Rosellen went farther afield than usual. "Meg and her, hnn, opinions on life."

"That's supposed to drive him to drink?" Kate sounded skeptical as only she could. "Huh uh, I still say it's only ever a short stroll for him."

The window beside them shook so hard it chattered. "Listen to it bluster out there." In businesslike fashion Kate rubbed a peekhole in the frost as if to check on whether the river had blown away in that gust. "At this rate, it's going to be a while until skinny-dipping season."

"Oho! That's next on the mad pash list? Lunch at the old swimming hole?"

"Hey, why am I the skinny-dipping expert here?" Kate tossed off. "It's the same river where you grew up."

Marriage and Neil and instructive joking with Kate quite often gave Rosellen the short-of-breath feeling that she was catching up on a lot about life but still had a ways to go. The rueful grin she sent Kate now outright admitted it. "See, though, you didn't grow up with Charlene for a boss."

After Charlene big-sistered herself off to commerce and romance in Bozeman, the Missouri River in an odd way took her place with Rosellen. In the drabness of Toston, the loneliness of that scissor-simple Tebbet household, Rosellen often turned to the river for company, slipping away for hours at a time across the highway bridge to the opposite bank. There on the west bank, the ospreys nested high in the cottonwoods and fished the river with their talons; around town, they would be shot at as fish thieves. Just under the osprey nest, a particular eddy at a bend of the river always looked tempting for skinny-dipping; but Rosellen never quite gave in. She knew Charlene had been right about that much, the danger in the water, that swimming alone in this river was asking for it. Rosellen's answer was to hug the Missouri as closely as she could without slipping into it. Telling herself she would go only a little farther, trace the riverbank around one more bend, she always ended up following its course all the way upstream to where it wound out of the stony hogback hills a couple of miles above Toston. They were the ugliest hills in Montana, she was pretty sure (Charlene had been totally sure), but the Missouri pranced out of them high, wide and handsome, its waters freshly braided together from the Gallatin, Madison and Jefferson rivers at the Three Forks headwaters. The steady-stepping river sought into the

247

valley around Toston as if just released,
and while she did not yet know how to put
it into words that was Rosellen, too.

"Uh huh. She's a little hard to outgrow,
I suppose," Kate left it at. Whereas she did
not particularly *dis*like Charlene, she did
not feel compelled to *like* her either. She
figured there probably was not much
wrong with Charlene that, say, putting in
a nightly eight hours as a waitress
wouldn't cure in a hurry. Yet she knew
from Rosellen that Charlene had worked,
clerked, and so maybe it really was not a
matter of job, it was more a matter of
Charlene. Generally when it came to the
sister issue, Rosellen in front of all the
Duff in-laws acted as though Charlene
was not too bad a bargain, but privately
she agreed with Kate that Charlene could
stand to have her nose brought down out
of the clouds. Along that same front, there
was Fort Owen for the two of them to try
to puzzle out. Owen they still were doing
some deciding about, whether it was just
intrinsically fascinating to have a high
mucketymuck brother-in-law wrestling an
entire dam into place or whether his brain
sometimes was too big for its britches, so
to speak.

Assuming spring ever came, Owen was

vowing this very minute in the small pool of illumination from his droplight, he in this office was going to be goddamn good and ready, the dredging setup was going to be doubly goddamn good and ready, to move an average of three million cubic yards of earthfill a month. Nineteen thirty-five was going to have to be the year this dam took shape, big unmistakable god-damn shape.

And then Bruce.

"Something's on his mind, besides the part in his hair," Kate reported. "Can you always spot that, with Neil?"

"You better bet," Rosellen testified. "When he's hauling, I can tell how his trip went by how the truck pulls into the yard."

"Mm hmm. Whoops, I'm about on." Kate gathered their dishes in a professional pile and went behind the counter to start her shift. Rosellen assembled herself into heavy coat and overshoes and mitts and scarf and drove home. They put away tonight and set course for tomorrow's talkative supper together, these happy two, who were holding back from each other hardly anything under the sun.

Bruce had been thinking about this all week, a span of concentration that had his head buzzing.

A kind of tingle built up behind his ears as he at last reached the point of telling himself *ask, go ask, they can't any more than tell you no.*

The minute his shift ended, he tromped up the gangplank onto the workbarge.

The barge boss, Taine, looked at him questioningly. "Medwick want something?"

"No, I do." Bruce swallowed hard and nodded toward the bow of the barge, where a man in a diving suit was descending into the water. "I want to be the next him."

"That a fact," said Taine with supreme neutrality. "Ever done any diving, and where?"

"Uh, not yet," Bruce said. "But I'm ready to give it a try, right here right now."

"Are you," said the barge boss. "And your qualifications are what?"

Bruce seemed genuinely affronted. "Doesn't being crazy enough to do it count for enough?"

Taine sized him up with more interest. "Just how old are you?"

"Twenty-two," Bruce vouched unreliably. "Like the rifle."

"All right, then, hotshot. I'll clear it with Medwick for you to report here in the morning. We'll try you out as diver's tender for Bonestiel. Then if you still think you want to go under the river, Bonestiel can show you what crazy really is."

Actually, Bonestiel, a Louisianan, was more than willing to show Bruce the ropes of diving. He himself, Bonestiel proclaimed, was directly headed back to Louisiana's warmer waters, not to mention its warmer air, warmer earth, warmer food, and warmer women. And so Bruce marked his true immersion into Fort Peck by apprenticing in the under-river world as murky and slow as Bonestiel's accent.

Meg acted as if she wanted to scold Bruce but couldn't figure out where to start on the size of the chore. Hugh announced that he had lived too long, punished now by this spectacle of one of his own sons drawing actual money to parade along the bottom of a river. Owen was surprised to find himself for once proud of Bruce; diving was serious going. Charlene figured Bruce was as bull-goose loony as usual. Rosellen was torn between concern for Kate's sake and a guilty thrill at having a diver for a brother-in-law. Neil only warned Bruce to keep his window shut in that diving suit.

Kate put it to him without any such preamble:

"So, are you trying to kill yourself?"

"Honeybunch, you know I wouldn't ever —"

Bruce paused. Beside him on the noon bed, Kate, calm and lanky and thoroughly undressed, was looking at him as if she simply wanted to know, one way or the other. That was another thing that tickled him about her. She didn't try to shoo him away from the interesting parts of life.

He lay back and searched the ceiling for some way to tell her the extraordinary feeling, the for-once right fit, that diving gave him. "It's better than about anything but you, hon. It's . . . scary."

She studied him sideways. Owen had pointed out to her that, in a diving suit with lead weights slung on him and the short tether of the air hose, at least there would be no question of where Bruce was and what he was engaged in.

Waiting for him to say more, she finally recognized his silence for the confession it was. She propped herself up on an elbow and made sure:

"That's what's so good about it? That it's scary?"

"Uh huh. Is that too crazy?"

"It's up there pretty far. So you *are* out to kill yourself? Have the diving do it for you, that's the idea?"

"Huh uh."

"What, then. If all you want is to get a kick out of scaring yourself, you could just walk a trestle blindfolded."

Bruce cast her a look out of the corner of his eye, but otherwise stayed unmoving on the bed. "I better explain," he said, "before you get too excited about being the Widow Duff."

"That wouldn't excite me," Kate said. "I prefer a husband alive."

"That's just it." Bruce's forehead furrowed in unaccustomed concentration. "See, that's kind of what diving is for me. It's spooky to have all your air coming through a little hose, and never quite knowing how strong the river current is going to be when you get down there, and then how you have to handle stuff real careful, not rip the diving suit — that's what I mean by scary. But scary in a good way, can you savvy? A way that says, 'Hey, do this wrong and you're fish food. But do it *right*, and you're Mister River himself.' See what I'm getting at?" He was up on his side, earnestly turned toward her now. "It's a mix, is what it is, scary and okay along with it. And not just anybody is cut out for that, you know?"

She was starting to.

Kate took stock as Bruce's hand found its way to her thigh. Of all of life's dangers, she was married to a man who was choosing the river. Third time in a row, in the line of Millay women. *Third time lucky.* She weighed the saying, wondering how it applied.

She touched him commensurately where he was touching her. "I should have married Neil. I'd only have to savvy a truck."

"Neil in his birthday suit here, instead of me?" Bruce's hand busied on her. "Talk about scary."

Something approximating spring, at last, and as work at the dam site stirred in 1935's first days of thaw, so did the towns.

For a place barely past its first birthday, Wheeler showed atrocious age-spots where ashes and dishwater had been thrown all winter, wrinkles of ruts in every street and alley, and the general dishevelment of a veteran tramp. Its sibling downstream from the dam, Park Grove, had just wakened to the fact that whole neighborhoods were going to be eaten by the dredges, but the rest of the scatter of Fort Peck's shacky suburbs were starting to hear the sing of hammers again. The workforce, talk had it, was about to increase by another thousand wallets.

Second Friday of the month. Rosellen's day was rat-a-tat-tat at the oversize Blickensderfer typewriter, turning out paychecks. Every maxim of the Lewis & Clark Business School applied. Her chin up. Her spine straight as could be but not rigid. Her backside (which, seated or otherwise, was thoroughly admired by the male contingent of the Ad Building) snuggled against the back of the chair. Fingers downpoised into "tiger claws," as the L&CBS typing teacher sang out a dozen times every class. Steady rate of typing rather than fitful bursts. Kersplickety splick. Typewriter keyboard deliberately *qwerted* and *yuioped* by its inventor to slow down matters and prevent jamming, but Rosellen's fingers flew nonetheless. Dollar-sign number number decimal-point number number. Keynes crooning in the keys. The quick green wage jumps over the lazy Wall Street claque. Out the checks roll, deft translation by Rosellen's fingers of the Fort Peck Dam project into alphabet and dollars and cents, to be cashed at the New Deal Grocery or the Rondola Cafe or the Blue Eagle Tavern.

J.L. Hill, wages for his percussive tunnel work . . .

John B. Hinch, wages for dredgeline carpentry . . .

Charles S. Siderius, wages for resolution of land titles . . .

Kate slept. Night shift at the Rondola

provided her the schedule where she stayed in bed until noon when Bruce trotted home, scooted under the covers with her, they deliriously went at each other, then climbed out for a bit of lunch.

The dream she was having was an old one, out of that story of her grandmother. Kate was on the Fort Peck ferry. The river kept moving past, the ferry was slow to go. The man she was with, who was not Bruce, told her he was sorry but she had to be tied up for her own safety. Not both hands, Kate told him. One hand then, Not-Bruce told her. He took out a little rope like a piggin' string, such as was used to tie a calf's legs together during branding, and tied her wrist to the rail of the ferry. There, you can't fall off now, Not-Bruce said, like your grandmother. My grandmother never fell off, Kate insisted. That's because she was tied up, he said patiently. But by now Kate was looking down, into the river, and there was Bruce, walking along under the ferry. Not in any diving suit, just Bruce as nature made him, walking along under the water as if he was having the time of his life. Kate in her dream tugged against the hold on her hand — which in her sleep had got caught between the mattress and the beaverboard wall — and told herself, These people. I could be down there walking with Bruce if this other gazink would only let me. Who does he think he is?

Kate resentfully rolled over in bed and her hand popped free.

Charlene was madder than a wet hen or any other comparison that could be drawn.

This had been the day of the colonel's wife's social get-together; just a little Kansas Street do, as it had been described to Charlene. She changed into her best frock and promptly at ten that morning set off across the horseshoe to join the other wives flocking into the King's House. It wasn't until they were seated, circled like a spruced-up wagon train in Mrs. Parmenter's acreage of living room, that Charlene realized not all the other wives were here. These were the Corps officers' wives, from along the east loop of Kansas Street: bing, bing, bing, a major's wife, a captain's wife, a lieutenant's wife, you could go right down the roster of who lived where in the row of Permanent Residences. Except for her. So, she was here solely by dint of Owen and his job rank as fillmaster, was she not, was she ever. Which, she knew in the loyal fathoms of her heart, ought to make her unstintingly proud. Instead it panicked her. Already, first bite into a mysterious pastry with goop inside it, she was aware of steep graduations, mountainous social contour lines, in this gathering.

"— My Raymond is staying with my sister back there. We hated so to have him change schools and come out here where —"

"— No, we only hear from them at Christmas anymore. Poor him, he was passed over on the last promotion list again. You know what they say, the feast of the passover is no diet for a Pointer —"

It pretty quickly grew apparent to Charlene that a prior existence in Kansas City, headquarters of the Missouri River Division of the Corps, favorably colored a person's status here. Intermixed with that, though, was West Point or not. If your husband's career lacked cadet gray, you probably sat resignedly like Captain Haugen's wife, Minnie, and brought your petit point sewing with you. In contrast, Colonel Parmenter having graduated from Choate *and* West Point, *and* been a high-ranking Kansas City officer, Mrs. Parmenter sat there with an entire deckful of aces. And this was just what rubbed off from the men. There was a pecking order of the women's backgrounds, too. Being from the South, for instance, seemed to count for a lot.

"— Eula, did you hear that awfulness on

Ma Perkins the other day? The whole passel of them were caught out in a blizzard and the young man from the lumberyard, whose-his-toes, Lester I think it is, said right there on the radio, 'Ma, you walk behind me and I'll break wind for you!' For two cents I'd write in to Oxydol and give them a piece of my —"

By watching feverishly and saying precious little, Charlene sorted out the basics of what was going on around her. Of all things, calling cards regulated these people. She had peeked when the major's wife placed the major's card on the hall table with at-home hours for next Friday morning penciled in, and it did not take much to deduce that a captain's wife would lay down the captain's card for the Friday after that. She was able to figure out, too, that the other engineers' wives, such as Pam Sangster and Shirley Nevins, in all likelihood were going to be invited to these next Friday soirees one by one, like rotated orphans. Somewhere a list existed and she, wife of Owen Duff, had merely been plucked off first by Mrs. Parmenter. Worse, what she was beginning to suspect was that *Colonel* Parmenter had done the list-plucking, not stuffy Mrs. Parmenter at all.

Charlene, younger than the rest and more striking in her sunflower-yellow frock and as usual coiffed as if with black lacquer, thought she was coping reasonably well until the cookie platter came around, at last favorably laden with Jaarala's cookhouse golden-and-sugared finest.

"I've always liked ballinacrunchers," she announced, glad of something recognizable to eat.

Not a full minute passed, however, before she heard Mrs. Parmenter say with enunciation too distinct:

"Wouldn't anyone like some more *berlinerkransers?*"

Hours now after the so-called party, Charlene still had her mad on, and in fact was expanding it from Mrs. Parmenter to the whole kit and caboodle of officers' wives. The big-shot Missourians acted like they'd invented the Missouri River. Married to the elite of dambuilders, hooey; bunch of muddaubers here. This brought a guilty twinge in her, for Owen's sake. He would know what she meant, though. The time Owen had taken her into the Blue Eagle, when she'd said once she wanted to see what it was like, he did that imitation of the Duke of Wellington entering Parliament: *"I have never seen so many bad hats in my life."* Well, this morning she, Charlene, had never seen so many bad heads of hair in her life. All those moppy old frumps who thought

260

they were somebody; the "when we were in Kansas City" attitude of the Corps wives still incensed her. Most of them, anyway. Minnie Haugen seemed nice, but you couldn't spend all your life talking about petit point, either.

She gazed at the clock. Two hours yet until Owen would be home. Three or more years yet until Fort Peck Dam was done.

Face it, kiddo.

She sat herself down, beaverboard Temporary Residence walls around her, and for the next two hours did just that.

Owen came home practically cross-eyed from calculations on fill ratios of four different dredges operating at four varied distances from the axis of the dam. Charlene met him with a kiss that included a heated dart of her tongue. He visibly perked up.

"If that's what's for supper," he said, going to hang up his hat, "I have room for several helpings."

"There's something else, first."

He turned around still holding the hat. "Why, what's up now?"

Charlene drew a statewide breath and told him she thought the thing for her to do was set up shop in Wheeler, as a hairdresser.

261

* * *

Meg had plans for the house — with sunshine blasting in through the window this was the kind of day when you could not help but have plans. Paint was a priority. She was pretty sure she could get Hugh to paint the house by threatening to ask Owen to do it. Flowers, the place screamed for flowers, color of any kind to break the prairie-and-shack monotony of the dam site and Wheeler. How soon now could she put in marigolds? Petunias, geraniums? Tiger lilies, hollyhocks!

She sang a few bars of "Gammer Gammon's Needle" before catching herself at it and puckering up, amused at the day's menu of distractions. Resolutely she swept out the woodbox, not because it wasn't going to be used anymore but because it wouldn't be used quite as much, which today seemed a sufficient reason. The rest of the place required a general attack. Remembering that this was Friday, water day, she decided to splurge and set the pointer on the water card at fifteen gallons instead of the usual ten, the extra for scrubbing this place down.

On her way past from putting the water card in the window, she briskly confronted herself in the small square mirror hung above the washbasin. At least her complexion was back, now that her days were

262

not spent in a wind- and sunburned alfalfa field. But she looked at herself beside the eyes and thought, *Ouch. Is it possible for a person to catch wrinkles by just being around that face of Mr. Jaarala?*

But after that first regret over the crinkles at the corners of her eyes, she decided she would not have repealed them even if she could, they were earned honorably enough. Charlene and Rosellen and Kate could lead the skincreamed wrinklefree life if they wanted, but her generation had these stripes of life. People are said to have the face they deserve at forty, and Meg Duff was forty-five.

Not nearly as old as the troubles of the world, she told herself and contemplated the diplomacy of paint again. If she knew Hugh, he would soon start a spring offensive, launch some idea about quitting Fort Peck. The way he had punctuated winter with sprees, after Neil went to trucking on the spillway cut, surely must be leading up to that, Meg more than half suspected. He'd had to do his spreeing only on any of his wages that he could squirrel away from her, though, and she'd firmly added and added her own wages, and any of his that she could retain, into a stash safely hidden from him. If money indeed talked, Hugh Duff was going to have less of a say than he thought.

She smiled at herself; a plethora of sun-shine, after a Fort Peck winter, put a deserved face on lots of things. So, Hugh, his habitual self, and paint: ought she to wait until after they'd fought out Fort Peck one more time, or would it save time to tackle him sooner than —

She went to answer the knock, water delivery a trifle early, checking her apron pocket for enough coins as she opened the door. Not to the water delivery man. With the sun behind him, for an instant until she could shield her eyes she thought the familiar long frame was Hugh and could not understand why he would have knocked instead of simply coming in.

Oh Lord, the recognition flew into her. *Darius. Oh no and oh yes.*

Part Three

OTHER RIVERS

1935

You couldn't even believe a woman when she said hello, Darius Duff reminded himself.

He was seeing Meg now across a quarter of a century, the lines at the corners of her eyes mapping that length of time and maybe something beyond. After all that Scotland had done to him lately, it somewhat surprised him that there was any wear and tear left for the rest of the world, even on a woman who had chosen to marry his brother Hugh. But Meg still had the speculation in those eyes. The nurse-like sense of attention, the way of peering at you as if clerking for God. The Milnes of Inverley were that way from the reverend on down, he couldn't help but remember: preacher and preacher spawn. They wore well, though, Meg the latest evidence

265

of that — the set character of her face, as if certified for good and all by the nock in her chin. Not to mention the lithe build below.

And the voice, streambed of voice, deep and as dancing as ever. "Darius!" She gave his name the particular lilt, shiny crown-point of emphasis atop the middle syllable, knowing how he hated a flat-tongued saying of it as Derry-us. "Darius, welcome!"

Don't hear more than is there, he had to tell himself. Vast fool that you were those years ago, don't ever put yourself through that again.

"A while, Meggie," he spoke as if it was a discovery.

"At least that." She still studied him in a kind of appalled thrill. His eyebrows went up inquisitively, and she hurried toward manners. "Come in, come in. But what — you didn't let us know you'd be coming."

"I didn't much know, myself." That punctuating small smile from him, as quick as if it was the last letter of the sentence. Hugh without the gale-warning flags, this brother of his. Which had led to confusions before, she more than remembered.

Darius stepped into the house and halted as if hit.

"What in stone cold Hell — ? Blueprints?"

He let his suitcase drop and strode on into the second room, to the blue-papered wall.

"They . . . help keep the weather out." He heard a swallowing sound from Meg. "Housing is a bit rough and ready here, as you see."

Rough, he could definitely see. The two-room hutch, shanty, shack, whatever American shambles it was, showed damp-stained beaverboard at the kitchen walls where the blueprints did not quite extend, and the floor of unplaned lumber was stark except where Meg had managed to knit a rag rug for beside the bed. The bed in with the living room furniture made the room as crammed as the corner of a warehouse.

He felt fury toward Hugh, putting her in this hovel, and with it vindication. *She could have done other. I made that clear enough.* But then the thought swarmed in that if Meg had chosen him, she'd right now be existing out of the pasteboard suitcase at his side.

"Here, let me — we're still getting squared away," she said, quite near him now, as she swept a pile of clothes off a chair. "But sit yourself down. Please, do."

Instead he waded through the clutter to the topmost roll of blueprint Owen had papered across the back wall. Fingers out as if finding Braille, he traced the white lines of the plan of the dam. Meg saw a frown come on him, his fingers pausing at the dam's midpoint and then moving professionally down to the lower right corner of the blueprint, the title block that revealed the scale of the dam.

"My God, they'll be moving dirt for an eternity!"

"That's what they intend, yes. Tons — well, tons of tons. Just how much, you'll need to ask Owen."

"I'll do that," he murmured as if to himself. " *Pyramids and tall memorials, catch the dying sun.'* "

"Darius. What's brought you?"

"It came to seem time." He kept his eyes away from Meg's, restudying the walls of the shack. After a moment, he went on: "Scotland's used up. You and Hugh long since decided so, didn't you." His smile flashed again, showing the short square tooth, bottom left, that had been chipped off in a shipyard accident. Meg had thought at the time that nicked part somehow made this smile of his even more appealing, gave him a dimple in his mouth, and she thought it again now. "You remember me, Meggie," she heard him say. "Takes some while for me to catch up with the way of things."

But when you do . . . she recalled, too.

"You're here for good?" She couldn't keep the alarm out of her face.

Darius simply appeared amused. "I'm a pair of hands that knows tools, and they must need those here. Hugh, now, he's a man of the plow if there ever was one and they've even hired him, haven't they?" He was giving her more gaze than she wanted. She took it as a relenting when he nodded toward the dam blueprint and asked: "And the rest of the family — Matthew, Mark, and Luke, are they all at this, too?"

"They are, yes. Even I am. I help the — I'm on at the cookhouse."

"Ever an ambitious tribe, ours," Darius bestowed, and then was watching past her to the front door.

Hugh had halted in the doorway.

"Unfair," Hugh stated. "I've just had a day that would curdle holy water, and now here's this."

Courting Margaret Milne, he'd had his work cut out for him. None of the situation (except the extraordinarily blue-eyed Margaret; Meg as she was becoming whenever conditions seemed to permit) suited Hugh Duff at all. The manse where even the doorknocker sounded basso profundo to a gawky young farm laborer coming to call. The dispiriting strictures of when and where courtship of a reverend's daughter could be in session. And, vague but ever-near, the dousing personality that was the Reverend Milne himself. Those were only the start of the odds against Hugh, too. The Duff brothers were what was left of a railwayman's family, whom the Reverend Milne seemed to peg even lower on the social ladder than they already were. Stroppy young man that he was, Hugh did not take well to being looked down on.

"Were I you" — counsel by Darius, more veteran in the ways of the world by an entire year, was never in short supply — "I'd stuff the poorbox in thanks for the old spouter."

"What're you talking of? The man will barely let us graze our eyes across one another," Hugh reported bitterly. "He's got his religions confused, thinks he has nunnery charge."

"What better way to convince her," Darius pointed out, "that you're worth breaking down all walls for?"

Hugh ran in streaks, she had known that from early on. There would be all his obstinacy such as the Gibraltar's worth it took to withstand her father's campaign of discouraging him, then suddenly here would come a veer, so that you had to look twice to be sure this was the behavior of the same Hugh Duff. The differentiation made him a lively suitor more so than Meg had ever quite imagined. Nothing in Hugh's life became him like the weaving of that romance. Meg's breath, and much of the rest of her self-possession, literally was taken away by his ploy of enlisting Darius, lookalike from a little distance, to dawdle around within view from the Reverend's study window while Hugh and she were at the back of the house in extensive forays of kissing.

"This is —"

"— daft, I know." Hugh kissed the tip of her nose, then her cheekbone, then her chin. "Where were we?"

"You know perfectly well where," she murmured, presenting her lips for his again.

This is daft, Darius groused to himself, trying to appear ostentatiously nonchalant for the figure watching with suspicion from the leaded-glass window. Making a gowk of myself while Hugh is spooning her in like dilly sauce.

"That father of yours —"

"— believes you are interested in my hand," Meg backed off a fraction from Hugh's latest exploration. "Little does he know."

The more her father pounded away about Hugh's supposed lackings, the more she thought Hugh needn't be all of one metal.

271

That was the way her father was, after all; pure preacher in an impure congregation, the world, and she did not want to be fastened to that kind of absolute again. If Hugh Duff came with a dent or two already in, she told herself she didn't care; and she didn't, then.

By the time of their marriage Darius was off on his own, the shipyards along the River Clyde were more home to him than the farm-market town of Inverley had ever managed to be. Steel sang to him. The longships find their harbor in the head, *began the poem of the Clydeside he loved best, and Darius filled himself from the eyes in with the constant armada along the resounding industrial river. Great Britain was determined to maintain a fleet that would overshadow Germany's. The Asquith government's Chancellor of the Exchequer, the fateful Lloyd George, had contrived a tax on estates: "Every time a duke dies," he crowed, "we can build a dreadnought." Those crammed years when the shipyards were at full boom, Darius had to make his start low, as mere bucket boy, and next came the testing stint as rivet-backer, that earsplitting chore within the hulls. Then, though, to riveter, and the riveters were the princes of the river, the canny hands at crafting the seams that* held ships together and the bargaining voices that the others of the Clyde workplaces harkened to. And so for Darius Duff and his rivet gun, those years, the Clydeside work held results close to magical: the laying of keel plates, the curving rise of the hull, the cladding of steel onto structural skeleton; make one vessel and you could make any, you could rivet together any longship that could be imagined.

Darius on frequent visits down from the Big Smoke, Glasgow, from his aeries of steel, was a Darius with even more spice to him, Hugh couldn't but note. Keener, more glinty; honed against those shipsides of the Clyde, maybe it must be put. Not even to mention prospering. Hugh knew he could tend oats on the MacLaren estate from now until next doomsday and never keep up with his brother's pay packet. Be that as it may. The land took a while, Hugh was always capable of telling himself, but it and he would be there when Darius was deaf and doled.

Yet would it. The day came, in the spring of 1910, when Hugh arrived home dazed with fundamental questions. He walked in to find Owen, barely past his second year, seated manfully at a tiny desk and chair, Meg laughing and Darius with a lordly grin.

"Worth a try at getting a scholar, don't you

think, Hugh?" Darius knelt down to spider-walk his hand across the desktop, Owen's gaze avidly following. Desk and chair were both exquisitely crafted; the lathes of the Clydeside shipyard were the world's finest, Hugh had no doubt. "It skipped us a bit," Darius was going on, "but you put together that lamented father of ours and the late great Reverend Milne in this lad's background and he's likely to be apt at turning pages, wouldn't you have to say?"

"We surely would," Meg gaily provided as she swept Hugh's tea-can from him and kissed the vicinity of his ear. "Hugh, did you ever know you had such a lovely brother?"

"It's been generally well disguised," he said.

The only sound then was the pattycake of Owen's palms on his resounding new little desk.

"Hugh," Meg said in a voice that did not quite waver. "What?"

What, yes. The radical acceleration of these visits from Darius since Owen's birth? The embedded suspicion in Hugh that Meg's choosing of him had been a close decision in the first place, and now down from Glasgow every fortnight or less was a fresh reason for her to rethink that decision? The firm recitation in Hugh that he could not, did not dare, believe she *would ever actually toss him over for Darius? The accompanying fact that he could never quite remove the chance of that from his mind, either?*

Hugh shook his head, to bring himself back to the day's blow. "The MacLaren land. It's going to tenements."

Meg came to him without a word. What was spoken was pure Darius:

"This we can fix like that, Hugh." Fingersnap. Across the crown of Meg's hair, Hugh looked at his triumphant brother. "There's every chance waiting for you on the Clyde. I only have to put in the word for you with the right somebody, Monday at the yard."

Were you Hugh, you knew in that moment that you were going to have to put an ocean between you and the Clydeside.

"You're as even tempered as ever, Hugh," Darius let out with a smile and an extended hand as he crossed the floor of the shack. "Full steam all the time."

Hugh gave him a handshake, but during it demanded: "What's behind this?"

"The times," his brother said evenly, "what else."

Hugh cocked him a look they both remembered. "You can't mean to tell me even your blessed Clydeside is feeling the pinch."

"It's beyond pinch," Darius confessed.

"Darius, yes, tell us how things stand," Meg painted in, shooing the visitor toward the kitchen table and sending Hugh the Milne gaze that conveyed *As a last resort you could try manners, Hugh Duff.* "Sit, the both of you, and I'll —" she rapidly attacked the coffeepot and the firebox of the cookstove.

"The times, you were saying." Hugh would not leave this alone, Darius saw. "They handed you yours?"

Darius fought back the risings at the back of his throat, the anger and the other. *Do it as rehearsed,* he made himself hear himself. *You knew this has to be got past.*

"The Clyde and I parted company, yes. Out the gate, and so I kept going. Knew a fellow. He was able to make me a place on a ship. And then —" Darius jerked his head in the general direction of the railroad. "Old habits die hard, Hugh. Family seems to be one of the incorrigible ones. Worse than a sweet tooth." He carefully kept looking his brother in the eye. "Truth to tell, I didn't know where else . . ."

"You've come late to see us at our best," Hugh said tautly. "When we had the farm —"

"Yes, I've seen that. Tidy. Tucked away like a swallow's nest, though."

Something came on in Hugh's eyes, then went out. Meg and untouched cups of coffee had joined the two men at the table. Darius knew it was time to give Hugh the high ground.

"You were far ahead of me about America. I'll say it now: I couldn't see past the Big Smoke. Although —" the smile suddenly in there "— wouldn't you know they have a Glasgow here, too." *Such as it is.*

Hugh took this in; admissions from Darius had never been frequent. He turned toward Meg a moment. The sight of her on the same side of the table with him seemed to give him heart. *The weight of life is what holds us to this world, eh, Meg?* He cleared his throat. "So you're not here as a tourist, then."

"I haven't come as a charity case, either," Darius kept in tenor with. "I'd put some money by, I'm not hurting on that quite yet." He made himself go through with it. *Use the slow spoon, you've had to before.* "A job of work is what I have in mind, if you happen to know of anything about the hiring here, Hugh. If you could lodge a good word for me in the right somebody's ear, say."

Hugh shook his head, but then inclined it toward Meg. "She's your man on that, Darius."

"We keep on, the whole payroll's gonna be Duffs."

Medwick shuffled through his boatyard shift roster. "Owen, you know Montana residents get hiring preference."

"Sure, Cece, everybody and his uncle knows that."

Medwick glanced up at the figure standing beside Owen in brazenly brand-new Mighty Mac bib overalls. "Where is it you been living, mister?"

"Helena," stated Darius with confidence but also with an un-Montanan long *e* in the middle. Seeing the wince on Owen, he tried again: "I've a cousin there, she's a music teacher. Her name's Hel*ee*na. She lives in Hel*eh*na."

"Yeah, well, don't coincidences never quit." Medwick put a long look to Owen, then a longer one to Darius. "How long since you came across from the old country?"

"An age ago."

"You know how we are, Cece," Owen thrust in. "Anybody with the name Duff on him will work himself silly for you."

"Uh huh, Bruce was all the proof I needed on the silly part, at least." Medwick sighed, picked up a pencil and jotted on a roster. He said sourly to Darius, "Welcome to the Montana navy."

"CASCADE SPILLWAYS, THOSE'RE CALLED. YOU CAN SEE, WHEN WE PIPE THE FILL UP INTO THE CORE POOL THEN THE WASTE-WATER GETS DISCHARGED DOWN THOSE SO WE CAN CONTROL THE LEVEL OF . . .

"BITUMEN SPRAYING, THEY'RE DOING OVER THERE. THE SONOFABITCHING BEARPAW SHALE TURNS SOFT AND SLICK WHENEVER IT GETS REALLY WET, SO WHEN WE UNCOVER AN OUTCROP WE GIVE IT A COAT OF . . .

"TRYING OUT A THREE-BLADE BUTTERFLY VALVE HERE, SEE IF WE CAN CUT DOWN ON THE CLAY PLUGGING THE DREDGING SETUP WHEN . . ."

Owen's headlong, half-heard, nine-tenths baffling tour for Darius before delivering him to his shift at the boatyard had looped through nearly all of Fort Peck by now. This and that were pointed out with offhand pride as the biggest in the world, but Darius seemed most keen on sorting out the swarms of workers. "And these be — ?" he asked persistently as Owen drove him past site after site of vast construction that he seemed determined to find unastonishing.

Okay, bloke from the Big Smoke, be that way, Owen thought with some amusement, and kept on going after they had crossed the temporary bridge over the river, heading the government pickup on into the hills beyond the east end of the dam.

Darius did not appear taken, either, with this bouncing tour of the countryside, to flatter it with that appellation. Ash heaps in the earth's backyard, these gray dumpy little hills more looked like as the pickup zigged and zagged along the road that threaded their maze. He rapidly gave up on the dismal scenery and studied Owen. *However Hugh happened to come by him, this is a thorough one.* Owen's profile still unsettled him. Darius felt as if he had fallen among some complicated tribe wearing mocking masks of past history. Bruce and Neil looked so much like a younger Hugh that it was truly unnerving — the aspects of Hugh in duplicate! — while Owen alarmingly resembled both Darius's and Hugh's father *and* Meg's, the memorable Reverend Milne. *Wouldn't you think,* Darius mused, *life would refashion us more than it does.* The women at least weren't such a confusion. A set of inspections might have convinced him Charlene and Rosellen were sisters, but otherwise he wouldn't have known so without being told. And cinnamon-stick Kate, definitely one of a kind. But then there was Meg, who still looked like every expectation he'd ever had of a woman, and that was most complicated of all.

He suddenly felt the sideways scrutiny Owen was giving him.

Their composite Darius uncled in the dimmest back corners of the Duff sons' imagination, unstirring there for years at a time, until something abrupt from the direction of Scotland would trigger speculation or hearsay. The Christmas when the toy steam engine arrived from over the ocean, the younger two boys fingered it with mouths open while Owen, ten-year-old sprout, studied the machinery and asked: "Dad, what's it run on?" Hugh took a close look, then looked sharply again. "Alcohol," he had to intone, there in 1918, the year Montana voted itself dry. A few years on from then, Bruce had come across the engine again in a box under the bed and fired it up for an incessant half day of play, meanwhile pestering an outline of Uncle Darius from his mother. When Bruce abandoned the steam toy for adventure in the hayloft, that was the last time he'd given thought to the uncle in Scotland. Neil, after he had taken to teenage carpentry and someone remarked on his swift knack with tools, heard his father say once: "He comes by it sideways in the family — I've a brother with a canny hand that way." Only once; other times Hugh would say, "I don't know where he gets it."

In the nephew trio, then, Owen alone in grown life had never deliberately thought about the figure in the Clyde shipyard.

His junior year course Strength of Materials 321 had practically forced him to, with its provocative questions of steel against seawater; he had tried to picture the shipwright life, another Duff life of the moment but across the flex of the world. And then Owen's Panama voyage, his shifts as boiler fireman in the cave of hull, where he could all but read his phantom uncle's trade in the firelit lines of rivets. Now that Darius had sprung to life in Montana, in their net of attention to this family newcomer Owen's mesh was the finest. He had noticed Darius's slight ruffle when Bruce, lately in favor of universal matrimony, put the question: "We don't get an aunt along with you, huh? Never married?"

Darius had seemed to take Bruce's measure for a moment, then smiled. "Not so far. Applications are still being sought."

"Almost there." Owen eased his eyes off his uncle and back to the anonymous hills. "How about a jag of jumping bean?" Driving full tilt one-handed, he groped under the pickup seat and pulled out a thermos bottle of coffee. Every American whom Darius had encountered so far was a caffeine fiend. "You get the cup first, you're the guest," Owen decreed.

While Darius mastered pouring an unwanted beverage in a bouncing vehicle,

Owen glanced sideways at him and asked:

"How'd you know to find us here?"

"Process of elimination. I found where you weren't, first." Darius took one sip of the coffee and pined for tea. "The farmstead looked like just the place for Hugh. Somewhere private for him to pound the ground, make the earth say — what, not oats, some sort of fluffaloofa . . ."

"Alfalfa," Owen supplied.

Darius folded his hands around the thermos cup and watched Owen for the effect of this next:

"Someone's scavenging the place. The boards are torn off the buildings and stacked there."

"It's the Old Man," Owen said shortly. "And Neil. They take the truck —"

"My brother is scavenging his own farmhouse?"

"He didn't want to see it burned."

Darius was given no time to digest that. "You'd better toss that coffee into yourself or out the window," Owen was advising as he shifted into lower gear. "We go mountaingoat here."

He veered the pickup off the road and straight up the tallest gray hill, wheels spinning as Darius bounced like a ball beside him.

At the top, the Fort Peck country spread around them in billowing reaches. The rumpled land hid away even the dam project, and permitted the river out only in a single streak of glitter in the middle distance, the horizon beyond as far and sharp as the quit of a map. As Owen braked the pickup to a hard stop, a canyon gaped below Darius's side of the vehicle.

At once he took in the sawcut sides, the engineered taper of the huge channel wedged between the set of hills he and Owen were on and a similar lumpy range of them a considerable distance across the way. There in the tremendous trench-cut gap between, a series of forms was under installation, concrete being poured into them by truckloads. Cranes swung bindles of steel through the air, legions of workers were erecting still more of the giant pillar forms. Owen, absolutely unable not to look pleased with himself, watched Darius watch the potboil of construction below.

"What's this, then — another dam?" Darius at last hazarded. "Do you practice building them, between every two hills?"

"It's the spillway."

To Owen's satisfaction, Darius at last registered astonishment. "But it's to hell and gone, here, from your dam!"

"Three miles, that's true. But the water'll come here in no time. The lake will back up out into the base of those bluffs." Owen indicated toward the disheveled geography to the south, then cut an arc under it with his extended forefinger. "It's just about a perfect natural reservoir. And when the lake level reaches where we left the road down there, the spillway goes to work."

"Not at your dam itself, though, this spillway," Darius dwelt on. "Why's that?"

"The dam can be just what it is, this way," Owen began as if savoring music. "See, Darius, we're dealing with water here that's about as changeable as the goddamn weather." Darius watched him turn as intense as the small boy drumming on his new sounding board of a desk in an Inverley cottage. "The Missouri's big on floods," Owen was saying. "Exactly how big it can get, we don't even know because our records don't go back that far. What we do know is that there's a whole pot of things that can pour water at us here. A heavy winter. A late spring, thawing and freezing again all the time. Then how about, say, a cloudburst up in the Rockies, just to get the runoff really running. That, my friend" — Owen tilted his head toward Darius a bit but kept his eyes on the immense spillway — "is what we call a hundred-year flood. The spillway, out here separate, takes care of that, and the dam doesn't have to do two things at once — hold back floodwater and let flood-water through. Integrity of the design, it's called." Owen caught himself. "But you'd know that from your own line of work, wouldn't you."

"Fancy," said Darius as if mostly to himself, and peered again down the canyon-wall to where rocksaws screeched into the crumbly top layer of shale and the black fog of bitumen sealed the cutaway trench of unweathered Bearpaw bedrock beneath. "If you have all the room in the world to gouge around in, I suppose this is the sort of thing you can do." Owen was reaching to start the pickup when he heard Darius add:

"Can't say I blame you."

"Blame?"

"For not wanting water cavorting through the middle of your earthen dam, of course, Owen." Darius was giving him an understanding grin that Owen could have done without. "Concrete spillway or no, there'd still be moving water in the vicinity of your earthfill, wouldn't there. Water on the go, against even a dam such as yours — over time, I believe water cuts almost anything."

"It does," Owen said after a few moments of regarding him. "That's why we're trying not to do this river any favors in the dam design."

Somebody should write this down, she thought. *You can't go a day around here without something new stewing up.*

In the dredgelines, the earthfill gurgled and burped and sloshed. The winter-built dredges *Jefferson* and *Madison* had joined the *Gallatin*, the trio of them proudly towed upstream to designated borrow pit areas and, for Owen as fillmaster, 1935 began on the 15th of April. The dredging setup was new and stiff, and its myriad equipment needed to be learned by crews of farm- and ranch-raised Montanans whose experience with electric dredges was not vast. Arguments were the Fort Peck anthem that April. Neil, of all people, locked horns with a tough High Line Swede on the pipeline trestle crew and had been lucky to come out of it with only a black eye, a cut eyebrow, scraped knuckles, and a sprained toe. After a terrible first couple of weeks, when Owen seemed to be everywhere trying to settle down men and machines, the heaves and staggers of startup seemed to be cured. Each dredge's cutterhead ate into the riverbank or the bottom of the Missouri and then water was mixed in, and the slurry was pumped through the twenty-eight-inch pipeline, and cascaded up onto the suddenly visibly growing mound of the dam.

This family is like nine radios going at

once, it really pretty much is. Every Duff a different station.

Nobody liked dealing with the dredge-line's drain traps, where river trash and balls of gumbo accumulated and had to be periodically mucked out, until the first buffalo skull tumbled forth. The bone relics came out like clockwork from then on, horned ghosts of some herd, herds, disgorged with every cleaning of the traps; the upstream borrow pit where the *Gallatin* was dredging must have been a disastrous crossing for the creatures. In no time, shellacked buffalo skulls were a Fort Peck motif from one end of the shacktowns to the other; each of the four Duff households sported one over the front door, and Darius had his affixed as a hatrack above his bed at the barracks.

Look what it takes just to be a married couple. Then all the in-lawing on top of that. Family is a hard idea. Maybe we'd be better off just in herds.

That first season the dredging operation, now the wellspring of progress on the dam, sat for its photo virtually every day. Thus someone managed to click a shutter at the exact moment during the launch of the dredge *Missouri* when its long wall of hull displaced the riverwater in a rolling shove of wave, and the five Fort Peck workers named Duff were posed aboard with their arms around each other like a file of sailors. Aligned on the deck behind the hedgerow of water, left to right: Neil and Bruce in paired grins, dubious Hugh, Darius bemused, Owen with an anchoring grip on the structurework, riding the fourth and final dredge down the ways to its namesake river.

No, though. Who would want to go it alone in life if they had any choice? The four of us who made ourselves Duffs by marrying Duffs — and now there's this extra one from Scotland into the bargain — we're as bad as they are for pairing off, choosing up sides, getting each other's nose out of joint, patching it up until the next time. This family seems to live on next times. That's something else that needs written.

The sheriff stood in wait, his Marlin .12-gauge shotgun resting in the umbrella stand he had dragged over next to him.

Shouldn't be long now, he figured, and took another peek out front.

Keeson's gray head moved nervously, there behind the store counter. The sheriff could see where the wire earpieces of Keeson's glasses hooked down between cartilage of the ears and pompadoured gray hair. He never had understood why jewelers didn't go entirely blind, squinting at all the little stuff they did.

"Hang tight, Floyd," he said softly. "This is what it takes, with these types."

"Remember, God darn it, Carl, I get to clear out of here."

"I've allowed for that, don't worry."

The owl-like shiftings of Floyd Keeson's head did not seem to signify any less worry. The sheriff pursed his lips and settled himself again against the back-room wall of the Glasgow jewelry store. Once in a great while the telephone was a wonderful thing, Carl Kinnick reflected. It had been nothing much to pay attention to, routine adjacent-counties report, when the store in Havre got knocked off during the noonhour; fool kid of a clerk, for leaving the dressed-up guy who flashed a wad of cash and asked to see the high-priced stuff perfectly at leisure to scoop out the display case while the clerk was in back fiddling with the safe. But then an hour and a half later, just the time it took to drive from Havre to Malta, the next sizable town east on Highway 2, the jeweler there got knocked off and knocked out as well, coldcocked when he bent down to reach something out of the display case for Mr. Jewel Bandit. Next it was only an hour from Malta to Glasgow, and when the guy started to pull his stunt again in Keeson's Jewelry he was going to be in for a major surprise. Zipping along the High Line like he was picking berries, huh; we'll just see, the sheriff told himself. He glanced down at the Marlin shotgun waiting handy. Put Marlene to working on him, and the prospect of her load of lead would get his attention in a hurry.

"Carl, here —" he heard Keeson let out between clenched teeth.

"Shut up, Floyd," he whispered back, then heard the store door whisk open.

The sheriff listened hard. Really not much of a spiel the guy had. *Special girl . . . necklace'd be nice . . . something with quite a stone . . .* It evidently didn't take a hell of a lot to be a jewel bandit.

"— appropriate item for you in the back room," Keeson was saying, and in the next instant swept through the doorway curtain and past Carl Kinnick with never a glance and kept on going, out the wide-open back door as the sheriff had instructed him to.

The guy already had the display case jimmied open and was arm deep among the wedding rings when the sheriff stepped out with the shotgun leveled.

Neither of them said word one as the sheriff moved around to the same side of the counter as the jewel heister.

The guy, though. The sheriff stared at him with growing disbelief. The guy was like a super dressed-up mannequin of the sheriff himself. Not the clothes, that wasn't it. The body structure, the bantam-weight frame, the same doll-delicate bones. The guy was damn near a complete physical replica of him, Kinnick saw; small man's swift raccoon hands, and their diminutive handtooled footwear would have fit one another. There in the jewelry store, two little lockets of men.

Then the jewel bandit grinned about how they matched.

The sheriff lowered the shotgun halfway. Utterly furious, he said in case Floyd Keeson or anyone else was within hearing: "That's a move you don't want to make," and simultaneously fired both barrels into the offender's legs.

Bruce was speculating out loud that Charlene would be the mayor of Wheeler, next. Charlene was assuring him his hours were numbered if that ever happened.

The A-1 Beauty Shop stood two doors down from the Blue Eagle Tavern. The shop name offered itself discreetly on the front window. What could be read the length of Wheeler's main street, and then some, was the resounding black block lettering across the top of the storefront:

PERMANENTS
$3.^{50} $5.^{00} $6.^{50}

The Duffs stayed grouped outside the new shop, admiring the screaming sign and Charlene's sales philosophy behind it: that the wholly outlandish top price of $6.50 made the $3.50 hairdo sound like a bargain, and that when a woman felt like splurging, there in the middle beckoned the $5.00 job that sounded like a relatively good deal.

"Ownie, I'm going to borrow her to do the arithmetic on the truck payments," Neil acclaimed.

One thing puzzled Darius. " 'Permanent,' though — why's this spasmodic hairfixing called that?"

"If you think I'm going to advertise that I'm selling 'spasms,' Darius, you have another think coming," Charlene handled that and the expression of mischief plastered on Rosellen at the same time. *Grin all you want, but this isn't Toston warmed over.* The eye contact sobered her kid sister at least temporarily, and Charlene announced with a proprietary clap of her hands that the refreshments were waiting inside.

Owen handed around the bottles of beer while Charlene showed off the A-1's fittings, from shampoo sink to cash register. Meg applied herself to Hugh's drinking arm, Neil and Bruce clicked bottles and chorused *Here's looking at you,* Darius kept to himself his opinion that American beer tasted as if it came straight from the horse.

Without letting on that she would keep watch on something of this sort, Meg watched them come and go in the vicinity of Kate. The Duff men all, even Hugh by now, were taken with Kate, like stags acquiring a taste for a lick of salt.

Bruce meanwhile had not been able to resist adding to Charlene's agenda: "You get any rich widows in here, be sure and chalk them on the back for Darius."

Darius managed as loud a laugh at that as any of the rest of them and kept to his nominated role as bachelor curio, saying he'd found it the safest policy to tip his cap only to himself. Interesting it'd have been, though, wouldn't it, to tell them about Fiona and his years of connubial imitation with her. After all, wasn't matrimony but a sort of friendship recognized by the police? But his and Fiona's arrangement did have an eventual drawback, too; in the end, Fiona had pranced off with a Spanish anarchist.

No, news of Fiona would not help his situation with Meg any, would it.

"Owen," Meg stage-whispered during Charlene's demonstration of the croquignole permanent wave machine, whose dozen metal headrods and snake nest of electrical cords were holding the Duff men in appalled fascination. He stepped back out of the group and joined her at the front of the store.

"Owen," she said with intensity, "what times are available yet with Charlene?"

"Mother, I imagine they all are. Let's have a see." He turned the pages of Charlene's daybook for appointments. "Blank as Orphan Annie, so far. If you want, when Charlene finishes up horrifying us males, you can get together with her for sometime —"

"A regular time, is what I want. Right after work, every other Friday. Put me down for then, pretty please, Owen."

He picked up the appointment pencil as directed. "Paydays, yeah, those are always popular," he left the matter at, but glanced from his mother to his father. At the edge of the clan over by the croquignole machine, Hugh stood like a man with something on his mind, or, worse, like a man trying not to have that something on his mind.

Kate and Rosellen conferred while setting out the covered dishes of potluck supper.

"At least it's a better name for the place than our mother's was," Rosellen said reflectively. "TOSTON CURLY CUES." She shook her head.

Kate sampled a meatball in tomato sauce and licked her fingers. "Talk about a family gathering. Now we're bringing them in all the way from Scotland."

"Nnhnn. He's kind of like Hugh with the bark off, isn't he." Rosellen studied across the room at Darius, who was looking rapt as Charlene explained the principle of the marcelling iron. Beyond him, Bruce uncorked a wicked wink which Rosellen at first thought was directed at her, but realized it was for Kate, of course.

"You two," she kidded Kate in the woman-of-the-world tone they always used when the topic of mad pash came up. "In a beauty shop, yet." Kate couldn't help herself from wearing a goofy expression. "Guess what," she murmured back to Rosellen. "The family is on the increase, in more ways than just Scotch uncles."

"Katy, really?" Rosellen instantly had her by both forearms. "Oh, good, when? Have you picked out names yet? Aren't you going to tell the rest of the — ?"

"Rosellen, if I cut in on Charlene's party with that news, you know I'll never get a decent hairdo out of her again."

The sisters dealt with each other before starting on their plates of supper.

Charlene said under her breath, "It's on the tip of your tongue."

Rosellen grinned recklessly. "It's all over you an inch thick."

"What if I did say —"

"A million or so times."

"— you'd never catch me sliding around in —"

"Skating; you used to say, 'skating around in.'"

"— skating around in hair the way they did." Charlene tartly checked Rosellen for any further grinning. "There, does that satisfy you?"

"Some."

"You're certainly awfully interested in what I do, all of a sudden," Charlene let fall. "Are you by any chance jealous?"

Rosellen's eyes widened in a way that Charlene still did not know how to read. "Can't I be just curious?"

"What happened was, the Swede called me a bunch of choice names," Neil was saying across the tableful of potluck to Kate, "all of it over the best way to nail in a crossbrace . . . ."

"I wouldn't want that responsibility,"

Meg was saying to Rosellen, "of having to hit the right typewriter key time after . . ."

"Are you characters about to get my pump boat done?" Owen was saying to Bruce and Darius. "Or am I about to have to bail out the core pool with a teaspoon?"

Darius said nothing, rather than say that the forty-foot pump boat would have been about twenty minutes' work on the Clydeside. Bruce, though, let Owen have:

"If you'd quit squirting water on your dam, Ownie, you wouldn't have that big puddle of water in the middle of it."

Owen managed to laugh, and the table talk moved on. But Owen, overseer by habit, was studying Bruce. Whatever canary Bruce had lately swallowed, he couldn't keep the feathers from flying out tonight. *Ah, well, hell. Maybe it's that peppy home cooking Kate gives him.* Owen himself had been hot with pride all evening, watching Charlene, taking pleasure from her intrepid battleplans on the tresses of Wheeler. *Watch out now, world.* Once again he ran his eyes over her. Certainly she was her own best advertisement. Darius, he saw, evidently thought so, too. The two of them were in thoroughgoing conversation.

"Hugh and I are the type they used to try to keep out of parlors," Darius was confiding to her. "Now here we find ourselves, in a beauty one."

"You're not the only one surprised at you," he heard right back from Charlene. The woman was harder than dental enamel. "None of them can get over it, you know, you with us this way. Fort Peck isn't an easy jump from anywhere. You must have really wanted a change of scenery, to come here just like that."

"I suppose sometimes we want change and sometimes change wants us," he resorted to. "What of yourself, though? Where was it you derived from before here, dear?"

Charlene gave him a look, a substitute for the real reamer she wanted to unloose down the table toward Rosellen. Had the little snip been blabbing about Toston and the footsteps in the hair-strewn shop back there? Charlene had tossed Toston out of her chosen picture once and could again.

"Bozeman," she bit out.

"Yoze-mite, ah!" Darius exclaimed with vast feigned interest. "Seen pictures of it! Great towering cliffs there, haven't they, and some mountain thingy split half in two? I can see why you'd miss so grand a place."

"That uncle of yours is a strange duck," Charlene softly told Owen after they had taken their celebration home to bed.

"What's a family without at least one cracked uncle?" he responded, nuzzling her in a couple of favorite places. He wondered, though, how many Duffs at Fort Peck it took to amount to too many.

You do have to hope to Christ they don't erode a hole in it by staring at it," Sangster said tiredly.

Owen only nodded, abstracted. By now he hardly even noticed the tides of workers from elsewhere on the dam, tunnel muckers and shovel runners and carpenters and catskinners and all the rest trooping up onto the levee edges of the fill at lunch hour or change of shift to stare and tell one another it beat anything they'd ever seen, a lake sitting on top of a dam.

The core pool — there was no getting around it: Owen Duff's unruly core pool — was phenomenal no matter how you looked at it. The dredged material that was being spewed in to form the core of the dam needed time to settle, needed to have the water drained off it at a judicious pace, needed in other words this artificial basin in the top of the damfill. On a blueprint it could not have looked more clever and neat, a settlement pond that gradually worked itself out of existence as more and more fill jelled in it. In reality, which was to say here under the noses of Owen and

Sangster, the core pool was a wind-whipped, sloshing, leaky, fickle body of water half a mile long, up in the middle of the pile of earth which was supposed to become Fort Peck Dam.

"We have got to get —"

" '— that sonofabitching pump boat up here,' " Sangster chorused in with Owen. "I agree, you know. This isn't any too much fun, trying to sluice out just as much water as you keep pouring in." Sangster's current specialty, a sluiceway to drain off excess water from the core pool, was busy draining all the time and still not quite doing the job. The water level kept creeping up, the three times a day a sounding was taken. Owen hated even to think about what would happen if the water backed up enough to breach the levee of the core pool. He had both this worry of a flood *above* the river washing a goodly portion of the dam down into the river, and one all his own; his dredged material was staying soupy, taking longer to consolidate into firm fill at the bottom of the core pool than it was supposed to. He simply and utterly needed a way to regulate this mass of water on the roof of the dam more exactly.

The object of his and Sangster's irritation could be seen in the boatyard, most of a mile away: the white speck of pump boat which Medwick kept telling them was being built as fast as it could, which wasn't anywhere near fast enough for them.

"You've tried, I've tried," Owen mused. "I think let's sic Major Santee on Medwick."

"Oh, you bet. Why don't you toss a spitwad at Medwick from up here and do about as much good," Sangster expelled.

"I figured I'd sic the colonel on the major first."

Sangster chewed that over. "Go in to the colonel and piss and moan about not being able to meet your schedule the way things are, you mean?"

"That's what I had in mind, yeah."

"Only problem with that is, you don't want to get them believing you're in too much trouble on the schedule."

"Max," Owen said tightly, "it's about half true."

Darius went up onto the east bluff to watch the pump boat be moved to the core pool. He had asked Owen how they were going to get this famous vessel up the considerable slope of the earthfill and into the core pool. "We're gonna walk it," Owen had replied absently. And be damned if that wasn't precisely what they were doing. Fourteen bulldozers, the big crawlers called Caterpillars, were hitched by cables to the square bow and now the pump boat, the size of a respectable hotel, was going up the road behind its column of clanking Cats as pretty as you please. He shook his head. Americans seemed to operate on the principle that they could solve anything if they could get enough traction.

"Making it sail on dry land, aren't they." The unexpected voice made Darius spill a bit of the tea he was pouring from his thermos.

"Neil, sunbeam, I didn't know you were anywhere about."

"Had to come see what they're up to at Ownie's lake." The younger man helped himself to the other half of the little shale cutbank Darius was sitting on. "You too, huh?"

"The craft, there" — Darius nodded toward the pump boat still advancing up the side of the damfill in a cloud of dust and clatter — "does bear my tool marks, you know." *Crude a tub as it is. But there was no bringing the Clydeside and the true ships with me, was there.* He glanced aside at Neil, who had not been a boatyard participant but was the one who showed up to witness this odd crosscountry launching. "Bruce's thumbprints on the bonny boat, too, of course."

"Mmm hmm." Neil had opened his black lunchbox and was doing fast damage to a peanut butter and honey sandwich. The sandwich was fine — product of the cookhouse of Jaarala and his mother, it was better than that — but Neil wished he was having for lunch what Bruce usually had. Rosellen's noonhour at the Ad Building, though, and his on the dredgeline trestle gang didn't quite work out right for getting together.

Taking his tea sip by sip, Darius mulled the Neils and Bruces, the young men working here by the thousands. Empires, armies, crusades had been built on lads such as these. A willing set of hands, durability, availability — those were the pegs history made use of, if Darius knew anything about it.

"What was it like," he was suddenly brought to by the sound of Neil's voice again, "being brothers back in Scotland?"

"In what respect do you mean?"

His nephew swallowed away on the last of a second sandwich before specifying:

"Fight much?"

"Mostly around the tonsils," Darius mused. "Your father likes a good argument. And I suppose I'm not averse to one either, now and again."

It seemed to be Neil's turn to muse. "If you're kind of alike in that, how come you turned out so different? Him, over in this country, and Mother and us and all, and you staying the way you were?"

"Well, your mother hadn't a sister," Darius smoothed past that with his instantaneous smile, "and so I evidently was cut out to be bachelor uncle to the world."

Sudden quiet at the core pool made them turn their heads in that direction. The Caterpillars had been throttled down to lowest idle, a barely audible diesel throb. The pump boat was afloat in Owen's lake.

"How you doing?" Rosellen always felt like an awed delegate to a maharani when she visited Kate these days.

"Pretty pukey," Kate reported. "I don't see why they call it just *morning* sickness."

"Nhn. When you say 'pukey,' though, is that sort of an all-over feeling you have or more of a stomach thing?"

"Both. Why? You taking a census on ways to throw up?"

"Hey, I don't even need to ask if an owly mood is one of the symptoms too, do I."

"Speaks for itself, I guess," Kate relented. "So does my middle."

"You're not showing much yet."

"On me, it doesn't take much."

Rosellen mildly pooh-poohed that, her mind obviously racing for ways to find out all about childbearing from the resident expert, peaked-looking Kate. "When do you start being a lady of leisure?"

"End of this week." Although what the Rondola's customers were going to do without her there to joke with about being bitten by a trouser worm or finding a surprise in the oven, she didn't know.

"Oh, already?" Rosellen let out without thinking.

"Listen, I don't care how they do it in China, I'm not." The part in *The Good Earth* where the woman worked in a rice field all day until it was time to pop into the house and have a baby was, according to Rosellen, certainly interesting. That was one word for it, Kate thought. She stated from experience thus far, "Getting started on a kid is no picnic."

"At least you've managed to," Rosellen flared.

Kate drew up in surprise. *Who's the owly one now?* "If Bruce were here, he'd tell you it's just a matter of doing it until you get it right."

That only reddened up Rosellen even more. Quickly they changed the subject, and their squall passed. But Kate still wished she could take that back about practice making perfect in a family way.

The day already had been about a week's worth of contentious hair. In came a naturally curly, not too bad to start on although too much curl will fight the set, and Charlene managed to push in enough wave, with liberal use of the marcel iron, to make the woman's head of hair stay reasonably calmed down. But then in walked two women together whose hair behaved like porcupine quills. It dawned on Charlene that these had to be Cactus Flat residents, showing the effects of the sulphury wellwater in that particular shantytown; and worse, the duo inevitably wanted only a wash and a wave. She forbore from informing them that the only hope for doing anything at all with the broomstraw condition of their hair was to chemical the bejesus out of it, and instead put it that they were in luck, the A-1 was offering bargain permanents today.

Watching the pair of them, happily permed, go out the door several hours later, Charlene wondered what follicles she was going to encounter next. By now it was interesting, though, what she could tell by her customers' hair. Who used rainwater to wash in at home. Who was sickly even if they otherwise didn't look it. Who had seen the latest Jean Harlow movie and who held on to the creed that Theda Bara's was the hairstyle forever.

She hadn't even started on Meg yet.

Their two faces stared at each other from the oval captivity of Charlene's wall mirror. Meg spoke up first:

"Anything short of a scalping, please, Charlene."

"Meg, as it is, you always look . . . nicely put together." As she was saying so, Charlene's fingers exploratorily lifted a tendril of her mother-in-law's sunned-brown hair. Plenty of life to it, if not much snazz in how it was worn. "Do you want to keep it that way, with just a wash and a wave? Or —"

"I want this," Meg stated with what seemed to be some difficulty, "to be a, a kind of treat for myself."

Charlene came around the chair. Directly in front of Meg, she put her hands on her knees and leaned down and in, looking in Meg's eyes and then around the verges of her face and the waiting frontier of hair. Halfway through her inspection, Charlene began to grow excited. "Meg," she blurted. "Let me give you the works."

"Whatever are . . . those?"

"This is going to sound like the dog's dinner, but it'll all fit together on you, I just know it will." Rapidly Charlene outlined the plan of attack. First, a croquignole permanent. Building on that, a marcel wave swooping to one brow. For a finale, antoine pincurls down the side and back. "Meg, I guarantee you'll scarcely know yourself."

Meg peered past Charlene to the mirror

again, as if to give her reflection a last say in this. After a bit, she announced: "Bang away, Charlene."

She confronted herself again in that mirror when Charlene was fussily finishing up with the pincurls. Under Charlene's ministration her hair now looked like fine-carved teak, its scrolls of perfect wave and curl making the little nock in her chin fit right in, sculpturally. If she did say so herself, Margaret Milne Duff looked like a new woman, royal make.

Charlene couldn't hold back a giggle at the thought. "Hugh is going to be thrown for a loop when you walk in that door tonight."

"No, he won't."

"Well, whyever not? Meg, take it from me, you look absolutely —"

"It's his time of the month," Meg said caustically.

Charlene's hands halted. After a moment, she went on with fixing Meg's hair, determined not to be dragged into Duff family matters any farther.

"So, business lady, how you doing?" Owen greeted her when she at last managed to close up shop and deposit herself home.

"Busy says it."

"What you wanted, right?"

"Mmmhmm." She went directly over to the easy chair where he was tallying daily dredging timesheets, sat on the chair arm and hugged the crown of him to her chest while telling him, "This is the head I was wishing for all day."

"Hey, you do know some pretty interesting things to apply on hair," he answered comfortably as his head inclined there between her breasts. Charlene bit her lip, and did not tell him that his father was off on a binge again.

"Hnnfp? What're you — don't, mmpf —"

"Shh," came a soothing whisper, at odds with the hand clamped forcefully over Darius's mouth. "Don't wanna wake up the whole menagerie."

The figure sitting on the edge of his bed seemed so dedicated to not disturbing the peace of the darkened barracks that Darius made himself lie there soundless. When the hand eased up a millimeter, he wrestled free from it and got his own heartfelt grip on the visitor. "Hugh, what to Hell?" he furiously whispered. "What's this about?"

"Wanna give you a treat. Take you out on the town."

"I've already *been* somewhat on the town." The couple of payday beers Darius had downed after work seemed to have

310

taken place innumerable hours ago, and the blackness outside the barracks windows didn't scale down that estimate. "Entrails of Judas, man, what time is it?"

"Friday or Saturday."

"Hugh, listen, now." Darius tried to make himself sound more patient than gritted. "You've had one too many. What you need to do is merely go home and find your own tender bed and —"

"No. Gonna take my brother out on the town, if I have to skid you there."

In the abrupt stillness after that, they could hear the breathing of each other.

"That shouldn't quite be necessary," Darius answered at last. "Remove yourself from the bedcovers, though, please, so I can at least put some clothes on."

Whatever the calendar said, payday always hung a full moon over Wheeler.

Traffic, afoot as well as automotive, was thick enough to be a hazard to the two men as they dodged across the main street. Evidently the clientele was beyond local. Up from chasing sturgeon in the dredge cuts, a fat fisherman in chest-high waders arrived at one of the saloons in front of them and stood, massive rubber bulge filling the doorway, for a moment. The flavor of Wheeler seemed familiar even if he had never tasted the town before, and he exultantly clopped on in.

Good grief, Darius thought to himself, does the drink run so deep here they're prepared to wade in it?

He did not yet know his way around town thoroughly, but Hugh could have guided the blind through his accustomed route. With much regret he was avoiding the Blue Eagle these nights, because Tom Harry had shown a tendency to waylay him while Owen or Neil or sometimes even Bruce was sent for. Thus Hugh's current port of call during a binge was the Wheeler Inn, which met the two Duffs with a noise level that would have taken the skin off lesser men.

No sooner were they inside the door, Darius already somewhat uneasy in the press of flesh, than a hawknosed little man popped from the crowd, piping out in a high squawk, "Hey, Hugh! And, uh, Hugh's brother! Need a lifesaver? I got extras." He reached down to the large sidepockets of his bib overalls, where the necks of several beer bottles protruded, and drew out two.

"Church key, too, Birdie?" Hugh inquired, as if topping off the transaction.

"You betcha. Never go without." Birdie Hinch found the bottle opener in another pocket and pried the caps off the beers for them.

"Here's mud in your eye," Hugh began to thank him with a toast, but Birdie was already veering out the door, clanking glassily as he went.

"These'll maybe hold us until we can fight our way to the bar anyway," Hugh evaluated, taking a healthy swig and starting to writhe his way through the crowd, Darius more or less in his wake. Nobody took exception to their progress, elbows evidently a part of the commerce here, and Darius managed to put some attention to the sprinkle of taxidancers and their partners carouseling within the general mob. He and Hugh passed within an inch of one couple so snugly together he would have sworn they were lodged in each other. Next came two women dancing together while they awaited customers; Hugh and therefore he resolutely ignored their wisecracks about being in the market for a tall matched set, and passed on by. As to the Wheeler Inn's other item of business, Darius had seen savage drinking in his time, at least by fabled Glaswegian standards, but this was bacchanalia.

When they were finally at the bar, Hugh had forged a spot and was finishing his beer by the time Darius squeezed a place to put both feet down.

"Cozy pub, this," Darius tried to enter the common mood.

Hugh seemed intent elsewhere. He unpocketed a silver dollar and tapped it indicatively on the bar until a bartender put up two more beers in front of him. Positioning one of the bottles squarely in front of his brother, Hugh with tipsy dignity insisted: "Here, have another lift of this."

Crawfurd, that fool Crawfurd, spun up unexpectedly in Darius from those words. Something like sickness filled him as he stared at the dark glass shape. *Whyever did he . . .*

"Darius?"

He was summoned back by Hugh's swooping tone of curiosity. "Are you going to drink that," he heard the prod sharpen in Hugh's voice, "or admire it to death?"

"Sorry, drifted a bit, there." He grabbed up the bottle, rattled off a toast of "Confusion to our enemies," and tipped a sizable quantity of beer into himself, while Hugh blinked. Within himself Darius raced for the safety of a conversational topic.

"None the neverless," he brought out sonorously. "Hugh, do you remember and how can you not?"

Hugh laughed so helplessly beer went up his nose.

"The great pulpiteer! The unstillable Reverend Milne!" The High Street church in

Inverley, not to mention the extent of the town within his vocal range, had famously resounded with the reverend's paragraphic alternations of "Nonetheless" and "Nevertheless" until the inevitable Sunday when the phrases amalgamated.

"And the time," Darius was in fine roar now, "he caught you and Meg in the darkened room and you claimed to him, 'This isn't what you think it is' and he drew himself up and said, 'It's going to continue not to be what I think it is, too.' "

They both had to set down their bottles in this quake of laughter, Darius managing to chortle out as a finale: "The man could have put in a patent on jabberwocky!"

"Eh," Hugh said after they ran out of snorts of mirth. "I miss the old goat."

"Your Owen," Darius hazarded, "resembles him. Facially."

"As long as that's all." Hugh was lurching a little, but seemed reflective. "Oh well, our Owen. I must have been reading Greek the night before."

Darius stood patiently to see if there would be more, and Hugh provided it. "Brains by the pound, Owen has. The ration of sense in him is another matter."

"He's on his way to being a worldbeater," Darius decided to contribute, "at this dam."

"He's always been on his way to five places at once." *And that Charlene wife of his has twice as many in mind for him.* Hugh, confused, stopped to sort out what he'd said aloud and hadn't.

"They're quite a set," he heard Darius offering, "your flock of sons."

"Neil, now," Hugh seemed to be counting carefully from a list, "he'd have held our name to the farm. Whereas Bruce —"

"That one bears watching, Hugh, or he'll die facing the monument."

With sharp puzzlement, Hugh stared at Darius. Then the saying came back to him, from Inverley. It had to do with the instructive way public hangings, when there were such, were performed in the town square, with the miscreant facing the statue of Queen Victoria, and it tripped readily off an Inverley tongue any time anyone was observed behaving like a scamp.

"He's young and full of himself, is all," Hugh claimed, although there were times when he himself wanted to read the riot act to Bruce. Determinedly he turned the matter, along with a fresh bottle of beer, toward Darius. "And when are you ever going to get yourself some posterity?"

"I'm still apprenticing at it," Darius joked smoothly, and Hugh had to laugh. As quickly as he could recover, though, he gibed:

"Palmistry, at your age?"

"Now, now. Doing the nasty by oneself isn't necessarily in the picture around here, is it," Darius amplified, making reference to the Wheeler Inn's commercial tinctures of blonde, brunette, redhead, and jet-black, although truth be known his own gambits had been in the straightforward brothels of Happy Hollow. Next he intoned, "As the Bible says, 'Better to put your seed in the belly of a whore than to spill it on the ground.' "

Hugh took a deep thinking drink. "Where exactly does it say that?" Darius gave a shrug. "On the flyleaf?"

Hugh roared a laugh. "That's where your mind has always been at, all right, your fly!"

Do I owe him this much of a listen? wondered Darius. *Do I owe him a damned thing?*

"Hugh, do you suppose we could find some other burning topic than my —"

"Serious, though," Hugh plunged on to. "There's much to be said for the married state. You ought to give it consideration sometime. For one thing, being married saves on all the beforehand —" Hugh woozily searched for the word he wanted "— kitchy-coo. And it holds up well. The

317

fucky part, if you take my meaning. Darius, you know, they say even a mouse grows tired of going in and out of the same hole. *But I never have.*"

In the hard moment that followed, the contempt that swelled up in Darius stoppered him from saying anything. His huge first impulse was to smash Hugh, which he fought down to an urge to hurl something viciously vulgar in return; but finally, swallowing with difficulty, he made himself confine to:

"That's maybe enough of your bedroom secrets for one night. Thanks ever so much for the pond of beer and now if you don't mind, I'll head back —"

"Drew your attention, didn't it."

Hugh's tone made Darius swing around and take a fresh look at him. He appeared appreciably less drunk than half a minute before.

"I wondered if you couldn't stand some reminding," he was going on, "that we're man and woman, myself and Meg, and not the spring greens you were nibbling at in Inverley."

As Darius eyed him, Hugh put a hand on the bar and pushed himself a bit straighter.

"Darius, this isn't then. It hasn't been some interlude you can whistle just like that, since I cleared out of Scotland with

Meg. I've done considerable, and maybe failed at more. Hard to keep count, when something of this sort" — he gestured in a way to indicate the saloon, Wheeler, the dam project — "comes down on you. But I made a place. I made crops. I made three sons. Meg and I, we made our life, out of not much more than a boat ticket. And I won't have you parading over here to undo that, if that's what you have in mind."

Bottled courage, Darius registered, *or is it more?*

In the paynight millrace of the Wheeler Inn, the brothers faced each other closely, one putting his huff to strongest use, the other waiting for him to abate. Tactics. Always the great question, those.

"I'm not out to, Hugh," Darius gustily refuted *undo.* "The same years have gone by for me as for you, there's a pile of life I've had since Inverley. My matrimony was with the Clydeside, my work there. You've never credited that in me, have you, how much I loved those bloody bedamned ships." He paused. "Everything I was — involved in there went on its back like a beetle. But I still had a brother, didn't I. You're what's left." He chose to pivot the matter on that. "We both know there was a moment when I'd have gone around the world on my knees to gain Meg. No sense denying that. But she went with you, didn't she. So, you won, then and there."

"Went with?" Hugh seemed to be tasting the words. "She was my wife. She *is* my wife."

"I can grasp that," Darius concluded levelly. "If our parents raised a dim child, it wasn't on my side of the mirror."

Owen had not much more than come home from work and closed the door when there was a strenuous rapping on it.

He opened it to Bruce.

"Didn't hear you roar in," Owen said, taking a peek past Bruce toward the street. "Where's your motor-sickle?"

"Kate made me give it up," Bruce reported sheepishly. "She says if I'm going to be a father, I can't go around with bug smushes on my incisors."

"Cramps your style, all right, I can see that." Owen made a pretense of inspecting Bruce's mouth area. "Well, now that you're afoot, better come in and rest."

Inside the house, though, Bruce stayed on the balls of his feet, rambling from one side of the living room to the other as if he was there to visit the walls.

"Bruce, not to put too fine a point on this or anything — but what in pluperfect hell is on your mind now?"

"Ownie, I've got a shot at being the government diver."

"No fooling." Owen's tone escalated as he grew sure that his chronically fooling-around kid brother for once wasn't. "That's pretty good going, buddy. It really is. Congratu—"

"First I need to buy Bonestiel's outfit." Bruce came up close to Owen. "See, Ownie, the diver has to have his own equipment. The government furnishes the, uh, air."

"What are we looking at here then, just a diving suit, right?"

"And the air hose."

"Well, sure, otherwise you'd have to practice holding your breath for some long time, wouldn't you."

"And the beltweights and the diving shoes and the telephone gear and the lifelines and the underwater lamps and the helmet."

"Bruce. Let's hear the total."

Bruce named the figure as coolly as he could, but his Adam's apple bobbed significantly afterward.

Owen also did a gulp.

"About as much as a Ford Triple A Truck happens to cost, you're telling me."

"Ownie, I hate like blazes to have to ask you for it. I'd —" Bruce fidgeted but kept his eyes straight into those of Owen "— I'd rather take a beating. But with the kid coming and everything, I can't swing this myself. You'll get it all back, I guaran-damntee you. You have my word and you can have my hide after that, if you want. See, though, it takes money to make money, don't they say? So if you'll back me on this, then the quicker I can start diving, the faster you can get re—"

"Don't hemorrhage yourself trying to convince me here," Owen shut down that spate. *The strength of conviction. Hard labor or a sizable sum, said the judge.* Owen had already visited his choices in this, turn this hitherto harum-scarum brother down or give him a possible leg up. He was not sure how it would have come out if this were a case of Bruce solo, but with Kate and the impending baby in the picture too, that wasn't nearly the question, was it.

"All right. You win. I'll put up the do-re-mi, and we'll work out how you fork it back to me."

Bruce all but tattooed his thanks onto Owen, then left. In the quiet house, Owen did a very rare thing, pulling down from the canned goods cabinet the pint of Four Roses that he and Charlene kept on hand for a hot toddy whenever one of them had a cold, and pouring himself a short swift drink.

He could already hear it with Charlene. *Owen, how long can you keep laying out money to them this way?*

Nothing I intend to make a habit of, he'd say.

Then why do you keep doing it, she'd say.

And she'd be right.

Something new has been added. You look like glory in its Sunday best."

Meg spun around at the sound of him. The cookhouse kitchen, empty at this time of night except for her, and now him, suddenly seemed central to everything.

"Aren't those pretty words." She caught her breath a little. "You always could embroider with your tongue."

"It is pretty hair, to go with the rest of you," Darius said as if sincerely explaining. "My compliments to the imaginative Charlene." By now he had covered most of the length of the kitchen and was lounging against a meatblock not far from her. "Not that my imagination has ever needed any adding to, Meggie, where you're concerned."

Now that this had come, after all the years, she found she still did not know her own mind. Or did she. At first she said nothing. Then:

"Darius, I have to scoot on home."

"On payday night? When the rest of the citizenry is on the town?"

"I only dropped back by because I'd forgotten to take these for Kate." Meg showed him the Mason jar and couldn't help smiling a bit. "She's at the stage of crazy cravings, and nothing compares with Mr. Jaarala's pickled crab apples."

Darius's own smile came on instantly, and the half laugh that was the same as Hugh's. "We'll hope her tyke isn't born puckered up."

Meg was looking steadily at him. "And why are you in this particular vicinity, Darius, this particular night?"

"I was hanging about, is all. And am rewarded with this wonderful coincidence."

"Really," she held to her decision. "I have to be going home."

"And what's there for you?" he asked, all reason. He had been storing up for this since the standoff with Hugh the previous payday. *It holds up well," does it. So does what I feel for her, you drifting tosspot.* "Unless I miss my guess, Hugh beetled downtown as soon as he was off shift. He'll be some while yet, drinking the town dry."

"I'm surprised you're not at it with him."

"I'm surprised that you don't see Hugh's only my brother, while you're you."

"Darius, we're not those peppered-up youngsters anymore."

"We're not down in our graves yet, either."

"We may be if Hugh ever finds us like this."

"He's otherwhere, though, isn't he. Meg, heart, let's look at this matter afresh. We don't have an ocean and the family you were raising and considerations of any other sort between us now."

"That's your idea of a fresh look? Going back to the bind we were in, before Hugh and I left Scotland?"

The noise of the door in the dining room made them both jump. Whoever had come in was still out of sight around the corner from the serving window.

Meg looked wildly around. The next thing she knew, Darius's arm was around her and they were ducking into the pantry, out of the wide-open area of the kitchen.

She had to listen over the drum of her heart for the sounds out in the kitchen. Meanwhile Darius's arm had not gone away.

There was some clumping, which came nearer and nearer, then stopped.

Then she could hear the almost sound-less whistling, the blown air of the only tune Jaarala seemed to know.

"It's the cook," she let Darius know in the barest whisper, unsure whether to feel relieved or twice as alarmed.

Darius speculatively kissed her fore-head.

Jaarala rummaged in the breadbox. Next he could be heard slicing, twice.

By now Darius had moved his hands under her arms and around onto her back and, having met resistance at her lips, was kissing through the neighborhood of her hairline along the side of her head, occasionally ranging his tongue into the delicate grooves of her ear. She tried not to think about how many other teases he could employ on her. She could feel the most definite one at the front of him.

Pasteboard carton being opened, gummier slicing. Velveeta cheese.

Jar lid coming off, tink of knife against its mouth. Slathered with mayonnaise.

She willed Jaarala to go eat his sandwich snack somewhere else, but no. He could be heard chewing, and he was a thorough chewer. That meant they had to be utterly still in the pantry, and Meg hung there in Darius's clasp of arms, cheek to cheek and much else to much else.

At last came the sounds of Jaarala washing up his plate and breadknife, then the whump of the dining room door as he went out. Meg put her hands flat on Darius's chest and pushed herself back far enough to see squarely into his face. She thought she felt commendably calm, considering.

"That was unfair," she said when she had the breath for it.

"I wonder if it was." He put the tip of a finger into one of the curls coiling at the corner of neck and ear.

Meg surprised him. She put her own index finger against his breastbone like a small but substantial pointer and pushed herself away more effectively.

"If I ever do walk off from Hugh," she said, "it will have to be in the open." She gave him that look as if she were taking God's inventory. "Not, Darius, in the pantry."

She wished she knew how much the names mattered. It was a harder part than she had thought, making those up. But if she were to call the woman 'Blondina' and him . . .

Call them Ishmael, Heathcliff, Hester Prynne, Swann and the Duchess de Guermantes, Huck and Tom, Antonia Shimerda, Molly Bloom, Puck, Hamlet, Goneril, Regan, Cordelia, Flem Snopes, Lord Jim, Anna Karenina, Eugene Gant, Mrs. Dalloway: they answer, faultlessly, each time making us a gift of all their wordly possessions.

Flaubert sends notes tinkling from Emma Bovary's piano and at the other end of the village the bailiff's clerk, "passing along the highroad, bareheaded and in list slippers, stopped to listen, his sheet of paper in his hand" and we listen there with him ever after.

Cather prompts an anxious young Santa Fe seminarian to say, "One does not die of a cold," and the Archbishop in the winter of age responds, "I shall not die of a cold, my son, I shall die of having lived," and we accept that as true for us, too.

Mayakovsky, Russia's cloud in trousers, jots to Lili Brik from his Crimean tour, "Lilik, I go off in all the directions there are!" and from London she postcards to him "Volosik, I kiss you right in the Parliament!" and we believe with them, there in those ever-lasting fevers of correspondence, their creed that love is the heart of everything.

Writers and the written, they haunt us as we most want to be haunted, in fogs of ink.

Rosellen knew little enough of this, yet she was on an updraft of it all. Her writing hand agonized, and cherished the agony. Time escaped, and she minded not at all.

It first came to her in the Ad Building, one of the times when she was turning out those reams of paychecks. *The names, all these. If a person could know . . .* She had sat up even straighter in her typing chair, posture of the thoughts suddenly pushing at her. *And what the money will let them do, make them do . . .* The idea went home with her and produced a tablet and a pencil, and she had been slaving away in stints ever since. Searching her imagination for grist. Lately she had been reading

Now in November, and she thought Josephine W. Johnson had it ever so right: "Words and days and things seen that lie in the mind like stone."

This was an evening when Neil's trucking run had been only to Glasgow and back, and so when she came out of her haze of concentration over her pages and heard him cut the engine, she thought now was as good a time as any to let him in on her endeavor.

"Writing? You mean — like what, that penmanship they made us do in school?"

"No, stories. The kind in magazines."

"No kidding? You been doing that? Let's see one."

Heart knocking on her breastbone, she handed him the little set of pages.

Neil slowly read of the people named Blondina and Merritt. He wasn't sure whether he had heard the precise story before or not, but it was the type that practically stood in the air at Fort Peck: a High Line farm couple who had been grasshoppered out, the man desperately going halfway across the state the next spring to a wage job on a road project, the woman having to do the farming on her own, climbing off the tractor after each round of the field to go over to the pickup and check on their baby in a fruitbox cradle on the seat; the story ended as soon as they heard there was hiring at a place where a great dam was to be built.

" 'Shod in Weary Leather.' You thought that up yourself, huh?"

"Nhn."

"Well, I think it's the greatest thing ever. You got any more?"

"I will have, the next time you're away."

She saw a look on Neil which said is *that what it takes?* and hurriedly told him, "I fill the time with it when you're off trucking, is all, Neilie. When you're here, so much the better. The writing can go hang, then."

"Okay, sure, you seem to be going strong on it."

"It's hard, though. I keep wishing I knew more about, oh, situations. People's behavior and all that, the times when I can't be around them to see."

"Well, you watch when you can and use your imagination a little, and don't you get to know more?"

"I don't just mean more, Neil. Everything, I guess you'd have to call it."

"Rosellen, honey, I'm all for you on this writing of yours. But you maybe don't want to set our sights *that* high."

"No, no. I won't, I promise. I knew even while that was coming out of my mouth it was going to sound batty." And that made twice, already, tonight. Her tongue needed to hear from her, she resolved. "What I meant was, trying to do these stories makes me think things over, in a way that I didn't even know things *had* to be figured out before I put them down on — oh, fudge, Neil, that's right back to batty in a hurry, isn't it. But don't you ever have that?" She put her hand on top of his, hoping he would follow suit. "Wanting to see on through the everyday run of stuff?"

To her relief, after a moment his broad hand came up and rested on hers. She chuckled and rapidly put her other on top of his. "Sure," she heard him say as they grinned at each other and slappily piled hand on hand, "a hundred percent of the time."

Hugh and Birdie were on the dredgeline drain traps now, transferred there by some Ad Building wiseacre whose initials Hugh was quite sure were O-w-e-n. The drain traps were mucky work, digging out cuds of clay and other obstructions, but Hugh Duff had dug into Missouri River earth plenty of times before, and Birdie came to each of these openable pockets of the pipeline with the interest of a weasel approaching a nest of eggs. Some of the damnedest items were being dredged up from the bottom of the river. They'd opened one trap to find it clogged with rusted barrel hoops and a very battered chamber pot, and lately there had been a chunk of the nameplate off the old sunken steamboat *Far West.* And fairly often the pipeline still would cough out a buffalo skull. Hugh cleaned those up and Birdie lugged them into Glasgow and peddled them. Hugh tucked away his share of the split as drinking money, while Birdie untucked his along with his dress shirt with the horseshoe embroidered on the back in Wheeler's temples of temptation.

"Tell you, Hugh," Birdie was confiding at high pitch as they unbolted the next drain trap, "I've done it with all nationalities and some from Texas, but this blonde number last night, she just makes you want to die and leave it in there forever. You know the one I mean? That kind of milk-haired one, there in the Blue Eagle —"

"Snow White there in the Wheeler Inn, you mean," Hugh responded, grunting as he opened the catchment in the pipeline and began breaking out the clay clog with a shovel. "I've laid eyes on her, yes." Birdie's bedtime history had to contend for attention with his own, lately. After the night there in the saloon where he had told Darius in no uncertain terms how things stood, he felt he had better do his part at home, too. He'd made up with Meg, and cozied her under the covers these nights in a kind of second honeymoon. Strut in here from Scotland as though he were God's gift to Meg, did Darius think. Hugh Duff would show him, how a man and a woman weathered the little jangles between them. "Eyes only, mind you, Birdie," he went on in this new spirit of things. "I'm severely married, you know."

"Uh uh, not that Snow White one, this's another — what's those there, Hugh?"

Both men got down on their knees on the muddy riverbank.

Hugh meticulously scooped the small round objects out of the scum of sediment in the trap bottom, spat on them and rubbed them between his palm and his fingers. Tiny planets of glassy blue.

"Beads." Hugh fondled them, thinking. "From the fort, wouldn't you think? When they were trading with the Indians here?"

Birdie too was looking speculative. "Wonder if they'll work on that blonde number."

The duded-up one is Plimpton, the newspaper guy," Jaarala whispered to Darius as people milled into Plentywood's clapboard Temple of Labor. Darius mentally marked the plumpish editor, in a pearl-gray suit and vest, there at the end of the front row. From issues slipped to him by Jaarala in the barracks, Darius knew that

The Producers News was a wordslinging fiesta, even by radical standards. "He gets against somebody in that newspaper of his and he tears them a new asshole," Jaarala favorably critiqued Plimpton's journalism now. "Him and Mott have worked together a long time."

The crowd grew, and Jaarala kept on naming off the ones he knew, abundantly Scandinavian from the sound of it, as Darius tried to make himself at home in the Red Corner of Montana.

Clydesiders were said to spoon the politics of the left into themselves along with their oatmeal, and the young riveter Darius Duff hungrily sat up to that table. His first feast there was the rent strike, when the city streets boiled with marching people; Scotland had found its feet at last, Darius exulted. The columns from the factories and the shipyards poured into Glasgow, passing a column of soldiers embarking for the war in France. "Down your tools, boys!" shouted the civilian army to the uniformed one.

Then Darius, tall in the human swell, could see the lines of the tenement women who had fomented the strike, and the great crowd that packed the streets around the Sheriff's Court. Faces by the thousands and thousands, a maw of mouths and eyes for the powers that be to look out upon, festival and class war feeding each other as they disbelievingly watched.

Each new minute of the massing forces brought a bolt of excitement to Darius. By then he had been in attendance at a hundred meetings, a dozen committees, a thousand arguments over Georges Sorel's doctrine of the general strike ("to render the maintenance of socialism compatible with the minimum of brutality," Darius could reel off by heart) versus parliamentary gradualism ("Having been preyed on does not entitle one to prey back," Ramsay MacDonald kept scolding them from Westminster). And now here it was, exactly as Sorel, in the densest of the arguing Bibles of the left, had prophesied: mass belief, passion, mania, whatever you cared to term it, the ingredient that forged the early Christians against the Romans and that turned Paris upside down street by street in the French Revolution was working in this epic strike of 1915. Chapter and verse, the workers triumphing with the weight of their numbers.

Waken Darius Duff from a coma at the age of one hundred and he still would remember the taking of Glasgow, those few high hours. In street after street, bobbing atop rafts of posterboard, "Red Willie" Gallacher and other speakers held forth, held

335

the moment, held poised the human mass that could pull down the city stone by stone if it took the notion. The ruling powers buckled. The Sheriff's Court session was called off, the government in London promised a law against rent-gouging.

But from that day, Darius was to see more and like it less. Periodically the Clydeside would writhe and rise, and nothing lasting would come of it. Like a stick driven into the beach of history, the rent strike marked a high tide of worker power. The next two tries at a major strike were met with barrings and arrests, and when the "forty-hour strike" was called in 1919, machine-gun nests were waiting at Glasgow's strategic street corners.

So, were you Darius, you learned to await the next chance, and the one after that.

As if having saved the most for last, Jaarala inclined his head toward front and center of the meeting room and said:

"The highpockets one, that's Mott."

Darius and Jaarala both were tallish men. Mott overtopped them and everyone else in sight by at least six inches.

At first Darius thought Lawrence Mott was the most awkward specimen he had ever seen. Hands the size of stallion hooves, big flat feet, that towering body as knobbly as if made up out of pipe fittings;

the face, otherwise unevenful, shocking for its eyeglasses, lensed thick as milkbottle bottoms. Mott's world, as a boy, had amounted to an unedged blur and he had been put into a school for the blind until it was discovered he was hardskulled enough to get by in life, blurred or not. Ultimately a grinder of optical lenses was reached in Germany who could accomplish the thick goggles Mott's eyes required, and with that weakness corrected he behaved as if no other was conceivable. Mott's term as sheriff of Sheridan County, along with the slate of other barely concealed radicals he pulled along with him into other offices, was rough-and-tumble even by Montana political standards. According to widespread whisper, he had funded his left-wing political machine on the gratitude of bootleggers whom he let traverse his jurisdiction into the liquid riches of Canada.

If Mott as a tactician sounded promising, on a speaking platform the man was an absolute revelation, Darius now found. Mott was an unerring picker at society's scabs. In a pitiless brass voice, one you would not want to hear if you had your hand in the cookie jar, he gave the audience the faces and figures of their enemies.

The Wall Streeters, as fatuous as they were fat.

The copper kings of Butte, the muscle-mined wealth of Montana engorged in them as unmistakably as a pig going through a python.

The lumber barons —

Abruptly Jaarala was up out of his chair beside Darius.

"In the woods during the war, the god-damn bastards wouldn't even let us have living conditions the same as what was called for in prisoner-of-war camps."

It was the longest sentence anyone had heard out of Jaarala.

Darius stared at his companion traveler, realizing that Jaarala hated the world's bosses all the way down to bedrock. Hard to think of Timmo Jaarala ever having been young, or of the century's issues not rolling off his round shoulders, but the lumberjack camps of his early years had turned many, like him, into fervents of the Industrial Workers of the World, the argufying street-fighting song-writing Wobblies, the I-Won't-Work agitators who preached one big union and the downfall of capitalist bosses that would flow from that. Usually silent Jaarala putting himself up for political adoption of this sort? Bedbugs, lice, maggoty bacon, murderously indifferent new machinery, unstable wages and hours, and long evenings in drafty bunkhouses to talk it over might do that to a person.

Jaarala sat down, looking shy and mute again. Mott gave him a long, slow, dramatic approving nod, then tore on into the rest of his list of oppressors, the grain cartel, the railroad nabobs, the whole Rockefelling Morganatic gang. A few minutes of Mott at his hottest and you could absolutely see into their mansions, viciously luxurious.

And this audience did at least half his work for him, Darius saw. As they listened to Mott, their faces wore the hard set of righteousness: of those who worked the land and could not understand why they had to sell a truckload of wheat to be able to buy a barrel of gasoline. Work your fields and yourself and your family until all were played out, and then some gut-robber took the gains? And grasshopper infestations on top of that? And blizzards of dust on top of those? Things shouldn't add up that way, it wasn't right, this audience of seared-out farm people said with their set faces.

The New Deal was a raw deal too, Mott thundered to them next. There could be no true new deal under capitalism, any honest shuffle of the deck had to have some of the reforms that the Wall Street ruling class yipped about as socialism. And that's where he, Lawrence Mott, and the Fusion ticket came in. Fusion, taking ideas from the left but holding to the pocketbook interests of workers and farmers, was the only sane route, he told them as if giving directions to Eden. *The man knows how to play these people like the pipes,* Darius marveled at the audience's raptness and his own. Roosevelt was not going far enough, Mott now reached. None of them in Washington or Helena or for that matter the county courthouse right next door here in Plentywood, by Mott's unsparing lefthanded yardstick not a one of them was going far enough.

Darius stayed at Jaarala's elbow afterward, waiting for their chance at Mott. As the crowd filed by to shake hands with the peering bone-rack figure, Darius put the thought of the moment out loud:

"The man is as clever with his tongue as a hummingbird, Tim. How the devil did he ever lose office?"

"They pattycaked him in '32," Jaarala stated, elaborating that the Democrats had not run candidates for a number of county offices in exchange for the Republicans not putting up anyone for sheriff, the combined voting strength of both parties against Mott and his slate. "But those buggers don't trust each other enough to cut that kind of deal every time."

"Mister Jaarala," Mott greeted when the others were gone, clapping him on the shoulder with a hand that whopped like a skillet. The gargantuan eyeglasses found Darius's face and took it in, whether in sheriff style or comradely appraisal Darius wasn't sure. "And you've brought us help from across the pond, you say."

Plentywood Temple of Labor or not, this was oddly like a tea-time visit, Darius being ceremoniously introduced to Aagot Mott next and then their bright-eyed eight-year-old son, Harald, who had sat quietly next to his mother in the front row while Bolshevism rolled over him like Sunday school scripture. It could not hurt the cause, Darius thought, that Lawrence Mott had married into this community of Danes and Norwegians; the word *socialism* was not likely to scare these Scandinavians into a tizzy. Darius knew he still had to feel his way in America, but so far so good, here. A sharp-toothed newspaper. The golden mouth of Mott. A following fed up with half measures. They had the apparatus, here.

Mott's hand cradled the lad's head against his leg as he talked with Darius and Jaarala of timing and tactics. "Next year is election year again," Mott led to, as if telling them the grain would be gold. He leaned back beside a windowframe shorter than he was and goggled down at Darius. "Mister Duff, are you a veteran of election battles?" Mott somehow crooned it with the unspoken but resonant note of *too?*

"I have nothing against elections," Darius said, "so long as we win them."

"That's the stunt," Mott agreed, grimacing. "That winning." Then, as if it was all part and parcel, he asked Darius the outlook for organizing on the quiet among the damworkers. The Communist Party of the U.S.A., a perfectly legal organization but frowned upon when it worked in the open, would be keenly interested in anything that could be done with a workforce such as Fort Peck's, Mott hardly had to tell him.

"Right now it would be worse than herding cats," Darius estimated. *Nor do I dare take on that sort of attention to myself just yet, do I. Thanks to Crawfurd. I've pitched in with the Bolshies times before, they won their scars along with us on the Clydeside, but thanks to damnable Crawfurd I need time before —* "Wouldn't you say so, Tim, Fort Peck is not ripe quite yet and the best we can do for the cause is to stay available?" Jaarala provided a sad affirming bob of his head. "Everyone at the dam is in one kind of a scamper or another," Darius elaborated. "They're up nights, trying to spend their wages fast enough."

Mott looked both unsurprised and disapproving. "Roosevelt and his crowd can't shovel money to them forever. When the makework runs out and people see that nothing has gotten better, then is when they will listen. Bide your time, Mister Duff. In this calling, we have to do a lot of biding."

"I dunno, Bruce, do I have to watch this? My money going to the bottom of the river, with you wrapped inside?"

"Come on, Ownie. Do you good to see how we do things here at the business end of the river."

Uh huh. I've seen disasters in the making before, Owen thought, but went onto the diving barge with Bruce.

Taine, the barge boss, obviously wasn't any too thrilled to have the fillmaster looking over his shoulder as he broke in a new diver, but Owen took care to tell him, "Nothing official about this, Al. I'm not even here, okay?"

Bruce already had started soaping up. The vulcanized rubber cuffs of the diving suit had to fit so tightly onto his wrists that water could not work its way under. Watching, Owen began to savvy that he had been wrong in a major way about Bruce needing him here as an audience. Bruce was his own audience.

343

Before the eyes of the barge crew and Owen, he began turning both rubbery and metallic. The diving suit was sheet rubber sandwiched between tough layers of twill, but over the top half of that went the corselet, the metal breast plate. A good deal of fuss surrounded the corselet; it had to be bolted to a strap arrangement around the neck of the suit, clamping the rubber collar against the corselet rim to make a watertight joint. *Or you're liable to get a drink of water you didn't ask for, huh, Bruce?* Owen was intrigued in spite of himself with the daring that this took.

When the tender and Taine himself finished grunting and tugging and bolting and backed away, there sat Bruce, or rather his head, wearing a leather cap with telephone receivers embedded to fit down over his ears, looking like a pilot in a huge Katinka doll.

I wonder how many dollars a pound this comes out to, Owen brooded as he scanned the bulky diving suit. He and Charlene had had words over his loan to Bruce. Hers were: *I'm not sure, Owen, I can rake the money in as fast as you can shovel it out to them.*

Now the tender gingerly lifted the copper helmet in both hands and stepped directly behind Bruce.

Owen realized he was watching a crowning.

The entire atmosphere on the diving barge had changed. From Taine's more attentive regard, to the tender's softer tone of voice, the figure in the diving suit was drawing something out of the crew that had not been there before. No one joked now. No one moved unnecessarily. Owen uneasily wondered whether this brother of his could carry off all that seemed to be expected of him. Wouldn't it be just like Bruce to get under forty feet of water and call upstairs, "Hey, I thought I was signing up for the balloon corps!"

The tender put the helmet over Bruce's head, the front glass turned eerily a bit toward Owen as if a Cyclops was eyeing him askance. Then the helmet was turned an eighth of a turn in the corselet joint. *My God, is that all?* rose in Owen. *It just snicks into place, against all the water in the Missouri?*

Through it all Bruce had behaved as though Owen was nowhere around. But the amphibian apparition turned now and gave Owen a stubby thumbs-up.

Owen stayed for the descent into the river, nervously watching the barge crew nervously handle Bruce's airhose, and found himself still staying, gazing down into the river, even after the water darkness hid Bruce from sight and the only sign that he was down there was Taine's constant telephone conversation.

"Can I?" Owen asked, gesturing.

Taine squirmed, caught between the unwelcome request and Owen's status as fillmaster. "Generally not a good idea to break the diver's concentration in any way. But this is more of a tryout run. So, okay, this once."

Owen went over to Taine and was handed the telephone headpiece. "Bruce? Can you hear me?"

"Yeah, I'm right here, Ownie."

"Now I know we've got this river whipped. Top to bottom."

But the river fought him on the arithmetic every day of every month, on through that spring and summer.

The number that Owen Duff lived by, and regularly wondered if he was going to perish by, was three with six zeroes after it. Three million cubic yards of earthfill a month had to be dredged, piped, and poured out into the core pool atop the dam, and by the sacred writ of Fort Peck, the schedule, it needed to be done for seven months out of the year, winter or no winter, high spring runoff or no high spring runoff, breakdowns or no breakdowns.

"Marchette, I wonder if you could get right at my monthly report for me. The colonel's going to have kittens if I don't hand him —"

"Owen, I'm so sorry," the gray-haired secretary indicated the heap of paperwork she was typing up, "but he already was by here and had a batch."

April, that horrid half-assed half month of startup, had been as close to a write-off as Owen ever wanted to come in this business of dredging. April of '35 he just wanted to kick under the bed of the river and forget.

"BJ, I'm kind of up against it here, I need this monthly report typed up for the —"

"It's lunchtime, Owen," Betty Jane of the henna hair told him serenely. "And then I have to take dictation from Major Santee."

The month of May gave him hope. The dredging still had a hiccup now and then, but they had met the 3,000,000 cubic yards goal. In June, he'd thought he had the job knocked, absolute easy stuff this around-the-clock dredging: the total of cubic yards moved was a fat 10 percent above goal. But now July, here in his hand, made bad reading; at the bottom of his compilation of daily dredging averages the number was three million, but damn barely. Owen Duff did not like to scrape by that way, and with August-September-October-November yet to come in his dredging year, and right now when he should be out there on the dredgeline trying to figure out how to boost the flow of fill, he was having to stomp around here in the Ad Building trying to find somebody, just anybody, to type —

"Rosellen, hey, glad I caught you before — uhm, you went to lunch."

Her fingers had jumped off the keys when she heard his voice behind her, and she swung her head around toward him and swooped blank paper onto the top of whatever she'd been typing, all at the same time.

Experienced as he was with Charlene, who never liked a surprise unless she was delivering it, Owen hurried to say:

"Excuse me all over the place. It's just that I'm in dire need on my monthly report, and saw you sitting in here, and so —"

"No, no, that's all right. I eat in, these days. I'm —" she vaguely indicated toward her typewriter and its hidden contents "— practicing my speed."

Owen didn't buy that at all. *Christ, woman, you get any faster, they'll have to invent an asbestos typewriter.* But while he was standing there trying to keep his face straight, Rosellen crinkled her caught-kid grin at him and gave him the joshing turn of words that Charlene sometimes did:

"What can I do you for?"

Pesky just that quick, was she. Owen stuck tightly to business instead of repartee. "This blasted report, that has to go in to the colonel half an hour ago. Can you whiz through it for me this once?"

Rosellen plucked it from him and told him she'd see what she could do. Owen walked off to the clatter of her typewriter resuming behind him, still wondering about her noonhour secret pages. *Neil had better-to-Christ hope they're not love letters.*

Three envelopes, long and white.

Independence Square in Philadelphia, the first return address.

Arlington Street in Boston.

Park Avenue in New York, New York.

Rosellen wildly wanted to rip them open right there in the post office, but thought no, take them home. Tingly suspense. Then giddy triumph. She could use this, in another story.

At the kitchen table, she slit open the envelopes and the worst messages of her life fell out. *The Saturday Evening Post* regretted it had no use for "The Steel Daisy," the *Atlantic Monthly* was rejecting

"Janie's Doll," and *Collier's* had turned down "Expectations."

The rejection slips stunned her, but under her mortification there was a greater panic: what had they done with her stories? A second slip lay under one of the rejection notices: *Due to the numerous submissions we receive, we cannot return any manuscript unaccompanied by a self-addressed stamped envelope.*

Rosellen felt herself blush, probably to the roots of her toenails. So these were the ground rules of being a writer. Her carefully typed stories had been thrown in wastebaskets in Philadelphia, Boston and New York. Thank heaven she still had the notebook pages.

Nothing fazed Neil. When he came home and found her red-eyed and blurty with the triple bad news, he kissed her enough to start taking her mind off Philadelphia etcetera, then sat her down.

"You keep at it," he instructed as Rosellen hung on his every word. "That's the only advantage, with people like us. Just keeping at it, until the other ones drop."

Bide.

Most definitely, Darius was biding.

He could perform the Missouri River boatyard tasks with whatever the mental equivalent of a little finger was, and devote the rest of his thinking to the other matters.

Tactics.

At the moment, there did not seem any exertion great enough to bring Meg his way, but he was willing to wait and see whether the leverage ever changed, there.

As to the politics at Plentywood, well, that passion couldn't be requited instantly either; Mott himself had told him as much.

Meanwhile the time had to be passed some way. There was always that about biding.

He persevered in the taverns of Wheeler, impossible though it was to become accustomed to the glorified water that Americans called beer. Taking care not to cross payday paths with Hugh, he favored the Buckhorn, one of the smaller and more orderly drinkeries, until the evening when he was on his way there and a human form flying out of the Blue Eagle nearly bowled him over.

The figure, one of the tunnel gang from the look of his mucky overalls, ended up woozily on hands and knees in the gutter after hurtling past Darius. In the doorway of the Blue Eagle stood Tom Harry, the majority of his white shirt torn off but his bow tie still in place.

"This ain't Butte," Tom Harry stated to the ejected customer. "You don't hop up on my bandstand any time you feel like it and sing 'Mother Machree.' "

Doctrine always interested Darius. He headed into Tom Harry's realm.

A three-instrument band called the Melodeons was blasting away, behind a contributions box with a sign reading prominently FEED THE KITTY. Dancing was epidemic. Darius secured a beer from a hamhanded man behind the bar and settled in to watch.

His attention went at once to a white-blonde head of hair; or rather, his attention glanced off that of the woman, who gazed around the Blue Eagle as if judging donkeys.

Darius watched her as she danced snugly with a young damworker, smiled her way out of his paid-for grasp as the dancetune wound down, then went back to her stool at the far end of the bar. She wore trousers, or whatever silly thing were they called in this country — slacks? Darius saw nothing slack about the way her form molded out the fabric. Upward, her breasts were silkily held by a blouse with a midnight sheen to it.

Darius headed down to the end of the bar to work out the rules.

Just then the saloonkeeper appeared, fresh white shirt on.

"The real money here is in being your

haberdasher, Tom," the woman was saying to him. "When you bounce a guy like that, maybe you ought to just do it in your undershirt."

"Shannon, you concentrate on peeling the shirts off these —" Tom Harry broke off as Darius materialized at her side. "Customer for you, looks like. Another beer to wet the other end of your whistle too, chum?"

"Assuredly," Darius said.

Tom Harry thrust him a bottle, then vacated to a short distance down the bar.

American propositioning tactics still were none too clear to Darius. The lewd old music hall joke — *The Honorable Member from Groinwich . . . is rising . . . to a point of order* — by now was pertinent, but he wasn't sure that was the best approach here.

The woman had been looking him over in quick, crisp glances. "Care to dance?" she recited. Warm as an ice pick, thus far, but everything else about her was attractive enough.

"No, dancing isn't my field."

"Whichever, you're supposed to be buying me a drink first."

"Ah." Darius called out to Tom Harry, "A dram for the lady, please, Prime Minister."

The drink came and more of Darius's money went. "Are you his?" Darius indicated Tom Harry, now stationed at the cash register, with the slightest nod of his head.

"No." She gave Darius a dead-level stare. "I'm mine."

"You're luckier in your ownership than most, then," he said drily. "What I meant was, how does this transaction work? Does he" — Darius did the slight nod toward Tom Harry again — "provide the premises?"

"I use his car, out back," she said. "Packard DeLuxe. It's got a backseat the size of an ambulance."

"I'm not much one for doing it in vehicles," Darius said. "It sounds a bit rushed, for what I have in mind."

"Isn't this my lucky night, the only man at Fort Peck who's proud to be a slow-poke," she mocked. "I suppose you can come up with someplace more leisurely?"

"I was counting on you to. After you finish business for the evening."

Until two that morning, quitting time, Proxy Shannon couldn't help wondering what she had waiting for her in this odd duck of a Scotchman. Most men hated the idea of any other man being with her. This one simply sat there and watched as she worked, a little amused look flitting across his face once when a tunnel mucker, still in his rubber boots, arrived in what was obviously a flaming hurry and sped out back with her. Hardest thing about the business, as far as she was concerned, was the male conviction that they were all something rare; but this specimen waiting patiently for her didn't seem to mind the rest of the parade.

Just before two, she caught his eye and indicated he should meet her in back of the saloon. Darius went out the front and around the building, and she was waiting beside the car. "Borrowed it from Tom to go home in," she said, and held out the car key to him.

Darius hesitated. "Is it far? Can't we simply foot it?"

"Everything's far here," Proxy informed him. He still didn't take the key. "You really aren't one for cars, are you. What's the matter now?"

"I don't know the driving."

"Fella," Proxy told him as she opened the door on the driver's side and climbed behind the steering wheel, "sometime tonight, you're going to have to contribute something."

The Packard sped out of Wheeler, across into the smaller scatter of buildings called Delano Heights and on through the even more scattered and sarcastically named neighborhood called Lakeview, then downward toward the river. Proxy parked the car on the riverbank above a strew of boxy forms. As Darius's eyes adjusted to the dark, he realized they were houseboats.

"The one on the far end," she told him, and led the way, her slacks and hair moonlit against the dark of the river.

When she turned up the wick on the kerosene lamp, Darius saw that the inside of the houseboat was as mussy as a daw's nest. Amid the clutter, he had to search twice to spy the bed. The houseboat rocked slightly as the Missouri roiled past.

Darius chortled. "I didn't know seamanship was going to be a requirement, too."

Proxy had made no move toward the bed, and that wisecrack or whatever it was caused her to look sharply at him. Gaunt handsome joker, but that didn't count. Business did. She said only: "More than that's required, you know."

"Yes. Well, now," he studied her. "What is the tariff?"

Out back of the Blue Eagle it was two dollars a go, plus extra for French and on up the menu; but here, her own premises and all and this cluck fresh off a boat of a different kind, she took a calculated chance and announced:

"Five dollars."

He pulled out a pursy kind of wallet she

had never seen before and took his own good time about fingering through the American money which all looked greenly identical to him. At last he sorted out a ten-dollar bill and a five, holding them up to her carefully before putting the money on the table by the lamp. "Here's for three goes."

"You're a perfectly dreadful house-keeper," he observed from amid the tussle of bedcovers the next morning.

"House*boat*keeper," she corrected him in that mocking way. "Whole different deal, when you can just throw stuff over the side when it piles up and gets too rank. And anyway, since when does somebody like me have to come with doilies."

"I like it that you're on the river, though," he said as if thinking out loud. He turned and gave her a studying gaze. "It commends your taste."

"My taste in men," she figured she'd better begin letting him know, "never lasts until breakfast."

"That probably commends your taste, too." He gave her a surprisingly attractive thin-faced smile.

"No 'probably' about it," she notified him. "Okay, Bosephus. The circus is over. Everybody up, out, we all had our money's worth —"

"Wait. One formality." He put a businesslike arm across her as she started to roll out of bed. "What's your name, then?" He'd heard the publican call her Shannon, but even in America a last name must be a last name.

"Proxy."

Darius stared at her, unsettled. *I hope to God I heard an r in that.*

"That's a new one on me," he ventured. "What, was your father a legal scholar?"

She hooted. "Him? Neither one!"

"What's it from, then?" Darius persisted. "I mean, it's perfectly fine by me, whatever you wish to dub yourself. Society oughtn't be permitted to put a person in lifelong irons by fastening onto you some name that you utterly don't —"

Wherever that was headed, she cut it off with:

"It's a nickname I picked up, is all. Short for peroxide."

She saw he still didn't have a clue, and wondered what century Scotland was back in. "My hair, stupe. How do you think I get this blonde?"

"Ah!" He nodded and nodded as if he savvied everything about her now, which Proxy entirely doubted.

"You're one to talk," she pointed out sharply. "Dah-RYE-us. Where's that kind of fandoodle come from?"

"My father was in his Persian period,"

Darius said. "He went nights, ancient history classes at the Mechanics' Institution. I've always told my brother Hugh he was lucky that was over with by the time he came along, or he'd have ended up Xerxes."

He turned back to her. "What's your real one, though?"

"Oh," she mulled a moment and with a skewed smile brought out: "Susannah."

"Susannah Shannon?" He looked inordinately pleased. Men will always go for anything sappy enough, Proxy found confirmed for the hundredth time. "But that's utter music, woman!" he enthused. "Person could dance a reel to that."

"Proxy," she said uncategorically, "is what I go by."

Two nights later, he was back for more.

Something for you, Meg, Hugh had been meaning to say. Hand her his share of the trade beads, make a joke about having gone all the way back to old Fort Peck to shop for jewelry for his wife. But he didn't, not quite yet. He knotted the azure trove of beads in a corner of one of the oil rags Neil kept behind the truck seat, then tied the little bundle to one of the coil springs up under the seat, out of sight. Save them, he could just hear that fancy tongue of Darius saying, for when the time is propitious.

In bed is the only way he knows how to make up, Meg mused. *The Hugh Duff definition of* everything, *is that? For that matter, is it going to be mine?*

"You work too hard," Charlene was telling Owen.

"That's how hard it takes," Owen told her tiredly.

"Gotta be your carburetor." Bruce had his head under the hood of the truck alongside Neil's. "That or your gas line. Probably both need blowing out."

"Wasn't I born lucky," Neil said, "to know somebody who's full of government air."

"How you doing now?"

"I feel big as a house."

"But Kate, does it feel like there's an honest-to-goodness person there inside of you, or some kind of other thing that'll, you know, turn out to be a person?"

"You ask stuff that most people don't even want to think about, anybody ever tell you that?"

"Oh, are you back in that awful mood? Does that come and go, or do you generally just feel stinko?"

"Rosellen, I'm so pregnant I could bust. If I'm *lucky,* I'll bust. So, okay, then? That satisfy your curiosity?"

"Let me borrow your office, Tom."

"Shannon, what you haven't thought of to borrow from me hasn't been invented yet." Nonetheless he waved her toward the back of the saloon and turned his attention to the bar commerce again.

Proxy locked the door behind her, then stepped to the office's sole window and yanked down the greenblind shade.

Privacy thus insured, with one hand on Tom Harry's desk to balance herself she whipped off one shoe and then the other, then took down her slacks and in a practiced quick unbuttoning was out of her blouse as well. Underwear and stockings she didn't wear on the job, they only complicated matters and besides, the joes fell for that in a big way, naked lady under a couple of pearl buttons.

Barefoot all over, she dippered water into Tom Harry's washbasin and began using his washcloth on herself. Ran the chilly soppy cloth over her breasts first, there was always some reassurance in how quick her nipples stood up and saluted. (Another thing the joes fell for.) She scrubbed on downward, flinching but thorough. Told herself what she had to keep telling herself in this line of work: *Take care of the merchandise, Prox. Don't let it show wear and tear.* Wurr and turr, would be Darius's version. She wondered whether all Scotchmen had their voice-boxes in their noses.

She didn't often do this, take a spit bath before going home with an overnighter. But there was no real chance to clean herself up at the houseboat, these nights, before the bed went into gear — this nightly tomcat was no different from the rest of men on that, naturally inclined toward the horizontal — and besides, sacktime with this one counted for a lot. Darius Duff unhesitatingly paid for extra stuff, and extras onto the extras. Whatever — more likely whoever — this joe was trying to get over, he had it bad.

Only problem was, he was running through his money as if he had haystacks of it, which Proxy doubted. She hated to slow up on him. Beneath that bed in the houseboat was a suitcase which held neat rows of the pocket sacks Bull Durham tobacco came in. A used Durham sack would hold exactly twenty silver dollars, and Proxy was filling them assiduously; the only bank she trusted was the bank of the Missouri River. Yet how much good would it do her to pump money out of Darius so fast that even he would catch on; a John D. of this sort didn't often crop up. So, string him along, or grab it off as it comes? *Come on, Prox, make up your mind, this shouldn't take a frigging Act of Congress.*

She toweled off, then reassembled herself into the silklike blouse and snug slacks. Doing up her face in Tom Harry's mirror, Proxy Shannon was short of beautiful but more than qualified as provocative. She had a spoilsport diagonal smile, which, paradoxically, the sharper she slanted it, the broader its force on the male recipient. Look very closely and there could be found a few battlelines at the corners of her hazel eyes, but again, these simply confirmed to the male order that she knew what to do with all this arsenal of hers.

This could not be a sound idea, Darius told himself, this amount of Proxy.

Yet could it.

He examined the matter. The other Duffs shared him around at Sunday dinner — once a month for him and Hugh to be at the same table seemed to be about the right interval, just now — but otherwise he didn't much cross paths with any of them except for Owen, busy bee whose overseeing often brought him to the boatyard. Darius was quite sure he was not missed during his traipses to Plentywood with Jaarala every second Saturday, so why would a nightly hour or two, well, all right, several, in somewhat dubious company be noticed either?

Besides, the kind of company he was finding on the houseboat was its own best argument. He still ached for Meg, and Proxy expertly extracted that ache, at least the physical portion of it.

He stirred himself, back to giving her a listening smile as she was telling him about — if he was following this correctly — her stint as personal nurse to a bootlegger.

"It was real too bad, but he was one sick pup," Proxy's narrative had reached. "His own homebrew did it to him. Fusel oil poisoning — see, he didn't get all that junk out of his brew and when he tasted it some, that's all she wrote, Buster. You ever see anybody with fusel oil poisoning?"

He shook his head, rapt.

"They turn blue as a robin's egg," she told him in a confidential tone.

Darius shuddered and decided he was getting off easy with only ill-tasting American beer.

"What became of him, then?" he urged her on.

"I brought him out of it. All I could do. Day and night, I stayed with him, kept making him sweat that stuff out of himself." She rolled her head back and forth on the pillow in evident wonder at the memory. "You know what? He paid me double what he was supposed to, he was just so hopped up with gratitude."

Incredible woman, really. She had already told him about the time an Indian chief on the Fort Peck Reservation had wanted to make her one of his wives, and the episode of, if he understood it right, an alphabetical elk who had been roped during a cattle gather near her uncle's ranch in one of the Dakotas and branded one end to the other with cattle brands from Lazy A to Flying Z. True, Darius had detected a bit of a tendency for Proxy to be cast large in her own stories, but then aren't we all.

"Proxy, where do you come from?" he suddenly wanted to know. "Originally, I mean."

"As much as anywhere, the Twin Cities."

"And those duo are — ?"

Proxy raised her eyebrows, then gave him a laugh. "Wheeler and Fort Peck, can't you tell by looking?"

"Enough about nativity, evidently." He cast a glance across her to the alarm clock. "I'll need to be going, won't I. First, though, as the Irishman said on his wedding night, 'Could I trouble ye again, Miss Shannon?' That bit we were doing last night, I could stand another session of that."

"A sixty-nine?" she asked with professional consideration. "Or the sidewinder?"

"Well, one and then the other, what about." He raised up on an elbow, though, grimacing in the direction of a dog's nightsplitting barks. "Blast that cur. A man can't hear himself function." He climbed out of bed, went over to the window and called out, "Quiet down, pot licker."

"Don't you know anything? Dogs speak German." She padded to the window and let loose at the top of her voice, *"Raus!"*

The barking stopped.

"Devastating." Darius gave her an appreciative chuckle, then a caress that started high and ended low. "But then, you naturally are, Proxy." He stepped toward the chair where his pants and wallet were. "While I'm up, I'll tend to the pecuniary —"

"Never mind," she said, "I'll take it out in trade." She saw his face light up. "Not that kind, pudhead. Do some chores around here for a change. Split some wood, pack out the ashes. Start just about anywhere." She turned her naked back on him and started toward the bed, then said as if it had just occurred to her: "Make breakfast."

Charlene was pretty much right about how draining his workdays were, Owen had to admit. The start of October, now, and so far today he had managed to be snappish to Rosellen (*"What,"* she'd asked when he took a look at the freshly typed September dredging total and swore. *"Did I make a mistake?" "Maybe this whole sonofabitching process is a mistake,"* he'd said and stomped off, leaving her mystified) and had riled Major Santee by insisting on Sangster for some booster pump engineering when the major wanted him on something else (*"Glad I married a nurse,"* Sangster said of the Ad Building atmosphere, *"she can help me put my straitjacket on"*) and he was only now getting to his ostensible task, troubleshooting the dredging. Owen jounced down the bluff from the Ad Building, digging his heels in to keep his balance, toward the wall of soupy earth that was his dam and the temperamental maze of pipes and pontoons and trestles that were his dredgeline. He could not help wondering what the engineers at Grand Coulee and Bonneville and Boulder were doing at this moment. Probably sitting around in carpet slippers, solving crossword puzzles.

But Fort Peck was making monthly average progress of three million cubic yards, just. They still were atoning for April. A strong August had made up for some of that early lag, but September didn't pick up the monthly average as much, which was what had set Owen to cussing earlier this morning.

So now we got Octember left to go, he put his mind to. *October, November, and whatever December will let us have before snow piles up to our belly buttons again. One nice sixty-day month out of that, just maintaining a hundred thousand yards of fill a day, and there it'll be, sufficient unto the goddamn year. Won't matter what the calendar says, just see it all as autumn on the Montana Riviera. Take it day by day, sixty more times out of about the next seventy-five, is what I've got to do. Move the mud, that's the daily drill, Duff.*

Owen was up onto the west half of the dam by now, the broad and brown Missouri flowing through between this and the east half, and upstream in front of him lay the quadruple sprawl of pipelines and timbering stuck in muck and clawed-out pits where the dredges were cutting and sucking.

Yet wasn't it pretty.

The pipeline-trestle strutworks strode across the distance like cadets with a palanquin on their backs.

The four pipelines themselves were each two-mile-long thongs, lacing the river valley to the new bluff of dam.

The white dredges, and the four brown

fields where they were digging away, looked almost like diligent farms.

And all of it, the long pendants of pipes and machinery, day and night flickered with light where arc welders were rebuilding dredge pumps and cutterheads: Owen's constellation of blue flashes.

At the day's start of business in the Blue Eagle, Tom Harry let drop:

"You've got an admirer."

"I thought I had nations of them," Proxy said warily.

"Judging by the wear and tear on my Packard, that could be. Watch it, though. Don't go tooting that Skywegian's bagpipe for him so much you forget our arrangement here."

"He's after-hours."

"I can tell. At one minute to two, he straightens his cap, says to his pecker, 'Hello, down there, ready for another ride on a houseboat?' and off he goes with you."

"Tom, you don't run me after I pack up out of here for the night."

"Then don't be letting some bughouse lawyer run you either, all I'm saying. That's not like you, Shannon."

Tom Harry turned away from her toward his cash register, but then flinched and uttered, "*Jesus,* what the — ?" Reaching behind himself, he plucked the beer-soaked back of his white shirt away from his hide.

"Sorry about spilling all that perfectly good beer," Proxy was telling him, empty glass aslant in her hand. "That's not like me, is it."

Even Darius, chary with any credit to the Fort Peck way of doing things, was taken with the implication of the dredgeline.

"It's an aqueduct, isn't it," he said to Owen during their daily lunch joust. "For muck, instead of water."

"That's kind of a cockeyed way of looking at it, but yeah, basically," Owen granted.

"Does that make your Corps of Engineers the new Romans?"

"I forget, Darius, didn't they kick the crap out of the Persians once?"

The dam was a foolkiller, they never dared forget that.

Hugh and Birdie were clearing a trap in the section of dredgeline nearest the diversion tunnels when hubbub broke out at the railroad trestle just above them.

The two of them climbed the side of the dam to see what was up. One of the gravel crew had stepped down into a dumpcar of pea gravel, where his hat had blown off

370

to, just as the dump-doors sprung open. Between the drop to the diversion tunnel portal below and the beating he took from the gravel, the poor sap never had a chance.

A foreman, looking green around the gills, came up from the tunnel portal and told everybody to knock off the gawking, get back to work.

"Them tunnels aren't any too good a luck, are they," said Birdie as the pair of them slowly made their way back down the dam. Hugh knew what he meant. Tunnel pneumonia was rampant among the crews digging the four huge diversion boreholes that the river was destined into. The dynamiter J.L. Hill, next door to Bruce and Kate, had lately come down with it. Between that and accidents that could happen while you were reaching for your hat . . .

Hugh had to say, "You do wonder if there are pockets of that kind of luck, yes."

"Incredible, really though, Owen, how your Roosevelt can put a Corps of Engineers bit here and a WPA piece there and a pack of contractors in around the edges, and it's all supposed to stand in one stack."

"Whatever works, I guess he figures." Owen started going through a sandwich as if he was famished. *He even hurries his digestive process,* Darius was convinced. "You take that prunehead Hoover," Owen provided between rapid munches, "his notion of things was, 'Don't just do something, stand there.' "

Owen was never on hand for long at the boatyard these noons, but the two of them crammed in a remarkable amount of the world's doings. There was plenty to go around. Spain. Ethiopia. Germany. As usual it was not clear what was going on in Russia, the Union of Soviet Socialist Republics rather, but Darius had edgily agreed with Owen that Stalin seemed to be knocking people around a bit much. Occasionally they even brought the discussion down to Fort Peck.

As now, when Medwick strutted by them with a curt greeting. *Belly on him like a burglar's sack,* ran Darius's thought, but he phrased it down to:

"There's a man with 'boss' written all over him, in his own hand."

"Yeah," Owen agreed, "there are times when I'd like to bring the full force and effect of a two-by-four down on Cece. But he does come through with my pontoons and pump boats, eventually."

"On the Clyde," Darius mused, "we'd have had a standing committee on Medwick."

Owen had finished off his food and was tanking up on black coffee. He blew lightly onto his thermos cup of it for a moment before saying:

"Tell me something, Darius. How come you chose here instead of someplace like, oh, say, Dnieperstroy."

The rivers faced each other from opposite pages of the world. The Missouri longer and arching and more sinuous, the Dnieper blunter and right-angled and to the point. Two hundred Ukraine miles above the Dnieper's discharge into the Black Sea, the Dnieperstroy Dam took the river in through teeth of sectioned concrete, the greatest power feed that had ever been achieved. Each river no longer a moving road, but something more like a giant hose, the Dnieper through its dynamos and the Missouri through its diversion tunnels were to hum out the bragging rights of each government. Dnieperstroy's peasant thousands of workers were meant to announce Communism's capability, the Soviet achievement: We have abolished Sunday. *The Fort Peck project was using the Missouri as its writ of ever-contriving America:* We deal with tomorrow as it comes.

Darius gave Owen the swiftest of looks, then tried to joke past the question. "But

Owen, my man, I don't know how to speak a word of Dnieperstroyski."

But from what I savvy about the Clyde-side, uncle of mine, you've probably talked some leftski of some kind. He told Darius as much with simply his return gaze.

Darius studied him back, then reached for his thermos bottle and took his time about pouring a cupful of moderately-toned tea. "Along the Clyde, political wrangle was simply everyday conversation."

"Any particular brand?"

"Basic as springwater, is all," Darius lilted. "A lad of parts, such as yourself here, must know that there are mountains of reading on this all the way up to Marx —"

"Marx? The man's dead, Darius — what does he know about anything anymore?"

"— and I've done a fair bit of that reading, you can bet your Sunday britches, Owen, my man." Owen had noticed Darius's tendency to grow more fancy before coming to the point. "But me, now, I know it most by gut," he was arriving at. "That the working class has always been hounded by the owning class. There does seem to me a clear bit of adjustment available there. That if they were one and the same, there'd be nobody to do the hounding."

As with everything else he had ever read, Owen's college course on political economy had sopped in and stayed; even before Darius was done, he had found the term for this particular pie in the sky.

"Syndicalism," he murmured. "That what you're about, for crying out loud? Sorel and his general strike, that's just going to topple everything neatly into your — excuse me all to hell, the working class's — lap? The Wobblies were for that, in this count and all it got them were some good songs and lots of jail sentences."

" 'Neatly,' now, I don't think that necessarily applies to —"

"Jesus H., Darius, that *syndicat* setup of worker committee this and worker committee that, wouldn't it be like trying to build a locomotive on a bicycle frame?"

Darius blinked, and in an instant of instinct, decided what he had better confine himself to in this scrimmage with Owen.

"I've been in more strikes than you've had hot breakfasts," he confessed ruefully. "But again, Owen, what's a man to do? Strikes were the way of it on the Clyde, they're how we brought up wages and conditions."

"Sorel's big idea, as I remember it, was more about bringing down governments than bringing up wages."

"What can you expect of a Frenchman, they never think small. Now, a Fabian female acquaintance I once had —"

"Let's whoa on the theory stuff," Owen decreed, "right about here. I don't have time to go through all the spectrums of Red with you." He hesitated. "For that matter, I don't think I even want to know some of what you maybe believe. But what you better keep in mind is that you aren't back there in the Soviet of the Clyde now." He did not bother to indicate the gray dromedary hills in the direction of the spillway, the high silent bluffs overtopping the river valley, the six-square-mile scatter of the dam workforce at their separate projects like tribal encampments.

"Peckerstroy I don't think is in the cards here, Darius. Detroit, the waterfronts out on the Coast," Owen named off for him, "Butte, even. If strikes are your game, that's more the territory. But not here. Hell, people here are flat-out grateful just to have a job."

"As am I." Darius gave him a quick keen smile. "Owen, about my being here. Maybe it's an interlude. Maybe it'll prove to be an entirely new tune. But I can't not care about what I've worked for. I think I'd do away with myself, before that."

"Strong talk," Owen remarked. "You take your politics awful damn seriously."

"The running of the world, I take seriously, yes. I've never seen why it has to be left to the big bugs. Even this interesting Roosevelt of yours — all this work here, the wages, the whacking great dam itself, it's all rather something he and his crowd are doling out, isn't it."

"Darius," Owen told him stonily, "I'm only a medium bug, okay? Some guys give me orders, and I give orders to other guys, and I don't know how the hell else to make anything work. I'm in this because the Fort Peck Dam is going to be built, and that's what I do, figure out ways to build. Sermons are never going to help me at that."

Kate strained.

"You keep that up, dear, it's coming," the nurse said.

The watermelon bulge of herself and the baby rose before her in the hospital sheets. Along with agonized and exhausted, she was madder than hell about how long it takes to put things together. All her life she had seen things be born, kittens by the carload, pups every time you turned around, lambs sliding out in a wet slink and the more difficult calves and colts, and it had not once occurred to her how the puzzling act of delivery would be with her. Too casual about it to take

377

that "twilight sleep" dope they'd offered her, but how about some kind of *mid*-night anesthesia to put her out cold right now? *Didn't matter, didn't MAT-ter,* she raged, *too late UHH now,* it was occurring all at once now, like pain of a lifetime's ailments concentrated between her thighs.

She hung on to the bed rails and convulsed the lower half of her body, feeling as if she was taking the biggest grunt of her life and it was not enough, not yet . . .

She closed her eyes so hard that the corners of her eyelids hurt, so she let them shoot open, staring at the hospital room ceiling, *beaverboard, why do the idiots call it that, it's not made of beavers . . .*

The doctorly advice that she ought to concentrate made her peeved on top of angry: as if a person *could* think of anything else but this, this delivering, unloading . . . *Giving* birth — if she could just *give,* she would — it had to be grunted out, it had to be . . .

"Here comes the head. Here we go, nurse." We? If *we* were having this, why was she getting all the grief? "I have it, nurse, I have *him.*" Doctor's voice, cheerful as cherry pie. "Mrs. Duff, you have a son here."

Kate panted, swallowed, shuddered.

They repeated to her that she was a mother now.

The Duffs piled into the hospital room the next noon. Beat up from the hard birth as she was, Kate on her pile of pillows gave them a pale grin. For his part, Bruce looked like parenthood was a tune he had casually written by himself. Everybody crowded around the bed to gauge the red-faced bundle in the crook of Kate's arm, and they unanimously declared him the best ever.

"What do you think we named him?" Bruce asked. "Give you seven guesses."

Donald, Meg hazarded.

Pasquale, and *Squally* for short, Hugh joked, making Kate mad at him for weeks to come.

Junior, Owen thought for sure, and was genuinely taken aback when Bruce smirked and shook his head *huh uh.*

Probably something like *Robert, Roderick,* or *Ronald,* said Charlene as if that was the way it ought to be.

Merritt, offered Rosellen.

Brewster, Neil came up with.

Tim, Darius surprised everyone with.

The parental couple shyly grinned back and forth over the baby, as if giving each other the christening privilege. It was Kate who revealed:

"Jack. He's Jack, aren't you, hon."

"As in crackerjack," Bruce could not resist adding.

In bed, Darius reported:

"All of a damned sudden, I'm a great-uncle."

Proxy reached down on him and fondled. "I'd have said a little above average, maybe."

"Madness, though." In the darkness of the houseboat she could just see the profile of his face, upturned as if the ceiling and beyond was being read from. "Bringing a child into this world, what with all the fixing the damnable place needs."

Proxy didn't say anything, and her hand did not stay there long.

The mother and child both were fine, fine, the newest father at Fort Peck learned to recite to the diving-barge crew and Kate's co-workers at the Rondola and any other interested parties, the doctor merely wanted her to rest up a few more days before letting her come home.

Her absence, though, left Bruce unmoored, drifty in both mind and the rest of him. The house seemed to him dead as a tomb. The thick silence of noon followed him into the kitchen, where he halted and tried to get his bearings for this lunch hour. He crossed to the breadbox, opened it, snapped it closed again without taking out so much as a crust. He was hungry in a different way than food could satisfy.

Tense with that feeling of not quite knowing himself, he went and stripped the sheets from the bed, bundled into them the dirty clothes Kate had told him not to worry about because Rosellen had offered to do them with hers on Saturday, and plunged out the back door and across into the Hills' yard. Best route against anyone seeing him, there between Nan's lines of laundry. Schooner sails of sheets and pennants of undies danced whitely on the wind as he passed. His heart going like a piston, he rapped on the Hills' back door.

Nan opened, surprise turning swiftly into her tidy smile. "I understand you're a proud father."

Neither of those fit how he felt at that moment, but he managed a grin. "Yeah, so they keep telling me."

"Here, those can go in the basket there," Nan steered Bruce's armload of bedding and such into an empty wicker clothes basket. She did not have the heart to tell him she had offered to Kate to do this wash and been told it already was taken care of, thanks a million anyway.

Bruce deposited the clothes and stepped back, but not awfully far. *I hadn't oughta*

381

notta, the damned lines of a song were going in his head like a radio that wouldn't shut off, *but I really gotta gotta . . .* Trying to sound like a natural neighbor, he asked:

"How's J.L. getting along?"

"Better. They want to keep him in the hospital to watch him a few more days yet." Nan kept her smile, but was poised in a way suggesting she had a Himalaya of laundry to get to.

"Quite a thing, isn't it," Bruce said as if amazed by the sudden thought of it. "Each of us on our own like this."

Nan Hill did not blush, did not look away in any melting maiden style, did not even entirely drop her smile.

"Speaking of that," she said, "I'd better get on with my day so you can get on with yours." She added in a tone that brought red to his ears: "I know I'm keeping you from your lunch."

As if it was a given, Darius went over and sat with Proxy at a relatively quiet table along the far wall of the Blue Eagle whenever she took a break from dancing and other activities, these nights. Along with his beer, this Friday night he carried what he had just heard from Jaarala.

"Plimpton's out."

"What's that mean, 'out'?"

"Been expelled. From the Party. He claims he quit, but . . ."

"Tim. I'm not in this for these damnable arguments over your Trotsky and your thisky and your thatky. All I want, all I've ever wanted, is a full say for the workers."

"How you get to that, without all this other, I just can't help you with." Jaarala's baggy face looked bleak, but then it generally did. He eyed Darius as if testing a board on a bridge. "Both of us've heard the choir break up before. I figure I'll go over there tomorrow like usual and see how things stand."

Darius said nothing for a moment and then told Jaarala yes, of course, that made sound sense, he'd accompany him. So tomorrow there would be the nearly half-day journey to Plentywood again, hour after hour of Tim Jaarala's wearying old-maidish driving across the dun geography. Damn the geography, geography was the blubber of America, great fat spaces between the human clusters. Darius almost felt nostalgia for Great Britain's vertical class system, kick it in the shins at the Clydeside and draw an immediate yelp in the House of Lords, whereas here everything went bending away out of sight over ridge after —

"Think the rain'll hurt the rhubarb?"

383

Proxy's tone practically crackled in Darius's ears.

"Sorry. I was a bit drifty there." Realizing he had better put away politics for the night, Darius made eye contact across the table to her. Encountering cool weather there, he sent his gaze on south toward what looked like the warmer clime of her nearly sheer blouse. He cleared his throat. "Proxy, love, any chance you can make an early evening of it tonight? Tomorrow —"

"— 'I canna manage to be aroond,' " she flourished the mockery before those words could troop out of him. "Naturally, you can't. Which is real too bad, because I had a Saturday night doozy I wanted to tell you."

"I hope it'll save?"

"I don't know that it will. See, it's one of those you just can't stop yourself from thinking about. Mystery, kind of. There's this bird who shows up, pretty much out of nowhere. He manages to get on at the dam, does his job, doesn't call any attention to himself. Sugar probably doesn't even melt in his tea, he goes about everything so hushy. Then along with that, he finds somebody enough of a stupe to take him home with her. Snuggles right in with her, night after night after night after night, except every other Saturday. Poof, he's gone, every other Saturday. Funny,

384

isn't it, for a guy who likes a helping or two of nookie all those other nights. Doesn't come around, ever, those every other Saturdays." Proxy addressed the night at large. "Where do he go, and what do he do?"

"Proxy, I've told you. An extra shift —"

"Extra shift, your earhole. I've asked around. Nosiree, no sign of Darius Duff on the boatyard crew those Saturday nights. What somebody did see, though, was Darius Duff toodling down the road with that sad sack who cooks at the barracks. I suppose the two of you go off on baloney picnics together?"

"It — has to do with political things."

"People like Tom Harry keep yapping that everything does." Proxy had on her ice pick expression. "This big dam out in the middle of where there's never been nobody but gophers, Tom says is a political thing. Whoopedy-do for political things, then. You trotting off with a bean-burner every couple of weeks, though, that doesn't sound like political generally does."

Darius was looking more unstrung with every minute. This was a front he hadn't expected to have to defend himself on. Even to himself he sounded wounded and lame: "I can't really tell you, Proxy. It's, don't you see, it has nothing whatsoever to do with the pair of us, and so I need to ask you to not —" he broke off raggedly and grimaced upward. "And what do you want, sonny?"

A young roustabout, red-haired but otherwise green as grass, had mustered himself enough to approach their table. Shifting from one foot to the other but standing his ground, the kid managed to sing out: "A dance with the lady?"

The pair at the table seemed to take a long time to digest this request. The kid fidgeted. "I didn't want to butt in or anything. But I been waiting most of an hour, and I'm gonna have to go on shift pretty quick."

"I'll give you a shift up your —" Darius furiously lurched from his chair and made a roundhouse grab which would have taken the red out of the kid's hair if it had connected, then started for him around the table. Proxy jumped up and with veteran skill interposed herself.

"Snookie pie, this actually isn't the best time for us to foxtrot." She propelled the kid toward the millrace of taxi dancers and customers at the far end of the bar. "One of the other ladies will be glad to dance your socks off, okay?"

She turned back to Darius. He still was poised there motionless, halfway around and half across as if he had run aground on the table. It didn't take much of a guiding shove from her to put him back blindly into his chair. "Try not to take on the world," she instructed, "while I go get you some nourishment."

She went to the front of the bar, absolute farthest from Tom Harry, to order a double whiskey. He marched down on her there anyway.

"Shannon, what the bejesus is going on over there, Latin lessons? You're supposed to be out on the floor —"

"He's a little riled up, Tom. I'll —"

"— dancing, not gassing the sonofabitching —"

"— make up the difference on the dance take and —"

"— night away with some yayhoo crying in his —"

"TOM, I HAVE TO!" Proxy divulged at not quite the top of her voice, but near enough. She stared nearby customers back to whatever they'd been doing, then leaned across the bar toward Tom Harry and said into his face:

"I'm the one who got him going on — what he's going on. So, I'll buy out my frigging dance take tonight, and I'll tell frigging Darius not to show his mug around here tomorrow night, and you won't have a thing in the frigging world to howl about, now will you."

Muttering, Tom Harry headed back to his cash register. Proxy sipped the double whiskey down to where it wouldn't spill, carried the glass across the room and deposited it in front of Darius. "Here. Nerve medicine."

Darius looked as if he was about to pop out of his skin.

"Drink it," Proxy tapped a fingernail indicatively against the oversize shotglass, "or I'm going to rub it in your hair."

Not seeming to see, Darius automatically closed a hand around the glass and drew it up for a gulping drink.

"Here." She frisked him until she found a handkerchief in one of his hip pockets, planted it in his hand, then lifted his hand to the wet trail down his cheek.

"You shouldn't look at a crying man," he managed to say as he dabbed, "it's seven years bad luck."

"They'll just have to stand in line with the rest of my luck." She folded her arms beneath her breasts in the *I'm waiting, stupe* gesture recognized by Tom Harry across the entire length of the Blue Eagle. Darius took some time at it before words were found.

"Jaarala knows some persons somewhere who're interested in changing matters," he started in.

"The Red Corner," she said impatiently.

"Puh-lenty-wood."

Her short circuit of the apparatus of explanation he was building up to knocked him speechless for a minute. His voice, once he found it, strained out:

"I thought you didn't give a fiddle about political matters."

"Never bothered to ask, though, did you. Anyway I don't."

Darius studied her, wiping his cheeks with a sleeve. "Proxy, can we — this is a bit public for political elucidation."

"Everything sounds better on a house-boat, I suppose you think."

"So how come you have to sneak out of town for these politics?"

"That's where they are, that's the damned point! Don't you see?"

"Darius, there's some stuff I know that would curl your toes, okay?" More by habit than intention they had rushed to bed as soon as they reached the houseboat, and the now-familiar touch of their bodies along each other was simply part of the atmosphere there. But Darius realized that tonight Proxy was heating up in not the accustomed sense. "Maybe I don't give a flip about these politics of yours," her words struck him like pebbles of warning, "but you better not ever think you can write me off with 'Don't you see?' I see quite a frigging lot when I want to, Scotch-potch."

"I've no doubt of that now," he could say with sincerity.

"Keep it in mind then," she recommended. "So what's all this with you dipping your wick in politics?"

"Back in Scotland I was in the movement . . ."

"What'd you ever move?"

"Proxy, if Marx'd had to answer to you, he'd still be sorting his umlauts from his apostrophes."

"Sor-*ry*," she said derisively, but snuggled closer to him.

Wary, he waited a minute. Then the long struggle began unspooling out of him, litany of trying to find the political moment, the pivot of rule.

"We all but had the bastards in '14," he bitterly arrived at. "Proxy, I tell you, we had them like this." Above where she lay, she could just discern in the darkness that Darius had lifted his left hand and closed it into a fist. It was a good guess that fist was clenched so tightly the knuckles had gone pale. "The Triple Alliance," his voice journeyed on. "The railwaymen, the miners, and the dockworkers," he named them off like bellpeals. "They were readying to shut down the country, and that would have brought out enough of the rest of us in support. We'd have changed the face of history turnable whore that she is."

Proxy went tense as a cat at a fur show, but Darius shot on:

"But the war came. And before you could say Tommy, men lined up in ranks to kill men just like themselves."

She made no pronouncement about the world's majority of stupes, but almost.

"We nearly had them again in '26, the General Strike." Darius lightly pounded his fists together, knuckles against knuckles, like rams' heads meeting. "That was to be the time." His fury came and went again, with the rasping memory of the warships standing gray but distinct out there on the Clyde while ashore the strikebreakers wrested back the docks and power stations and tram lines, sailors and police and blacklegs conspiring to keep the General Strike from ever living up to its name.

"The hard times, that was the next chance." His chest rising and falling as if still catching breath from then, Darius recited to Proxy the hunger marches of '31 and '32, the Depression-desperate crowds that took to the streets and struggled with the police, the perfidy of Ramsay MacDonald's government, the flare-up along the Clydeside this past winter . . . there at

1934, his voice stopped for a moment, then stumbled out with:

"There was some trouble."

Alongside him in the wordless minute after that, Proxy puckered her lips and began to blow silently and steadily toward the side of Darius's neck, perhaps six inches away.

When that eventually drew his attention and he turned his head in her direction, she cut off the little stream of air.

"Unless I miss my guess," she said, "you were in it up to the top of your neck."

The crackdown had begun in '32, led by the London police. Up the length of Great Britain, the tactic now was to charge into the marchers and crowds of the unemployed, break their numbers with the swing of truncheons. The Clydeside had been delivered blows before, and by experts, but there was no sense having your brains scrambled on a regular basis. Darius, by then a member of his committee's flying squad — movement veterans who were dispatched into the streets whenever trouble or opportunity flared — adapted to the times by carrying a piece of lead pipe, just short enough to fit in the deep side pocket of his jacket, just long enough to have some effect against a policeman's club. He and others of the flying squad particularly watched for young coppers in the street skirmishes; catch one unaware and you could give him a shiver, the whack of your lead pipe against his oak truncheon stinging his hand. Doctrine lay behind even such street guerrilla tactics, after all: the minimum of brutality compatible with . . .

By the winter of '34, Darius's wing of the labor movement and the middle-of-the-road Trades Union Council were in blind alliance simply to try to keep people fed. There were those, Darius included, who believed the TUC couldn't find its guts with both hands during the General Strike, but resentment never made a meal; food tickets had to be distributed to the unemployed, and Darius was to spell his TUC counterpart at the Woodturners Hall the afternoon of doling out tickets there. He arrived to a mob piled against the closed hall.

Darius struggled, half-swam, through the swarm of men.

"I'm from the Clydeside flying squad! Let me through, we'll get the distribution going, LET ME FOR CHRIST'S SAKE THROUGH!"

He shoved and was shoved to the door of the hall, where he managed to negotiate the men there — some of them fortunately recognized him — into letting him unlock the door and go in alone. Then he had to push in against the resisting shoulder from inside.

"Crawfurd, you great fool, it's me, Duff!"

Darius wrenched through the narrowly opened door, then he and the other slammed it and leaned their backs against it, looking at each other. George Crawfurd was white as nunnery paint.

"We're in the shit," the TUC man whispered to Darius. "They allotted us but five hundred tickets. Christ only knows how many are howling out there."

An easy riotful, Darius could agree. Still, the pair of them had to do what they could.

"None the neverless," Darius intoned, then laughed. Crawfurd gaped at him like a beached fish.

"We need to get cracking at this," Darius told him as the outside clamor began to rise again, "or they'll be in here all over us. I'll pass them through one at a time, you hand the tickets."

Crawfurd backed away doubtfully, pulling a table and chair to one side, away from the direct sluice of the doorway.

Darius turned around to the door. Unlocked it, rammed it open and flung himself sidewise into the doorframe, his back straight and tight against one side and his right foot up as high as he could against the jamb on the other side, making a barrier of his cocked leg.

"One at a time, boys, under the leg!" he shouted into the mass of faces. "Our man

George Crawfurd, inside, has your food tickets. But we've got to do it orderly or it can't get done. Easy go now, here, you be first" — he reached out and tugged at a thick-shouldered man who appeared to be the most explosive of the bunch. "Under the bridge. If you'll fit, we can put through anybody up to drayhorses."

That drew a tentative laugh from the human wall. The thickset man hesitated, then ducked awkwardly under Darius's leg, his back bumping the underside of Darius's thigh as he waddled under and through.

"Easy go," Darius said again, to the next man. "It's the only right leg I've got, so scoot as low as you can, that's the way . . . Another, now." He reached out for a sleeve, any nearest sleeve, and tugged indicatively downward. "That's it, down to the scenic route. I know this'd be more interesting if my name was Fifi, but . . ."

For the next hours and hundreds upon hundreds of men, Darius stayed jammed in the doorway, a cork against the hungry human sea. When he spotted a particularly small man coming, he would make the switch and put his other foot up on the doorjamb, to rest the aching leg.

Twice, too, he had to drop his leg and fight off doorbreakers, men who lost their head whether from panic, fury or desperation it didn't matter, and lunged blindly at the doorway. Both times he had the luck that the nearest men on line instantly turned into his allies, swatting sense into the berserk ones.

Even a good many of the better-behaved men were wild-eyed, plunging into the arch of Darius's leg. Many others simply looked dog-miserable, ashamed of taking this dole, even if it came from their labor brethren.

Then out of the head of the line raged a man with a thin, pinched face, a twitchy manner, and a screeching disbelief.

"What's it to you whether we starve or not?" he unloosed from inches away.

"It would offend me," Darius railed back, "to see people die like midges!" Grabbing the man by the scruff of the neck, he ducked him on through beneath his leg.

Through it all he kept count, deliberately making it obvious, as proctorial as possible. If he would stay intent and orderly about this, the incipient mob would. Possibly. He let the running stream of numbers purl under his aching leg, his weariness and fear. He found his flat pencil, and each time that he had counted twenty men, he would reach up and score the lead across the doorframe above him.

At last the waiting men were a wedge several deep instead of dozens. Darius shifted his eyes carefully among this remainder, the last men which would mean they were the angriest. He let the next few go uncounted beneath his leg as he looked up at the doorframe and tallied the twenties. Twenty of them themselves, which it took him a groggy moment to work out as equaling four hundred. He swung his gaze back to the waiting remnant and, but for the vital matter of demeanor, could have cheered. There were going to be enough food tickets, by a sound margin.

Darius had the tortured back of a keelhauling victim. From his rump to the base of his neck, skin was gone in several places and what was left was red and raw. Crawfurd uncorked a pint of whiskey and handed it to him. The shirtless man swigged, shuddered, swigged again and nodded his thanks. Then with obvious pain he put on his coat.

"You're sure you want anything touching that back?" Crawfurd asked.

"No," Darius expelled, "but can't you see them arresting me for public indecency if I don't?"

"You did a grand job of work here today," Crawfurd said. "It was a near thing, too — we've only a dozen tickets left. Minus yours, of course" — he thumbed one from the thin sheaf and put it on the table beside

Darius — "and my own," putting that one in his coat pocket. "I'll turn these other few back to the committee first thing in the morning."

Darius stood silent, weaving just noticeably, the coat draped over his shirtless upper body.

"Another lift of this?"

Crawfurd held out the whiskey to him again.

"George," Crawfurd heard Darius Duff say coldly, "turn out your pockets."

The shorter man kept his gaze on Darius and tried a laugh. "What's this, now. Darius, man, you've had a massive day —"

"Give or take goddamn few," Darius's voice came to him wearily but fiercely, "I put four hundred and forty-eight men through that doorway. That plus our two plus that ten you're so busy showing off to me comes out at four hundred and sixty tickets, doesn't it. Where're the other forty-you've palmed?"

Crawfurd cast a disturbed look at the figure before him, damned ladder of a man. He was not predisposed in favor of Darius Duff, who according to gossip along the Clyde had a plentiful history of bedmates among his female Red mates. George Crawfurd, a bit of a trimmer in everything but family matters, wasn't going to be chided by a sleepabout.

"It's not that way at all," Crawfurd began to protest hotly. "You must've mis-
counted, or maybe I —"

Darius slammed him against the wall,
one hand holding the neck of Crawfurd's
shirt while the other felt at his pockets.
The searching hand found the extra sheaf
of food tickets in the inside pocket of
Crawfurd's jacket.

"It's none of your damned business!"
Crawfurd shouted. "A man has a right to
—" he broke off and swung an arm around
onto Darius's back, thumping as hard as he
could with his fist. Darius gasped and
arched his back, but wrenched out the wad
of tickets. Crawfurd grabbed that wrist, trying to make him turn loose of them. They
scuffled until Crawfurd pounded Darius's
back again, and as Darius groaned, Crawfurd forced his hand against the table,
clawing for the tickets. Too late he glimpsed
the lead pipe in Darius's other hand.

"Who, mannerly me?"

Darius swung off the bed, keeping his
face away from Proxy after that unmissing
guess of hers. In the trouble to the top of
his neck? More like over the peak of his
head. He went to the waterbucket and
drank from the dipper, the cold galvanized
taste going down in big swallows. He remembered the exact sound, like a dropped

sack of meal, of Crawfurd's skull splitting, he could trace out every inch of how that foolish death had come to happen. *Crawfurd, don't. This time, man, don't do as you did, and spare us both the . . .* But there wasn't a second time, was there, where Crawfurd was concerned. The once was the all.

Proxy could tell trouble a mile off, and Darius was only from her to the water-bucket.

Isn't this just ducky, she mulled over as she watched him, *I find one with a little money and who halfway has some smarts, and he's some kind of hoodoo in the old country.*

He knew she was calculating him. He tried to muster a smile but didn't nearly make it. "What obtains, do you think? Regarding me."

"You mean should I bounce your butt off this houseboat sooner rather than later?"

"That's the essence, Proxy, yes." He did manage a bit of smile now but of the sad sort.

"This Red stuff, and these tictacs of yours over there in Outer Nowhere," she gave a little thrust of her head in the approximate direction of Plentywood. "Are they catching?"

"Some people are quite immune," he admitted. "But you, I would hope —"

"Darius. If they pin something on you, will any get on me?"

He looked at her, in that dry way that she figured Scotchmen adopted at the time they were weaned. "Your reputation probably will not suffer, Proxy, even if mine should happen to."

Neil had made the discovery of coal. The seam of it was a couple of hours' drive straight east along the Missouri, to where Big Muddy Creek found its way down out of the Plentywood country and joined the river. As a mining operation it did not amount to much — the coal crew had to crawl in on hands and knees to dig the skinny seam — and neither did the coal, soft slightly brownish lignite junk that burned like punk. But Neil already knew life wasn't guaranteed to be a scuttle of anthracite, and so he garnered a ton of the soft coal at a time, all but living in the truck after he got off his dredgeline shift. Wheeler and the other matchbox towns now were showing coal heaps in backyards where he and the Ford Triple A had deposited woodpiles the autumn before, and Neil told himself that if he didn't turn into a zombie and drive the truck off the bridge into Big Muddy Creek one of these dark evenings, he and Rosellen were going to have the world by the tail after a few more trucking seasons.

He blew in for supper now, though, to find Rosellen looking both excited and perturbed.

"Get a billydoo from one of those magazines?" he barely had to guess.

"Really did, this time," she said, somewhere between rueful and thoughtful. "Not one of their printed-up rejections — an honest-to-God letter from the editor."

"Well, that's progress!" He studied the mixture of expression she still had. "Don't you think?"

"It is and it isn't." What Rosellen had dreamt of was an editor's letter, a telegram would have been even better, saying *eager to publish whatever you care to send . . .* "He said my endings need work." In fact, the sentence that stood out in the actual editor's message was, *There is an adage, Miss Duff, about the writer's requisite scrutiny of his previous tries: 'Employ the eraser.'* "He said they're too much like O. Henry."

"Who the hell is Old Henry?"

She saw how instantly angry Neil was on her behalf. Before she could say anything, he was telling her:

"This guy, editor or whatever he is. Write *him* a letter. Right now, why don't you. Tell him to go take a flying jump."

She charged over and hugged him,

coaldust and all, coaxing each other out of their mood with the familiar press of body against body. But there still was a trickle of fear in her, that the editor might be right. Not only right, but that she maybe could not do any better with endings or any of the rest of it than she already had.

"Scurf," Meg said. "All babies get scurf."

"Yeah, but — " Bruce looked at Kate and she at him, mutually dismayed over the ugly patch of dry scaly skin on the exact top of Jackie's head.

"Kate." Meg's commander-in-chief tone. "It is no lasting reflection on you as a mother."

"Thanks. I think."

"A little scurf on him or not, he's a beaner," Hugh declared. He grinned across the bassinet at Kate and said, "The family line has taken a distinct upturn," suddenly convincing her of the virtue of Jackie having grandparents.

"Hey, didn't I have something to do with —"

"No offense intended, Bruce."

The night after going off to Plentywood again with Jaarala, Darius hove into the Blue Eagle at his usual time and there was no Proxy.

"She said to tell you she's out finding gold tonight," Tom Harry relayed. "I were you, I wouldn't wait up."

"Ah," Darius digested this news. "What's that name you and she have for a customer with a heavy purse, a John Q.?"

"John D.," Tom Harry provided drily, "as in Rockefeller."

"The very one, of course." Darius shifted from one foot to the other, casting long-faced gazes around the confines of the Blue Eagle. "Well, then, now." He put a hand in his pocket toward coinage, upon second thought drew it back out.

"Cripes sake, fella, you look like somebody just took a leak on your leg," Tom Harry diagnosed for him. "Belly up here, I'll stand you a beer. Hate to see a man too bollixed to buy himself a drink."

"What's this under the category of 'The devil's good to his own'?" Darius marveled as Tom Harry uncapped a beer and positioned it in front of him. "Or have you merely gone mad?"

"Duff, I wouldn't trade you for a pinto pony. Come on back into the office a minute, there's something interesting you've got to see."

Darius and bottle strolled after him to the cubbyhole office off to the side of the bandstand. Tom Harry opened the door and stepped back. Darius stepped in and found himself facing a large man who wore the obvious item of interest, a badge.

At Darius's look, Tom Harry lifted his shoulders in a shrug and closed the door after himself.

"Name's Peyser," the man said, holding out a thick mitt of hand. On his hip rode a pistol with an ivory butt the size of a hunting horn. "I'm the undersheriff down at this end of the county."

Crawfurd, oh Christ, Crawfurd and Duff, you'll die facing the monument screamed a chorus together in Darius's head, but he managed to shake the undersheriff's meaty hand and drop into the straight-back chair the man indicated.

"Where'd you land in here from?" Peyser started right in.

"Glasgow," Darius said without specifying which nation.

Peyser grunted as if that was what he had expected. "Something you better know about," he said as if Darius had come to him for advice. "I was appointed to this badge by a sheriff who is hell on wheels about politics. He's hell on wheels about most things, but politics really fires him up. Particularly those that go pretty far in a certain direction. Off toward Plentywood, say."

Not Crawfurd then, sang in Darius. *At least not yet.*

Bold with relief, he mustered:

"I had no idea there's a law in America against going for a Saturday drive."

"If you're claiming that a man's political persuasion isn't against the law in this country, that's true, as far as it goes. But Sheriff Kinnick, if he was here, would point out to you that we can generally come up with some law that a person is on the stray side of." The undersheriff leaned forward as if getting down to business. "There's feeling that goes back a long way against radicals — Wobs and such. Troublemaking, wildcat strikes, sabotage — that's the kind of stuff the Wobblies got themselves a reputation for, in case you didn't know."

"That's their reputation, is it," Darius said as if marveling. "And here I thought the Industrial Workers of the World, to give them their rightful name, were known for being put in front of a firing squad in your Utah, shot on the docks in your state of Washington, and hanged from the nearest trestle in places such as your Butte."

"I won't say those didn't happen, too," the undersheriff said. "Lots happens." Peyser eyed Darius as if calculating how large he had to spell it out for him. All the way, he decided.

"If you get on the wrong side of Sheriff Kinnick," the undersheriff said unequivocally, "he's the type who will nail your pecker to a tree and give you only a rusty saw to get loose with."

"Ah, thank you, no," Darius said. "Point taken."

"But," Peyser patiently kept on, "Sheriff Kinnick isn't here, is he. So, to keep me from having to keep track of you for him, why don't you be a little choosier about who you hang out with."

By Clydeside reflex, Darius instantly set about to split that doctrinal hair. "Everywhere?"

"No, hell no, only around here. Up in Plentywood, I don't give a poop what you do. That's not our jurisdiction."

"So I'm to mend my manners when I'm *not* in a car with a certain party," Darius pursued, "but once we hie off together . . . ?"

"That pretty much ought to do it," the beefy undersheriff said in the same spelling-out voice. "As far as I'm concerned, Jaarala's okay. Some will tell you he's one of those bughouse cases, off the deep end politically. That's only the Scandihoovian in him, I figure."

Darius took a swallow of beer and carefully tried: "That sounds like perhaps a different tack from your Sheriff Kinnick's."

"This job's a job." Peyser looked impassively at Darius. "If I had to agree with everything any boss thinks, where the hell would I ever work?"

He always dealt with them naked, waiting in bed with only a sheet over him, lights off, his mouth a little dry with anticipation until whichever floozie it was this time rapped on his door.

When he heard the knock now, he raised his voice just enough to be heard outside. "You found it."

About all he could make out of this one as she stepped into the darkened room was that her hair was unnaturally pale, nearly the silvered-up color of the moon on a clear night. As usual he couldn't see the face in any detail and didn't care; face wasn't the part that interested him on these occasions. To his surprise, this one stopped there by the door and said:

"You do keep it darker than a black cat's ass in here, sheriff, sir."

He didn't say anything to that, as it was self-evident. He listened to the slidy sounds of her undressing. When she padded over to the bed, he asked:

"You're who?"

"Does that matter any?" Proxy had been all set to say something like "Claudette" as usual, but somehow decided the hell with it, brass would do. She still was huffy about Tom Harry having sent her on this,

408

even though she had dickered double the usual price out of him; if Tom and the other Wheeler nightspot owners had to slip some satisfaction to little Kinnickinnick here every couple of weeks, that was their problem, not hers. Quite where this risky attitude came from, she didn't know. Usually the thing to do was to tell herself a joe was a joe except when he was a John D. and then the enthusiasm could be found to exert herself on his wallet somewhat more; but tonight, she was in just no mood to pretend. Nor did she care what he was going to think, sheriff or no sheriff. After all, she had been run out of better towns than this.

This one isn't scared, the sheriff thought to himself, and wasn't sure whether he liked that fact or not.

"I need to tell you what's involved here?" he asked.

"I hear you like — you always want a trip around the world," she said.

As much as it galled him to know they talked about him, he was relieved not to have to issue minute instructions. "That's the deal, all right," he said gruffly. Then: "That sort of thing suit you?"

"That doesn't matter either, does it," he heard her say, and then her mouth began to make its ports of call on his small body.

Workforce roster in hand, around him dredgeline pontoons being built as fast as hammers could go and the swing shift about to come in the gate and keep the pace going, Cecil Medwick looked upon his boatyard and found it good. Except for one Scottish thistle.

Medwick watched Darius Duff handling work with an ease that, if you did not know better, could be mistaken for inattention. Most of these Fort Peck workers had cut their teeth on rural manual labor, so that the only style they knew was to tear into a job and muscle it into surrender. But Darius more — Medwick wasn't sure he even had the right word for it — *teased* away at the construction of pontoons and pump boats and the like. His work was good as gold, that wasn't the problem. He was just — different. And evidently going to stay that way, Medwick had found out. The time he caught Darius putting in a couple of bulkheads where he was sure one would serve, he asked: "Where the hell did you learn to do it that way?" Darius had looked at him with a perfectly serious face and answered, "Building the *Queen Mary.*"

Granted, a man could learn his boatbuilding trade on the Clyde River or up the Woogadooga and Medwick wouldn't care, so long as the guy really knew his stuff. No, that wasn't what was bugging Medwick. He couldn't put his finger on it, but something about Darius did not fit. The guy rang wrong as a solder dollar.

The shift changed, and Medwick traded gab with the men coming on, but he still watched the stiff-spined figure of Darius Duff until it went out the boatyard gate. Medwick knew in his sleep that the best way to can a guy was always FFI, failure to follow instructions. But that method of firing wouldn't work with Darius, because Darius *did* follow the goddamn things, he simply did so in a way that told you he knew better.

Maybe, though, just maybe there was another shot at showing him the road. Medwick had been feeling it in the air all evening, and its little stings of cold were starting to hit the backs of his hands with nasty regularity now. He took another look at his clipboard with the roster on it, thinking through the angles. Owen Duff was always a major consideration, but from what Medwick heard about the dredge averages, Owen was maybe having his own troubles. So Owen might not be so hot a hotshot from now on, looking out for every Duff on two legs. And if that was to be the case . . .

Medwick moved his finger down the roster and checked the letter after Darius's name. There it sat, the way to discharge him, good old S for *single.* After the dredging shutdown, and the Fort Peck fleet was tucked into the winter harbor, a proportion of the workforce would be laid off seasonally, so-called. Preference for being kept on went to the *M*'s, family men.

Satisfied, Medwick unclipped his roster and stuck it inside his coat to protect it from the faster falling snow.

"Well, fuck and fooey." In disgust Owen directed an angry heel at the frozen mud of the riverbank. His spirited try didn't even dent the substance. Overnight, with the help of a north wind and a dusting of dry snow, the banks of the Missouri had turned into brown iron. And his hope of dredging on into December hadn't even made it to November; this was the thirty-first of October, and it looked like shutdown.

Owen unloosed a few more stanzas of cussing, but absently, already studying the dredge fleet and the dull gray morning as if adding up a column of numbers and checking the unwelcome sum. "Max, what do you think the chances are of lucking out on a week or two of thaw?"

"Zero, or maybe just none," Sangster provided.

"You're telling me to stash it all in winter harbor, just accept shutdown six or seven weeks earlier than we had to last year."

"Uh huh."

"You're telling me I could get my tail in real trouble if I fiddlefart around and get the whole dredging setup frozen into the river."

"You bet."

"What I like about you, Max, is the way you present an argument." Owen shoved his hands even deeper into his coat pockets, pulled his chin into his coat collar and peered from under his brows up the bluff toward the Ad Building. "Isn't the colonel just really going to love this news for breakfast." With Sangster in step beside him, he set off to deliver the word of shutdown.

Wouldn't you know it. Last year I had only the one dredge and the weather let us peck away on the fill until Christmas Eve. Now I've got the four of them up and going and it's the earliest winter since the Ice Age. Okay, okay, take it easy, Duff, these things happen. Next year is what I better start worrying about now. Figure out April, this time.

Holy cow, though. For that matter fooey and fuck, again. All of a mighty sudden there's three million cubic yards of fill that I'm short this year. That ain't canary feed, as Max would tell me. Next year we — we, hell; me, myself and I — are going to need to move mud like it's never been moved before. Meanwhile, welcome to winter harbor, everybody.

The dreamwork of Fort Peck built through the November nights, turbulent, drifting on the dark change of season and work and prospect, restless inside the bone hulls of fate, thousands of sleep-made privacies tossing and turning. Wheeler, with its alcohol content, tended toward inward uproar: showdowns, arguments won on a second try, woozy otherwise unimaginable sexual situations. In the Fort Peck townsite along Officer's Row, the dreams held a tendency toward hierarchy, Colonel Parmenter's vision of a command post in the blissful sweltering Philippines and Mrs. Parmenter's nocturnal jaunt backward thirty years and thirty pounds to her cotillion debut both overriding, say, Captain Brascoe's delirious armwaving scene with garbagemen who were *delivering* garbage into his tidy streets instead of *hauling it away.* Across a few of those streets, in the barracks, Darius dreamt back to Scotland. One floor up from him, Jaarala in his slumber was shaking dice against Tom Harry and Ruby Smith, and winning.

414

In both towns, in the course of any night, more than one man dreamt of Proxy Shannon.

Within the walls of the Duffs, Hugh was on mental horseback, riding a workhorse — it seemed to be the broad-beamed dun nag they had called "Hippo," back on the homestead — through the snowdrifts of the road between Fort Peck and Glasgow. He thought it odd he was drawing a wage for this, merely riding around in the snow, but who was he to complain. Meg, beside him and not, was on the bandstand of the Blue Eagle, where she could peer over the heads of the crowd, watching and watching, until finally she saw him come in through the door, the tall familiar figure of Hugh. It was Hugh, wasn't it? Bruce slept the sleep of the underwater walker, stupefied but unalarmed, while Kate wanted out of the dream she was in, where she was trying to wait on customers in the Rondola and feed Jack on her breast at the same time and the smartasses along the counter kept saying, *I'll have what Jackie's having.* Meanwhile Rosellen was stalled in a reverie version of the Wheeler post office, waiting for the mail. Every time she went up to the wicket window and asked *Is there any for me?*, the postmaster would say *Did you bring a gunnysack for it?*, then laugh and turn away. Minutes before, Neil woke up on a rancher's approach road halfway between the coal mine and Fort Peck, having pulled over to doze when he thought he might fall asleep at the wheel, and now had climbed out and was walking around and around the truck to get himself warm and awake enough to drive home. Charlene, by contrast, was steaming in her dream, trying to run a beauty shop the size of Cunningham's department store, customers in chairs even up on the mezzanine, and the only help she had was Meg who kept asking, *Charlene, tell me again what to do when they say they want the works.* And working at sleep next to Charlene, in sessions that were more like naps linked together, lay Owen, perpetually trying to get somewhere on a train, but every single time the conductor came by and demanded his ticket, he could not find the thing.

Owen stood it until the Monday before Thanksgiving, when with the holiday ahead and the weekend and a couple of compensatory days off for the overtime that was owed him, he was going to be a man of leisure. None too soon, either. The recessional of the dredge fleet, off the river and into hibernation in the winter harbor, was over and done with, but after that first hard freeze and whiff of snow, the weather had turned infuriating. Persistently cold and nasty but not *that* cold, not enough to form meaningful ice on the Missouri River. And he badly wanted the evidence of ice, immediate thick humped-up drastic ice, to ratio the shutdown of dredging. More than evidently, so did the Corps mucketymucks. He had been tromping around overseeing the dismantling of the dredge hookups on a gusty cold afternoon (but not *that* cold) when a message was brought down to him from Major Santee, asking whether current conditions weatherwise warranted reconsideration of shutdown decision. Back up the hill to the Ad Building went the message with Owen's familiar dashed penciling in the margin CONTINUE RECOMMEND SHUTDOWN BUT UTY. Up To You: Santee was one peeved marshmallow at having the decision bucked back to him that way, but he ended up not countermanding Owen on shutdown.

And since then, Owen's work had consisted of a lot of staring down the road, so to speak. Next-year calculations to be done on piping the fill in from enough dredge-pits to keep the dam inexorably growing, and the question of how to regulate the waterlevel in the core pool which would be bigger and trickier than ever, and the guessing game of where to pick up enough added dredging output to make up for this year's three million cubic yard shortfall. Owen by that Monday before Thanksgiving had noticed he was jiggling his knee pretty much constantly as he thought over the year that lay ahead.

Charlene was home when he reached there these days, shutting the beauty shop earlier as winter layoffs sobered Fort Peck's expenditures. After they had kissed and she started to turn back toward making supper, his hand and arm caught her waist again. Before she could even reverse her direction, she heard:

"Maybe we better go across the mountains and have a look."

It took her a moment to catch up.

"Live it up in Spokane, a night," Owen was saying his way toward it. He met her eyes with his. "Then go on to Grand Coulee and see what we think."

Excitement knocked under Charlene's ribs. "I'll write the Everetts, right tonight." They'd been friends with Connie and Ev all the Bozeman years, before Ev latched on as one of the first engineers hired for Grand Coulee Dam.

"Yeah, do." Owen hesitated. "For now, let's just tell people here we're taking a trip through Glacier Park before the snow really starts to fly."

He felt they had to tell Max and Pam Sangster the truth, and she could not bring herself to up and go without saying at least something to Rosellen and therefore Neil. But otherwise that was their leave-taking of Fort Peck, few words to anyone and those less than fact. Half a dozen days ahead yet before anybody, even the rest of the Duffs, would know they had gone off to climb a fresh ladder. The two of them (mostly Charlene) worked it out that by taking all their clothes, they wouldn't even need to come back for their other things; Rosellen and Neil could send or store whatever was wanted. A telegram from Owen to the Ad Building — COULEE JOB UNPASSABLE UP — would do the rest. The A-1 Beauty Shop could be advertised for sale, and Charlene could come back by train long enough to handle that whenever there was a taker.

So, truant from the world, they aimed themselves west toward the Rockies, swapping at the wheel of the Chevy every hour or so as the railroad towns of the High Line gazetteered away behind them, MALTA HARLEM ZURICH HAVRE KREMLIN, and the mountains slowly defined into crag and timberface and snowfield in front of them. Through Glacier National Park, the cliff-clinging curlicues of Going to the

419

Sun highway kept Owen grinning at the ways the engineers had managed to graft the road onto the mountains, Charlene enjoying watching him at it. The night in Spokane, they made love in an auto court, feeling fantastically free to create all the rumpus they could, what with only vehicles in garage stalls on either side of their room. After sleeping in and a leisurely late start, at last they were on the plunge of the road to the Columbia River, dark with afternoon shadow. In a mile-wide gorge, amid the slate color of the riverwater, the dam at Grand Coulee was rising like a scaffolded cliff. Grand Coulee's construction town appeared to be a diluted Wheeler, but Charlene was determined to think the best of it.

The next morning Ev Everett sneaked a job button and an inspector's hard hat for Owen, and with them on he could prowl the huge project of concrete. He knew Grand Coulee Dam in theory, but a look around said it more strongly. Canyonwork, this was; the ends of the dam anchored into cliffs, granite bedrock at its base. The organizational lines were altogether different from Fort Peck, too; this was a Bureau of Reclamation dam, no puffed-up Kansas City colonels, majors, or captains. While Owen inspected Grand Coulee, Charlene visited two years' worth with Connie Everett, and learned to her delight that other Bozeman couples she and Owen had lost track of, the Lowells and the Krebses, were here on this dam, too. The men came home for lunch, then Owen went off with Ev to be introduced around the Grand Coulee version of the Ad Building. Conversations there confirmed what Owen mostly had heard already, that the Columbia was on its way to becoming one massive generating device, an entire sequence of dynamo-feeding dams that could be regulated with a few flicks of a few switches. The feed of power, he was shown on charts, was potentially colossal, from the little reddened coils of toasters on a million breakfast tables on up to the new potline method of cooking up giant amounts of the light metal called aluminum. *Of time and the electric river, huh,* ran his thoughts. *Well, maybe it is time. Hook up an entire river drainage and see what it can be made to do, maybe it is time to get in on that.*

When the men returned after work, Connie and Charlene cooked rib eye steaks for supper and afterward the two couples drank beer. Close to the end of the second bottle apiece, Ev reiterated that he was positive there would be no problem in getting Owen hired on. A little dreamy with the beer, Charlene was watching out the living room window at the nighttime lattice of lights on Grand Coulee Dam, as if even the swing shift crew was helping to dim away Fort Peck. And then Owen was saying:

"We're going back, first thing in the morning."

The two of them lay on the Everetts' fold-out davenport, Owen catching sleep in those chainlink naps of his while Charlene was stretched beside him stiff as a post, waiting and waiting for the night to be over. She wasn't going to fight in whispers.

Nor did her stormiest tones make any difference on Owen, the next morning when they went out to the car.

"They've got this dam knocked," he told her. "They'll be at it for years yet, but they've already reached the point where they can build it like they're reading off a grocery list. And that's — that doesn't feel like it fits, for me. I feel like I'd be throwing away Fort Peck."

Well, yes; Charlene had thought that was the whole point.

"Can't blame you for getting worked up over this." He himself was considerably that way, she saw. "But we came and took a look, and Charlene, damned if I could see myself just stacking concrete on top of concrete. I know coming here got your hopes up. It did mine, too. But huh uh. I stood around here listening to these juice jockeys talk about how they're going to be able to electric-up your zipper of your pants, if that's what you want, and all I could think about was how many of those watts it would take to cure the pump lag in my poor sonofabitching overworked dredges."

Facing around from the steering wheel to her as he was, the set of his mouth told her as much as his words; the quizzical underline he had brought to Grand Coulee was gone.

"I know it's tough," he said to her. "But let's go home."

Neil came humming home late for supper because of delivering coal, and Rosellen didn't care, and when he kissed her she knew his nose would leave a coaldust smudge on her, and she didn't care about that either. He headed to the washbasin to clean up and she had intended to let him get done with that and sit down for supper, but she couldn't hold it any longer.

"I sold some writing."

"You didn't." He spun to her, his expression lighting up. "You did? Wahoo! Which — how much —"

"To the *Grit* paper."

"Uh huh!" He was eagerly toweling coaly water and wettened dust off himself. "So let's have a look at it."

She handed him *The Weekly Grit*, full of pithy tales and kernels of wit, with her thumb next to a line in the "Oh, Say!" column.

Neil read out loud:

"The wind, dancing in a dust dress."

"Uhm?" He peeked inquiringly at her, shaking the pages of *Grit* as if more ought to fall out.

"That's — what they took, from my 'Dry Land' story. But they paid twenty-five cents a word."

"That beats the pants off hammer wages," Neil rallied loyally. "Rosellen, this is just great. Gives you your start. Grab your coat and let's go tell everybody. Bruce and Kate first, then —"

"No, wait. Not yet. They'll think I'm . . . putting myself too high. It's, well, it is only seven words, Neil."

"What the hell about that, though? Old Shakespeare must have started with seven, sometime or another." He watched her expression, which was an odd confessional smile amid firm shaking of her head. "What, you need this writing to be a secret?" he puzzled it out.

"For now." Rosellen went to him. "You

know about it. For me, that's everybody."

"Airplane ride, Jackie! RRR RRR ZOOOM RR RREAUGH!" The baby laughed down from where Bruce's hands were holding him aloft. "Doesn't he have a smile on him like a million dollars, Katy?"

"He's a honey," she agreed over her shoulder, still trying to pack their things and Jackie's to go to Bismarck, the car nowhere near ready.

"So are you, Katycat, you know that? You really goddamn are."

"And you're a windjammer."

Thanksgiving supper at the cookhouse, Hugh showed up when the rest of the eaters were starting on their second helpings. Thoroughly Hugh-style, Meg thought, dispatching herself across the kitchen to the serving window to tell him so.

But he shook his head when she started to dish up turkey and fixings for him. "I'll wait and lift a fork with you, if you please, Margaret."

After the dining hall had emptied out and the servers shed their cranberry- and gravy-wounded aprons and one lone morose pearldiver was beginning to scrub away at sink load after sink load of dishware and cutlery, Meg's head appeared in the serving window again. *She does still*

look like the top of the line with that hair,
Hugh noted to himself one more time. She
called over to him, "If you still want a
witness to that eating habit of yours, come
take a plate."

He went up for the laden plate, Meg now
busy dishing her own. In through the
serving window, he could see Jaarala over
by the stove, stirring this and shaking
that. Hugh hesitated, then spoke out:

"Care to join us?"

"No, gonna eat off the stove. There's
always cookin' needs watchin'," came the
response. But then Jaarala more or less
looked at Hugh, and fleetingly even toward
Meg. "Thanks anyhow."

Meg and Hugh ate, across from each
other at one of the long tables that seated
forty-eight. Bruce and Kate were spending
the holiday at her parents' in North Dakota, to show off the baby. Neil was working a shift of overtime, since so many
others of the dam force were off for the
day, and Rosellen said she had something
she needed to finish up at home. As to
Darius, in circumstances such as this Meg
was apt to mention him only in cautious
general terms and Hugh to speak of him
not at all. They did have the food to be
comfortable with, turkey a la Jaarala
roasted to a moist succulence and smooth
mashed potatoes and heavenly gravy and

426

cranberry relish with tiny taste nuggets of orange peel and corn pudding an ecstatic taste of which would put you to wondering with Hugh:

"What does old Cookalorum in there" — he nodded in the direction of Jaarala — "do to this?"

"Don't I wish I could figure that out," Meg said.

At pie, mincemeat that made the mouth water helplessly for more, it was her turn. "I was just thinking, what Owen said about Kate that once? That if Roosevelt his very self were to come into the Rondola, she'd wait on him as if he were anybody else until he was through and then tell him, 'Save your fork, President, there's pie.' "

"She would, too," Hugh agreed, with a slightest chuckle.

When they finished the feast, Meg got up and brought back fresh cups of coffee.

Hugh took a strong sip, looking off out the window at the dam lights haloed by the frost in the air.

"We'll soon have winter here again," he said.

"We will," she acknowledged guardedly.

She nursed her cup of coffee, wondering about the long nature of this marriage, while Hugh went into the other room of his mind.

427

He did not want to deal with his suspicion toward himself that had been building as he went to work on the dredgeline traps day after day, but it was growing inescapable. The furrowed path all the way from Inverley to the Missouri River homestead — had he been an impostor, all those years? Worse, a dabbler? A doubt such as this cut to a man's core, that's what it did. No reason it should, he kept insisting to himself. A drop of sweat, produced on hourly rate of pay, ought to be the same as any other drop of sweat, seasonally induced on a farm; but the sun-warm sweating done in a greening field surely somehow — *Christ on a slick raft, man,* Hugh told himself, *you'd better not start trying to sort out sweat.* Yet he found himself doing exactly that, these days. He was beginning to suspect that damwork was growing sinfully more comfortable to him than farming.

"A penny for them," Meg said, to try to draw him out of his well of silence.

Hugh shook his head. "They're worth positive millions." He looked across at her, a familiar look that said his thoughts would not make themselves known until later, if ever.

Hugh is otherwhere, though, isn't he pierced back to Meg from that pantry session with Darius. While she waited,

428

waited, waited. Sometimes she had the patience of an imbecile, she thought.

"It would help on the employment, I'm told," Darius stared at the houseboat ceiling and said, "if I were married."

How can they be such total bastards without even half-trying, Proxy asked herself although it was no longer even a question, *men. They swarm all over us and they want to play house on a houseboat with us and they tell us about every time they cut their finger with a jackknife when they were little boys, and then they slink off and marry some stupe who's still got her cherry. That tightfart sister-in-law of his must've found him somebody. Neaten up the famn damily by marrying him off to whoever-the-hell. Jee Zuz, I'm so sick of the way they behave. I could just pigstick —* everything furiously piling through Proxy all but blocked out the next from Darius:

"Do you suppose you could arrange to be there?"

Proxy stayed silent, the ceiling receiving a scouring stare from her. Finally she said:

"This is some kind of Scotch joke, right?"

"Isn't this just the way of the damnable world?" Darius asked the ceiling. "Here I am, ready to enter marital bliss at last, and my intended chooses now to turn back into a coy virgin."

Proxy raised on an elbow and looked down at him. "I hope I wouldn't have to go that far." She studied him like a skeptic buying wild honey in molasses country. "Are you serious? You're serious."

"I'm at least that bad. One stipulation, though." He reached up and grasped a handful of the short hair at the back of her neck. "If you've had any proposal before this one, don't tell me the comparison."

Proxy didn't say anything for a bit. Then: "Say we go get licensed. What am I supposed to do with myself then, weave brooms?"

"You can do much what you like. I need some leeway myself, now and again."

"The Bolshie business, you mean."

"Ah, well, some of that. Then too, I'm a bit long in the tooth to be thoroughly domesticated. Simply because we'd be married doesn't mean we need oversee each other every minute, does it?"

"I could stay on working for Tom? The dancing, I mean?"

"Assuredly."

"If I once in a while see a John D., maybe a little backseat driv— ?"

"Proxy, don't go down a list with me! There's such a thing as quitting while you're ahead, woman."

She moved over onto him. She licked a

tantalizing course along his collarbone to the base of his throat, tongued a humid kiss into the hollow there, brushed the effective tips of her breasts across the rise of his chest once, twice, and again, then lingered above him with a diagonal smile. "Since when?"

Part Four

THE SHERIFF

1991

Bastard of a case, that truck-in-the-river shenanigan had been. Long after he had lost office and everything else but age, the sheriff thought his way back and forth through it. Staring out the window of his room in the Milk River Senior Care Center, he would take moments from 1938 — that sight of the pair of bodies naked as Creation; or that clodhopper undersheriff, what was his name, mewing *"Married, you bet; only not to each other"* — and pull those pieces of time apart. Lay them out, conversations, expressions on faces, all the puzzlework of investigation, and sort them over. Try again to find his way into when he was just starting on the tricky process of figuring out what Duffs had done to Duffs.

"We can't account for what happened any

more than you can, Sheriff."

One of them, one of that damned family, had made that baldfaced claim to him back there at the outset.

"And don't think we haven't tried."

Huh, they hadn't seen trying until they saw Carl Kinnick.

Beyond his window, same as ever — samer, it somehow seemed to him anymore — Glasgow streeted off below the bare northside hill the Senior Care Center sat on. Daylight at least alleviated one of his aggravations, the rooftop sign at the east end of the old downtown. Up there on daddy longlegs supports, in the dark before dawn it was sometimes burned out to EL VELT and other times it blazoned in full pink HOTEL ROOSEVELT. Either way, that name poked at the sheriff like a neon pitchfork. He always waited until daybreak took care of that sign to do what he did now, employ the wooden coathanger he used for opening the window by fitting the hook over the handle of the stiff latch and giving a both-hands pull to unlock it, then shoving a wooden end of the hanger against a corner of the glass to push the window as open as it would go. Air the place out, let in what he could against the institutional stuffiness. Even bad weather improved this place. Actually this appeared to be a good enough day outside, although you never knew, even here in September, if the clouds were going to build in from the west and by one o'clock be storming hard enough to knock down a nun.

Glasgow looked weathered in a lot of ways.

Up and down was the history of towns like this, of course, but it had been a while now since up. Things had boomed when the SAC air base came in, north of town — B-52 runways the fattest construction payroll since Fort Peck Dam. Then when it seemed as though we weren't going to have to atomize the Soviet Union after all, the flyboys picked up and went. Empty base, bigger than the parade ground of Hell, just sitting there, weeding up. Concrete all over the prairie, while the dam holding back the Missouri was of dirt; it took a lot of government doing to get things that backward, the sheriff thought.

Grimacing, he slightly shifted position, there in his supposedly mobile confinement. He had been hating this wheelchair from the precise moment his fanny first met it.

"The two of them, out there that way — none of us knew anything like that was going on. Sheriff, we're a family who've always had our differences. But you never can expect something of this sort, can you.

It takes a lot now, for us to hold our heads up." How hard that Duff case had started off. And kept on being. He could still remember how his heart stopped a little, there on the boulder face of the dam, when he grasped the fact that the two drowned bodies in the truck were not a simple pairing. How he started, on the instant, trying to reconstruct the chain of events. The watchman heard the splash at such and such a time, then the lapse with the diver grappling down there in the dark, then the truck coming to the surface nose-first on the crane cable, water sheening from it. But the greater water, the river, shut off the scene of before that. Of what had drawn that truck to the bottom. The only sure thing he had then, in what had gone abruptly from a vehicular mishap to a full-fledged case of probable homicide, were unclad bodies — one of each, naturally — there in the truck cab. Intact-looking people, yet the spark gone from beneath the woman's crown of hair, and from behind the man's span of forehead. For his own benefit the sheriff had needed to study up some on forensic medicine in his job — the oldest dodo of a doctor always was appointed county coroner, and about half the time couldn't even be trusted on cause of death — and so he knew that each brain, under the bonecap

436

of each person's head, was shaped something like a low leafy tree, a canopy of cortex. Under that canopy rested the brain's constituent parts, rootlike. Looked at that way, the *person* was the family tree, in and of his or her self Carrying everything that had gone before, family-wise, back all the way to the dawns of history, there in that personal mental spread of tree. And for all that to just go, vanish — how people could let themselves be pruned out of life, through some weird situation they had put themselves into, was beyond Carl Kinnick. But then maybe that was why that man and that woman had ended up as victims, there in that sopping truck cab, and he as sheriff.

Ex-sheriff.

Xed out of the political picture in the '74 election. He'd done every kind of election-eering he could think of in his own county that year, then gone down to Billings for the Republican congressional candidate's last-gasp rally. This is what politics had come to, dragging yourself halfway across the state to try to get glimpsed on television along with a swarm of other tie-wearing stiff-smiling office-holders or would-be's. Back in 1952 the sheriff had managed to switch parties in good style, declaring himself an Eisenhower man and contending that he of course would have been proud to remain a Democrat if that party'd had the common sense to nominate Ike instead of that eggbrain Adlai; pretty shrewd alibi, if he did say so himself. But it cost him in '74. As he drove home from that Billings rally to Glasgow on election night, defeat drummed down on the Republicans, the car radio reporting the Democrats had obliterated the GOP congressional candidate, taken most of the state legislature, won across the board. Watergate and that creep Nixon; the sheriff drove north through the night listening to every detail of the national crapstorm cascading down on anything Republican, the moment at last arriving when the radio voice said *"Even long-time sheriffs are being turned out of office in the Democratic sweep. Up in Valley County, Walt Jepperson is leading the incumbent Carl Kinnick by nearly five hundred votes . . ."*

Half a thousand votes. Good Christ, in Valley County a losing margin like that was as bad as five hundred million. As if the population of China had swarmed to the polls and all voted to kill him off as sheriff. Abruptly the tall grass at the edge of the highway danced in his headlights, the car drifting toward the ditch while he was in the trance of that election result, and he'd had to sheer the steering wheel hard to keep the car on the road. Wouldn't that have been something pretty, too, giving the bastards a chance to say he couldn't take defeat and went and committed suicide.

A knock on his room door shunted aside that train of thought. Two quick raps, by knuckles that knew what they were doing. Flinching all the way, the sheriff wheeled himself around to face the door, then said merely, "What."

The nurse came in to check on the LP as the old sheriff was called by the staff.

When she'd started working here she assumed it meant Long-Playing, like an old phonograph record, because of Carl Kinnick's seemingly neverending longevity. Soon enough, though, she'd heard somebody refer to him as the Little Prick, and by then she understood. Just when you thought he couldn't possibly surpass his record for orneriness, he found some way to. The time when the recreation director Doris, new on the job then, planned a surprise birthday party — must have been the LP's eighty-fifth, ninetieth? who the hell could tell, or cared any — and gone to the trouble of digging around in the Valley County Museum to find a poster of Carl Kinnick running for election in the 1930s. Framed between his name on top and DEMOCRAT FOR SHERIFF underneath, pearl-gray Stetson tugged down in a businesslike way, he made quite the picture of a lawman, everybody thought. But he took one look at it and cussed out the recreation director unmercifully. It ended up with him shouting at Doris that if he ever wanted to be surprised, he'd let them know about it first.

Now Kinnick appraised the nurse's body as he did every time she came into his room, aware that she didn't like being looked over but also knowing he could get away with it. No sense being so old and crippled up if you couldn't at least run your eyes across an attractive young flank.

Shitheaded old poot, the nurse thought, but said:

"How's your hip today, Mr. Kinnick?"

"Hurts," he reported, the same flat way he did every day.

"You're supposed to exercise it more, you know that," she said as she did every day. She herself could not see why a hip replacement had been done in a person this ungodly old. For that matter, why this contrary little man had agreed to undergo the operation. But old age is some other kind of territory, people exist in it by their own lights, she always had to remind herself in this job. At least Kinnick didn't paw at her, the way the old grabber down

440

the hall in 119 always tried.

"So are you going to?" she asked.

"Going to what?"

"Exercise-your-new-hip-joint," she stipulated as levelly as she could.

To her surprise, Kinnick squinched up that dried-apple-doll face and seemed to think over the matter. But then he pronounced:

"Doubtful."

"Mr. Kinnick, you're a case in more ways than one," the nurse spoke in a sweet-sour tone which she knew couldn't land her in any trouble, and went out of his room.

He hated to see her go, as always. The little spots of time when she was in his room were the only sample of real woman he had, anymore.

Peyser.

Norman Peyser.

That was the overgrown undersheriff's name, it came back to him now, along with the guy's football-shaped face. Naturally the big lummox hadn't had a shred of a theory as to what happened in that truck at the dam and so he, the sheriff, had to do it all on the Duff case, from scratch. The undersheriff wordlessly in tow, Carl Kinnick traipsed the Fort Peck Project and its rickety towns from one end to the other — good God, one set of Duffs lived like badgers on a houseboat; what kind of

441

people were these? — as he tried to figure out that truck shenanigan. Go around and question them all. Work on them, make them account for every minute of their whereabouts that night of the drownings. Sort through the possible motives, although the Duffs were a bunch you could not easily nail down; every time you thought you had a motive clear, some new angle popped out from another Duff. And while he was working on them, plenty was going on amongst them, he could sense. Against him, against the world of justice he represented, they closed ranks. But he was as sure as anything that they were having some pitched fights, and there were obvious silences; the, what, eight of them surviving the drowned pair were trying to sort out what they had left, which even the sheriff could see amounted to one another, not the most comfortable sum after what had happened. Dealing with that family of Duffs, the sheriff for the first time in his life entertained the thought that maybe orphans did not have it so hard after all.

Well, what the hell can you do, though, when you come right down to the pussy-purr question of how people are going to behave.

Almost a dozen terms in office, and he still hadn't been able to predict with any real certainty. He had sheriffed as hard as he knew how, given his every day and far too much of his nights on behalf of law and order in Valley County, and in the end they threw him out just because he happened to be wearing the same political eartag as Tricky Dick Nixon. Sure, he knew that some were saying, even then, that Carl Kinnick was older than bunions and ought to be tossed onto the retirement heap. But didn't something like his perseverance on those Duffs, that truck, the river, go to show that he —

He moved wrong on the hip, and gasped with pain. God, how could his own body jab him so. He considered buzzing for the nurse, ask her to dig out a pain pill from the bottle in his top dresser drawer. But he detested pills, about as much as he despised asking for help.

Slowly he caught his breath and waited out the misery in his hip, taking a look around his room for the how manyeth time. This place. Not much to recommend it, life in here, but he was doing what he could with it. Meals, which everybody else in here tried to make a big deal, he merely went through with because he had to. Ate alone whenever he could, and purely silent if somebody ended up having to share a table with him. And only one good television night in the week, when he could watch *America's Most Wanted*, with the sound off. Give himself a chance to study the wanted-poster faces, and try to guess ahead in the crime reenactments the actors did.

Beyond those few things, getting by in here was a matter of maintaining his orneriness the way he did. By now he had a full theory of it: a philosophy of why to be difficult, if anybody ever took the trouble to ask him. All right, there were those who'd say he did not even need to work at being mean, it came as natural to him as a morning piss. But that radically underestimated the effort he was making, if they only knew. Huh uh, this was an entire new deal, the extent to which he made himself stay furious against the walled-in world. Everything else had shriveled up; his pecker no longer worked, his hip gave him constant torment, he sat here at the mercy of white uniforms twenty-four hours a day. (Yet people thought he was in a problem mood because he was lonely; the dumb bastards, they didn't even know he always had the Duffs.) So this was what he had arrived at, careful and constant exercise at staying stubborn. Crabby, contrary, owly, behaving like a mean little hyena: whatever term you care to call it by, he would tell you that the capacity for being ornery was the one power left to a person in old age.

Finally Carl Kinnick checked the calendar again, and this circled day. September 22nd again. That and the fancily printed 1991. Huh. The century had reached the point where it read the same forwards or backwards. He wouldn't be that way himself for another eight years yet, would he, at ninety-nine. There had been a spell of years when he hated aging, could not figure out why people shouldn't just conk out at some given point, like car batteries do the month after their warranty is up. During that time he half wished that he had not corrected his patrol car's veer toward the ditch that Watergate election night. But ending up as blood, gristle, and windshield shards didn't appeal, now that he could study back on that alternative. No, Carl Kinnick had got over wanting death's quick cure of everything. Traveling with the century wasn't easy, but so what.

Part Five

PLUGGING THE RIVER

1936–1937

It was the middle of February and the wind had been shoving at the north side of the house all of 1936 so far. This morning, the stillness woke Meg up. She burrowed out from under the six blankets heaped over her and Hugh, just far enough to raise her head and listen into the crystalline silence. The cold of the air pinched inside her nose.

"Hugh!" She turtled her head back under the load of covers and desperately nestled herself spoon-fashion against the length of him in his longhandle underwear. *"Hugh-it's-freezing!"*

Groggily he rumbled: "Margaret, it'd be news if it wasn't. We've had freezing weather since around October, for God's sake."

"I mean, in here! The fire's gone out!"

Hugh absorbed this. Then said in the tone of a man wronged: "Goddamn that soft coal."

He lurched from under the mound of bedding toward the stove and could tell at once this was not merely the feel of a fireless house, this was deep cold. He rattled open the firebox of the stove and swore at the dead ash of the coal he had banked the fire with at bedtime. Crumpling yesterday's entire *Glasgow Courier*, he stuffed it in the stove, grabbed up a double handful of kindling and chucked that on top of the paper, and, shivering hard now, made himself position dry sticks of wood atop it all so the flame would draw. He struck a match and lit the paper and hovered miserably until the kindling at last caught fire too. Then he lunged back to bed. Meg rewarded him with a clasp of warm arms. At that moment, the thermometer outside the Fort Peck Administration Building read 61 degrees below zero.

Bruce was goddamned if he was going to walk anywhere in this kind of weather. Before getting the stove going, he dumped the cold ashes in an empty lardpail, then used the kerosene can to sop them. In his cap and mackinaw, he ran out to the car, knelt in the snow, shoved the pail under the oilpan, leaned back as far as he could and tossed in a match. When he was reasonably sure the flaming kerosene was settling down enough not to burn up the car, he jumped back in the house to wait for the crankcase oil to thaw enough so he could start the engine and drive down to the winter harbor.

Owen was goddamned if he was going to fool around with a car in this kind of weather. He put on dress socks, then worksocks, then wool socks; piled on two pair of pants over long underwear, and a flannel shirt over his work one. He molded some newspaper into his overshoes for insulation, put them on, wrestled into the buffalo hunter coat he'd bought for just this eventuality, clapped his cap on with the earflaps down, bandannaed a scarf across his nose and mouth, stuck one of his office oxfords in each side pocket, pulled on thick mittens and walked to work at the winter harbor.

" '19, that was another cold bastard of a winter," Tom Harry reflected. Proxy had not been in the sin business long enough to have other big winters for comparison, so it seemed to be up to him to forecast the economic climate accompanying such cold. "On the one hand, this kind of weather, you'd think guys wouldn't have anything better to do than drink and diddle," he set out. "Hell, people even manage to do it up north in igloos, after all." He paused, then asked with a rare note of uncertainty: "Don't they?"

"How the frig do I know? This place" — Proxy indicated the frosted-over front windows of the empty Blue Eagle — "is the only igloo I've been in."

"I about went bust, though, there in '19," Tom Harry recounted. "Guys holed up, wouldn't come downtown just because it was a little cold. A lot like now, Shannon." He still called her that, even though she regularly pointed out that she had a married name now.

"Things are tough all over, Tom," she gave him with her mildest mocking smile. "Even the birds are walking."

"Shannon, what would you think about a buddy night at your end of things, maybe once a week — What're you looking at me like that for? The moviehouse does it every so often, has one guy pay and lets his buddy in free. Builds up the trade."

"Speaking for myself, I'll go take up choirwork before I ever let two guys have a poke for the price of one."

"Okay, okay, just an idea, all it was. Jesus Christ, though, you're getting awfully particular since you had your knot

450

tied." He gave her a sidelong look. "How is married life anyway?"

"Not half bad."

"Holy state of maddermoany." He shook his head. "I could never see it, myself."

"That's sure frigging astonishing to find out."

"Sarcasm never got anybody past St. Peter. Now come on, give me a hand with the thinking here."

"How would hot toddies go?"

"They wouldn't. The only time a Montanan will sip a toddy is when he's halfway to pneumonia."

"Rum, then?" Proxy began to take on a faraway look. "Did I ever tell you about my uncle who raised St. Bernard dogs and the time there was this coyote in heat and —"

"No, you didn't and you're not going to. This is a goddamned business meeting, Shannon. Besides, where the hell would I get rum? Half the time I can't even get the Great Falls beer trucks to come up here, the way the roads've been." He shook his head. "You call that thinking?"

"O-*kay*, Tom," Proxy intoned, "you show me what real thinking is."

Tom Harry passed a hand over his face, turned around, dusted off his cash register, turned around toward Proxy again, and studied off into the empty barroom and dance floor. Finally he said:

"I don't think it looks good, until spring."

"So should we close up shop?"

"Hell, no." He looked as if she had insulted him down to his shorts. "What kind of a way is that to run a saloon?"

Back at the onset of winter, in the courthouse at Glasgow, Proxy had needed to think madly to recall "Susannah" as the given name she'd furnished Darius and then she had to give him a dig with her elbow when he started to fill in "Renfrewshire" as county of residence instead of "Valley," but they managed to do the deed, nuptially.

"What now?" she asked him a little nervously when the Justice of the Peace was through with them. "Give each other a bath in a washtub of champagne?"

He looked surprised. "We get the family over with, of course. Then we settle in like old dozing spaniels." He pulled her to him and there on the Justice of the Peace's front porch gave her a kiss that she felt to her ankles. "Don't you know thing one about married life, woman?"

But the jitters caught up with Darius as soon as groom and bride began making the rounds. Inches inside the doorway at Owen and Charlene's, an exceedingly thin grin plastered on him, he introduced Proxy. "I've gone and got you an aunt.

452

Please may I present Proxy, ah, *Duff* she would be now, wouldn't she."

"Uh huh," issued out of Owen as he gave that night's first blink of recognition. *Jesus, that one.* Perfectly vivid in memory was the evening Proxy flattened the red-headed taxi dancer. "Well. Congratulations. Come in. Uh, sit down."

"Yes, do," said Charlene, all interested. *Here you go, Owen. You wanted Fort Peck, here's a case of it in the family for you.* She looked Darius in the eye and then Floozy, no, Proxy it was, wasn't it. "You've got to get over being bashful newlyweds sometime."

"No, no, we're not staying," Darius interjected. "We merely called by to enlighten you."

Proxy studied Charlene. "I've seen you."

The altitude of Charlene's eyebrows said it was mutual. "I operate the A-1," she responded. She studied Proxy's bottle-blonde hair. "If you're ever in need."

"Anything off for family members?"

"Proxy, love," said Darius, "we've to —"

"Sit down," said Owen again, "take a load off, why don't —"

"I wouldn't think discounts are a good idea," Charlene said cheerily, "in any business."

Proxy laughed, and her smile began to skew treacherously. "Dancing the dimes

453

out of joes doesn't leave much room for bargaining, you're right, but —"

"Really, we've to be going," Darius hastily stepped in. "Calling in on Bruce and Kate next," he explained, as if it were a continental journey. Capturing Proxy by an elbow, he steered for the door.

"Hey, wait."

Darius and Proxy turned around at something in Owen's blurt.

What the hell do I know about a combination like this, or you either, Charlene, hmm? A bareheaded decision about how we act, that's all that's up to us. Darius and a wifey who could kick the giblets out of Joe Louis, that's his problem.

"How about if we come along?" Owen said, Charlene beside him nodding keen agreement. "Make it more of a family shindig, that way."

By the time Bruce and Kate and the baby snowballed into the procession and the whole bunch of them reached Neil and Rosellen's, they were too many for the Packard that Proxy had borrowed from Tom Harry, but Neil and Bruce charged out into the night to rig up the truck so they could all ride in that. They crowded and kidded, and their every sound carried on the cold night air to Wheeler neighborhoods half a mile away. It having been unanimously voiced that brides and mothers with small children rated the cab of the truck, Proxy scooched in next to Neil then Kate next to her with Jackie in a bundle. *Jee Zuz! A papoose, too, even.* Proxy always figured she had her work cut out for her in trying to be sociable with women who weren't in the trade; but at least the Charlene one could dish it out, and the other two didn't seem any slouches either. The men she had noticed separately around town before, but seeing them in one bunch tonight made her realize they were all Darius's basic Duff frame of rake handles and doorknobs. And if Darius was a fair sample, they had the stamina of wolfhounds.

Now banging broke out on the roof of the truck cab, along with urgings to Neil to tromp on the gas and at least give the frost a run for its money. Charlene and Rosellen and Darius and Owen and Bruce, in caps, coats and blankets close to mummification, stood up behind the cab and held on to the boxboards, giddy with the purified air of the winter night and the colder glitter of starshine overhead. Every one of them knew that in chasing off on this makeshift shivaree they were showing about as much sense as a pan of gooseberries, but was it their fault if nonsense was suddenly contagious?

They piled out at Meg and Hugh's house,

calling mock warnings ahead that they had lovebirds out here.

Hugh took the announcement with a prudent if not successfully deadpan expression, Meg took it like a pin under the skin. What was to be done, though, with the entire family grinning in the doorway?

"Come — come in. Sit yourselves. Kate, Jackie can be tucked in our bed. Hugh, take their coats while I —" The production of coffee began. Hugh insisted they all move on into the Blue Room. Gamely confronting the blueprint decor, Proxy declared it real interesting, it somehow reminded her of a place she once worked in that had mirrors everywh— Darius asked if the coffee was ready yet. Speaking of ready, Hugh tossed back at him, Darius had taken a scandalous length of time to gird himself up for matrimony, had he not? Sounding as valiant as he could, Darius maintained that he had been converted overnight by the example of the other husbands in this room attaining such magnificent mates. *Tell us, Jealous!* one of the men chimed above the general acclamation, he thought it might have been Owen. Just then Rosellen, clued in by swift whispers from Charlene on the way over in the truck, wanted to know from Proxy how she ever got into taxi dancing. Oh, Proxy generalized, from pretty early in life she had been on her own. *On her back is more like it,* Charlene thought and smothered a giggle. Owen, his arm around her, gave her a complicit hug; for his part, he was looking ahead with fascination to the mixed tints of Red and peroxide. Neil was pondering the avarice of love, how it was capable of snatching the socks off anybody at any time. Bruce for once was tongue-tied; to him Darius was old as the hills, but here he was, fixed up with the kind of woman who could do it to a guy until his eyes popped. Kate meanwhile was wondering what the various ways were that Darius and Proxy reached mad pash, as much practice as they'd probably both had; Bruce in bed pretty much had one gear — true, it was high gear — and so a person could not entirely help wondering, could she, how others went about matters. She thought to herself, *I wonder if Rosellen knows what I'm thinking . . .*

"And here I thought you were a confirmed bachelor," Meg said in lowest tone to Darius when he happened to drift over next to her while the others were carrying on.

"I thought that too, Meg. We were both off."

Proxy was making sure to watch, with quick little angled glances, as Darius and Meg traded something else too low to hear, and then Darius conspicuously rejoined the general ruckus. *So that's where that stood; behind bottled brother Hugh's back. Darius, you're quite the family man. But you didn't get very far with her, did you, or you wouldn't have thrown in with me. Serves you right; that drypuss sis-in-law there looks to me like a lost cause from the first.*

Hugh was watching his brother with something like vexed admiration. Darius had always been the kind who'd send one present to cover three boys and could get away with it; the same way that steam engine toy sailed in from the Clydeside, here courtesy of Darius Devilment Duff was the latest plaything from the Blue Eagle, tossed in the family face. *Owen, there with your instruction-manual look on you: it runs on peroxide, doesn't it, this one. Quite the device, really. What's that wife joke — "You screw it on the bed and it makes mince of you," eh, Darius? Of course it may depend on how easy you are to mince.*

For once Darius was hoping Hugh could see under the surface of him. *As of today, Hugh, the old question is over. We are quits, in the matter of Meg. I cede and concede. When I uttered "I take thee, Susannah," we each gained a wife. Man, will you not credit that?*

"Least we can do is give her a chance," Bruce said after they were home.

"She looks like she knows what to do with a chance when she gets one," Kate said.

"Huh!" was all Neil said, afterward.

"I guess!" said Rosellen.

"That look on your mother! I thought she was going to give up the ghost, right there!" Charlene said the instant they were home. She yawned and added: "I don't know, I kind of got a kick out of Mrs. Darius Duff."

Owen, busy mulling everything, said nothing.

February's glacier of cold air slid down from the north until it covered Montana from corner to corner, then stood there for two solid weeks.

Her fingers waiting at attention on the keys, Rosellen read that over. Owen had given her a funny look when she poked her head into his cubbyhole and asked how a glacier behaved. But he reeled off enough of an answer that she could give the next part a whirl:

Temperature readings were its cutting edges, red stubs of mercury in the bottoms of thermometers across six hundred miles, saying —

Pushing with her toes, she scooted to the window in her typing chair, its rollers raucous in the noonhour-empty office, peeked out at the king-size Ad Building thermometer, then trundled speedily back.

— repetitiously 35 degrees below zero at noon, 38 degrees below zero at dusk, 45 degrees below zero in the night.

With a slight frown she looked that over, yanked open her desk drawer and thumbed through the used edition of SAY IT WITH SYNONYMS that Neil had given her for Christmas. Fingers at the ready again, concentrated on the keys, then kersplickety, taking out *repetitiously* with an overstitch of *xxxxxxxxxxxx* and tapping above it the substitute *monotonously.*

People tottered with the cold when they had to be out in it.

Herself, to name one. Merely to come to work, a person had to load on so many clothes she felt like she was traveling in a closet.

Fort Peck's around-the-clock moviehouse gained new patrons, workmen bundled with everything they could get on, clumping in to stand behind the back row until they thawed out enough to trudge off on their errands again.

Neil. Shivering in, for each day's hyp-notic five or ten minutes of gray-and-white newsreel. (What's this Hitler? How does a place like Spain get by with everybody fighting everybody?)

A diesel boredom —

She backspaced and put the *x* key back to work.

A diesel monotony broke the silence of the frigid spell and simultaneously made Fort Peck go even more groggy — the engines of the bulldozers were never shut down in weather this cold, merely throttled onto idling all night long.

Kate swore that the most effective lullaby on both Bruce and the baby was a Cater-pillar D-8.

Mealtimes at the cookhouse, the air went stale with cigarette smoke and

461

the accumulated pack of not recently bathed bodies —

Meg swore she was going to don Bruce's diving suit for her job, if winter and odor didn't let up soon.

— but then the instant you stepped outside, the air's keenness would all but take the lungs out of you.

As if reminded, Rosellen stilled the machine-gun chatter of her typing, threw her shoulders back and took a seismic breath. Here it was, keys and brainstorms going together at last. If Owen sat in there sopping up everything about the dam and glaciers and whatever else came his way, if Proxy was an obvious whiz at the, hnn, tricks of her trade, if Darius knew how the *Queen Mary* was put together, if Neil recognized every rattle in the truck, she was just as much on top of her vocation today. Drunk on writing, she couldn't believe the clock telling her that lunch hour was nearly over and she was about to have to go back to manufacturing paychecks. She hit the carriage return with ecstatic force, there were enough minutes left if she kept slamming away at the words on the paper.

So, in the shacks of Wheeler, the shanties of Park Grove and McCone City and New Deal, the sod huts of Free Deal, the tidy but not overly warm houses of the Corps townsite —

Charlene, the poor abused thing, claimed you could get frostbite from the nailheads in their walls.

— the houseboats along the wintered-over river —

Darius scraping a peekhole in the iced window of the houseboat so that he could look out at more ice.

— the parlors of the Happy Hollow brothels and the saloon precincts of taxi dancers —

Proxy. Woohoohoo. Talk about a family addition.

— in beaverboard kitchens and drafty living rooms, Fort Peck's people fed fires and hunkered in to wait out the record winter of 1936, the year they had all been looking for.

He rattled when he coughed, and he was coughing a lot.

Never one to let a little thing like a bad cold get him down, Hugh rode out the spasm, cleared his throat and blew his nose, sucked in as much breath as he could, and, glad that the weekend was nearly here, put his mittened hands to the wheelbarrow's handles again.

Here at the mouth of the tunnel the river would one day siphon into, along with the three other huge boreholes through the base of the dam, outcroppings of crumbly weathered shale still were being shaved down with rocksaws. The men who had been assigned onto the barrow crew for the winter merely had to trundle the saw-cuttings to the conveyor, which —

To his surprise, all at once his wheelbar-row was on its side, and he was on his, too. His head, light as a balloon, seemed to be somewhere above his fallen body, watching, taking note of the confusion, the scream of the rocksaw suddenly shut down and the rest of the crew shouting for help. He went in and out of conscious-ness, and in the moments of light-headed clarity he felt quite offended. Technically speaking, he was not even in the tunnel, where pneumonia bred.

Over the weekend, Hugh Duff grew old.
Owen saw it immediately in the white whiskers salted among his father's stub-

ble, when he and Charlene stopped by the hospital again before work on Monday morning; his father had always been an immaculate shaver. Recuperation, this was supposed to be, the oxygen tent having done its part, Hugh's lungs clearing and his breathing better, but the grizzled figure in the hospital sheets had a long way to go yet to reconstitute into anything like Hugh Duff.

"How the hell are you?" Owen let out before realizing it was not the best sickroom hello.

"Pretty well done in, if you want the truth."

"Yeah, well, it'll take a little time for you to mend," Owen said uneasily. He cut a quick glance to Charlene, wishing she would pitch in; women were better at this convalescent kind of talk, weren't they? When she simply kept on the automatic smile you send someone you don't like but have to have sympathy for, Owen had to do the next part, too: "How long are they going to keep you here?"

"Don't know yet." Hugh went into a coughing fit that was hard to watch. Then his chest heaved a few times, and he was having to breathe with his mouth. "Until I can whistle opera, I suppose."

"We ought to at least get you a shave," Owen said in a bothered tone.

"Your mother says she'll tend to that," Hugh coughed out, then shifted in the hospital bed, twirling his finger to indicate he wanted it cranked up some. When Owen brought him up to a semi-sitting position, the heaving lessened and he managed to finish: "It's her best chance to scrape me and see any real result." He brought a hand up to his face and paused it there, as if surprised at the seriousness of the bristles. He scratched his whiskery neck while he considered his visitors again. "How's the Charlene?"

"I'm getting by, Hugh," Charlene produced. Dressed for business, hair done in exemplary fashion for her day's customers, she looked slick as a racehorse. "Where is Meg anyway? We figured sure she'd be —"

"She went off to the cookhouse to smuggle me a real breakfast. The food in here is a threat to one's health."

"Jaarala's grub is bound to help, yeah," Owen laughed. "Anything else we can bring you? Name it."

"Years off my life, Ownie, would be all. I swear to Christ, this time last Friday I was your age." Hugh's voice was reedy, but reporting to its pulpit. "I don't know whether it's me or —" he grimaced at the hospital window to indicate outside, all of Fort Peck. "But I went through winters on the place that would frost the tallywhacker off a brass monkey — sorry about the language, Charlene — and never came down with anything like this."

"Dad" — Owen was exasperated without quite knowing why — "this is the worst sonofabitch of a winter any of us have ever seen. If it's any consolation, that's what it took to get you down."

"One more record, eh, Ownie?"

"I have to run." Charlene's words were meant for Hugh, but she was looking toward Owen. "It's almost opening time. Don't do anything in here I wouldn't do, Hugh."

Charlene had barely gone when Owen checked his watch. "I'm going to have to clear out of here pretty quick, too."

Weak though he was, Hugh jumped all over that. Owen didn't like being around sick people, did he. Well, Hugh didn't either, particularly when he was one of them. "Christ in his nighty Owen, stay until your mother gets back, can't you at least?"

"Sure." Owen watched him in some alarm until Hugh's breathing calmed down, then went over to the window. He was surprised at how hard it was to discern the dam from here. In fresh snow camouflage, the plateau of fill nearly blended with the bluffs of the valley, chalk-ings of outline against the greater gray of sky. Blots of gravel showed through on the dam in a few places, and the frozen crater lake that was the core pool could be picked out if you knew where it was, but the prairie's flat winter light didn't give much of a sense of scale. Owen turned away, moved restlessly around the hospital room. "You having plenty of company?"

"Everybody, yes. Except your uncle and esteemed aunt. No, that's not quite the case. They must have been here while I was asleep. Darius left me some high-toned reading."

Braced for Marx, Engels, Sorel, or THE LITTLE RED SONGBOOK, Owen picked up the slim olive volume from the bedside stand. William Blake. POEMS AND ILLUMINATIONS.

" 'Tiger, tiger, burning bright,' " Hugh rasped, "isn't he the one?"

"Yeah, other stuff too," Owen answered slowly, holding open the pages marked by a slip of paper. "This, ah, your place marked here?"

And did the Countenance Divine
Shine forth upon our clouded hills?
And was Jerusalem builded here
Among these dark Satanic mills?

Bring me my bow of burning gold!

Bring me my arrows of desire!
Bring me my spear! O clouds, unfold!
Bring me my chariot of fire!

I will not cease from Mental Fight,
Nor shall my Sword sleep in my hand,
Till we have built Jerusalem,
in England's green & pleasant Land.

"No, Darius must've left that in." Hugh seemed to go deep into thought. "Darius has never given me so much as a whit before. I must really be a goner."

"You're not any kind of a goner, damn it," Owen slapped the book shut, "you're going to be up and around and ornerier than ever in no time now. Then you're supposed to take it easy for a while, is all. Make you a deal, along that line. How'd you like a new job come spring? I'll get you on as a watchman. Give you a chance to build yourself back up and —"

"No."

That first word was more than audible, but Owen thought he heard wrong on the rest of Hugh's answer. It had sounded as if his father wheezed out:

"I quite like poking traps."

Hugh, do you know there are times when this is the way I most love you? Absent.

469

Meg attacked the chores the instant she got home from the hospital each evening, woodbox–coal scuttle–waterbucket, windowshades drawn down even though they waved discouragingly in the drafts around the window casings, a rag rug flung against the bottom of the breezy door for all the good that would do, too. Hugh's regular hand at the shack, she did miss. *But not your main habit. The drift that starts in you, so that you begin to be not yourself even before you're off onto one of your jags and then draging yourself home looking like death warmed over. Absent entirely is preferable to that, Hugh, and although I hate to speak ill of the ill, I am relieved when this skimmed version of you in the hospital is out of my sight, too.* The water in the kitchen stove reservoir was warm enough, barely, to wash herself up a bit before going to bed. *I remember, in one of our fights about leaving the homestead, or perhaps it was English Creek or even Inverley, you told me I could dampen spirits at a funeral. Maybe I am not much good at mending the world. My father did think he was a tailor of souls — what can a reverend think if not that? — but in the end he could not even fashion mine, a stroppy young kissing fool named Hugh Duff did that for me.* She undressed there in the kitchen by the stove and shimmied her flannel nightgown on as fast as she could, then raced for the bed. *But Hugh, what I mean about love for you in absentia is that the hard parts of us do not rub together then. In memory or for that matter anticipation we cushion each other to ourselves, or at least I do you. Of course, under these covers — when there's not such a mountain of them, anyway — we manage it, too. You tell me I am sweet to the bone, here, and I in all honesty can say the same for you. But elsewhere — otherwhere — the veers you make . . . What is there about the Duff squad of manhood? You with a will to drink the world dry, while Darius falls for a dyed mopsy at the drop of an eyelash. "Don't be so high and mighty, Meggie," he said to me on their shivaree night. That was uncalled-for. I do wish now though, that I had not told him back, "Better that than the other — low and insipid." You see, Hugh, there have been times when Darius seems to fasten in where you curve away from me, when Darius and I . . .* That avenue was gone now. Or was it. A man's term with that Proxy was normally a matter of minutes, not a lifetime of marriage. *So, Hugh, I hate your habit of risk. But I perhaps grasp it better than you think . . .* Meg, curled in the middle of the bed, sank into the chilly sleep of the alone.

471

* * *

When the weather moderated — it had no other way to go — and the temperature at last was up around zero, the dam crews picked up at their usual schedules, except in special cases.

"We do what?" Bruce asked incredulously at the winter harbor. "What the hell for?"

"You're putting us at what?" Darius asked at the same moment in the boatyard. "Whose bright notion is this?"

"What the dickens can I tell you?" the foreman answered, so swaddled it could have been either Taine or Medwick, and gave a not-my-doing shrug. "You guys have been detailed off to this, until spring gets here. You're icemen now."

"Take a seat, Duff." First names did not come naturally to Major Santee.

Owen sat and watched the major frown at his memorandum. *He wouldn't know a good idea if it came along and bit him in the butt.* This was the Friday before ice became the new career of Darius and Bruce, and Owen's idea had not yet made its way through the channels of the Corps. God only knew, he thought, how furrowed up the major would be if the memo called this ice plan what it actually was, the Murgatroyd process.

It had come to Owen while he was passing the first morning of March by staring alternately at the white river and the mostly white calendar leaf, equally unyielding. Now a mere six weeks until dredging was supposed to start, and there lay the river under a lid of ice thicker than a railroad bed. In Owen's most pessimistic moments he figured this big winter's armor of ice would be off by about Labor Day, and in his optimistic ones he thought it might only take until the Fourth of July. In any case, an April 15th startup of dredging gave every indication of being a long way out of the picture. *So, okay, if the Archangel Murgatroyd right this minute came along and asked what you most wanted done, it would have to be to melt that sonofabitching ice off the dredging areas, wouldn't it. Murg, my friend, that would do nicely, get the damn stuff out of my way by the fifteenth day of Ap—*

Owen sat up then. Huh uh. No. Christ no, melt didn't really matter. Just *get* the SOBing ice off, so the dredging material would have time to soften up and the dredges would have a clear channel to move in. The right kind of crew, of ice cutters and haulers, could do that.

"You've already been to the colonel, I suppose?" Major Santee said now, wafting the one-page memo up and down a little as if trying to guess its weight.

"Unofficially," Owen said carefully about having gone over the major's head, and with even more care: "He's made it known the dredging schedule counts for quite a lot with him."

Santee passed his frown over Owen and on out to the Missouri. "There's a world of ice on that river. How do you expect to cut enough of it to make any difference?"

Owen did not smile, didn't even grin, but nonetheless his expression was that of someone fortified by all the aces in the deck.

"I've been talking some to Sangster about that. Seems to us, we ought to just use the buzzsaw process."

The contraption resembled a mammoth nasty insect. A long low chassis, two wheels at the back beneath an engine out of a Fordson tractor, and at the front where the stinger would be, a three-foot-diameter buzzsaw blade. Ungainly and makeshift, when the thing was started up it blared like a captive motorcycle and when the whirling sawblade met the ice there was a ceaseless ear-reaming whine, and as Sangster and Owen had guessed, it could cut ice like nobody's business.

Bruce, for one, was unimpressed. "I still don't savvy what good this is gonna do," he maintained, obviously reluctant to put his effort into either savvying or ice hauling.

Darius did see the principle of the job he and Bruce and several dozen others were about to be put to, clustered out here on the river like Dutchmen who'd forgotten their skates. But that did not make the task any less dismaying to him, either. Wrestling blocks of ice from the stiffened river was going to be cold heavy work.

"Aw, Walt," Bruce tried on Jepperson, their new foreman, "we probably can't even haul ice out as fast as the river'll make more."

"One way to find out," Walt Jepperson told him, telling them all.

They sawed the ice out in slabs as big as steamer trunks, then grappled a sling around one end of the slab, then signalled to the operator of a windlass which slid each ice block up a long ramp onto the riverbank, where a stacking crew built a careful pile of them. You'd have thought ice was the latest in construction material.

"Duff, you be the rigging slinger," Jepperson had assigned to Bruce. "Other Duff, you might as well help him out with that," he told Darius, perhaps moved by how miserable the older Scotchman looked while standing around between the transit of slabs.

The two of them took turns trudging back from the ramp with the sling and tow rope. Darius steadily tromped around in a circle to keep from freezing while waiting his turn with the rigging. As Bruce approached with the sling over his shoulder and the length of rope snaking behind him on the ice, Darius thought out loud:

"Have a guess as to what I'd rather be doing."

Bruce did not always fathom this uncle, but he figured he had a pretty good chance on this. "Warming your toes on Proxy's tummy."

Darius quit stomping and peered at Bruce. Then he downright giggled. "Toes!" The rest of the day, every so often he would hoot, "Toes!"

The river found one last way to give the Fort Peck winterers a bad time.

Darius and Bruce had been watching the situation build, out in the main current downstream from their ice pond, and wondered. Owen had been eyeballing the middle of the river the past week and didn't even need to wonder, he knew too well what this was adding up to out there. Huge chunks of ice were mounting and mounting, a jagged barricade clogging the flow of the Missouri.

"Just what we always wanted, a dam out

ahead of the dam," ran the sarcastic re-action around the Ad Building. Came the day when the Corps officers trooped up onto the bluff to have a look, their over-shoes buckled firmly so that their pants bloused out like jodhpurs and their breath making an echelon of little clouds. The eight men of the civilian engineering staff formed a motley covey around them. A little off to one side stood the colonel's silent, ever-present driver. As usual Owen took a ribbing about his buffalo coat, and as usual he was the only one of them complacently warm as they stood around in the snow.

Colonel Parmenter studied the ice jam with distaste and addressed them com-positely:

"We weren't thrown off schedule by the other ice jams, the other winters. What's the worst this one could do?"

An alarming number of the civvie engi-neers had versions to offer. Nevins from the tunnel project lost no time predicting some washout, he couldn't specify how much or how little, along the diversion channel banks if the ice jam caused real flooding. Owen pounced in to point out the possibility of delay in the dredging startup, after they'd spent a month's worth of effort in clearing out ice to avoid precisely that. A couple of others had their dire say. Then Sangster, not wearing his glasses because the nosepieces hurt his nose in the cold, squinted and formulated:

"How about, it'll take out the truss bridge."

Fourteen trained minds simultaneously calculated what a sheer mess that would be. If the railroad truss bridge went, swept away by ice floes on the rampage, the dam construction would be stopped in its tracks for nobody knew how long, the diversion tunnels would be stopped, the spillway would be stopped. Everything they could think of would be stopped except the instructional chalk in engineering classes which would be studying this fiasco for the next hundred years.

Everyone on the bluff knew what Colonel Parmenter was going to say before he finally puffed out an exasperated plume of breath and ordered:

"Blow the bugger."

Bruce never after was sure how J.L. Hill roped him into the job of dynamiting the ice jam.

It *seemed* to happen in as purely simple a fashion as J.L.'s neighborly stroll over to him there on the ice-cutting pond and borrowing him like a cup of sugar. "Kind of like to have somebody along who knows the river," Bruce was suddenly hearing out of J.L., "and you've been on both the top and bottom of it."

"Yeah, but —"

"Danamite," as J.L. said it, "is best to handle when it's cold." He looked at Bruce as if that should take care of all worries.

Stunned, Bruce tried surreptitiously to check J.L.'s mittened hands, see if he still had the trembling. Tunnel pneumonia had been only the half of it, that time last fall when J.L. was hospitalized; from what Bruce had heard, something on the packing paper of dynamite boxes had given J.L. Hill a shaking affliction. "I thought you still weren't feeling any too good."

"I'm not. But if you think I'm going to pass up a crack at blasting something like this" — J.L. jerked his head in the general direction of the frozen river — "you've got another think coming."

"Yeah, well, it'd be up to Jepperson or not, whether he can spare me," Bruce stalled.

"Jepperson says it's jake with him. Already transferred your pay record for tomorrow. You draw an extra thirty cents an hour, working with danamite."

"Thanks all to hell, J.L.," Bruce managed to express. "That'll make me feel a lot more prosperous in my coffin."

J.L. nodded as if in acknowledgment, still looking straight at Bruce. *Lunch his way out of this one, why doesn't he.* Aloud, J.L. said: "We'll put the danamite to it in the morning."

The morning came without horizons, a milky sky fading down into the snowy bluffs above the valley of the Missouri. From the east bank of the river where J.L. and three other men from the powder gang and Bruce were grouped, the ice pack in midriver was ghostly, slurred.

Since J.L. was not supposed to be around the packing paper, two of the others were prying open the wooden box which held sticks of dynamite. Bruce nervously watched back and forth between the dynamite box and where a man named Quincy was fondling blasting caps. A trudge of half a mile or more out across the corrugated river lay between them and the ice jam.

"We just . . . walk out there with this stuff?" Bruce asked.

"Walk kind of careful, is a good idea," J.L. answered without losing count of the coils of detonation wire he was shakily accumulating.

None of these detonationists, it turned out, had ever dealt with ice before, although they assured Bruce they had blown up most other known substances. Quincy had helped to blast out a log jam once. "Logs went flying pretty as any-thing," he reminisced. "It's just only a matter of placing the charge right."

"Yeah, but where's that" — Bruce nodded toward the jumbled geography of ice out in front of them — "in a deal like this?"

"You're the river guy," J.L. said, the flint-gray eyes straight at Bruce again. "That's where you come in, showing us where the channel's the deepest and fastest and so on."

Smithereens, ran in Bruce's mind. What are those? Little smithers, but what's a smither? Nothing he hankered to learn about from firsthand experience, he was dead cer— he was certain of that much.

Steady, he told himself as he kept abreast of J.L. and the other three as they trudged across the ice with their explosive goods. The motorcycle didn't get him, he went on telling himself, the mud avalanche in the pump barge didn't get him, the diving didn't get him (*yet* crept into that last one), so why should one little excursion with dynamite get him?

Because! Because (a.) J.L. Hill trembles like an ash grove in a high wind, and (b.) there was that highly unfortunate pass Bruce made at Nan Hill and (b.1.) Bruce didn't even know this part but the neighbor across the alley, Tarpley, had figured

481

it bore mentioning to J.L. that he'd seen Bruce Duff slinking home from the Hills' house one noontime, and (c.) the competence of the other three here in the blast crew was a totally unknown quantity to Bruce except for Quincy's pleasure in causing log-size items to fly, and (d.) this was not some piece of equipment that Bruce himself was in charge of, such as a motorcycle or a diving suit, this was the cast-iron winter river and a guessing game of dynamite.

Bruce wished he had not yet been born.

The cold river air, meanwhile, was damp and penetrating. He felt it meet the sweat on his body, and resignedly figured pneumonia next onto his list of mortal hazards here.

"Somewhere around here, you think?"

J.L. was addressing him, he realized.

"Uh, let me study this out a little." Bruce sighted through the two halves of the dam to the dark steel webwork of the railroad bridge, trying to put together in his mind his underwater hours and this vast ice lid, to divine where the channel ran strongest.

"Back a ways toward shore, is where I'd do it," he at last suggested. He took a chance and pointed at a pyramid-pile of ice chunks, a hundred yards in that direction. "About there, maybe."

The four dynamiters gazed back along

their tracks in the snow, then at Bruce. One of them who had not said anything so far scowled and stated: "What we don't want is to have to come back out here a second time, and try blow this."

"Yeah, that'd be tricky," J.L. agreed. "Quite a lot better not to be prancing around on ice you've already used danamite on."

Bruce felt all eight eyes on him. "You're downright sure," J.L. was asking, "that's the fastest part of the river?"

"Pretty sure. Now, *downright* sure, J.L., I don't just know how to be *that* sure when there's all this ice on top of —"

"What we wanted. Right, boys?" J.L. hefted his plunger box. "Advice from the horse's mouth."

The other three snickered mightily and fell in line like elves behind J.L. as he headed for the ice pyramid.

The detonation preparations went fast, as though everyone wanted to get this over with.

While two of the men embedded the sticks of dynamite and J.L. began affixing the blasting caps, Bruce and the other man spliced wires from the caps into the firing wire and began unreeling it all the way to the plunger box. "Don't be letting that wire touch those terminals until I get there," J.L. warned over his shoulder, and Bruce definitely didn't.

When all was in readiness, the dynamite quartet plus Bruce gathered around the plunger box on the welcome solid ground of the riverbank. Spectators flocked up onto various high points. In the Ad Building contingent on the crest of the dam, Bruce could discern shaggy-coated Owen looking like the world's tallest leanest buffalo. At the end of another lineup of gawkers stood Neil, arms folded, probably with a grin on him like a Chessy cat; if people insisted on getting Neil and him mixed up, Bruce considered, conscription into the iceberg squad would have been a good time for it. Actually, though, Bruce was starting to feel better about this dynamite deal. Originally he'd thought of invoking the fact that he was freshly a father, although J.L. Hill and Fort Peck foremen in general didn't seem overly impressed, and he had almost gone to Owen to get him out of this, but goddamn it, if he was the government diver he was the one who was supposed to know the course of the river, wasn't he. Now he nodded in synchronization with the other blasters when J.L. Hill asked, "Everybody happy with this so far?"

J.L. looked in every direction, twice, then shouted out the warning of blasting:

"FIRE IN THE HOLE!"

As soon as that had echoed away, he pushed the plunger.

The explosion was a healthy boom, and a satisfying shower of ice hunks rained down in the middle of the river, and the ice pack massively shifted, grinding and groaning. Then jammed again.

"Goddamn/sonofabitch/bastard!" was heard in mixed chorus from the other three, but neither J.L. nor Bruce spoke. Until after a minute J.L. provided:

"A little bit off, on that one. I think I know where to set the next one by myself."

Bruce knew he could not let that be the case. "I'll go with," he said shortly.

Out they trudged again, J.L. Hill with his plunger box under an arm and a sack of blasting caps swinging from one quivery hand and coils of detonation wire in the other, Bruce two steps behind carrying the dynamite charge in both hands like a museum vase.

The icescape in front of them had been stirred around marginally by their first try, but mainly it was still jumbled, still jammed, still massively more ice than the river seemed to know what to do with.

J.L. halted well short of where they had set the previous charge and said, "Let's think this out a little bit."

He put down his detonating equipment, Bruce gladly doing the same with the dynamite.

As J.L. walked off a little way to squint at the ice conformation ahead, Bruce trailed him but kept his mouth conspicuously shut as though giving J.L. more thinking space.

The two of them heard the ice groan, then a sound more ragged than that. They could not see any difference yet in the pile of floes ahead of them, but it sounded for all the world as if the heavy winter load of the river was shifting.

"Whoa, a minute," Bruce heard out of J.L. "Maybe we aren't even going to have to give it another shot of dan—"

The ice cracked at their feet. Then crumbled, mushed up and fell away, beneath J.L.

He was in the water to his waist, arms flung out on the slushy edge of the unbroken ice where Bruce was backpedaling away. For the first time, J.L. Hill looked perturbed.

Aw, don't river, was the full thought that came to Bruce and stayed with him. He hated having to, but he flopped down in the slush and wriggled his way on his belly to the ice edge where J.L. was clinging. He got his mittened hands under J.L.'s armpits and pulled for all he was worth.

J.L. was gripping into Bruce's coat at the shoulders, clenching so hard that the coat bunched onto the scruff of Bruce's neck and half over his head. "Let go . . . up . . . there!" Bruce got out in gasps, slush against his face and down the front of his neck. "Elbows — put your . . . elbows . . . to work . . . damn it . . . J.L. . . ." J.L. hung on to him, his eyes oddly calm as they stayed locked on Bruce's from inches away; then he let go his grip and began levering himself up onto the ice with his elbows as Bruce tugged away.

Upright on the ice and lurching for shore, J.L. soaked from the waist down, Bruce from the waist up, the mismatched halves of a freezing being were met by those who had been onlooking from shore and were bundled into Colonel Parmenter's staff car with the heater turned up full blast. After the pair of them were thawed and looked over at the hospital and declared not much the worse for wear but delivered home with orders to rest up, J.L. turned to Bruce, before Bruce climbed out of the ambulance to go in to Kate and he to go in to Nan, and said:

"All right. We'll call this even."

They all thought spring couldn't come fast enough to suit them, but whatever it was about 1936, the melting season highballed in as overdone as winter had been. Toasty chinook winds billowed in all the way from Hawaii, it felt like, warm gales from the west that would pin your eyelids back.

Christ along the Yukon, though. Can this be right? If this keeps up . . .

Fort Peck's snow enthusiastically degenerated into Fort Peck's mud. Clods of clay like squashed bricks were churned up everywhere by the crawler tracks of the bulldozers. Tough damworkers watched their chance to sidle off alone and stand for a minute as if looking around for something, actually just to sniff the talcum smell of spring.

. . . and there's no reason that I can see yet why it can't keep up . . .

Wheeler looked leprous, its usual state at the start of spring. With snow going off in patches, rubbish resurfaced from the previous autumn, usually squarely amid a backyard swamp of mud, and the thaw also revealed the gray remains of that slaggy soft coal which all winter long had produced more ashes than heat.

. . . we're going to be moving fill as easy as passing the butter.

From startup on the fifteenth of April until only the first of May, Owen's quartet of dredges moved nearly a million more cubic yards than in the same span of time that had been so cruel and fumbling the year before. Week by week after that, he checked and rechecked his figures, and unmistakably they kept jumping. The holy average of three million yards of riverbottom muck to be dredged and piped up onto the dam every month, hah. Owen could see ahead now — it would be August — when the dredging pace would reach an exalted total of four million yards a month.

"Toston? Oh, my cousin lives there — Etta Drozner? I bet you must know her. I'll have to write to her that we met up, here of all places."

You just do that, old biddy, Charlene thought, and resisted the urge to frizz the back of the woman's head to a fare-thee-well. Here was one more reason why Charlene wanted out of Fort Peck and for that matter Montana, everybody knowing everybody else's business in the entire state. She had gone all through school with horsefaced Etta Drozner, you bet, and could have enjoyably enough passed the rest of her life without ever thinking of her again. Now the word was on its way back to Toston that Charlene, Helen Tebbet's older girl, was hairdressing, too.

Fiddlesticks. But what can you do, if somebody insists on being a fool. When she closed up the beauty shop at the end of the afternoon, she told herself she had better walk home the long way, give herself a spring airing. See if that would help the merry month of May at Fort Peck, anthill of the construction world, any.

That roundabout route drew her along the side of the neatcut Corps town which was nearest the river, the blufftop view there the same one of the dam site as Owen had first shown her, except that instead of Christmas white everything for miles now was the color of unsuccessful fudge. As she always had to do with the dam project, which changed all the time as mammoth things were being built and things twice that size were being gouged out, Charlene scanned through the scraped-brown sprawl until the railroad truss bridge gave her her bearings. A long lattice box of steel which spanned the Missouri with nothing under it but two hundred feet of air and water, *Sangster's running jump across the river,* Owen called it. Whether or not the truss bridge was as miraculous as he said, she could always read the dark VVV of its girders from up here.

Owen's dredge fleet, she knew, lay out of sight upstream behind the west half of the dam, but she was proud of herself for managing to pick out, even at this distance, the dredges' constant input into the core pool; the piped waterfalls that unloaded the fill material in their steady gush. And right there near each of those cascades, the human specks that were the dredgeline maintenance crews.

What maintains love?

Every night anymore, she and Owen threw the supper dishes at each other. No, they didn't. But they might as well, the battle of Fort Peck seemed determined to go on in all guises. Owen was flying so high as fillmaster this time around that he looked ready to crow with joy when he totted up the fill figures each night. *That's fine, well and good,* she had tried on him a time or two, *then why wouldn't this be the best chance to clear out with everything you came here for? You whipped the dredging setup and the boost problem and the ice. They'll write you up as the engineer who got the kinks out of the Fort Peck project. Owen, why not take all that now as ammunition onto the next job?* And regularly back from him, the vocal equivalent of a volley of crockery. *Huh uh, we've got to see it through, Charlene. I wish to Christ you could get that in to your head. To build a dam you've got to build it all, there's no halfway that's even worth talking about. And nothing is really whipped here. We don't even have the river plugged yet, for crying out loud.*

Crying out loud, mm, Ownie? Their situation could stand more of that, too. This was not the time of day to be thinking about sheet music, the bedtime variety, but what was she supposed to do when the thought kept at her? The Bozeman memories — for that matter, one from Glasgow — of the rumpus Owen and she used to make, the outcry of coming to each other in the bare skins of dark; then, as they lay spent, she would ever so slowly provide her hip and leg in a cat rub against his and he would respond to the luxury of that, or if not, then her hand, seeming to drift, touching there where he went hard; and then a second go. She couldn't really say it was an exact comparison, but she and Owen needed a second go at sorting out Fort Peck.

Somewhere down there in the dam confusion, rocksaw teeth started cutting into shale with a piercing howl, stopped, started up again, stopped, started. The playful shriek only added to her theory that they liked the commotion of Fort Peck, the excitement when things went wrong, even the dangers of it, men did. While she herself just could not see the attraction. What she yearned for was the day she and Owen would leave here, climb in the car and go. No, wash the car first. She didn't want to take even Fort Peck's dust with them.

But for now Charlene stayed, hands thrust into the pockets of her frock, there on the bluff a minute more and looked steadily at the truss bridge, the one item of the Fort Peck Dam she knew something sure about.

Across from Toston, the river wide between them and the adult world, the girls stalked in the willows until they could peek upward to the osprey nest in the big dead cottonwood tree. They did not have to wait long before the fish hawk flew in, a trout in its talons to feed its young. The Tebbet sisters watched a while and then Charlene hugged her arms across her chest — her breasts had begun to come and she monitored them frequently that way — and said it was time to go home. Rosellen was still only a slip of herself, pesky, curious about everything. When they got back to the highway bridge from this osprey outing, they met a cattle drive, cowboys from the Sixteenmile country in the mountains back of Toston. Charlene hurried Rosellen and herself across the bridge and over to a telephone pole they could stand half behind to watch without spooking the herd of cattle. The bridge was a trio of trusses with dark steel girders up its sides and overhead, and the cattle did not like the look of it. The bawling herd wadded itself up at the approach to the bridge. A slender rider wearing spectacles guided his horse into the cows and with the end of a lariat fought a little bunch of cattle out onto the bridge. Instead of pushing the bunch into a trot, though, the cowboy reined back to the foot of the bridge. He did this three times, nudging a bunch of cows out a little way but then retreating, which disappointed Rosellen no end — she wanted to see what it would be like if the whole herd hightailed over the bridge at once. Charlene had to agree that this seemed like a dumb slow way to move cows. The rider wasn't very far from the pair of them when he backed his horse around for the next batch of cattle, so she spoke up:

"Why do you fool around with a few at a time, if you want them all to go across?"

The cowboy winked at her. "Easier to show you than tell you, sis. Hop up behind. Then I'll give Missy there her turn." He slipped his boot out of the stirrup, the empty U of it now an open invitation for her to climb on behind his saddle.

For an instant Charlene wished somebody else was there to nix this. His back that she would have to hold on tight against, her new chest and all. The cowboy was old enough to be her and Rosellen's father. But not as old as their father.

"Oh, Charlene!" Rosellen hopped with every word. "Can we? You first! Then me! Aren't we going to?"

"You have to stay right here," Charlene issued, "until I get back. If you so much as move, I'll spank you inside-out." Her little sister could be a real handful when she put her mind to it. Rosellen might have her nose in a book one minute and be inspired to climb the dizzying fire ladder on the grain elevator the next. "Promise, now? You won't —"

"I won't move an inch!" Rosellen hugged the telephone pole for proof.

In the next instant, Charlene was up onto the horse and riding double behind the cowboy as he worked a considerable number of cattle out onto the bridge and this time hazed them into a dead run. But midway across the bridge, centrally atop the Missouri, the cowboy reined the horse to a standstill and glanced half over his shoulder toward Charlene as if to say, You wanted to know.

She could feel it, all right, even up there on the horse: the shivering of the bridge. The mass vibration set up by the cows' running hooves, a thunder shaking the bridge from inside its plank roadbed and metal girders.

Quickly the cowboy spurred his horse around toward the approach to the bridge *and shut down on the next cattle who tried to run, deliberately breaking the dangerous quaking rhythm. Push some, hold some. Charlene swung down off the horse onto the bank and boosted Rosellen up behind the cowboy's saddle so that she, too, could go onto the vibrating bridge and know something new. That everything trembles, sometime.*

Rosellen was about ready to give up. She had sent out "Glacier of Mercury" to every magazine from *Country Gentleman* to *Woman's Home Companion* and the editors must have been waiting behind the mail slots like baseball catchers, the rejections came back so fast.

She knew she shouldn't let it get her down; *Nome wasn't built in a day,* as everyone at Fort Peck went around saying when the square winter palace of ice slabs piled up and up on the riverbank. Maybe writing, getting anything taken by one of the numbskulls in charge of magazines, was like that. Sling the stories out, and eventually one of them would stack up properly with the ice blocks that were editors' hearts. Right now, though, she wished she could have a chin session over this with Kate, who of course was scarce anymore, having her hands full with the baby. But she knew anyway what Kate would say: "So if it makes you blue, don't do it." Which to Rosellen didn't seem to cover the trying-to-write dilemma, somehow. Only Neil, and not even him entirely, savvied how depressing the constant stream of rejection letters were for her. "It about drives me crazy, to do the absolute best I can and they shoot it right back in the next mail," she had burst out. "They'll catch on someday," he had said back in his steady way. "You put in your time at it and you'll get there eventually."

On this Saturday, though, instead of getting underway at the writing, Rosellen doodled. Black squares, midnight in a coal mine. Zigzag mountains, terra firma going vice versa. She sat there and sat there at the kitchen table, trying to cook up stories, but it was all succotash today. She wished she had climbed in the truck and gone with Neil on his run to the Duff homestead.

Neil was experiencing gumbo. He had been around oceans of it, every spring while he was growing up here, but it was still amazing how mud could wad up on the rear dual wheels of the Triple A until you had to get in there with the end of a tire iron and more often than not your own bare hands and claw the stuff out. By this point of this trip he and the truck were both painted with the gumbo, but the load he'd put on ought to give him enough traction to make it up the long slope out of here, he was reasonably sure. Now that the homestead was reduced to lumber, he had promised the Old Man he'd haul it all, they'd leave the place clean as a bone, but that didn't necessarily mean he had to do it all in mud season, did it. If he pecked away at it in loads when he had no other trucking to do, he'd still be able to finish up here by summer's end. For right now, he wished he was sitting at home watching Rosellen write.

"Yours is all ready." Nan Hill produced the large bundle of freshly done laundry. How and under what circumstances, Nan could only guess, but women of this sort went through clothes even faster than the damworkers. "Did you want to take Mr. Harry's shirts for him, too?"

"Makes no nevermind to me," Proxy assented, "as long as you collect from the tightwad rather than me having to try to." She took the stack of shirts wrapped in butcher paper and tied with string, and set it atop her own bundle. She kept on peering next door, though, toward what she could see of Bruce and Kate's house through the lines of laundry kicking up in the wind. Hard to figure, how things take the cockeyed turns they do. "I'm in-laws with your neighbors now," she tested on the washerwoman, as if saying it out loud would make it sound any less wacky.

"So I hear." Nan Hill gave this latest Duff a neutral smile, thinking that the biblical remains of old Ninian Duff must be churning loudly in his English Creek grave.

Proxy eyed the small, neat woman, pretty in a somewhat worn way. Married to some guy with a case of the dynamite shakes, from what she'd heard. *That must make it interesting when he eats his peas.*

"Tell me one damn thing," Proxy blurted, then indicated with her gaze the mass of laundry that this wren of a woman had drudged at today, drudged at every day. "Why do you go around here smiling?"

Had anyone else asked, Nan might have lightly recited the sunny day, the stimulating breeze, the glad sight of the day's loads of washing done and hung. But she found herself saying to Proxy Duff:

"So that I won't forget how."

Proxy watched the sails of garment bucking on the wind. She saw a shirt with a large pattern of a horseshoe sewn on the back, and laughed. "We've got at least one customer in common."

At the early show that night, gathering

499

their strength to go dancing afterward, the three couples nudged and chuckled among themselves as the cartoon came on with a typewriter keyboard busily going SPLICK SPLICK SPLICK as a cockroach wearing a porkpie hat hopped from key to key to introduce himself as *archy* and his friend, the cat from the alley outside the newspaper office, as *mehitabel.* Rosellen giggled the most of any of them at archy's bouncy typing as it splatted onto the bottom of the movie screen, and whispered along the row to the others that she could use a crew of bugs like that for paydays. Neil and Bruce sat back grinning like grade school kids again; every movie they ever saw was their favorite the minute it came on. Folded comfortably into his seat Owen relaxed as competently as he did everything else, and even Charlene loosened up appreciably on these get-together nights, in Kate's considered opinion. More than any of them Kate, after the past half-year of tooth and nail motherhood, was ready for a night out. She wouldn't want anyone to get the wrong idea, she was simply glad of a whole babyfree evening at last, with Bruce's arm cozily around her and the funny stuff occurring up there on the screen with mehitabel, who was convinced she had been Cleopatra in an earlier life (*cleopatra* was of course the best archy could do for her because he couldn't work the shift key), and the big brute of a rat named freddy. Then, though, came mehitabel's lament of her current life — *what have i done to deserve all these kittens* — and Kate shrank a little lower in her seat as though singled out. She knew she had all the right feelings for her baby, there was no way she would trade Jackie for — well, *not* having him. But mehitabel's yowl hit home in her, if a person was going to be honest about it and Kate habitually was. When Jackie wasn't spitting up he was producing at the other end, it seemed like, not even to mention the crying, the feeding, muss and fuss of all kinds. You could love that kind of a little mess-maker, Kate with weariness had come to believe, but you couldn't necessarily like one every minute of every day. It wasn't like mad pash with, well, Bruce on their old noonhours, where the feelings took care of themselves, no complications. So, she sank into that seat as if taking cover, a little wary of mehitabel and herself. It ended up not that funny a cartoon anyway, because it was the one where freddy the rat, full of poisoned cheese, took on the banana-boat tarantula who had got loose in the newspaper office and was making everyone's life miserable. After the brave rat triumphed and succumbed, archy batted out a key at a time, *we dropped freddy off the fire escape into the alley with military honors*. Resolutely Kate looked forward to going dancing.

Next thing to useless. Shame to have to admit it about himself, but there was no getting around it. Take tonight. Payday night, and him with no pay. Had to resort to the pretense of walking for exercise. Not that she made any great show of believing him. But she didn't have to bother to, did she. Wageless as he was, she plainly counted on, he couldn't inflict much on himself. She had a point. There was that about being an invalid, it didn't pay worth a damn.

If he were the decider over it all, he would stamp himself underfoot like a grasshopper. On the other hand, not so fast. Hugh had never been one to write himself off entirely. In lieu of life, there was always some other plan. And for once he had been ahead of himself, putting the trade beads away when he had. True, tonight it took a little doing to find the truck among everything parked at the recreation hall, but he had persevered. In there at the dance, he well knew, were Owen and Charlene and Neil and Rosellen and Bruce and Kate and combinations thereof; they ought to get together more, someone of them had the bright idea, and so Jackie was left with him and Meg (well, Meg at the moment) while they kicked up their heels. *Dance up a storm, you six, before the time goes . . .* When he at last tracked down where Neil had parked the truck, he had only to feel around under the seat until his hand found the handkerchief bundle of beads. Next stop, downtown Wheeler. He still had to shun the Blue Eagle, where Proxy's presence virtually guaranteed Darius's. Unto the Wheeler Inn, then, barter the beads there. Bargaining with Ruby Smith was like gnawing the bark off a tree, but at last she scooped the tiny blue beads into the palm of her hand and told the bartender how many beers to set him up, not nearly as many as he liked. Craved.

So, then, now. Only half in the bag, are you, Hugh, eh? he estimated himself. And the walk home, in the night that was pitifully early yet, was causing even that much to wear off. The intoxicating air of Montana. Didn't he wish it were so.

Half was some, it wasn't none. *If I had the money for it,* his thoughts ran to where they had become accustomed to lately, *I think I'd do the thing. Outright damn do it. But it takes such a considerable . . .*

Ask Owen? Not ready for that yet, not that hard up. *Yet.* No, work was the largesse from Owen. Darius, now, Darius at this late date was showing signs of wanting to be a charitable big brother. *Frogs will be kissing princesses, next.* Hugh had let slip something about his money wish and Darius quick wanted to know *Hold on, Hugh, what would you do with the wherewithal if you had any?* Be damned if he'd spill his guts to Darius. Back at work soon now, how recuperated did you have to be to poke traps on Ownie's blessed dredgeline. Maybe find treasure there. Right, Hugh, depend on it, he chided himself. Pirate gold on the tropical Missouri. No, find a way, he'd have to, to put his pay away until he had enough. He had priced it out, the necessary sum, and it amounted to a lot of putting away. Not easy. Never easy.

Home before he knew it, and now Meg inspected him as he came in. That ditchline of mouth on her and on Owen. But she couldn't help showing a bit of pleased surprise. Hugh looked not much the worse for wear. Turning off the money on him maybe worked. (Among other steps, she had cornered Birdie Hinch and threatened him with dismemberment if he lent Hugh funds to drink.)

"You're good and early," she commended.

"Early, at least," he gave her, overdignified as always when he'd had a few.

She decided to risk it. There weren't even the makings for breakfast in the house and besides, now it seemed safe enough to cash her paycheck at the grocery store, with Hugh off his prowl. "I need to run to the store. Quick and back."

"The coast is clear now, Meg, eh? All along the shores of Bohemia."

Maybe he was not quite as sober as he looked. "Hugh, understand me. Jackie is asleep. Can you take care of him for just a few minutes, or can you not? Are you — feeling all right?"

"Margaret, woman, I am perfectly capable of minding my own grandson," he asserted.

"I'll be no time," she told him.

But coming home, from two streets away she could hear Jackie squalling, and hastened toward the house to comfort him and afflict Hugh.

I will beat on him unmercifully, she vowed, *I will throw him piecemeal into the street. If he has let harm come to that child —*

Before she could yank the screen door open, Hugh's voice came, and the sound of him walking a slow back-and-forth as he had done when the crying baby he held was named Owen or Neil or Bruce.

"Where begin and where end, Jackie-jack. Here you are already, the next Duff, while those of us so far barely know how to breathe circles on a looking glass. Were I you, Jack, I'd be bawling all the time about this crew you've come into, I would." The child obliged with a screech of *Eaahh!* "Yes, yes, yes, that's the boy. Cry it out." Jackie's bawling began to lessen as Hugh soothingly talked on. "You've a grandfather, myself here, who's had practice at being a thorough fool. Did you know that yet, Jack? And your father is something of the same, and vulcanized and underwater about it to boot. We have to hope he'll stay in one piece long enough to bring you up. Your mother, by some wild accident, is at least somewhere in the neighborhood of common sense. Whether Kate as Momma will outweigh the rest of this family, we shall have to see, Jack my man. You've one aunt who's as sharp as a pinch, and an aunt and an uncle who think motion must be progress. Then there's your grand-uncle, who in a wild-ass way chases after the wrongs of the world. Not that the world doesn't need chasing. And we've taken into the family, or she us, your great-aunt Proxy. An approximate — how should we say, Jack? Dancing doxy, foxy dancer? Your Aunty Proxy will give you tales to tell in your old age, Jack lad." Hugh's pacing and the little patting sound on Jack were the only sounds for a few seconds, and then the murmuring of the child and Hugh's musing again. "The only one of us making a real go of it is your uncle who knows how to stop up rivers. Just now the world thinks that's something that needs doing, and so here we be, Jack, the lot of us dabbing away at Owen's great dam. Ah now, right you are, to squall over that." As Meg reached for the handle of the screen door again, she heard: "Your grandmother, did I think to mention, Jackie? Your grandmother I am still trying to figure out after battalions of years."

It was pith helmet summer at Fort Peck now, too hot for hats. All those, including the five male Duffs, who hooted at the light bowl-brimmed headpieces the first day the Corps officers sported them were fervently wearing them by the end of the first week of swelter. Shirts off, torsos oiled with sweat, ten thousand men, the most ever on an American dam, clambered in and out of the diversion tunnels and across the trench floor of the spillway and along the serpentine miles of dredgelines and everywhere on the sloped face of the dam-fill as if it were Tut's tomb. There were groans throughout the Ad Building when Major Santee won the office pool on how

507

far the mercury in the thermometer traveled up and down at Fort Peck that year: 175 degrees, from February's 61 below to July's 114 above. Another record, naturally.

Jaarala, baggy-eyed as if he was at the end of a long choring day instead of just beginning one, came by for Darius on Saturday with the latest poker-induced loan of a vehicle, this one an olive-green Nash which bore a distinct resemblance to a tortoise. They set off for Plentywood with Jaarala's serene foot on the accelerator.

Coarse weather again. The sun like a ladle of molten steel swinging over them the next many hours. The big car's wing windows drew in hot moving air in place of the one other choice, hot motionless air. Wincing constantly against the road glare and the rush of air like convection off a stovetop, Darius understood why Americans are a squinting race.

Out of nowhere, which was to say the interminable equator of highway beyond Wolf Point, Jaarala imparted:

"We'll maybe get the goddamn bastards this time."

Darius's eyelids, half-drawn shades, opened for business. Evidently 1936 was going to be the year Jaarala had something to say.

"There's a bin of them to be got," Darius responded. "That's certain."

Jaarala nodded a fraction. "Their time is about goddamn up. People are gonna catch on that the bastards who been running things run it all for theirselves."

"How far up the slate do you think there's any hope?" Darius took the chance to ask. As best he could tell, the election that coming autumn extended from thimble inspector to Roosevelt, that mountain of cork. In such universal running for office, Lawrence Mott taking control of a county would be one thing, but for the CPUSA to make a broader showing would be monumentally another.

"That I can't really say," Jaarala answered slowly. "So goddamn many people think it's only a matter of who talks the slickest."

"There's a color of truth to that, Tim."

"I wouldn't necessarily say so. Mott at least bow-wows in the right direction. That's pretty much where we need to start from, don't we?"

And go where. Up the teetertotter on thesis and down on antithesis, and sweetly level on synthesis. And then deciphering that, the map to the dialectical holy land, past Marx's desk and out onto the cobblestones with Sorel and by way of the Clydeside, where I put in a soldier's years, and across here to the timberbeast camps where you slaved, Tim. And how far have we come? The movement is stacked up with bloody apparatus in Russia, and it's being warred on in Spain, and in this America when we back a Mott we have to call him a Fusion candidate. But against *is at least a direction of some sort, isn't it, Tim. We do this against the bastards who own and run it all. How dare they. How goddamn dare they, in your terms, Tim. Push comes to shove, someday. We're to help it come, aren't we . . .*

"Are things okay with you?" Jaarala had turned his head from the road to look at him in concern.

Darius ran a hand over his eyes. "The weather's a bit on my nerves. Montana doesn't seem to have seasons, merely Hot and Cold."

Peter Stapfer was nervous without his Hutterite cap, new as he was at putting together enough of a fib to explain where it had gone.

Clad in communal black, knowing he was as obvious as an overgrown crow in this strange town, he hastened back toward the vegetable truck, the two younger men from the Colony peering fretfully down the main street to see what had become of him. Ears of sweetcorn, tomatoes, cabbages, snapbeans and peas in the pod lay boxed, each lovely in its row, in the back of the Studebaker truck, and a barrage of customers impatiently milled around waiting to buy. Peter was the bearded one in charge of this venture, the vegetable boss of the Frenchman River Colony, and in the Hutterite way of doing things he alone would handle the money here. He knew he also had to be the firm example of how the Colony, one of the communes born of Anabaptism in Moravia many generations ago, could deal with the outside world and yet not be of it; could stand under God's wing but go forth with their wares; each of the younger Hutterites had been along on selling trips to Saskatchewan towns such as Shaunavon and Swift Current, but they had never seen anything like Wheeler, Montana.

Peter Stapfer ostensibly had gone into the Blue Eagle Tavern to get American money for making change, in the vegetable selling.

"Excuse me. I haf Canadian money." He held up the much-folded little batch of bills the Colony boss had entrusted him with for this trip. "Can I gif it you, for United States?"

Tom Harry studied the black-trigged man who looked scared as a caught kid, in spite of the beginnings of gray in that chinline beard on him.

"Don't see why not," he muttered finally. "We need some of the Canadian dinero every so often." He took the bills the man thrust at him and started for the cash register, then turned back. "What are you, fellow, House of David?"

"N-no," Peter Stapfer said unsurely. "Hutterite. Our *kommune* — our colony iss in Saskatchewan."

As the saloon proprietor resumed his way to the cash register, Peter Stapfer became aware of the woman whose hair reminded him of cornsilk and whose blouse knew neither shame nor restraint. She was boldly sizing him up and down, in a way he would not ever dare to with her, and her gaze seemed to be lingering in a vicinity unexpected to him, the top of his head.

"Spiffy cap," the woman was saying, right to him. "Where do you get one like that?"

"Ve . . . ve make them. All our wear, clothing, iss our own hand."

"I know somebody who's got just the head for one of those," Proxy decided with a wicked grin. "I'll buy yours from you, Jasper, how about." Peter Stapfer's heart nearly stopped then and there. He had hoped for this very thing, although the cap was not what he had meant to part with.

512

Down his right pantleg, from his waist into his boot, was hidden one of the short stock whips made at the Colony. Cattle ranchers prized them for their handiness in the shipping pens, and Peter Stapfer had intended to bargain the whip for what he wanted. But no one in this house of Hell resembled a cattle rancher.

Indeed, the saloon proprietor now made mockery by calling down the bar to the woman: "Jiminy Christmas, Shannon, you gonna get religion next?"

"Tom, blow it out your —" Proxy veered, but then came back to business. "Come on, fellow, how much are you asking for that cap?"

Peter faced the woman and managed to utter:

"Money iss . . . no use to me."

Proxy returned his look with a mixture of resignation and scorn. "Sure. I ought've known. Another Holy Joe who wants to take sin out in trade. All right, deacon, you can come have your little diddle. Let's go. But that better be a good cap."

As he grasped what the woman meant, Peter Stapfer blushed to his heels.

"No! No, not . . . that."

He cast a glance over his shoulder, worried that one of the younger men would come searching for him and find him talking to this Jezebel. "I gif you the cap for

513

a picture." He spun his hands in search of the fuller word. "Photograph."

"What of?" Proxy asked, eyes sharply narrowed.

"Me. To haf."

"That's all you want? Just your picture taken?"

Peter Stapfer bobbed his head.

"Just a picture of yourself," Proxy made doubly sure, "not of us doing — any funny business."

The man bobbed and blushed some more. Proxy called out, "Tom. Let me borrow your Brownie a minute."

"I must trust you," Peter Stapfer said to her rapidly. "The Colony, they cannot know of this. Ve do not . . . haf such things, images, photographs. Mail it, please, in this." He thrust at her a seed company envelope of the sort that came to him as vegetable boss of the Colony.

Nodding slowly, Proxy took it from him.

Minutes later, completing his hurried return to the vegetable truck, Peter Stapfer panted up to the pair of younger Hutterites awaiting him. He gestured to his bare head. "They are thiefs, here."

There. He had not actually *said* his cap was stolen, and among this awful collection of people surely must be some who qualified as thieves.

The younger men did not even seem to

notice. They were asking Peter Stapfer in frantic German if now they could begin selling the summer's vegetables.

Returning from Plentywood, Darius eased open the door of the houseboat so as not to break Proxy's sleep.

He immediately saw he needn't have bothered.

In the lamplight Proxy was sitting up in bed, on top of the covers, stone naked except for the cap on her head.

"Got something for you," she greeted him, her smile at its crooked best.

Darius blinked it all in, only a little red star lacking above the blunt proletarian brim of the cap. Although Lenin likely never wore his like this.

Darius's smile now was at its utmost, too.

"Yes, I see that," he said, going to her. "And a cap as well."

The decompression chamber was the one thing about diving that Bruce had never liked, but that was before today. Today he lay in it gratefully and more than a little scared.

Other times, only a few, he'd asked for the chamber more as a precaution, whenever the ascent back to the barge didn't feel quite right. At only river depths, the bends weren't supposed to be much of a problem. This time, though, blooey. He'd been tightening a big hex nut on a brace-plate forty feet down when the next thing he knew he was wondering what the wrench was for in his vulcanized gloved hands and the barge boss Taine was in the midst of a conversation with him on the helmet squawk box and when he casually said he was feeling a little woozy, Taine fished him up in careful stages and clapped him into the chamber.

What spooked Bruce was that missing time, between when he was nicely going about his business with the wrench and waking up, so to speak, in midyarn with Taine. Hadn't happened before. *Alertness* was always what happened to him there under the river. In the diving suit he felt as if he was at last wearing life; as if existence had come and found him and wrapped itself plumply around him. The top moments of motorcycle speed, sure, they'd been fine; but the transformed gait beneath the river, where he went along as solemn as one of those old pharaohs, *that* suited him so much better. According to how the river was running, leisurely and normal or fast with runoff, he might be weighted with as little as twenty pounds of lead or as much as eighty. Bruce would never have thought so beforehand, but the

516

eighty-pound days were the ones he especially liked, the surge of the river meeting
him strong and tricky as he descended
from the diving barge and made his way
down to affix a brace on a piling. Then the
rooted feeling, from his fifteen-pound
shoes and the lead weights on the belt of
the diving suit; the calm, contained view
out the circle eye of the helmet; he
couldn't have invented it better himself.
The only hard part was the time limit, only
two hours of diving work allowed and then
two hours of bunktime in the barge cabin,
gathering strength again. Or as now, in
the decompression chamber, letting the
effect of the river work out of his blood-
stream. Lying here this long, he was pretty
sure he was getting over being scared, but
he still was curious. Those moments that
went missing; he wondered where they go.

Another day, another surprise out of
Proxy. When Darius got off work and came
home to the houseboat to burn himself
some supper, she was still there instead
of at the Blue Eagle. More precisely, she
had set up shop at the table, operating a
little hand-machine which took cigarette
papers and loose tobacco and rolled them
into cigarettes. The American genius for
perfecting the trivial never ceased to
astonish Darius.

517

"Tom's giving me his Durham sacks these days if I roll him his cigarettes," Proxy said, sounding quite pleased with the deal.

"Generous Tom," Darius restricted himself to, not wanting to be drawn deeper into the topic of Bull Durham sacks and their contents. He was about to start rummaging for supper when he saw that Proxy had something more on her mind.

"One of those spitshine Army birds was just here."

"Ah? Wanting what?"

"Us out of here."

"Out . . . what, off this — ?" Darius's words stumbled. "Off this houseboat? But we live here! It's ours!"

"Houseboat and all, they want gone." Proxy concentrated on her cigarette rolling. "Moving a dredge in. They're going to take this whole part of the riverbank."

"But I quite like this vessel of ours." Darius sank into a chair across the table from her and the cigarette makings.

"Somehow I don't think that matters a smidge to the Army birds, Darius."

He passed a hand over his face. He tried to imagine how it would be, living in one of the shantytowns. His comings and goings would be evident; the feel of being watched, nosed at. Whatever living quarters they could find, likely to be no better than that hovel Meg and Hugh were in. "Proxy, I'm not sure I can —"

"Could be fun," she cut him off, "when you think about it."

He stared across the houseboat at her.

"Anybody can make a boat rock on water," she said. "How are you at getting one going on dry land?"

The bulldozer crew foreman Vern Bantry glowered at the quintet of Duffs. Any of the four restlessly ranked behind Owen he would not have lent a rollerskate to, let alone a bulldozer. Owen the fillmaster was a considerably other matter, though. But even so . . .

"Does it really have to be one of my D-10s?" Bantry demanded.

"Afraid so," Owen tried answering minimally. When Bantry kept eyeing him, Owen provided: "We've got something we need to move and it's going to take a sonofabitching lot of pulling power."

Bantry looked twice as suspicious now. "What's the something?"

"It's nothing anywhere on the project," Owen assured him and mentally added *unless you include the river.*

Bantry was back down to merely skeptical. "A D-10 Cat doesn't run itself. Who's your catskinner here?"

"I —" Bruce brightly started to speak up for himself.

"No," Bantry declared.

"Neil can operate it," Owen said fast.

The dozer foreman ignored the rest of them and told Owen, "Get it back here by next shift or they'll fire all our asses." Then thought a moment and amended, "Fire *and* jail all our asses."

The ten-cylindered Caterpillar bulldozer, Neil proudly at the levers, detached itself from the turmoil of earthmoving at the upstream face of the dam and like a stupendous bumblebee began lurching along the west bank of the Missouri.

At a roaring pace, the big dozer bore down on the setting-up crew for the dredge *Jefferson.* Once there, the bright yellow machine and the five tall skinny men perched all over it tried nonchalantly to rumble on past.

"Hey!" called out the startled foreman there. "Where the dickens do you think you're —"

"Got a priority order," Owen called back in a voice twice as loud, "to clear something off the site, up the river."

Charlene and Rosellen and Meg and Kate and the baby and, hostess to it all, Proxy were already waiting at the houseboat.

It took some doing, not to mention some splashing and cussing, but the men managed to loop a cable around the houseboat at waterline and winch it up taut to the idling D-10. Watching back over his shoulder, Neil eased the Caterpillar ahead and the houseboat was drawn up through the soft mud onto the bank.

Bruce cheered and Rosellen clapped and the rest enthused in other ways, even Meg joining in a bit at the feat of this. But Darius was shouting to Neil, "Wait, wait, wait."

When Neil halted the tow, Darius sprang up onto the houseboat and delved inside. After a minute, he reappeared with an empty beer bottle and hopped down to the ground.

"I've been in on the launch of a good number of them into the wet," Darius was in high good humor, "but this is the first time in the other direction. It's what I would call an occasion, is it not."

He knelt to the river, holding the bottle neck tipped into the flow. When the bottle had filled, Darius held it out and said quietly:

"Do the honors, love."

Proxy's cheeks colored. She sneaked a look around at all the Duffs to see if they were going to make fun of her on this. None showed any sign of it. They were the damnedest bunch to try to figure out. Tear into each other at the drop of a hat, but stand together if the world so much as looked cross-eyed at them.

Proxy came over by Darius, took the bottle, and turned to the houseboat.

"O-*kay*, then I christen you the —" and she stopped.

"*Prairie Schooner*," Rosellen provided, which Owen thought was really pretty good.

"Damn right," said Proxy, and smashed the brown bottle over the stern.

The houseboat slid on the prairie grass, the bulldozer leading it up the ridge. Neil was quick-learning enough as a catskinner to steer clear of dips and cutbanks, although occasionally the houseboat plowed through a mound of dirt around a gopher hole or badger den. Hugh and Meg volunteered to take Jackie with them in the truck to the crest of the ridgeline. The rest chose to tag along beside the tow job, kidding, laughing, the great bald blue sky of summer's best evening over them.

At the top of the bluff, Neil maneuvered the houseboat to Darius's orders and Proxy's counterorders, walking it into place with careful yanks on the D-10's steering levers.

Owen, who had backed off to watch this emplacement process with a professional critical eye, all at once broke out laughing.

"What," Charlene asked, coming over to him with crossed arms and a little smile. "What's tickling your funnybone?"

"Nothing," he had to maintain to her, had to keep the jingle of it to himself. What had hit him as he watched the siting of the houseboat, afloat on the grass above Wheeler, above the river, above all of Fort Peck: *Proxy and Marxy's ark.*

The fingerprinting of Fort Peck occurred the next Monday, a day hotter for some than even the soaring Ad Building thermometer indicated.

"New regulation from the alphabet guys in Washington, D.C.," was all that anyone in charge could tell the workers. That, and to line up at the personnel annex to the Ad Building first thing that morning.

The line tailed out onto the prairie. Word was rapidly passed back that inside the annex the government types who had come over from Butte to do the fingerprinting were tripled up on the job, funneling people to three separate desks at a time. Even so, everybody griped about how long this was bound to take and about having to carry the new identification cards with their thumbprint on it — the paperpushers must have worked their tiny minds overtime to come up with this, it was universally agreed in the long line.

Several ahead of him there in the impatient rank, Hugh recognized a beaky nose in profile. He asked the man behind him to save his place, then stormed up and pulled the figure away, behind the nearest parked car.

"Birdie, you great fool! What do you think you're doing here?" There already had been a perceptible evaporation from Fort Peck of those who did not want the arm of the law registering any more about them than it'd already had occasion to.

"I checked with that undersheriff guy," Birdie whispered. "He says he never heard of them getting fingerprints off of feathers."

Hugh's mouth came open, but he had nothing to controvert that. Besides, Birdie was staring at him and wanting to know, "Was we supposed to dress up for this?"

Uncomfortably peeking down at the white shirt prominent beneath the bib straps of his overalls, Hugh furnished: "Must not've noticed what I was putting on. The morning after can be that way."

The fingerprinting was supposed to have come without warning, but of course Fort Peck's tide of rumor ran days ahead of anything. So, Darius had plenty of chance

524

to think through the matter. Let the American government make its daub of his flesh in its ink and take the chance that the imprint would never wend off to Scotland Yard and the *Crawfurd, George* HOMICIDE case file there. Or pack up himself and Proxy and go. Neither appealed. Which had brought him here, a dozen spots behind Hugh in the shuffling and conversing throng of men, as the line snaked slowly into the propped-open double doors of the personnel annex. As soon as he could crane a look in from the corridor, Darius had a panicky moment when he saw Rosellen there in the office. He tucked himself as thoroughly as he could behind the broad-shouldered pipefitter ahead of him in line and watched. Evidently Rosellen's was one of the desks commandeered by the fingerprinters and she simply needed something out of one of the drawers. Spying Hugh, though, as he lent his right thumb to an inkpad at another of the desks, she waited to walk out with him. Buttonbright at his side, she kidded Hugh about having a black thumb now instead of a green one until he declared to her he was going to wash off Uncle Sam's ink this very moment. As Hugh veered into the men's restroom and she went on down the corridor, Darius relaxed slightly. No one else familiar was in the office or on line around him now.

He began coughing as he stepped toward a desk, a different one from where Hugh had gone through, and tried to smother it with his hand as he gave his name and address and nearest relative — it still startled him a bit to designate Proxy — to the card-typing male clerk. When told to put his signature on the identification card he managed to do so despite the spasm, but as he started to provide his thumb to the man doing the fingerprinting, a really wracking outbreak hit him, gagging him, doubling him over with his hand over his nose and mouth.

"Hey, now, take it easy," the fingerprinter said, coming around the desk to whomp him on the back. Darius at last straightened up, eyes running and nose sniffling. "Catarrh," he pronounced, which in his burr sounded perilously like the onset of another glottal earthquake. He looked apologetically at his damply slimed right hand, the fingerprinter giving it his full regard too.

"The old handkerchief's a bit full," Darius croaked and snuffled, drawing out of his pocket a ghastly yellow-mottled limp rag, "but —"

"Oh, for cripes sake," the government man broke in on him. "Go clean that off with water," he ordered with disgust, setting aside Darius's identification card and fingerprint form, "then come back and cut in line so we can finish you up."

Obediently off to the restroom went Darius. To the figure at the sink next to him, wearing a shirt as memorably white as his own and identical bib overalls, he said: "Confusion to our enemies, Hugh."

"Yours, anyway," Hugh told him tightly, went out and edged back into line, bracing to present his well-scrubbed thumb in place of Darius's.

"Where've you had your thumb that you don't want anyone to know about?" he had asked when Darius waylaid him the night before.

"It's, well, I'm embarrassed to even tell you, Hugh, but it dates back to the Clydeside. An old matter of politics, a person would have to say."

Was Jerusalem builded here. *Whinstone streets and roundheaded walls of rock and every second Scot granitic with an idea to perfect the world, that was the land he and Darius derived from.* Will not cease from Mental Fight. *It surprised Hugh less than he would have expected — somehow he now had the translation of something familiar — that Darius had been into the thick of it at the Clydeside. Old Ninian Duff and that telegraphic bombardment from the*

527

Bible, Darius and his Blake and who knew what other songbirds of dogma. Men of the word, his uncle, his brother.

Darius now told him as if making a clean breast of everything since puberty:

"They barred me from the shipyards, there at the last. You remember they liked to make a habit of that, the big bugs — bar a person if he'd been too active in favor of a strike. And I'd become a bit active. So you can understand I don't want them matching me up here with any of that over here — I'm not honestly one of you preferentially hired Montana specimens, am I."

Hugh understood enough; that Darius for whatever reason would vanish off the map of Fort Peck rather than undergo this fool fingerprinting. He was thinking over the advantages of that when Darius came out with:

"Money, you mentioned a time back, Hugh. This stunt would be worth that to me." (And to Proxy, although she did not know it. A certain size of metal washer exactly matched that of a silver dollar and, while Darius regretted it, whatever necessary of Proxy's stash of Bull Durham sacks were about to hold washers.)

Hugh knew his needed sum to the very penny. To make sure, he doubled it in what he named to Darius.

Blowing his nose vigorously, which provided his face some cover from his handkerchief and his left hand, Hugh barged his way to the head of the line, right thumb at the ready.

The man in charge of the inkpad glanced up, recognizing the telltale white shirt and the general lineaments of the snuffly figure, and said in annoyance, "Hold your horses, mister." He processed the person at the head of the line and seemed about to go on to the next one, leaving Hugh standing there prominent to the world.

"AHAHARGHH!" Hugh cleared his throat in mucous-churning detonation, making as if to bring his right hand up to the phlegm supply.

"Oh, for —" the fingerprinter grabbed his hand, drawing it down to the inkpad as he fumbled for the paperwork that had been set aside. Taking hold of Hugh's thumb, he rapidly made the impression of it first onto the identification card and then onto the employment record of Darius Duff. "You want to go invest in some cough medicine, fellow," the man muttered to Hugh without giving him so much as a look.

"You're pitching in on this pretty enthusiastically." No sooner was Hugh outside the Ad Building than the voice made him jump. He shot a glance along the line, now longer than ever, and found Owen's face there.

As Hugh came over, Owen, appearing bemused, jerked his head to indicate the army-size column behind him. "I thought I saw all your dredgeline crew together back there somewhere. You're the first guy in the whole bunch I've ever been able to get ahead of me on any schedule."

"Figured I'd get the nuisance over with early," Hugh held to.

"Yeah, I know. Nobody's favorite thing, more paper plastered on us." Owen gave a little grimace. "You know the deal about Fort Peck, though, don't you? The weight of the paperwork has to come out even with the weight of the dam."

His father laughed at that to an extent which surprised Owen. Then Hugh went on his way, fortified in the reasoning he and Darius had reached the evening before, that if ever it was noticed his thumbprint was on Darius's identification card the assumption would be clerical error, a mix-up somehow because of the same last name, a piece of paper somehow handled wrong; in paperwork was their foe, his and Darius's, and in paperwork was their salvation.

Not even the fingerprinters themselves would have disagreed with that proposition. On through the day, whorl after whorl, professionally and automatically they did what they had been sent to do, compile the shadows that men left whenever they touched anything. Even at the end of the day when the last damworker was given back his smudged thumb the fingerprint crew did not start home for Butte, but simply went across to the Fort Peck hotel for the night. They knew from experience that they would have some business tomorrow, too, men who would show up on the job claiming they'd been sick or hungover or otherwise detoured and now, sheepish or resigned, would be told to go get fingerprinted or keep on going. The fingerprinters, and the authorities behind them, were realistic enough to accept the paperwork bargain, that either an identity be registered in lasting ink or its possessor perform a vanishing act.

Among those already gone for good was Tim Jaarala.

MARY HAD A LITTLE LAMB
AND IT WAS MADE OF MUTTON.
EVERY TIME IT WAGGED ITS TAIL
IT SHOWED ITS LANDON BUTTON.

The sheriff sighed. He passed on by the political ditty neatly lettered and tacked up beside Tom Harry's evidently permanent Franklin D. Roosevelt campaign poster, and made his way toward the bar. You wouldn't catch the sheriff arguing against that writing on the wall, actually; the only way Alf Landon and the Republicans were going to see the White House was if they got in line with the tourists. But what a hell of a note elections were, and this one in particular, as far as Carl Kinnick was concerned. That Red goon Mott was running again over in Sheridan County. The Democratic congressional candidate from across the mountains, O'Connell, was another wildman. The whole country seemed to be turning pink around the edges. And Carl Kinnick, who to be sheriff had to be elected, knew nothing to do but tuck himself under the wing of Roosevelt again.

It had taken the proprietor of the Blue Eagle about two seconds to cotton on to the sheriff's presence on his premises; the sheriff often wished the rest of the citizenry was as swift on the uptake as bartenders and prostitutes.

While Sheriff Kinnick picked his way to the bar, Tom Harry was doing a rapid inventory. Shannon was on a day off, couldn't be her bringing this little law dick down here from Glasgow. Birdie Hinch was nearby guzzling a beer, but Birdie always took off like a shot if he didn't like the way a cop looked at him, and today

Birdie was eyeing the approaching sheriff with merely professional curiosity. Crossing off suspects, Tom Harry didn't like how the list narrowed toward himself.

"Help you, sheriff?" he asked, hoping he sounded just dubious enough.

"You could put up this poster." The sheriff had tried this both ways, making Peyser or another undersheriff or some so-called campaign worker traipse around with this stuff, or do the traipsing himself, and the evidence was clear. His campaign posters went up and stayed up if he inflicted them in person.

Tom Harry held the poster out at arm's length and went over it as if it were an eyechart. "Heck of a likeness." The head-and-shoulders picture of the sheriff with his Stetson cocked down didn't reveal how much of him was hat.

When he realized that Kinnick was going to stand there frowning until he saw the poster go up, Tom Harry plastered it on the big mirror behind the bar. When the sheriff still stood there looking edgy, Tom Harry took over the frown and asked:

"Something else, sheriff? Bring you anything? Blonde or otherwise?"

Kinnick was finishing up his estimate of the saloon, not very crowded at this time of day. "On the contrary," he said, straining to be civil. "I figured I'd buy a round for the house. Goes with this campaign crap, you know."

Tom Harry all but smiled. "Big of you, sheriff. Everybody in here will vote for you early and often. Got one thing to attend to, then we'll get your round of drinks set right up." He stopped by Birdie Hinch and whispered something that sent Birdie sidling toward the door. By the time the first of the Blue Eagle denizens had a drink in their hands and were shouting thanks in the sheriff's direction, crowds were on their way in from the Wheeler Inn and the Buckhorn Club and the other joints where Birdie was spreading the word. The sheriff stoically pulled out his wallet at each fresh onslaught. Just because he hated Wheeler didn't alter the fact that it was full of votes for a Democratic candidate for anything.

Hugh dropped into a chair at the kitchen table, not knowing whether to hoot or commiserate.

"Fired from government work? Meg, I didn't know you had it in you."

Elbow to the table, chin propped to her small tight fist, Meg said as if prosecuting: "The man could not even crack an egg properly. It was unbelievable."

He clucked his tongue against the roof of his mouth as though that was certainly the case.

With her free hand she moved the salt and pepper shakers into alignments until they shouldered together in the center of the table with a resigned *clink.* "Besides, I will have you know I was not so much fired as quit."

Hugh kept his eyebrows up in interest until she burst out:

"Hugh, really, the end result was some of both." It had come to war between her and Jaarala's successor, a sallow ex-Army cook named Platt, with due speed. "The man is a . . . a . . . a beanburner. I finally had to tell him in plainest English — well, you needn't know what I told him."

I can about imagine, though. "Where, eh, would you say this leaves us, Meg?"

On the spot. Very much on the spot, is how I would describe it, at least in your case, Hugh. Aloud, though, she kept to: "With you as the provider of the paycheck now, naturally."

The truck beetled down the middle of the spillway cut, at uncertain speeds and evidently trying to follow the haul road, although tending to drift off one side of the roadtrack and then the other. As the river end of the spillway grew near, the vehicle sped up, slowed, sped up again, then jerked to a halt as if lassoed.

"How was that?" asked Darius, still

standing on the brake.

Proxy unbraced her arms from the dashboard and caught her breath. "Darius, you drive like a man with a paper ass."

Forehead furrowed, he said: "I thought I was beginning to catch the knack."

"It'd help," she stated yet one more time, "if you'd remember-to-use-the-frigging-clutch."

"Ah, *Ah*," he said sagely. "The *other* foot-lever. Depress that one together with the brake, do I need to?"

"Scoot your tail over here," she instructed wearily. "Watch me again, okay?" She climbed over him and nestled behind the steering wheel, backed the Ford Triple A around, and drove up the huge excavation toward where the spillway gates were under construction, reciting the gears to still-furrowed Darius as she shifted through them, calling his attention to the clutch the whole while.

"How do you come by this?" he eventually asked about her automotive teamstering ability.

Proxy lit up at this chance to embroider out loud as she gunned the truck back to the head of the spillway. "That bootlegger I told you about?" she launched into. "That I was the private nurse for? Learned all the driving tricks there are from him. I drove loads in from Canada for him while he was laid up. At the border crossing they wouldn't suspect me, see. They'd ask what I was hauling and I'd bat my baby-blues and just say, 'Crockery. My missionary aunt died in Lethbridge and left me all the family dishes.' "

"That definitely explains everything," Darius remarked.

"Your turn again, chickadee," Proxy said, wheeling the truck around so that it faced down the spillway cut to the distant river again. Before switching places with him, though, she thought she ought to offer: "Tell you what — if you want, I'll go to Plentywood with you this next time while you're getting used to this over-grown flivver of Neil's. Share the driving with you."

Instantaneously, "No."

Proxy gave him a look.

"I need the driving practice, don't I," Darius tried to clothe his naked refusal. "And I know you're never much one for political doings."

And I'm not good enough for your Bolshie band? Is that it, too? She debated with herself about whether to pitch into him with that, but decided it would save her a lot of trouble — not to mention some excruciating hours of watching Darius herd this truck along a highway — if she left the Red Corner to him.

"Mother, I didn't know you had it —"

"Owen. Never mind, please." She was dandling Jackie on her knee, his doll-like hands in hers, cantering him to Banbury Cross; the more deeply solemn she promised him "rings on your fingers and bells on your toes, Jack shall have music wherever he goes," the happier the gape of smile on the child.

Righty right. Never mind. Owen fidgeted, inside and out. *This household is so famously well off, almost up there next to the Vanderbilts. You and the Old Man are just going to have money to burn, sure, uh huh. He'll burn through the only wages you've got left, anyway, and does he ever know how.* For the third time in as many minutes, Owen wondered why he was expending his lunch hour this way. Meg was minding Jackie while Kate had her hair done; ergo, Kate was off gaining a fresh perm, and probably a good time in the blankets as well if this was one of the noons when Bruce popped home, while he, Owen, was perfectly welcome to share a nursery rhyme. He tried to stow all that and concentrate on the business at hand. "Let me put it like this, then, Mother. If you've sacked the cookhouse, what the deuce do you think you're going to do from here on?"

Meg bucked Jackie on her knee some more. "This," she said.

"Bruce is actually going to let you?" The news that Kate was going back to waitressing intrigued Charlene, who wondered what kind of campaign it must have taken. "What'd you have to do, Katy, kick him in the slats?"

"He talked himself into it after a while," she responded, streaming water as Charlene finished the rinse. Even as wet as an otter, Kate looked imperturbable, life floating no surprises past her, or so she seemed to Charlene. *But what the heck do I know, though,* Charlene thought. *Maybe being married to Bruce is interesting in a way. Dessert all the time, instead of what's supposed to be good for you.* "Last night he reached the point where he said if I wanted to go back to herding flies at the Rondola, he supposed it was up to me," Kate's report went on, "and so I am."

"Mmm, and our ma-in-law and Jackie are a good match, at least until he gets old enough to talk back to her," Charlene said while turbaning Kate's head with a towel and bringing her up out of the rinse sink. "Handy."

"Owen will have the dam done by then," Kate said offhandedly. "We'll all be scattering."

"That's supposed to be the case." Charlene did not say aloud *and I for one can barely bear to wait,* but it conveyed itself. Vigorously drying Kate's hair, she heard her say something. "Katy, sorry, I didn't quite catch that."

"My working — we always need the stupid money," Kate said in a clear and level tone. "It just goes."

"Mmm," said Charlene, cosigner with Owen of notes financing Neil's truck and Bruce's diving rig, and delicately left it at that.

"Ever hear the one about the kid in school?" Proxy asked, not waiting on an answer. "They've all got their teeny-tiny primers out on their teeny-tiny desks, and little Johnny raises his hand and asks the teacher, 'Is this readin' or is it writin'? Because if it's readin', it's sure writ rotten.' " Nervous as she already was, Rosellen's giggly *nhn* came out almost a hiccup.

"Hey, though." Proxy ran her eye down the listings on the cover of THE ALABASTER QUARTERLY. " 'The Wreck of the Prairie Schooner.' Sounds like this place." The houseboat, because she and Darius were the only ones ever here, presented just two spots to sit amid the spill of tossed clothes and random groceries and much else that had never been put away, and Rosellen was meticulously drawn up on that other perch. Proxy glanced curiously at her, then back at the little magazine, with the curiosity distinctly turned off. "Well, thanks, Boots, I can always use some reading material. I'll get to it sometime when —"

"Proxy, I have to ask. Will you read it right this minute? Please."

What, just because some other smarty thought of calling a high-and-dry houseboat a prairie schooner, too? Proxy shot her a pinsharp look, then shrugged and began perusing the story.

"Uh *huh*," eventually she pronounced, Rosellen breathless for more. But Proxy flipped back to the first page and with a little mocking smile read off: " 'By Nell DuForest'?"

"That's my nom — I used a pen name."

"Oh, one of those. I've known people who ended up in the pen for how they used names, sure." Seeing the panic on Rosellen, Proxy said: "Kidding. Come on, don't go goosy. How come you did that, though, hide your name? Don't the rest of the tribe know you wrote this?"

"Neil, is all. Plus you."

"Naturally I'm honored all to hell." Proxy's tone was more amused than piqued, but some of both. "How come you

541

chose to let me in on your little nommy plume?"

"I didn't feel right, about your not knowing I'd written something with, well, sort of you in it and so I —"

"Don't kid me," Proxy demolished that, rough as a rasp. "That's not why."

Rosellen surprised her with a flinchy grin, still looking a little guilty and perched-on-a-pincushion but grinning most definitely. Rosellen, Proxy had always figured, had to know the score more than she let on, but from her own veteran standpoint she couldn't help but regard her as primarily still a cute kid, although now that she stopped and thought about it Rosellen had been married ages longer than she herself had, and reportedly Rosellen ruled the roost over there at dam headquarters with that lickety-split typewriter of hers — Proxy redid her estimate before the bright-eyed younger woman even finished owning up:

"You've got me, on that. I guess I didn't care a snap whether you knew I'd drawn on your, humm, past career. You maybe want to throw me out on my ear. But I need to know, does it ring right? The sound of things there in the story?"

Proxy pursed her lips judiciously. "It's kind of . . . watered-down."

"Well, you bet. I can't put in every last

little hotsy-totsy detail."

"Nah, not that." Proxy thumbed through the story. "I mean you make it sound like a doctor visit or something, the business with the joes. Me in here —"

"Proxy, no, she's not exactly y—"

"— what's the name . . . 'Easter Russell.' " *There's one I'll have to remember to use sometime.* "It sounds in here like I don't care if any of the bastards know their way around in bed or not, I just herd them through. That's not quite it." Proxy stopped to think. "Okay, it's a *lot* of it, but it's not *all* of it — any line of work has its complications, huh? Men have got those things on them for a good reason. So, a hobo girlo like Easter and me, we might as well make the most of it whenever we can, don't you think?"

Rosellen looked as if she wanted to be writing this down on something. "So you don't just herd —"

"Matter of attitude, is all it is," Proxy proclaimed. "Men are like anything else, you could throw away the majority of them and no loss. But that doesn't mean they can't do you some good, if you play your cards right." Proxy paused for obvious thought. "Take Kate," she said matter-of-factly. "She has to play kissynums with a short deck, now doesn't she."

Rosellen's blank expression — in fact,

what was more than blank? — made Proxy impatient. She pressed her hands flat onto her breasts to proportion them down to Kate's size, which took some doing. "Fried eggs, is about what she has to work with, see? But that Bruce of hers is all over her, all the time, from every indication. So she must make up for it in attitude, that's what I'm saying."

"And you never run short on attitude?" Rosellen sounded as though her throat had gone a little dry.

"*These* days, I get a lot of help," Proxy gave a self-mocking laugh and tossed her hand around to indicate the marital houseboat. "Far as I can tell, Darius can hang his cap on the front of his pants about any time of the day or night. Some guys are just always ready to go." Proxy stopped to reconsider. "Well, not *always,* maybe, but pretty damn —" She broke off upon noticing that the expression on Rosellen's face still wasn't the greatest. "I guess this isn't doing your story any good, though, huh?"

Proxy dipped back into THE ALABASTER QUARTERLY, but then glanced up as if in afterthought. "How's Neil?"

"Fine. Busy."

"Huh uh, how is he at the needful? What we were just talking about. The jazz in bed."

"Oh. Good. I guess." As Proxy kept

544

watching her, something flared in Rosellen's eyes. "I don't have a whole set of comparisons."

Vitamin G. Guts. "Okay, I asked for that," Proxy said, sounding a bit pleased. Once more she put her finger and attention into the literary block of print. "Listen, though. This part where I —"

"It's not really you. I mean, I changed *lots* about —"

"— tell this Pierre shitepoke that if he's going to get tough with me —"

"— really, you're not the —"

"— he better have his casket clothes on. I like that part."

Rosellen knew from a hundred missives from editors what the next word was, going to be.

"But."

On that creed Proxy seemed to be gathering her forces.

"Truthfully? The whole jigaree, Rosellen? I don't get how it comes out." She frowned intensely into the last page of the story. "I mean, this." In a Sunday-school reciting voice she read: ". . . *their two shadows across the prairie like reflections pendant in water before them.*"

"See, but, what that is," Rosellen mustered, "there's meant to be a sense of everything sort of hanging out there ahead of them —"

"Honey, I know what a pendant is. But you mean that's all? Easter and Pierre just end up there stuck with each other, like clothespegs on a line?"

"It's, well, implied."

"I guess I like mine a little more plied."

Employ the eraser hnn, Proxy, you're telling me, Rosellen thought. Drat the endings, how to work out a version of people that was — well, conclusive. What were the cusswords Neil and Bruce let loose with whenever they were good and mad at something? *Cat shit, rat shit, and guano.* She'd like to have used those now.

Finally, though, she puffed out her cheeks, then let the exasperation leak out in a rueful grin. "All right. I wanted to know. Now I sure as the devil do."

Before Rosellen could gather to go, though, Proxy lifted a finger inquisitively, as if testing a breeze. "Now you tell me something, okay? It's probably no big secret I — work extra at the Blue Eagle, some nights. When I come in here, those times, Darius is dead to the world and we don't, umm, get up to anything until the next morning or noon or sometime." To Rosellen, for the first time since the shivaree night Proxy seemed jumpy. "Listen," she was asking urgently, "this married stuff — would it be better if I hurry my butt home and be here when he comes off work, do you think?"

"It maybe wouldn't hurt," Rosellen said conservatively.

"I ask you because that Neil of yours is gone so much. I mean, I know it's not his fault, in a way. But *he* doesn't seem to figure *he* has to be on hand, any particular time. And *you* seem to put up okay with that. So, I wondered. Whether it matters a hoot or not."

"Proxy, I . . . every . . ."

"You're going to tell me we have to free-hand it as we go along, like everything else?" Proxy laughed, but it sounded salty. "Major news, huh, Rosellen?"

"I don't know about everything else. But in marriage, yes, I guess that's the news."

Summer turned its corner at Labor Day, the heat records and giant days of work and long blue evenings under empires of stars behind now.

On the holiday itself, the three couples and the child were on a picnic at a place better than it sounded, Nettle Creek. Up-river from Fort Peck far enough that the dredges looked like white trinkets, the overlook offered a pleasant grassy coulee below and the soft rattle of cottonwood leaves over the jumpable little creek. They knew cold weather would have its way before long, but this first September Monday was well behaved, perfect early fall. Ample supply of picnic sunshine for them, with a few pantaloon clouds shelved in the sky off to the west.

"This is more like it," Neil approved.

By now they were full of food, sated with Kate's fried chicken which everyone swore they could taste before they even picked up a piece and Charlene's salad specialty with noodles broad as a finger and rich with a seasoning she refused to disclose, the feast topped off with pie of the venison mincemeat that Rosellen made from deer neck, magical. Owen, eldest, had had to do a mock recital of the Old Man's inevitable pronouncement after such a holiday meal: *I have had an elegant sufficiency, any more would be a detrimental superfluity.* Earlier the men had hunted, not very far nor ambitiously, for Hun pheasants. The women had traded war stories from work. Jackie had been passed around among the six of them like a lucky charm.

Rosellen tickled Neil's ear with a piece of grass until he batted at the imaginary fly, and they all got a charge out of that. She sat up and took in the scenery again. Gazing over into the coulee and cottonwood grove, she asked: "So will this go in the lake?"

Owen sent her a look.

"Hey, I'm not being critical," she said

with a hasty laugh. "I was just thinking about, when the dam is done —"

"— and the gophers get this country back," Bruce chipped in —

"— when the dam is done," Rosellen threw a pinch of dust at Bruce, "what the valley will look like, all in through here. It'll be like the sea came back, won't it?" She hoped that was the way to put it, to show Owen he and she had a meeting of minds on the glory of the dam. Charlene could yawn all she wanted about Fork Peck, but anybody with any imagination could see that the dam was going to redo this part of the world.

Owen sat up now, too, enough to study the capacious river valley and the join of the coulee. "You got it, we're building an ark lot here," he ratified Rosellen's little rhapsody. "I'd estimate it'll fill up along this stretch about to the base of that rimrock. Couple of years from now, we can picnic up top there and be catching fish at the same time."

"Not yours truly," vowed Bruce from flat on his back and hat over his face. "Off to the *deep* sea by then, for me and you and Master Jack, right, Katy?"

"Why not, you were pearldiving when I met you," said Kate.

"I can see it now, 'TREASURE CHESTS FOUND FOR YOU AND YOUR DISHES DONE AT

THE SAME TIME,' " came from Charlene, who never missed a chance on Bruce.

"Sure, pick on a guy when he's down," Bruce droned drowsily under the hat.

"Somebody else is about to go down for the count, aren't you, Jackson," Kate scooped the little boy in. "Squirming won't get you out of it. A NAP, a NAP, a nap *nap NAP*, for Jack *Jack JACK!*" she nuzzled at him until he reluctantly chortled. With the child corraled in her arms, Kate looked over at the truck parked facing into the sun.

"I'll pull it around," Neil volunteered. "Get Snickelfritz a little shade." He climbed in and started the engine.

"Hey, wait!" Bruce yelped, remembering. "I stood the Hun gun —"

His yell came too late. The truck had driven over the .22 rifle he had left standing against the front bumper.

"Aw, horseshit!" When Bruce scrabbled the rifle up out of the grass, there was a noticeable bow in its barrel.

"Could be good for shooting around corners," Owen called over to him. "You might need that capability, when the Old Man finds out what you've done to his gun."

"Yeah, sure, pour it on," Bruce said bitterly. "Damn it to hell, Neil, why'd you have to go and move the —"

Without a word Neil snatched the rifle

from Bruce. He took it around to the front of the Triple A, inserted the long gun barrel between the bumper and the truck frame, and pried. In what seemed still the same motion he pulled the .22 back out, sighted along the barrel into the air, then gave it another, gentler pry against the truck frame. He squinted along the barrel once more and handed the rifle back to Bruce. "Try it out."

The three women and Owen were all sitting up straighter than they had been, watching this. Bruce now looked dumfounded as well as angry.

"Seniority," Owen announced, getting up and coming over between his brothers, past a quick grateful glance from Kate. "If you two are done bending things, better let me see how it sights in."

Owen took the rifle, leaned across the hood of the truck in a steadied position, and aimed at a lone old fencepost across on the bank of the coulee. The rifleshot was instantly echoed by the *tunk* of the bullet hitting wood.

"Shoots like a charm," Owen verified. "Neil, you ought to set yourself up in the gunsmith business."

The grin on Neil could have been seen for a mile. "Fluke of luck," he murmured, but the bask of it for him wasn't the justright straightening of the rifle; it was the private delicious feeling that he had known he could do it. Not known how; but knew, some uncallable way, that the gunbarrel metal would come out of its bow if he put muscle and eye to it; that he would show Bruce. Maybe that was as much name as the impulse had.

"All right, now," Bruce was abruptly all business. "Let's do some real shooting. Pair off, how about, making it interesting." He glanced toward Charlene and decided to risk his neck. "Vas you dere, Sharlie? Come on, lady, let's show this bunch how to hit a target."

Amid everybody's hesitation after that, Kate was heard from. "Neil is the only one of you I've seen do anything special with that gun," she tossed behind her as she went over and bedded Jackie down in the shade of the truck. "I want to be on his side." That left Owen and Rosellen to uphold the pride of the Ad Building during this gunnery, they gamely agreed.

"You're stuck now," Charlene notified Bruce with a shake of her head. "What's that little ditty of Darius's — 'Don't let the awkward squad fire over me'? I'm it."

"And then for the grand finale —" Bruce in full impresario flourish went to the picnic supplies in the back of the truck and pulled out his lunchbox. He opened it to show them it was stuffed full of rags, and nestled in the rags lay a blasting cap. "Followed me home from work the other day," he explained.

"I thought you had enough blow-'em-up last winter," Owen said, amused.

"Learned my lesson," Bruce claimed. "Leave the dynamite alone, stick with the small stuff. Okay, let's get this shooting match going. Duffs against Duffs against Duffs. Heads up, world."

The men banged away, marksmen all, but Bruce measurably the best, the other two in vociferous agreement that the Old Man had always let him sneak off to do the deer hunting while they did all the work on the place. When the women's round came, Kate proved to be a decent shot, having learned enough gunhandling as a youngster to cope with rattlesnakes and skunks around the ferry landing. As she plinked the majority of her shots into the silvered fencepost they were using as a target, Neil took the opportunity to slip to Bruce: "Ought to make you think twice, being married to somebody who can shoot like that."

But Rosellen in her turn showed a tendency to squint the wrong eye or both eyes. "Where're the keys on this thing?" she spoofed as her bullets plowed around the fencepost in no predictable pattern. "Looks like you're safe enough, anyway,"

Bruce laughed to Neil.

Up next, Charlene heard Bruce say so softly it was intended only for her: "You can do okay at this, if you let me lay out how."

Ordinarily, she would have felt duty bound to flippantly question that on both counts. As much in honor of Bruce taking the trouble to be sly as anything else, Charlene tossed her head back and told him:

"Show me, then, Sergeant York."

"You need to get down on your belly," he said, with what sounded to her like actual apology in his tone.

She and Owen were always the clothes-horses of the bunch, and she had on nearly new gabardine slacks and a Brigham light-wool shirt much too good for wiggling around on the ground. Besides, both Rosellen and Kate had done their firing standing up, using the hood of the truck as a gun rest. Charlene made sure of Bruce for some judicious moments, then went to her knees, and silkily stretched facedown in the grass.

"Woo-oo!" Neil let out, but the others stayed silent, watching.

Kneeling next to Charlene, Bruce held the rifle where he wanted it against her right shoulder and instructed her to squirm until she got herself comfortable in the prone position. And she did begin to feel cupped to the ground, the shapetaking sensation of it meeting her from her bosom and diaphragm down her middle to the pelvic press of earth.

"Shift your — lower half out to the left," Bruce's voice came.

She maneuvered her legs in that direction.

"Not quite there yet," Bruce again, then a pause before she heard him ask Owen: "Okay to show her by hand, mister of the house?"

"You're the family sharpshooter, but be a little careful where you aim those hands," Owen's retort drew a general chuckle.

Then typical Bruce, he yelled the warning "Everybody close your eyes!" as he guided her hips with his fingertips, showing her by touch where to make move. "Keep your shoulder where it is and the gun straight ahead like that," he directed, voice back to normal, "but the rest of you has to angle out some more to the left, there, that's it."

Kate looked on in wonder. Miss Fastidious was getting dirt down her front, cheatgrass barbs in her slacks and socks, and she didn't even seem to care.

Neil was watching as if wanting to memorize Bruce's hands and Charlene's anatomy. Why couldn't he have been the one to think of this? Look at the leeway instruction gave a guy, right out in the open.

"Almost nearly ready, just about," Bruce funned in encouragement to Charlene. "Bring your right leg up some," he tapped the side of her knee, "to jack the pressure off your breathing, okay?" She felt her chest lift itself just enough. By now Bruce was administering her ankles. "Toes out — there you go, stabilizes the legs." Her feet, in his prescribed imaginary triangle from the resting toes up through the in-turned heels, all at once did become invincibly anchored.

"Last little tricky part next." Now she held the rifle firmly, Bruce steadying the length of it against her shoulder and below the bone of her cheek and out to where the gunstock and its slim barrel resided in her hand, saying as he did so, "You need to plant your elbow right under the gun, line everything up along your arm. Feel it come to rest?" Immediately, she could: the angle of her arm magically taking the weight of the rifle and propping in place as firmly as strutwork.

"You look pretty solid," Bruce couldn't help sounding pleased. "Now all you got to do is take your time and aim."

While she did so, she spoke up for the

556

first time, over her shoulder but obviously to Owen:

"How about letting me have a couple of practice shots, on account of it's such a nice day?"

"What're those," Owen wondered, "Toston rules? This is the part the rest of us never get in on," he advised the other three onlookers, forgetting that it applied to Rosellen, too. "To be a Tebbet."

One side of the coin of Rosellen was transfixed with the story, right in front of her eyes, of Bruce coaxing Charlene into markswomanship. The opposite side wanted to know what was going on, where did Bruce come up with being this slick at gunnery instruction and since when did Charlene care whether she could hit the broad side of a fencepost or not? But after the remark Owen had just made, she felt she had better pitch in for the sisterly side of the family a little. "You bet, a Tebbet knows the angles. Show these gorillas how it's done, Charlene."

Charlene aligned the .22's sights by fractional movements, adjustments as devoted as licks of love. The round pin top of the rifle's front sight steadied for her into the matching notch on the rear sight. She held her breath on the first shot, and it flew just high of the post. Murmuring from where he squatted beside her, Bruce instantly coached that she needed to take a deep breath, let it out ever so gradually, and squeeze the trigger somewhere in that relaxed slide of its outgo. She drew in air as he instructed, the ground meeting it under her. Her exhale coaxed the shot, which with a nicking sound tore a silver splinter off the fencepost. Her third shot thudded squarely into the post. So did her fourth. Her fifth, too.

"Okay, deadeye, hold your fire," Bruce awarded her the contest. He loped across the coulee to the fencepost and carefully placed the blasting cap in a split in the wood. He walked grinning back up to the picnic site, where Charlene still lay prone.

Bruce and the others all held their breaths as she took time in sighting, regulating herself. Then Charlene fired, and the post blew apart.

Why now?

He hurried up the ridge toward the houseboat, breathing hard, his tightened Adam's apple not making the process any easier.

Why in the name of the Nazarene couldn't this have waited until after . . . Of course, better if it hadn't ever happened, it's never a pretty thing when . . . But still, why now?

Proxy in bed yet, trying for a full morning's sleep, opened an eye as he hurled in.

"What now?" she yawned. "Forget your dingus?"

"I've to go to Plentywood," Darius let out between his teeth. "I'd like you with."

Startled, Proxy let loose her questions by the bunch. "You sure? Right this frigging moment? What for?"

"A funeral."

Near the top of the town, overlooking the square streets of Plentywood and the bends of Big Muddy Creek and turning a paintless cheek to the new county courthouse being built with WPA largesse, the Temple of Labor was surrounded with trucks and pickups, the Packard a distinct minority among them. Proxy had burned up the miles from Fort Peck, asking Darius only once if he didn't want a turn at driving. "If I so much as hit a mosquito with Tom Harry's vehicle, I would never hear the end of it," he begged off.

At the door of the hall Lawrence Mott met them, a leaning tower of grief. With a few quick blinks, Proxy wiped away her reaction and put on the straight face intrinsic to prostitution, poker, and other pursuits she had been around. Behind his thick eyeglasses Mott squeezed his eyes nearly shut to keep tears from brimming.

"Sorry to hear of this, Lawrence," Darius offered, along with his hand, which instantly was lost in Mott's grip. They stood that way, oddly like first lovers holding hands, until Proxy cleared her throat significantly. Darius indicated her. "My wife, ahmm, Susannah."

Proxy made herself look steadily up into the eyes, big as onions behind jar glass, while Mort leaned nearer and peered until he could take in the details of her face. "We thank you for this show of support, Mrs. Duff."

"Least we could do, seems like." Before she could come up with anything to tack onto that, Darius took her elbow in surprisingly formal fashion and they promenaded on into the meeting hall, where the crowd was already wall-to-wall. Slatbutt wooden folding chairs had been set up in solemn rows, and the people sitting in them were craning around uncomfortably.

Darius stopped short, all at once his hand tightening so hard on Proxy's elbow she reached across to make him quit. "Damnation," she heard him let out under his breath.

In the front row, Aagot Mott was crying in a way that would shear your heart out. It took Proxy no time to realize, though, that Darius was staring beyond the sobbing mother to the catafalque and the casket it supported. The cloth draped over those was the Red flag, the hammer and sickle centered squarely on the casket of nine-year-old Harald Mott.

As Darius stood frozen, Proxy by habit reconnoitered the entire room. *Wuh oh, he doesn't know the half of it yet.* Maybe she was not up on politics, but anyone with an eye in her head could see that the draperies which swagged the windows were also red with the gold hammer and sickle embossed, blazoning Communism out to the town.

Darius lurched from a clout on his shoulder, Mott's gesture as he passed them in the aisle and made his way toward the casket. Without quite knowing how he dropped there, Darius found himself sitting in the middle of a row of sunbaked men wearing their marrying-and-burying suits and stoveworn women in dresses of somber shades. Proxy now had a grip on him, and the voice at the front of the meeting hall, keening yet reverberant, could only be Lawrence Mott launching into eulogy.

Drowned while at a boy's delights, jugging minnows in the creek, Harald Earl Mott, beloved son.

Out these windows, Mott's pealing voice intoned, you could see to the sharp spot on the creekbank where Harald had fallen in.

Thus the swags, the proper frames through which to view a lost life of promise such as Harald's.

For young though this lost son was — Mott dipped his voice in the direction of his wife's suppressed sobs — Harald was a Red. A brave fighter for the day.

And if there was any solace, Lawrence Mott announced as though comforting a filled cathedral, it was that Harald now would forever stay so, the littlest comrade under the banner of the struggle.

There was more but Darius let in little of it, hearing instead the shifting of bodies on chair slats and stiff dress shoes flexing against the floor. Of all the audience, probably only Proxy sat still throughout Mott's performance, and even she peeked sideways every so often at the vein hammering blue in Darius's temple.

"And now, please, turn to page thirty-two," Mott brought it to conclusion at last. "We will sing the anthem of Harald's cause, and our own."

People reached under their chairs, then, after a moment of uncertainty, stood up to sing. Proxy with twin indents of intentness between her eyebrows flipped past "Joe Hill" and "Pie in the Sky When You Die" to the proper page and held the little songbook over to share with Darius. He didn't bother to glance down at it.

"THE WORKERS' FLAG IS
DEEPEST RED,
IT SHROUDED OFT OUR
MARTYRED DEAD."

Darius's voice quit on him after the first line. The Temple of Labor congregation was doing a morose droning job of the song, but there was no missing the gallant rhythm, no escaping, ever, the habitual little blown tromp of this anthem. Like a chanting wind in the forest of memory, Jaarala's whistling of this. *Tim, man, wherever you took yourself off to, you managed to miss the choir at its worst.*

"AND ERE THEIR LIMBS
GREW STIFF AND COLD
THEIR LIFE-BLOOD DYED
ITS EVERY FOLD."

Proxy thought it was a hell of a note that while Darius felt free to clam up, she was expected to keep singing along with this. She gave him a notifying glower, but nothing seemed to register on him right now, so she concentrated back onto the red-covered songbook. Stiff, cold, blood; these Bolshies were as grim as Baptists.

"THEN RAISE THE SCARLET
STANDARD HIGH;

BENEATH ITS FOLDS WE'LL
LIVE AND DIE . . ."

If only it would stay raised. Darius stared forward at the towering frame of Mott, songbook held up close to the milky eyeglasses. *Elsewise the folds slap us in the face, do they not, Lawrence.*

"THOUGH COWARDS FLINCH
AND TRAITORS SNEER . . ."

And Crawfurd. I killed you for flinching, did I not, George. For your treason to hungry men, forgiving in to yourself instead of holding to. For the sneer behind pocketing those food tickets, I took the lifeblood out of you. For the bloody words atop this tune.

"WE'LL KEEP THE RED FLAG
FLYING HERE."

"This tears it," Darius rasped out on their way to the car.

"I would sure think so," Proxy concurred. "Those farmers looked like somebody shat in their hat."

He seemed not to have heard her. "You saw the expressions on them. The churchly ones you could expect it of, even though Mott didn't seem to, poor damned sad baboon. But even those who aren't

Bible-habited . . ." Darius broke off. They might have swallowed Fusion, a dab of socialism-and-water, at first, these restless farmers. But undiluted Communism on a funeral day was bound to set their tidy moral Scandinavian stomachs to churning. *Damn Mott, poor Mott, poor everybody in the Red Corner now,* keened in Darius. Proxy knew his word for the miles-away look on him, the vacancy there: otherwhere. As if to himself, Darius finally murmured: "That — that in there shook them."

And not just them, Proxy thought. These politics of his always were the one thing he was a Holy Joe on, but Darius was going to have to do some adjusting now. "Listen, don't let it get you down. This isn't the only Bolshie outfit in the whole —"

He opened the passenger-side door of the Packard and slumped into the car seat, slamming the door in her face.

"Well, horse pucky, Darius, what've you got to be so frigging upset about," she lit into him, or tried to, through the closed car window. "The man lost his little boy, how can you expect him to think straight at a time like —"

"Evidently you can't," he intoned, although so low she couldn't hear it.

Proxy bit the corner of her lip and marched around to the driver's side. *Isn't this going to be fun and a half, driving home with him shut up like a constipated toad.* But as soon as the car started, so did Darius.

"Why does it forever happen? Almost more damned times than I can count, the movement has tripped over itself this way." Proxy had the Packard floored, telephone poles flicking by like fenceposts, but she let up a little to keep tabs on his expression and what he was saying. "You get people halfway lined up behind the cause," he was going on, "manage to make them see what a fraud the old order is, push things to a brink of getting some good done — and then it all clatters down."

"Hey, maybe not *all.*" Half by habit — she didn't usually have to perform this while steering a car — she reached across and put her hand on a friendly visit to the inside of his thigh; if that didn't cheer him up, she didn't know what would.

But Darius wasn't having any. "Mott. I know he's a grieved man," she heard him say as if to himself. "But he lost all sense of tactics with that funeral."

The camera came to town at the end of that summer. It took a look around, day by day, aimed by the famous photographer. First it found a metal-hooded welder at work on a dredge cutterhead big as a whale skull, and then a cow munching over a find in an overspilling garbage barrel in a spectacularly junky back alley of Wheeler. It registered Colonel Parmenter and Major Santee and Captain Brascoe spiffy and officious in their uniforms, but next Ruby Smith vigilantly eyeing the take in the Wheeler Inn. The camera seemed deliriously random, popping up on its tripod in unlikeliest places, but it knew what it knew. Into its film packs, on measured winks of light that would be distilled into famous magazine pages in New York City, were to be put Fork Peck Dam and the damworkers' shantytowns.

Extra early, Neil started the truck's long, low-gear climb out of the bottomland at the homestead, the morning fog off the river sealing away the terrain above so that only a steady amount of steep grade, about a hundred feet of sloping twin ruts, kept showing up ahead. The lugged drone of the truck was monotonously unchanging, too. Nonetheless, Neil whistled a bit, the warbly swatch of "Aura Lee" that it took a virtuoso to do; he could not help but feel he had the jump on the day, plenty of time to make this haul between now and noon when he had to go on shift at the dredgeline. Glad, too, to have the last of the floorboards and siding onto the truck and no more of these scavenger runs to the homestead. *The Old Man can kiss the place goodbye now.* He palmed the gearstick knob beside his knee for a moment, tattoo of vibration up from the gearbox into his hand. The Triple A took a beating on these hilly hauls, but he had it in mind to snag Bruce or Owen one of these soon weekends to help him take down the transmission, check the gearteeth and all.

The truck finally dug free of the fog, up toward the grass horizons of the ridgeland. Not quite dawn yet here, Neil was surprised to find; the sky was staying more inky than he expected, making him wonder if his watch was fast. Or maybe the fog had something to do with it. This last climb of the road from the homestead switchbacked into a long curve eastward, and even before the road topped the ridge, he saw that the lid of cloud lay on the river in that direction the entire way ahead. At Fort Peck they doubtless were cussing the damp gray morning, and he whistled some more at the prospect that the fog would burn off into a bright day by the time he hit the dam.

The sun came up now, Neil conscientiously squinting down toward the side of the road, same as he always did the first minutes of bucking the sun on any of these drives into dawn or dusk. Foggier than he'd thought; the cheatgrass along the bank of the road seemed dim today, not catching the first light in pastel flame flickers as usual.

Curious, Neil glanced up to gauge the sunrise and abruptly ducked his head as if slashed in the eye, both eyelids clamped shut but a green jagged arc of light under the left one.

Everything tipped. His hands on his eye had cost him the steering wheel, the truck off the edge of the road, then he balled himself up inside the rollover, hearing the sound of houseboards avalanching.

"What the dickens — ?" Birdie Hinch flung down his shovel and got ready to run, if he only knew where. "It's turning night again already!"

The dredgeline foreman himself appeared dumbstruck at the darkness falling at 6:30 A.M., until he remembered.

"Eclipse. It was on the radio. Couple of minutes' worth, is all, then it'll be regular light again. Everybody take a smoke, why not, while this gets over with."

"End of the world, Birdie!" someone on the crew teased in the double dimness. "St. Peter'll be sorting us out here in a minute, you better figure out which chicken you're going to start repenting on."

"Lay off him," the foreman called out. Then to Birdie: "But don't be gawking up there, in case that fog lifts. They say you can get your eyeballs fried by looking into one of those."

Nothing broken on him. Except there in the eye, the green wound blazing there.

The power of panic drove Neil up out of the toppled truck, wrenching the driver's-side door open into the sky overhead, then scrambling out like a frantic sailor through an escape hatch. He lit on the ground hard, the truck on its side hissing shrilly through its radiator. His back to the sunrise, he tried clapping a hand, then both hands, over the eye but it did not help any. The scald of color, the shape of a large glowworm, stayed vivid within the eye, no, *Jesus, brighter!* when he covered it that way.

Neil grasped by now that this was not from the shatter of the windshield, some sliver of glass. Somehow this was a slice of the sun itself driven into his eye. The, what was it called, corona, branded green into his vision; they'd been warned about it in school every so many years, blindness if you ever looked into an eclipse. But he hadn't even known this morning there was going to be an— The thing swam, maddeningly front and center, always just out from his nose. This wasn't blindness, this was maybe worse, something forever there you didn't want to see, couldn't stand to see but couldn't keep from seeing. Hunched, Neil stared down at the ground, the crooked crown of sunfire against it. His throat tightened so much he felt half-choked as he tried to think how to deal with this. My God, how could you ever even sleep with this smoldering in your eye.

In a jolting lope he ran down the road toward the river. When he entered the fog, the sting of color grew even more vivid again, lifting and falling according to his strides but never leaving his vision, never dimming from its hot turquoise arc inside his eyeball.

Panting desperately from his plunge down the ridge and from the terror of the brand in his eye, Neil reached the river. He clambered out onto a gravel bar, dropped to his knees and madly sloshed water, handfuls as fast as he could scoop, onto the eye. The cold shock of the Missouri made him gasp, shudder, but he kept applying the water until his hands grew too numb. The fuzzy green eyebrow still glowed in the center of his vision.

He lurched to his feet, gravel clattering

under him, the river purling past, and looked around wildly, trying to shoot glances here and there more quickly than the green tuft of fire could follow. But it was always there, in fact it seemed to squirm to wherever he looked an instant ahead of his sense of looking there. Impossible as outrunning your shadow, he realized.

But what, then — can't go through life like this, can't, this'd drive a person batty before — Got to do something with —

It hit him then, that maybe the only way to get the green burn out would be to have the eye taken out.

Doctors, do they do that? Jesus, though, can I even stand it long enough to get to a —

He knew nobody in his right mind could pluck his own eye out. What, though, if it drove him crazy enough to?

Quit thinking that! Don't even — I — That's crazy to even — But what'm I —

He was afraid to even cry, not knowing what that might do to the crippled eye. By now he had backed off the gravel bar, floundering up onto the riverbank. Dazzles of light came off the water at him now, the sun had cut through the fog. Neil ducked away, frantically turning his head toward the stand of cottonwoods. The green corona in his eye merged somewhat with the green mass of leaves.

Trembling, he tested this out. As long as he kept his eyes fixed into the cottonwood patch of green, the corona's clinging glow seemed not quite so bright against it. Every time he shifted his eyes to anywhere else, there it flared. The alfalfa field, when he tried it, produced too deep a green, the sun-molten one crawled floridly atop it. He snapped his gaze back to the cottonwoods again.

Quivering with hope now, he forced himself to sit still on the riverbank, knees hugged to his chest, and stare on and on into the leaves. Surprisingly hard, to make yourself do nothing but stare. Rosellen. He thought about her, craved having her here but in the next instant decided no, how could he explain even to her what was going on in his eye. He tried to occupy himself with the place, thoughts of the past life here. *Cold mornings, the boy him taking his turn at the chores starting with the milk cow, milking the first squirts onto his hand to warm them; Owen had taught him that trick. Bruce and him, twinned in even where they slept, those tussles the two of them waged over who was taking up too much of the bed, until the night the Old Man came into their room and laid a cedar fencepost down the center of the sheets for a boundary. The Old Man and*

573

Mother, their long devotion to disagreement about this place. The river chiming in, any season, road of water that the luck of a year either came on or didn't. Their last winter here, the big freeze that left this stretch of the Missouri and its tributary Go-Devil Creek like a series of ice rinks; the cows from the Austin ranch that the Duffs were wintering on shares slipped and slid on the ice, the calves were born backwards that hellish calving time. Then, though, the annual hope that was alfalfa, the melt in the mountains coming down the canyon as rapid tan water and perking into the river-bank fields to push up the green growth. But before spring was half off the calendar, summer was crowding in, the Old Man going hermity once more, Mother skeptical about everything, Bruce itching to pull out, himself trying to fathom where things were heading. Summer of grasshoppers again. The view from the running board during the poisoning, the tires of the pickup leaving behind twin slicks of crushed grasshoppers. Then that feeb in the government Chevy. Then the dam. And the truck. And this . . .

Gradually he could determine that the green squiggle was fading, just perceptibly. After many minutes, it turned to dull red. Wild with relief, when he shifted his gaze off the cottonwood canopy now, after each blink the glow seemed to go down a little in color.

When the last of the sun scar was finally gone, Neil, drained as he was, thought to check his watch. As best he could tell, the immense time it had taken for the green fire to fade from his eyesight was an hour.

"It's all beat to hell on that one side," Owen diagnosed the truck after they had righted it with a tractor borrowed from the Austin ranch. "But the garage in Glasgow can bang most of that out, don't you think?" He badly wanted Neil to think that, rather than notions toward a new truck. *Charlene will have my scalp for sure if we lay out money for another damned rig.*

Going through the motions with Owen of looking over the mistreated Model Triple A, while Rosellen tried to stay at his side and yet out of the way, Neil appeared both dulled down and uneasy. He still had trouble believing what had happened here had *really* happened. There was no telling how much longer Bruce was going to keep ragging the daylights out of him for trying to teach the truck to roll over like a cocker spaniel. His mother, on the other hand, stated "These things happen, Neil," without managing to give it a reassuring sound. The Old Man had simply looked at him as if Neil had turned back into a nine-year-old. Except for Rosellen, he had only told any of them that the sun got in his eye and the truck flipped over when he lost sight of the edge of the road. He knew it was like saying he had been singed with a match when he had been jabbed by a red-hot (*green*-hot) branding iron. But how could he say to them he had been singled out by an eclipse?

"Sure some mess, huh?" Neil muttered to Rosellen as if he hadn't heard Owen's prescription for the truck.

"You're not hurt, that's all that counts. Tell me again. The eclipse and all," she said yesterday after he'd had to hitch rides all the way back to Fort Peck and she was holding him.

She had begged to come with them on this salvage of the wreck and the interminable tow job ahead, and now she put her arm through Neil's, the way she figured a wife was supposed to furnish adhesive encouragement here, although she was close to bursting with the belief that yesterday would have been her real chance. She would have given anything to have been along with him when the sun struck his eye, when the truck somersaulted. By now she had thought up all different versions, how she would have raced on foot the five miles to the Austin ranch for help or stayed and cradled him in her arms while the thing in his eye went away, whatever was best for him. Never in a jillion years would she have said so to Neil, bunged up and feeling low as he was, but the same way she had been secretly a little thrilled by his inexplicable fistfight with the tough Swede that time, what had happened to him here put her imagination on full perk.

Past her, Owen snuck another hard look at Neil. It wasn't like Neil to spill a truck on a straight dry stretch of road like this; Owen felt half-embarrassed for his brother the minute he saw the wreck site. Maybe there was some angle to this that Neil wasn't owning up to, but it was an odd damned piece of driving.

"That's what you think we better do, then?" Owen applied on him again. "Give the guys at Moore Motors a go at pounding it back into shape?"

"Sure," Neil at last said, swallowing. "I guess."

The camera all but licked the lips of its lens when the big tunnel liners, plate steel culverts thirty feet in diameter and cobwebbed inside with crisscross support rods to hold them rigid until they were placed in the diversion tunnels, came into view. What the famous photographer was famous for were photographs of sections of machinery so abstract they looked like metal fossils, and here was a spiral pattern, seashell magnified by industrial design to the size of a silo, to make you dizzy with awe. Workmen, silhouetted, were climbing all over in there, hitchhiking on midair, on the support rods — the rods and the boltcollars in the middle into which they were cinched were called tension spiders — and even one man clinging on the outside of the big round form, upper left, as if he was at the ten o'clock point of scaling the clockface of Big Ben. The tripod spraddled out, the camera eye focused. "That's fine, perfect," called out the photographer to the men glancing down in curiosity, "don't look at the camera," and not more than half of them did.

Darius sipped thermos tea, hanging at the edge of a group of catskinners greasing and fueling up their bulldozers. He had been up on the opposite side of the tunnel liner, bolting down a flange at the two o'clock spot, when he spied the photographer coming. Now he waited, deliberately out of the picture, impassively watching the others ride the tension spiders.

Rosellen popped out of the Ad Building at quitting time, pretty as a bouquet, yanking her aquamarine scarf out of her coatsleeve to put it on.

He stood a moment, just admiring, then fell into step with her.

"Thought I'd walk you home. Now that we're afoot."

"This isn't the previous Neil," she gave him a grin and glommed on to his arm in a kidding way. "Coming up to a married woman in broad daylight. Next thing, you'll be asking directions to my room."

Catercorner from the Ad Building, the hotel of their first night drew a comical gawk simultaneously from them both, then they chuckled together and began walking up through the kempt Corps townsite toward Wheeler.

November's evidence was in the wind, chilly on Rosellen's legs, teasing at Neil's hat. This was nifty, though, she decided, sashaying home arm in arm, his familiar long frame the warmest thing in Fort Peck's larder of wind. There was no fancier word needed for it. Nifty *of* him, too, to think to —

"Maybe we ought to clear out of here," she heard come from him, not in any dreamy planning way but as if it had been pent up. "Tell Fort Peck we've had a sufficiency."

"Neil, no. Why?"

"We're going to need to eventually anyway. Trestle monkeys aren't long for this world here. About all that's left is the

579

channel trestle and then my kind of work shuts down to —"

"Mine'll still be going, though. The last two people on this dam will be one working and me doing paperwork and paychecks on him." That didn't bring the laugh from him she'd hoped for. A little wildly, she looked at him from the side, wondering where the Neil who always preached perseverance to her had gone. Clear out, when this place was going great guns? She couldn't even imagine anything to match the dam, the stories, the ingredients of life here. "And didn't you say yourself there'll still be hauling jobs when they start topping off the dam?"

"Yeah, I did," he said in a thin tone.

"Then, what? What, sweetheart?" she persisted. "Your accident? Is that what has you thinking like this?"

He bridled at her choice of words. What had happened, there with the truck, his eye, the green — he shook his head sharply. Beyond accident. Wasn't "accident" something that happened to you when you were about half-asking for it, like not checking your safety belt and climbing spikes before you scaled up a bridge piling? This other came down out of the fairy blue and slugged you. Tried to blind you.

"Rosellen, I'm not asking for static over

this. It was just an idea. I'll — we'll need to take a look at things before the topping-off gets underway, though."

"I know." She was still wondering how they had gotten into this nearest thing to a fight. "When we have to, we will."

How in the name of Holy Pete can a guy be expected to sort it all out, wondered Neil. What was it that Owen said, *To be a Tebbet.* Sisters didn't look to be an any more understandable proposition than brothers. Charlene would give just about anything to kiss off Fort Peck, Neil knew, and here Rosellen couldn't be budged from the place.

They walked on home, not saying anything.

The camera went up in an airplane to look down on Fort Peck. Glimpses, though, were all it could manage; the dam project from overhead proved to be simply too big and sprawling and, well, unphoto-genic. The four tall gatehouses that would regulate the river into the tunnels under the dam were being erected on geography that looked reptilian. The curved Fort Peck townsite, in its extreme regularities, looked like sets of false teeth in a rusty basin. So it went, uncooperative earth down there. The famous photographer was considerably less than pleased, but did manage to shoot a panorama of the town of Wheeler in underexposed glowery murk, which the editors in New York would have cropped off if they had not wanted a glowering murky sky over their notion of Wheeler. But how bright did New York look when it was two years old?

Owen watched the airplane make its circles. *There's what I should have done. Grabbed Charlene out of the beauty shop today, told her we're celebrating, hired us some wings and gone up for a spin.* Not that his mood could have been any higher, even up there.

He was on the deck of the *Gallatin*, the first dredge that had started moving fill onto the dam and thus his favorite, in a sidepool of the river where an immense borrow pit of dredging material had been clawed out. Exultant in every direction, he kept taking time out from everything he had to do and sneaking looks at the dam, which now stood in two distinct halves, marching ramparts with a single vee of channel between them. The west side's dike section, as it was called because the fill was being banked against the low hills there, was the harder to appreciate because it fit like a jigsaw into the existing geography, but that was exactly as planned. The east half of the dam, two full miles of engineered ridge with the core pool up atop it and every conceivable piece of construction equipment all over it, that eastern half was self-evidently prodigious. Owen, who had been to Gettysburg, knew that the piece of earth he and his dredges had patted into shape here was bigger than Cemetery Ridge, where entire armies fought.

This lovely fifth day of November, he didn't mind shutdown for 1936 at all. His dredges and pipelines had moved a magnificent five million cubic yards of fill in October. They had done the same in September. As far as Owen as fillmaster could see, they could pretty much do the same from here on, picking up in '37 at the same swift pace and pour fill around on the dam like gravy onto mashed potatoes after the plugging of the river, next summer, and keep it up right through the topping off of the dam in '38. No, never mind the airplane, and celebrating in thin air. This was where he wanted to be, this day. On the *Gallatin*. Amid the mosquito fleet of workboats, the plump booster-pump barges, the pack of power-feed pontoons, the dredgeline crews uncoupling the huge pipes from the *Gallatin* and the three other dredges, *Madison*, *Jefferson*, *Missouri*, the dredge crew here joking its way through the season's last tasks. Everywhere around him, the navy of Owen Duff.

Calhoun the dredgemaster had clambered down from the lever house and was standing next to him. Owen, still telling himself he really ought to go topside himself and buckle down to all the paper chores of shutdown in his fillmaster quarters — *got to get at that stuff, Duff; on the other hand, the hell with it until we're in winter harbor* — turned around to see what Cal wanted.

"The guys, uh, kind of would like to mark the occasion. They wonder if it's okay, though."

"Why, what do they want to do?"

Calhoun glanced aside as if just noticing the tan sidepool of the river. "Throw you in."

Owen shot a look to the *Gallatin*'s crew, two decks of grins directed at him.

"Hell, I'll do it myself!"

They cheered as he stripped off his short sheepskin mackinaw — he would need all the warmth he could get after that water — and tossed his Stetson down on it. He stepped to the very edge of the *Gallatin*'s deck, feeling giddy, feeling perfect. He turned around, his back to the water. The way kids did when they slung a big rock into a creek, he sang out: "And Billy Mitchell SANK the battleship!" And peeled off backwards, arms flung, legs out, falling body given over to gravity, smacking the water with a thunderous splash. When he came back up, even above his sputtering and chattering and thrashing he could hear the dredge crew laughing like lunatics, and as best he could while swimming for the *Gallatin*, Owen laughed crazily too.

The famous photographer, who was a woman, threw the Corps officers into a tizzy by wanting to visit Happy Hollow. When she asked about the brothel situation, the colonel, who had been providing her his own driver, hemmed and hawed that well, yes, it was only to be expected, construction boomtowns had plenty of whatevers. Then let's see one of your whatevers, the photographer said, and off they and the camera headed, to the Riding Academy.

The photo session in the parlor of the Riding Academy did not go particularly well — the only one who didn't look self-conscious was the house dog flopped on the flowered linoleum — but within the hour Owen and everybody else in the Ad Building had heard the story that when the photographer asked the names of the uneasy trio of subjects on duty in the parlor, she got back the jingle, "We're just three destitute prostitutes." Well, maybe. By the end of the afternoon, Charlene had heard from half a dozen different hair customers the tale that while the colonel's driver went into the Riding Academy first to clear the way for the photographer, a drunk tapped on the car window and asked if she was in the market for a man. "I already have one," she said. "He's inside." The drunk stared and said, "You are the most even-tempered woman I ever heard of." Well, maybe.

The night after the election, Darius was in a mood a crocodile would have spat out.

He had just paid off Proxy the ten silver dollars he had bet her, against the chorus of beery jubilation roaring around them. Landslide for Roosevelt understated it, even Darius could recognize. FDR had won every state in the Union but Maine and what was that other one, not Piedmont, Vermont. Locally, if the Blue Eagle was a fair sample, Wheeler was greeting Roosevelt's re-election as though it were the civic version of the Second Coming.

Darius groused, "I thought you told me you do not know squat about politics."

Proxy gave him her wickedest smile. "I don't."

"Guess what, though," she provided him next. "Had my picture taken. Gonna be famous," taffy it out to *fay muss*. When that didn't bring any kind of a rise from him, Proxy put her hand on his arm, trying to fondle him out of his grumpiness. "That photographer came in here so p.o.'d about the Riding Academy, she took pictures like crazy. Had me stand here at the bar all by my lonesome, toss down a few drinks. She said I'm a natural subject — so what do you think of your pretty-posey wife, bub?"

Darius passed a hand over the bottom part of his face. "I think, Proxy, that the camera is not nearly the only one who likes to lap you up — meaning myself, of course," he roughly tagged on, "and secondly, that I would like a series of drinks."

"Don't get too plotzed to polka, later on," she decided was the best she could do with him for now. "Listen, I have to go be dancing, this is the biggest night we've had in here since the Fourth of July." Darius felt her kiss on his temple, then was alone in the celebrating mob.

A very drunk constituent tottered in next to Darius, imparted "Here's to the greates' presdent ever, Frank'n Eleanor Roosevelt," clinked his beer bottle against Darius's before Darius could whisk his away, then surged deeper into the saloon. *May you have a dozen noses and pepper in your snuff,* Darius bestowed after him. Yet Darius had to grant, even through the beers he himself was polishing off, that Roosevelt was only the, what did they call it, proximate cause of his dreadful state of mind. Plentywood. Mott. The Red Corner that had paled out. Those were the real shafts in the ribs. Mott had been soundly defeated. No, trounced. No, ground into the dirt of Sheridan County. *So much for Fusion, the fuse that fizzled. Back to square one again. No, Darius, be honest with yourself; if you can't, who will? Back before square one, that's where the movement stands now, somewhere off the damnable political checkerboard entirely. That funeral . . . the boy . . . the same with Crawfurd . . . why does blind chance forever have to intrude every blasted time we . . .*

Darius brought himself to, and turned to face the next tormentor awaiting him, grinning sardonically down the bar. The election bet he had lost to Tom Harry amounted to *twenty* dollars, fortunately unbeknownst to Proxy.

Hugh had not intended to be drawn into the election celebration, but wasn't it forever being said that Franklin Delano Roosevelt was magnetic? Here in the screeching Wheeler Inn therefore Hugh was; attracted by the historic moment, joining in every toast to the shantytowns' favorite President, the begetter of Fork Peck Dam, the big wheel of the New Deal.

What was that joke, yes, he had it now: *A man's got to believe in something, so I believe I'll have another drink.* Beer providentially in hand. Bottle in either hand, now that he took conscious inventory. Hugh shrewdly put one back on the bar in reserve, pleased with his reasoning power. He had handed his wages over to Meg as usual, last week's payday; she'd be baffled how he had the money to go on this toot. *Confusion to our nemeses, eh, Darius?* Wiping beer foam from his mouth with the back of his hand, drunk but still capable, Hugh bit the skin there gently but firmly to keep from laughing aloud. Wouldn't do to laugh out loud at Meg.

The way Bruce had it figured, he was owed a little fun. Wasn't diving season all but over, now that Owen was putting the dredges into winter harbor? Hadn't he weathered the bends, survived the river again, soldiered through this tricky year, ice to overheated, like a good fellow? Kate wouldn't be home until after midnight from dishing out T-bones to the election celebrants, and he could swing by and pick up Jackie from Mother and the Old Man before that and put him snug abed, then be waiting up casually to hear how Katy's night had gone. Meanwhile, there was his own to be tended to.

* * *

Look, Tom Harry just had explained to Darius, think of the United States as a great big envelope, and the only states that hadn't voted for Roosevelt were the two pitiful little stamps up in the corner.

Darius had begun remarking what an infuriating bastard Tom Harry could be without even half trying, when he heard at his ear: "Hey, unk, celebrating the election? Old FDR sure showed them his rosy rear end, didn't he?"

Darius said with resignation, "Another country heard from." He made room for Bruce at the bar. "For the love of heaven, man, buy us a round before this barkeep steals the shoes off us."

Bruce in fact bought more than one, standing there spectating the fate of the world as argued by Darius and Tom Harry, but his heart wasn't in philosophy. Up on the bandstand, the Minstrelaires were braying out dance music. A nice familiar tension started at the back of Bruce's throat. He peered over a bunch of heads and spied the whitish-blonde hair.

"I haven't said hello to Proxy yet," Bruce let drop to Darius. "Guess I'll go pay my regards, maybe see if she'd like to dance with a relative for a change. Be okay with you?"

His uncle gave him a glance, then waved

a dismissing hand and resumed on the education of Tom Harry.

Maybe it was his imagination, but Bruce thought Proxy studied him like he was horseflesh when he went over to her. "Everybody is on the loose tonight, huh?" she met him with but included a slight smile. "You in here irrigating your way to health like the rest of them, Bruce?"

"A person can do better than lipping on a bottle," he observed, which cocked Proxy's smile a little sideways. "I know you get your fill of dancing," he went right on to, "but could you stand one more?"

She had to admit she was an eeny bit curious about Bruce. Kate hung on to this flirtface for some reason. Maybe the kid had something to flirt about all the way down, so to speak.

Checking in Darius's direction, she made out that he was deep into telling Tom Harry the history lesson of the workers at *The Times* of London coming back from tea break and finding that the owners had settled their labor dispute by wheeling in Gatling guns, The *bloody* Times *of toffee-nose* London, *man!* Which proved that not even the most elegant of the big bugs could be trusted, not FDR nor any —

To Proxy, history was one thing, commerce was another. "Sure, if you want to give it a whirl," she said to Bruce, taking care to make it seem a natural transaction. "If your money's no good, I can sic the rest of the family on you."

Hugh patted himself down three times, more surprised with each pat to find his pockets drained. Quite a feat, really, that the half of Darius's sum that he had set aside for this sort of liquid expenditure had already been expended, not to mention liquidated. He shook his head in wonder at himself. Wouldn't he be up a dry creek without a tiddle if he didn't know precisely and exactly — ah ha! prezactly — where to obtain further funds. Taking a woozy bearing toward an elaborately embroidered horseshoe on the back of a shirt, perched where its wearer could kibitz down at the Wheeler Inn's ceaseless poker game, Hugh began plowing through the press of bodies.

Proxy had danced with every kind of specimen, tall, short, neither, drunk to the gills, shy as virgins, obvious tomcats, puffy deacons in suits and vests, and once even with a traveling salesman with a wooden leg, and as far as she was concerned surprises were few and far between. Bruce was one. He danced like somebody who had been studying up on it since grade school.

592

"Will this do?" he asked as if he had a patent pending on it.

"Suits me," she had to admit. "In this job, people do more walking on my feet than I do."

Bruce gave her the winning grin of a kid who always counts on getting the large half of anything. "Your tootsies will get good care from me." He hugged her into him a little more, as other dancers squashed past on both sides of them. Dance steps were mostly only a matter of survival, in a crush of couples like this. Yet and so, Proxy could tell that Bruce had a first-class sense of rhythm, surprising in somebody with the male Duffs' customary build of long extremities joined with hard knots; her main complaint about Darius so far had been that his bony knees were wicked in bed.

"Not much running room on the floor tonight, is there," Bruce now observed softly, and pressed her close enough that she could feel the bump in his pants.

If Proxy wanted to lure a potential John D. out to the Packard, she could put herself on him like melting beeswax. That wasn't the case with Bruce. She wasn't volunteering much, but he was front and center on her and exploring for more.

"Speaking of room, how about a little breathing space?" she made it sound like a suggestion.

Bruce's concentration was elsewhere. Among his fascinations were Proxy's slacks. *Peter-cheaters. Is that why she always wears them, to string things out a while longer?* Then her bountiful blouse. *She's got a full house there, for sure.* Maybe it was his imagination again, but he believed that her nipples were standing out more and more at attention, the cozier they danced.

Proxy got his attention by pulling on his earlobe.

"This is not such a real great idea," she told him.

"Bought this dance fair and square, didn't I?" he murmured, looking at her as if spooning her up. "So I get to lead. Relax and put yourself on automatic, why not."

Instead, she lifted onto her tiptoes to peer around Bruce toward the bar. The back of Darius's head was still evident as he stayed busy being disputatious with Tom Harry. The swaying throng of other dancers was solidly elbow to elbow surrounding her and Bruce, which was the only way you could get away with this. She smiled her smile of long practice at Bruce and decided to give him a buckle job.

He appeared startled, then thrilled, then beyond that, when her right hand slid away from his back and crept around front and gripped onto his belt buckle, riding there jammed recklessly between them as they danced closer than close, then slowly the fingering reach down behind the buckle, touching exploratorily, skin greeting skin, the tips of her fingers cupping down over the tip of his hard-on and staying there.

There was not much motion to dancing like this, but what motion there was Bruce could feel with embarrassing intensity.

"Proxy, whoa," she could hear the strain in his whisper, "can we go —"

"Hnn nn. A little buckle-fuck will fix you right up, don't you think?" she whispered mockingly back. "You bought yourself a dance. This is a dance."

In alarm, agony, and a dizziness that seemed to extend all the way down to that place in his throat, Bruce thought the music would never let up. The instant it did, he was saying thickly: "Come on now, I'll wait out back or wherever until you —"

"Bzzz," Proxy said pleasantly but drew away, hand and all. "Buzz off, Brucie. That's as far as this merry-go-round goes." She crinkled her nose at him, which made her look like Delilah must have in her prime, with a peroxide rinse. "Think that over the next time you try buy a dance and turn it horizontal." The last he got from her was the sight of the provocative back of her slacks vanishing toward the dance line at the end of the bar.

As the Minstrelaires tore into another tune, unrepeatable thoughts filled Bruce's mind while he jostled his way back to the bar and more or less blindly came out at the elbow of Darius again.

Bruce blinked. On reflection, this was maybe not the best spot to have ended up. On further reflection, it might be even worse if he slunk out of here without putting up a front to Darius. Besides, Darius's back was still doctrinairely turned to the dancefloor and its FDR skipjays. Tom Harry had departed to deposit the first installment of the evening's take in his office safe, but Darius didn't really look as if he was in the market for a new arguing partner at the moment. Bruce squared himself up and moved in shoulder to shoulder with his uncle.

"Champ dancer," Darius greeted him and shoved a bottle of beer to him.

"Needed that," Bruce said after a swig and a sunshine smile at Darius.

"You're also a damn chancer," Darius said.

The smile dropped off Bruce as if cut free with a knife.

"Don't be fiddling around with Proxy," Darius told him softly. He took a beer swig of his own, but his eyes never left Bruce's. After a long deliberate swallow, he said: "As they say about suicide, there's no future in it."

"Hey, what. You've got this wrong," Bruce tried to muster. "A turn around the dancefloor is all it was."

Darius kept on eyeing him. *Couldn't face a fact if his life depended on it. Hugh's old failing.*

Birdie Hinch nearly jumped out of his skin, and did hop down from his perch in poker table territory, when Hugh spoke up behind him.

"Birdie, I believe you have something of mine."

Birdie rubbed at his nose with the back of his hand, taking a racoon-like peek at Hugh as he did so. "You told me don't give it back to you, unless you was sober."

"Sober is a relative term. Now, if you please, fork it over."

"Stone cold sober, is what you said."

"This is no time to turn scrupulous, man." Hugh stepped closer, teetered over him. His face was nearly in Birdie's. Breath like a brewery on overtime. Birdie bit a lip uneasily.

"Birdie, that money." Hugh was frowning, considerably at himself for asking back the safekeeping sum, the half that was left of Darius's payoff to him; but preponderantly at Birdie, righteous little banker all of a sudden. "I need it. Right now. Let's go, wherever you've stashed it."

When Birdie Hinch did not move, Hugh's control went. "Damn it!" he burst out. "Don't make me give you a knuckle sandwich! My money, go get —"

"Two can fight, Hugh." Birdie swiftly kneed the taller man in the groin, then turned and ran.

"*Whu* — *!*" Hugh let out, half doubled over. Birdie hadn't laid into him very hard, but it didn't take much there.

He stayed hunched a moment, until fury overcame his hurt. Still clutching himself, he slowly leaned back and craned as high as he could, to catch sight of the fleeing back of Birdie as it appeared and disappeared through the maze of people in the Wheeler Inn. Birdie was squirming through the outer edge of the crowd, nearly to the door, as Hugh took out after him.

"— didn't mean anything by it, that's the way people dance," Bruce was saying.

"— not accusing you of anything, merely informing you for your own health," Darius was saying.

"If it isn't my horseshoe honey." Proxy

gave Birdie the little tickle in the ribs reserved for regular customers. "Look, I'm real sorry, Oklahoma, but tonight has gotten kind of busy."

"This ain't about that," Birdie rattled out. Although he sorely wished it was. "Hugh is on a tear. Somebody better do something about him besides me." Birdie's words were still in the air as he ducked back into the Blue Eagle crowd and wove for the back door.

Hugh swayed in the front doorway, still fumbling at his pants. He'd had to pause at the alley to take a leak, dimly relieved that he still could. Now he sorted the sardined clientele of the Blue Eagle for Birdie. His inspection, though, caught on a piece of headgear visible just above the others at the bar. That Dutch-boy cap of Darius's, or whatever it was.

Everybody I know is sartorial but me, a great pity toward himself came over Hugh. Birdie forgotten, he lunged off toward the bar and the cap and Darius.

"— if that's the way you feel about it," Bruce was sounding hurt.

"— the only way there is to feel about it," Darius was sounding grim, "so the next time you think you can play twinkle-toes with —"

599

"The two of you better quit feeling around," Proxy broke in, "and get the net out for — Speak of the devil."

"With the tongues of men and of angels, and cymbals and tinkles and such, eh?" Hugh barged in to the bunch, proud to declaim with the best of them. Old Ninian Duff and the Reverend Neverless Milne, between the two of them hadn't they done the guts out of half a dozen Bibles? Family line. It always told. Which brought Hugh's thoughts around to Bruce, unexpectedly present. "Where's Jackie? Why're'nt you home?"

"Mother's taking care of him, don't goddamn worry yourself about that," Bruce fumed. "She can take a crack at you next."

"In due course," his father granted, giving him a tragic wink.

Darius, who himself had been putting away drinks like a camel this evening, looked perplexed at the load Hugh had on. "Hugh," he asked in wonder, "do you tamp it into yourself?"

By now Hugh had focused onto Proxy. His head nodding in grave consideration, he asked as though concerned:

"And how're tricks, Proxy?"

"Hey, farmer." As she spoke it, it amounted to a summons to etiquette. "The last I heard, it doesn't cost anything to be civil."

Hugh looked surprised, gallantly wounded, and sly all at once. Darius was about to say that they had all had enough of an evening when Bruce beat him to it. "Come on, Dad, FDR is probably already in bed, let's us —"

"The election!" Hugh exclaimed, remembering. "Darius, you've ever been quite a follower of politics, haven't you. Always trying to make new britches out of old curtains, back there at the Clydeside? Tell us, as a connoisseur of things political. What'd you think of the election?"

"Unk is in mourning," Bruce could not resist.

"No!" Hugh let out, all amazement. "Do you suppose the big bugs conspired at things again, Darius?" Hugh brought his right thumb up to eye level, looked at it with fixation, then tapped the pad of it significantly with his opposite forefinger. "As the moron said over the empty mustard jar, 'This has all the fingerprints of a hidden hand.' "

"*Hugh,* you —" Darius grabbed out at his brother.

"What's going on here?" a new voice shouldered in. "Been getting reports you people are about at each other's throats."

The undersheriff, Peyser, was big enough to obtain the immediate attention of even Hugh.

601

"Eh, the harness bull of justice! Watch out now, miscreants. Officer, sir, I wish to report a matter of considerable missing mon—"

"Hush, Hugh." Darius forced a smile at Peyser and squeezed the back of Hugh's neck as hard as he could with one hand.

Bruce, blinking a mile a minute at the sudden lawman, stepped in close on the other side, where his father stood wobbling. Proxy, the only one in the bunch who appeared to Peyser to be in a sane condition, was pursed up like a radish tester.

In the background, Peyser saw Tom Harry throw up his hands and stalk off to the farthest end of the saloon.

Shifting his weight, the undersheriff studied this collection of Duffs, then glanced over his shoulder. Sheriff Kinnick himself was in town tonight, trying to hold the lid on Wheeler. The sheriff was working one side of the street while Peyser was supposed to be laying down the law to the other. *These rangutangs know how to celebrate, so a certain amount of bottle behavior we just have to put up with,* Kinnick had enunciated the night's policy. *But whenever any of them reach the fuck-you stage, that's it. Toss them in the cooler.* On the other hand, the sheriff wasn't the one who had to live in the same town with these Blue Eagle hammerheads.

"You going to take him home and hang him out to dry," Peyser finally rumbled, "or do I have to?"

"We're about to have the matter in hand," Darius said quickly, "are we not, Bruce."

"Sure are," the younger man brazened. Peyser looked at him narrowly; he'd thought this was the trucker one, Neil, but no, it was the former madcap motorcyclist. With great obviousness Bruce was gripping his father's arm energetically. "Else what's a family for, huh, Dad?"

Hugh glared straight ahead at the undersheriff "WHERE'S MY MONEY, YOU TIN-STAR FUCKAROON?" he bellowed.

Peyser warily considered him, meanwhile putting a hand in his back pocket where he carried handcuffs. The guy really was as pie-eyed as a boiled owl. The undersheriff looked from the drunken one to the twitchy set on either side of him; Peyser would have felt a lot better about this if the high-powered bigwig Duff from the dam, Owen, was around.

"They can handle it, Norm," Proxy spoke up, not quite sure why she bothered. "Honest."

"They better. That sheriff of mine would just as soon billyclub a specimen like this as look at him."

"We're on our way," Darius vowed. "After you, constable."

Proxy, though, was the first to move in the wake of the big undersheriff. "Tom is going to cream his jeans if I don't get back on the dance line right now. Nighty-night, all," she left them with, one last pang to Bruce.

"If I help you steer him out of here, can you handle him home, do you think?" Darius asked as though thinking might be a new event for Bruce.

"You bet," Bruce maintained, stonily meeting his uncle's eyes.

Stepping around to start breaking a trail to the door, Darius glimpsed the open gap at the front of Hugh's pants. "Damn it, man, you're unbuttoned. You'll get us all arrested yet for letting your steed out of your barn."

"Eh?"

Darius let out a royal sigh. "Here, I'll do you up." He moved close in front of Hugh to shield the doing of it and began to button Hugh's fly.

Hugh swayed, then rasped out:

"Aren't you the clever whore, too."

Bruce froze, figuring this was it, Duff blood was about to cascade.

Darius's hands stopped, then did up the last button of Hugh's fly. As he stepped back from his brother his voice shook but he managed to say: "Better go home with the boy now, Hugh. You've had a mouthful more than you should've."

In the morning he met himself in the mirror and backed away. If beauty was skin-deep, Hugh Duff had definitely been skinned. Even his reflection looked shaky, and his facial color was off, except where it streaked like peppermint in his eyeballs.

Never given to easy confessions, even Hugh had to admit this was beyond dismal. The record for morning-after heebie-jeebies. Reluctantly he tried running his tongue around the inside of his cottony mouth, only half-hearing what Meg was telling him from the other side of the kitchen until he caught the words *cannot stand to be under the same roof anymore, when you are as you were last night. Hugh. Hugh, I am going to have to leave —*

"That won't be necessary, Margaret. I'll go."

"You?" Meg erupted. "*You?* Where is there for you to go?"

He turned around to her, her outburst stoppered at the sight of his face. Hugh had a look on him she had not fully seen since his days of courting her in Inverley.

Owen was as incredulous as she had been.

"He took off out of here just like that? Where the hell to?"

His mother deliberately looked away from him before she answered:

"He said to tell you he's gone to college."

The jag boss searched his suitcase, then the chest of drawers, then under the mattress, for the third morning in a row.

Hugh watched him, melancholy for them both. Since the jag boss, a thickset back-of the-Yards Chicagoan named O'Shea, stayed with him day and night, when exactly could Hugh have conjured alcohol into the room? Hugh all too well knew he had another twenty-five days ahead here at the Carteret Curative Institute, but O'Shea evidently was here for all time, inspector general of the satchels of drunks.

"Clean as an angel's drawers," Hugh's keeper announced, also for the third morning in a row. He cocked his ear to the sound of the cart in the hallway. "And here comes your slug of concrete."

Hugh wasn't saying much. The heavy gray concoction, which had to be taken every two hours, tasted like bad whiskey, hot malted milk, and chalk. It crossed his mind that not even Darius's money, soberly beseeched out of Birdie Hinch for absolutely this purpose, could buy flavor here.

In subsequent days Hugh Duff went through moods he hadn't known were in him. He jumped O'Shea the fifth morning — the relentless cleanliness of angel's drawers no doubt accounted for it — and after O'Shea pinned him and then stepped back with a grin, Hugh realized where he stood. *Christ, man, he could've cleaned your clock six ways to Sunday.* Watching his behavior from then on, Hugh without a stumble advanced to shots in the arm, hypodermics of pink something or other, and onward to jiggers of the nasty yellow goop which was the Carteret secret remedy; all of it dope of some kind, he figured, but he didn't care as long as it did the job on him. Outside the Institute windows, Chicago blared in the night. After the first week the jag boss was gone; in his place, dollops of wax which could be used to plug the ears if North Rush Street sang too temptingly. The Carteret philosophy prided itself on going hard on hardcase drinkers: this is the belly of the booze beast, this is Jonah's bed in the whale, and you had better lay stretched there scared and sober in the dark to make yourself know you can survive it. Hugh ingested on schedule, sat up straight in the Amen Corner sessions every afternoon along with meatpacking heirs and Southern cotton traders. After two weeks of this, the blessed midpoint, he was granted permission to go out to a movie with the other inmates who had been toeing the line. With a corporal's guard of O'Shea and a couple of orderlies, they trooped around the corner to the Windsor Theatre. To the bafflement of the other moviegoers, at nine o'clock sharp, fifty men simultaneously took out little vials and drank them in one toss, their community gulp of the Carteret cure.

When the first issue of the magazine reached him by somebody slyly shoving it along the counter of the Downtowner Cafe in Glasgow, the sheriff had a heart-stopping moment over the opening frieze-photo of taxi dancers and damworkers draped over one another and the big black-type underline 10,000 MONTANA RELIEF WORKERS MAKE WHOOPEE ON SATURDAY NIGHT. Then he remembered he'd just been safely reelected for the next four years.

Even so, Carl Kinnick felt as though he was being scrubbed down with gravel as he flipped his way through the magazine piece. *Cowless cow towns — rickety as git-up-and-git — saloons wide open — all-night whooperies — taxi dancers lope around with their fares in something halfway between the old barroom stomp and the lackadaisical stroll of the college boys at Roseland — Red Light suburb — the only idle bedsprings are the broken ones — Franklin Roosevelt has a Wild West —*

That last one, Wild West, the magazine smart alecks managed to use seven times in nine pages, by the sheriff's fuming tally. On the other hand, they counted up only six shantytowns for Fort Peck, missing the actual total by ten or so.

Sheriff Kinnick sat there not knowing what to think, looking at the dead-accurate pictures (including the one of some anonymous blonde number tossing down a drink under that damned FDR campaign poster in the Blue Eagle) and the haywire lingo, until he turned to the very front of the magazine. There the editors announced that in sending their camera eye to explore this exciting time in history that would be known as the American century, they were presenting Fort Peck Dam on the cover. Although it wasn't. The structure pictured, looking like the kind of massive parapet Mussolini would love to strut on while he made speeches, was the concrete piers of the spillway gates, three miles away from the actual dirt dam. This, said the editors and the cover of the new magazine, was LIFE. Well, maybe.

The truth is not in that woman.
Meg, masked with I-am-after-all-a-

Milne-of-Inverley manners, watched as Proxy held the attention of Hugh and Darius and even Owen and apparently even Charlene.

Although, really it must be — she doesn't expend any of it when she talks.

". . . but that's how those dance marathons are," Proxy concluded with a flourish, looking around the Sunday dinner table at them all. "Real long." This latest story had been about the time in Hibbing, Minnesota, when she and her partner danced for so many hours straight that the contest judges gave up and paid them to quit.

"You've got more constitution than I have, then," Charlene said as if comparing histories. "I'd have perished of boredom first, Prox."

"Just in case any of us take up marathon dancing, what did you do to keep yourself occupied?" Owen prodded Proxy along some more. He always liked to see how far out on a limb she would let herself get, when she started storying.

"Umm, nothing worth mentioning," was all he could draw out of her, though. Proxy tried to watch her step where Owen was concerned — after all, who in her right mind would want to cross tomahawks with Charlene?

"Spent the time reading the Good Book,

naturally," Darius interposed.

"You're one to talk," that brought him from Hugh. "You'd have parroted poetry the whole while."

"That reminds me," Proxy sailed on again, "do you know this one?" Prim as a spelling-bee contestant, she reeled off:

> "She offered her honor,
> He honored her offer,
> And so all night long,
> it was on 'er and off 'er."

Charlene giggled at that more than Owen thought was strictly deserved, but then he let loose a laugh, too. Hugh and Darius gave their indecipherable chuckles, so close to identical. Meg pasted on what she was pretty sure was the last Sunday-best smile in her and reminded herself that she had a full week ahead to get over Proxy before they all went through this again. For the benefit of Hugh, which was to say in the furtherance of his Carteret cure, she had enlisted Darius and Owen and Charlene for these round-robins of what amounted to sentry duty, and that meant putting up with Proxy, *bag of yarn that she is*. Meg fiddled with her spoon and then her fork and listened to the January freshet of wind in the kitchen stovepipe as the others razzed Proxy's taste in poetry.

611

So, happy 1937 Hugh Carlyle Duff. Year one of your Reform Act. When we shall see whether the mend holds. For now, she would shoo them all into the Blue Room and follow up with more coffee and pound-cake, whenever Proxy shut up.

She thinks she is somebody, Proxy retaliated against the fidgets of Meg's fork and spoon. *Face it though, Prox, there had to have been a time back in that thistle patch they're all from when she could have had her pick of Hugh or Darius. So maybe she is.*

Janus is the two-faced god, and while Kate could not have specifically told you that, she knew all about the fickle behavior of his namesake month. Snow and blow, clear away and then gray, with mocking icicle grins hung on the Rondola's eaves — this was January for you. Every start of every year of her life had taken place in such weather, Fort Peck weather, and Bruce's talk of Louisiana and California notwithstanding, anywhere with a sunshine coast and warm water to be dived, she would not be surprised to find herself still here when the next ice age came by. Although, she did mention to herself in this mood, there were women who punched their own tickets in life, got themselves to elsewhere; Proxy was well

612

traveled, you could say that for her in more ways than one.

January, though, probably made even Proxy hole up on the houseboat, Kate figured. Snuggle in there with Darius; breakfast, lunch, and dinner in bed, she wouldn't be surprised. Noontimes past, Bruce and herself used to about beat down the door getting at each other, hadn't they. Not so much anymore. Jackie's presence in the shack, that of course made a difference. But even on those occasions when Meg, bless her cactus heart, kept Jackie a while extra, it wasn't a sure thing that Bruce would find his way home in time for an opportunity together. Kate wanted to be fair to him on this score of settling down, so-called, in some parts of life and not others. Bruce was always going to go around inviting lightning, as Owen said about him. Yet he was a good enough father toward Jackie. Better than that, actually. When he was around.

For now, all that Kate decided was to take January in sips, times like this when meal business went slack and she could carry a cup of coffee for herself over by the cafe's front window. She rubbed the usual spot in the window frost to see out again. Out there, the river, iced and white, the source of her chronic dream of somebody — lately it had been Jackie and her, both — tied to the ferried wagon the way Grandmère Henriette had been. Kate didn't put much credit in dreams. Didn't think she did, anyway. Nearer in view, cut in a long channel pointing toward the Rondola, was the winter harbor, the dredges moored there. She remembered every detail of how her father, late each year when the Missouri grew dangerous with ice, would skid the flatbottomed ferry out onto the riverbank, drain the converted Fordson tractor engine that powered its windlass, take down the bridle pulley from the long cable across the river, and begin to wait out winter. All the harbors in the head.

Neil climbed down from the truck into the snow, only ankledeep here on the ridge above the Duff homestead. Winter had swept through without murderous cold, at least to this point of early March, and after testing the weather he decided he could work without his coat on.

He clomped across the ditch, his overshoes scrunching on the dry snow, and went over to the white lump on the prairie. Owen and he had taken care to pile the spilled lumber good and tight before they towed the truck in to Glasgow last fall, and the stack looked intact, but even in this mild, open winter it had collected a sizable bank of snow and so the boards were bound to be frozen to each other. The worst was going to be how wet his gloves would get, mauling the boards out of the snow, but he had a spare old pair somewhere under the seat of the truck.

He'd had every intention of plunging right at the work, but he found himself stalling, giving in. At last he turned around and took the look he had been dreading, down the long slope to the river and the stand of trees beyond the stark patch that had been the homestead buildings. The leaves, in the time since he stared so desperately into them that eclipse dawn, had turned and fallen and the cottonwoods stood bare and skeletal. *My God, what if it'd happened this time of year. That green thing would still be crawling in my —* •

He knew it was batty to resent the blind bad luck of being singled out by the sun. That one unerasable moment here when all he'd done was to glance up from the verge of the road in curiosity about the out-of-kilter sunrise, and bang: everything turned upside down and a hell of a repair bill on the truck. A happenstance he couldn't have done anything about, he'd told himself over and over. But there were times ever since then when he wanted to take a swing at something. While Rosellen had chosen the exact same time to turn fierce about sticking with Fort Peck, instead of seeing about life for themselves somewhere less treacherous. He couldn't put his finger on it, why he and she couldn't seem to connect better on this one argument. As he kept telling her, trestle work and hauling at the dam weren't going to last, so before awful long she was going to have to argue with the calendar as well as him about their time to go.

He discovered he was shivering, and turned and dived to work on the lumber pile.

In a land usually beholden to wind, today's breeze was only the gentlest of stirrings. Come, this breeze laughed, help me chase the grass and set the wildflowers to jigging on their stem legs.

Laughing along with it, Juanita and Gilbert next . . .

Nhn, what they do next, old Nita and Gil, about whom I barely give a hang? Leaning back from her typewriter, Rosellen ran both hands through her hair and checked on the sundial of spring she had been watching out the Ad Building window: a patch of snow, gone gray and ugly, which clung to the side of a coulee between the Corps townsite and Wheeler. That snowbank dwindled markedly these April days, but spring was coming more easily out there than it was on her pages. *So, are stories going into hibernation on me? That's interesting. What would be the opposite, when warm weather —* She got out KNOW YOUR ANTONYMS! and there hibernation's reverse was, "aestivation: a state of dormancy or torpor during the summer or periods of drought." She had to chuckle. That could explain a lot about Juanita's and Gilbert's reluctance to show any life on the paper this noon hour, they were out there aestivating.

Antonyms put aside, she glanced around again, needing to keep watch so that Owen didn't suddenly show up over her shoulder wanting his dratted monthly dredging report and become curious about what was in her typewriter. She'd tried to get the report off her desk and onto his, but Max Sangster was in with him and they were talking over something about the dam hot and heavy. The clock wasn't doing her any favors either. Why was noon always the shortest hour?

Daydreamy as a glazed figurine, Rosellen did not look like someone with all of life on her desk. Yet there she sat, steaming to know people's sensations, stories, the private roads of their lives. Right now what she really wished she had the story of, knew how to tell, was Neil running into the eclipse the way he had. But he was like a porcupine about that one topic. When she had tried to coax details out of him, he asked her right back whether she wanted to know about it or just write about it. *Both. All.* She was surprised he would even put the question like that. *Neil, sugarboat, why won't you turn loose of that eye episode? I know it must have been awful for you at the time. But it didn't even leave a sty, did it?* He shook his head. *Then why — ?* All he would say after that was that she should stick to making stories up.

Stickum wasn't the only ingredient, whatever Neil thought. Kate had told her last fall that the famous photographer ate supper in the Rondola every night with GONE WITH THE WIND propped open in front of her. That book was longer than the Bible, and a good deal more windy, despite its title. Yet people read it until they almost passed out from the effort. Disgruntled — *is there gruntled?* — Rosellen took a hard look into her typewriter at Juanita and Gilbert and the laughing breeze, and pulled out the sheet of paper and crumpled it.

Time to move the circus. Owen as ringmaster, fillmaster, scarcely took time to breathe; his figure, thin as a rake, but that beehive of a head, seemed to be wherever anyone looked while twenty total miles of dredgeline were being uncoupled in twelve-and-a-half-foot sections of massive pipe and hauled by an army of trucks to new strutworks waiting on the downstream side of the dam. All four dredges, Owen's great white wagons of the Missouri, were going to parade one final time through the river channel between the halves of the dam and take ready positions, downstream, to gnaw at the river's banks and bottom afresh. From here on out, all of the dredging would happen downstream, because after the start of this summer the river would be plugged. No more channel, once the boulder-and-gravel barrier was dumped into place at the upstream face. Even by Owen's impatient standards, the mouth of the channel there was already changing in startling fashion; an eight-hundred-foot trestle, sudden forest of pilings shooting up out of the water, was going into place in the gap between the dam halves.

With this final trestle and its railroad track being highballed into place, the dam site now from, say, famous-photographer altitude looked like a model-railroad layout: the track vaulting the bottomland and river on the high pilings of the new trestle and following the east bluff of the river around to the downstream top of the dam, then crossing back over the water on the steel truss bridge there. This oval was going to be used relentlessly for closure of the river, trains steaming out onto the trestle with barrier material and exiting back across the truss bridge, the go-round continuing with train after train until the river no longer flowed. Owen and Sangster and the other engineers looked forward to it like kids promised a train set for good behavior.

Yet, as he prowled his pipelines and booster stations and dredges, he had the sensation of leaving a neighborhood he loved, this upstream stretch of the river where the earth had been made to flow into new form. For certain, he and his tons of apparatus had changed the neighborhood no little bit. Dredging cuts lay around him like square flooded fields. Time, though, to go.

Owen paused, to pull out his Eversharp and then a notebook. He had two of them going now, one in each shirt pocket, for the day-by-day dredging and for the big move downstream. He quirked a little smile at himself as he made sure he had the right notebook. To readily tell them apart from here on, he wrote in crisp lead

on the cover of the one for the move:
EXODUS.

Someone on high, whom he correctly suspected to be Owen, had taken pity on Darius this past winter and instead of freezing half to death at ice cutting, he had been merely chilled to the marrow every day in a pour job down in the tunnel-gate shafts. Then and now, concrete was being poured furiously, and to Darius's surprise, with hoisting cranes going overhead and the operatic clamor of machinery and the odd crannies of workspots down in the shaft forms and the way the silolike walls took gradual curvaceous form, the work reminded him of shipyard life more than anything had yet at Fort Peck. Now that the weather was momentarily so winsome, though, he lingered up top before going down with the other two bullgang men for the next batch of pour.

"Duff, what the dickens they doing up there?" Rosocki called up out of the bottom of the shaft to him. "We been waiting forever on this pour. Tell them to get their ass in gear, would you, so we can be out of this gopher hole."

Darius peered around over his shoulder. Down the dam slope from him and the shaft mouth, a driver of a cement truck had swung out onto the running board to

621

take a dubious look at the rise where he had to back up. Darius watched the rear of the truck approaching as the driver revved it in reverse gear, but then the vehicle shuddered ahead, short of the pouring hopper, before the driver could get the brakes on. The foreman Miliron was on his way over, looking dire.

Darius reported into the shaft, "They're trying to teach the truck manners," then went down the ladder steps nailed to two-by-fours of the shaftwall form with the odd shambling grace that always made others stop and watch him, a scarecrow dancing ballet. As Darius touched foot to the bottom of the shaft, he heard Miliron yell at the truck driver, "We're behind on this pour! Damn it, get that thing up here!"

Darius chuckled and turned toward Rosocki and Cates to say something about the universal tone of voice of foremen, Clydeside to Fort Peck. As he did, a shadow fell over the three of them, instantly followed by the sound of metal slammed into metal.

Rosocki and Cates squeezed themselves against the side of the shaft as if papering themselves to it, Darius flinging himself into their clutching arms. The pouring hopper, struck by the truck, plunged into the shaft with a grating roar.

The crash deafened them for a moment,

then the stunned three stared at the shaft-wall. The hopper as it plummeted had scraped down the wall, breaking like matchsticks every step of the two-by-four ladder Darius had just shimmied down.

"God Almighty had his hand on your shoulder that time, Duff," Rosocki said shakily.

Darius said absolutely nothing. Even after an extension ladder was brought and he and Cates and Rosocki climbed out to the scared apologies of the truckdriver and the grudging commendation of the foreman for not getting themselves killed, Darius still did not have a word to say.

That night, someone lodged a wrench in the gearteeth of the project's biggest hoisting crane, crippling it.

By the tens of tons, rock was flowing onto the dam now. Trainloads of quarry stone were being brought in from two hours away, at Snake Butte — as the name promised, rattlesnakes accompanied the cargoes of boulders, and caused everybody at Fort Peck to think more carefully about where they stepped — and then the loads were discharged on the slope at the west end of the dam, where heavy equipment was beginning to place all this rock to form riprap, the breakwater-like artificial shore which would withstand the waves of Fort Peck Lake when the dam filled.

Bruce wished rock had never been invented. All spring, he had been diving to the footings of the new trestle, which straddled the river at the upstream face of the dam and in effect was going to be the haul road for the mountain of rock as riprap was emplaced on the full four-mile width of the dam. It was the middle of May now. The engineers, Owen very much included, demanded that the trestle be done by the start of June so that they could run their rock trains across it to the eastern half of the dam; then by the end of June, they wanted to be able to *stand* trains on top of the trestle and merrily dump boulders and gravel over the side until they had the river plugged. All well and good and dandy-fine for the engineers, it seemed to Bruce; for him, it meant underwater handling of braces and bolting in the hardest part of the river, the heart of the current. Unlike Sangster's truss bridge at the downstream end of the channel, an elegant cat's cradle of steel girders that suspended itself across the river, the trestle walked through the river on stilts, actually thick wooden pilings, and every one of them carried brace specifications that made Bruce sweat beads of his soul. If he messed up, went woozy from the bends and forgot to bolt down one end of a braceplate, then when the weight of a sitting trainload of rock came onto — he didn't want to think about it, and couldn't get it off his mind.

Up through the water, aloft in the strut-work of the trestle, Neil had been called in as brace monkey. Swaying over the river on a safety belt — he swore he could feel the thrum of the current, the Missouri humming in the wood of the pilings — he didn't like the channel trestle project any better than Bruce did.

Floodwater, they both gladly could have done without.

In that pleasantest spring, the water trickling down rock faces and soft coulees began to swell as the snowpack in the Rocky Mountains turned to mush. Down a 50,000-square-mile slab of the continent the trickles began to feed the creeks, Blacktail and Newlin and English and Cut Bank and Hound and Cow and some hundreds of others that were the capillaries of the vast geography of drainage from Bozeman to St. Louis. One by one the myriad creeks began to lift the rivers, the basic trio of Gallatin, Madison, and Jefferson in their collecting-basin valleys of southmost Montana; then, beyond where those three formed into the headwaters of the Missouri, north across six hundred miles, other river after other river muscularly began to contribute high water, the Dearborn, the Smith, the Sun, the Teton, the Marias, the Judith, the Musselshell. By the time the water reached Fort Peck, several hundred brimming creeks and ten enlarged rivers were running as one.

Great, just sonofabitching great. The one spring when we could use a little cooperation from the river, it's running twice as much water as it did other springs. Where does it even get it all from, the colonel and the major peeing their pants about the schedule? Sangster is going to have conniptions if they have to shut down on bracing that trestle. I'm going to have something myself if all this sets back the plug date. Where the hell am I supposed to put fill by then if the channel isn't —

"Eh, Owen. A minute of your time?"

Hugh had headed him off before he could reach the government pickup and start for the briefing at the trestle. "Dad," he acknowledged, trying to think why his father wasn't over at the dredgeline poking traps. Christ, was the dredgeline clogged? Had the Old Man and Birdie let —

"There's a job I want on," said his father, just like that.

At long wonderful last. Owen tried not to

spoil this by looking too pleased. "Well, sure, good. Anything short of my own, just name it."

"Snakecatcher."

"Sn— ? Are you out of your pickled mind?"

"Not pickled anymore, remember?"

But what's the difference, if you're going to behave like this. Owen worked his mouth without saying anything, trying to study his father afresh. Now that Hugh had turned dry, he went around with the willed aplomb of a firewalker. But, thought Owen, refurbished dignity or rectitude or whatever the blazes it was didn't particularly qualify him for — "Dad, listen. Since when do you know anything about handling rattlesnakes?"

Unfazed, Hugh told him:

"My idea of it is, it would give a man something to concentrate on."

Snagboats were on busy duty upstream from the dam channel, grappling out the most threatening tree trunks and logs before they could build up dangerously against the shins of the trestle. Still, everyone aboard the diving barge was keeping half an eye on that stretch of the river, colonel's briefing or no colonel's briefing. If, say, a floating forest of big cottonwoods suddenly showed up around that bend of the Missouri, there was going to be a unanimous footrace for the high ground of the dam.

By now even the color of the river looked mean, a sullen muddy tone as if lava was corrupting the water.

"But you can see enough to work down there?" Colonel Parmenter asked.

"Yeah," Bruce answered with untimely honesty. "Just enough."

All in God's world they wanted from this day, the Corps officers and the engineers and the apprehensive diving barge crew and for that matter Bruce, was the one more diving shift it would take to finish bracing the footings of the channel trestle. If they could get the bracing done, in Sangster's estimation, everything ought to hold. If they didn't, and higher water and a jam-up of snags and other trash found the right pressure to put against an un-braced section, then — Sangster mourned out in *Dear John* tones — that's all she wrote.

"I still say we need to wait and see how long before the flood crest is due to get here," Owen maintained. He watched for the effect on Colonel Parmenter, never easy to gauge either. Then he swung toward Bruce. *Come on, Bruce. For once in your life, take it a little slow.* "What does our government diver think?"

"'That this would be a nice time," Bruce said as if the idea had just hit him, "for about a two-week vacation.'"

The bullgang, languishing along the top of the dam next to the trestle, heard the round of laughter come up from the diving barge and wondered to each other what was so funny down there in the big drink. Neil had shed his climbing gear and was lying back with his hands under his head, trying to just listen to the laughter come and go or to nap or anything except to think about the trestle and high water and random danger flicked down like a playing card out of the sky, but the thinking would not go away. Next to him, unusually untalkative, sat Darius, watching down the slope of the dam to the diving barge and the specific figure of Bruce.

"You know, though, sir," Bruce spoke up again, with Owen snapping a look at him, "I'd kind of like to get it over with. I'm ready to go down" — he a little theatrically peered at the lusty water — "whenever you say."

Jesus, where does he get it from, piped in hot from the Old Man? Owen was trying to hold his temper, knowing himself already riled about the screw-up in the pipe hauling. If he could get his hands on the joker who poured sugar in the gas tanks of his haul trucks . . . Bruce, though, was the immediate issue. *Here's Bruce Duff for you, world — never happy unless he's in trouble up to his bottom lip.* Aloud, actually quite loud, Owen said:

"And I think we don't want to go off half-cocked here. Look, how about this, everybody," by which he meant Colonel Parmenter. "We get the noon reading from Tansy Creek" — the nearest measuring station — "and if the river is cresting at Tansy, okay, we'll know it'll hit here a couple of hours from then. That'll make it tight, but there'll still be time enough for Bruce to go down and finish his bracing. Right, Bruce?"

Sure, you bet, Ownie know-it-all, if everything goes right. If I don't drop my wrench in the silt. If I don't black out any too many minutes at a time. If this and if that. "I'd still rather start the dive now," Bruce argued, "and have a little more time down there just in case everything —"

"Damn it, though," Owen broke in, "what if we get the noon reading and the crest is past Tansy Creek? What if it's at about" — he took a breath and looked bleakly at Bruce — "the Nettle Creek coulee? Then it'd hit here while you're down on the dive. That wouldn't be such a hot thing to have happen, would it, Bruce?"

"I can't guarantee holding this barge in the middle of something like that," the barge boss Taine spoke up.

Bruce cut Taine off with an angry swipe of his hand. "Hey, here," he was still directing his argument to Owen, "I'm the goddamn one on the spot who has to —"

"I still say it's a matter of timing," Owen insisted, "we've got to know when the sonofabitching crest will get here and work from —"

"Gentlemen."

Both Duff brothers appeared startled at the word from Colonel Parmenter. The colonel gazed back and forth between Bruce and Owen.

"I don't wish to lose a diver, I don't wish to lose this barge, I don't wish to lose the trestle," he solemnly enumerated, even if those didn't particularly add up. "Everyone take a break. We'll wait for the noon reading from the Tansy Creek station."

Looking steamed, Bruce climbed the face of the dam as though he was charging up San Juan Hill. Near the top, the sight of Darius slowed him considerably; he had been treading with care around his uncle, not to mention Proxy's volcanic vicinity, ever since the night in the Blue Eagle. *Aw, hell, he can just hunker up and stay sore, if that's what he wants,* Bruce decided. "Unk," he acknowledged stiffly.

"Nephie," Darius returned commensurately.

Neil was sitting up, yawning but impatient. "What's the deal?" he asked Bruce. "You bigwigs got the river figured out?"

Bruce stopped short. *Christ Jesus, now him.* Neil seemed to be on the prod pretty often, anymore.

Holding his temper — there had to be some limit to how many brothers, uncles, and whatnot a guy could take on in one day — Bruce laid out river matters for Neil, primarily in profanity, then glanced over his shoulder as if the barge argument was following him. "Let's clear out of here until Owen gets off the warpath," he concluded. "Come on, I'll stand you to coffee and pie."

Tactics. Take care of those and they'll take care of — "Mind if I tag along?" Darius spoke up.

Bruce thawed so visibly Darius was almost embarrassed. "You bet, Unk. You can explain to us how one Duff can be such a horse's patoot" — he jerked his head in the vicinity of the barge and Owen — "while the rest of us are so perfectly nice."

The Rondola was brimming with customers as usual, but places at the end of the counter were being vacated by a railroad crew, and the three Duffs moved right onto stools still warm from the gandydancers' fannies. Bruce winked at the waitress. "We came to brighten your day,

Better Half."

"Surrounded, am I," Kate greeted them, dealing out three cups and pouring coffee. "Won't the dam fall down without you characters leaning against it?"

"We left Owen in charge," Bruce muttered, "so it wouldn't dare."

"Hi, Kate, how you doing?" Neil was pleased to get her in on this. He had forgotten she'd be on shift or he would have proposed this Rondola sideshow himself to try to settle Bruce down some. "Been trying to drill some common sense into this husband of yours, about how much water it's wise to walk under."

"Better get a big auger," she said.

Neil shot a glance at Bruce, expecting him to blow up. Instead, looking less riled than when he'd stomped away from the river, Bruce said so soberly it was comical: "There, hear that? This is what she does to me."

"Kate, merciful," Darius flashed in with. "Tell us, what's the pastry prospect?"

"There's pie, and it's rhubarb."

"Saves on the strain of deciding, anyway," Bruce said. "Hon, put this on our tab, will you — I went out of my mind and told these guys I'd treat."

Neil and Bruce watched restlessly as Darius poured cream and sugar on his slice of rhubarb pie, then dug into theirs unadorned. While Bruce and Darius — mostly Bruce — talked trestle through mouthfuls, Neil let his gaze drift after Kate as she wielded the relentless coffeepot and swept dishes to and from customers. That little exchange between her and Bruce, wham bam; nothing moony about the state of their marriage, it looked like. Watching her at waitressing, he liked the way she never scurried, just covered the territory. Kind of interesting, actually, to rest the eyes on Kate's long silky build, although he was reminded of Bruce's original assessment that you couldn't see her coming around a corner.

On her next pass along the counter she came over to them again with the coffee-pot.

"Not I," Darius declined again, one cup of the stuff more than adequate with him.

"Had all I can stand, too," Neil said against another refill. Which sounded stiffer than he'd intended, so he glanced up at Kate and kidded: "Bruce claims there's something in the coffee here and that's how you got him."

Kate judiciously looked in the pot she was holding as Bruce chortled and the other two sat there grinning.

She killed off Bruce's chortle by pouring Neil's and Darius's cups to overflowing and skipping his. With all the nonchalance in the world she told him, "You already had some, remember?"

The noon reading of the river depth left no further room for argument. The flood crest had just passed Tansy Creek, it would hit Fort Peck in another few hours, and while Bruce could grind his teeth all he wanted, he also had to hustle into his diving suit. There was time enough left for a standard dive, Owen had been right about that. *But where the hell does he get the idea,* Bruce was still thinking furiously as his helmet snicked into place, *that this'll be a standard dive?*

"The damned knothead of a kid did it, Charlalene! Bruce goosed the moose!"

Owen bounced into the house so full of strange beans that she at first thought he had come home drunk. Now she recognized it as engineer elation. "You're pinning medals on Bruce?" Charlene checked to make sure. "Since when?"

"The trestle! He —"

"— got done with the bracing in jig time," Neil was telling rapt Rosellen, "he didn't even take his whole diving shift. The barge bunch looked like they couldn't believe it, him signaling already he had it whipped, down there. You should've seen

635

him, though, when that helmet came off him — old Bruce looked like one relieved puppy." Neil himself looked as if he was thinking back step-by-step on the history of Bruce.

"Oh," he thought to say, though. "Saw Kate today, too."

Darius was kissing places on her, lingering here, darting there. Proxy nibbled her lip in pleasure. He did know how to get a woman's attention. She could feel every least maneuver of his mouth, tongue practiced as a cat's. Charting planet to planet on her, slow delicate orbit of first the aureole on one breast and then same on the other, then on to teasing each erect crest, somehow finding time in the soft valley between to say things. God, you wouldn't think a Scotchman could make love talk, would you.

"Hnn*nn*?" she brought herself out enough to respond. "What, sugarbush?"

"Laid eyes on Kate today," he was saying as if just reminded. "She's a bit flat in the netherlands, isn't she."

Hugh had to admit he didn't care much for their rattling. *Far, far better to hear the buggers than not, though.*

By the nature of things, each rattlesnake was peeved, stirred up at its boulder cave being derricked away or yelling men tres-passing into its vicinity, by the time Hugh was called to the scene. He was assigned the west half of the dam, which had the headstart in rockwork on the face of the dam and thus more snake business. Now that the riprap loads were rolling across the trestle to the east half too, a second snakecatcher had been put on over there and Hugh had heard practical jokes were being pulled on him, a dead rattler cozily coiled behind his lunchbox when he went to pick it up, for instance. No one pulled anything on Hugh Duff.

He stayed perched judiciously on a stone slab and scouted around for his latest poisonous customer. Invariably the snake was reported as being the size of the Loch Ness monster, but they were damnably hard to spot, the pattern on their backs blending so with their surroundings. In a way he was grateful to that angry buzz of the rattle, as a warning device. Poised there, he was outfitted with a sheephook, its seven-foot handle a healthy length, while the narrow springsteel neck of hook designed to snare the hind leg of a sheep did nicely enough around the circumfer-ence of a rattlesnake. Hugh's procedure was elemental but not necessarily simple. Yank a rattler out of its striking position, like a coil of enfevered rope. Then pin it down (make *sure* it's pinned down), in back of its wedge of head, with the flexible neck of the sheephook. Then reach in and employ the machete, which he carried at his waist in a scabbard that would have suited an admiral.

And so now I am married to the St. Patrick of Fort Peck. There he goes — Sir Hugh, of the Serpent-Ridding Hussars.
She had Jackie on an outing, on a walk along the bluff where they could look down and see the trains run. The boy attended closely to anything that went on wheels. Unfortunately, thought Meg, he seemed to be thoroughly his father's son in that. Bruce and momentum, kidskin and glove. She hoped Kate wasn't tiring of his velocity. Not that she herself was the leading expert at keeping up with the demands that were men. These days, these lovely walks with Jackie, Meg spent the major share of her attention on the lanky figure with the shepherd's crook, there on the boulder dike in the middistance. *How then can he keep being the same Hugh, having traded himself in wholesale as he did in Chicago? Are we stone, under it all as Owen's dam will be there at the lake-water?*
"See Gramp?" she tried to point him out to Jackie. "Gramp, down there letting daylight into the snakes — see him?"

The child, though, had caught sight of color dancing by in the air. "Mum Mum," he called for her attention, pointing after the dancing thing. "Buttafly."

"Jack. I'm glad you brought that up," Meg said to him, as usual speaking to the child as though they both were Prime Ministers. "There now is something I have never understood — a butterfly does fly, I grant you, but do you see anything the least bit buttery about it? Would you not say, Jack, a better name for the lovely tiny beast would be 'flutterby'?"

Bright-eyed, her conversation partner considered this with the quizzical smile that reminded her so of Owen.

"Fluttaby," the boy agreed.

Ah, now he saw the adversary, patterned-green circles of itself under it as the snake lay looped to strike. Pink mouth hotly open, twin fangs prepared, the better to dagger and poison you with, my dear.

Quick as a pirate, Hugh grappled down with the sheephook, spilled the nestled snake sideways into a curving series of writhes, pressed down with the neck of the hook, then delivered the chop with the machete.

His heart and breathing always sped up by about twice during this. Hours at a time went by, though, in snakework, when he did not think about a bottle of anything.

Now he employed the other item he carried on this job, a fisherman's creel. With another slash of the machete, he lopped the rattle off the defunct snake and dropped it in the creel with the others. "I don't see how you can go those snakes, Hugh," Birdie had said to him more than once. In the spirit of enterprise, though, Birdie shellacked the rattles Hugh provided, glued them on little wooden bases and sold them. Already the tails of rattlesnakes were showing up all over Wheeler beneath the mounted skulls of buffalo.

Four days before the river was to be closed off, in the middle of an already complicated enough afternoon of jigsawing the dredge-lines back together downstream from the dam, Owen was called to the field telephone.

"Sangster. Sounds like he's got a hair crosswise," the pipehaul foreman warned before handing him the phone.

"Owen," said the thin voice on the other end, "you better come see something."

"What, at the trestle again? I'll be right —"

"Huh uh," the fieldphone voice now sounded as if it was having trouble believing itself. "This is at the truss bridge again."

His first look at the slumped earth, within spitting distance of the truss bridge, sent Owen white-faced. Sangster's was whiter.

The slipped section of fill resembled a muddy scallop shell perhaps two hundred feet long and a hundred high. It had slid, still in one arched piece, several feet down into the river channel. Scoured away underneath by the flood, loosened by the rapid fall of the floodwater, who knew what the precise cause was: it had slid. The arc of gap where the shell edge had pulled away from the dam was spookily neat, as if a hill had just taken an innocent step forward from the mountain of earthfill. There was nothing innocent about it. The shifted heap of fill was throwing enormous weight down against the main pier of the railroad bridge.

"It holding okay?" Owen tore his eyes away from the sickening dam slippage to ask about the health of Sangster's bridge.

"Not really." Sangster even still sounded pale. "Out of line about a foot already, and more to come. That pier's cracked."

Owen spoke six or eight expletives, rapid-fire.

"I agree," Sangster said. "But we've got to do something besides cuss at it."

They knew they had only minutes before the official car delivered Colonel Parmenter and Major Santee and general hell.

They already had the gravel cars going by the time the Ad Building contingent descended. First thing first, everyone could see that much. If they lost the truss bridge they lost the railroad loop, the key to plugging the river; they would lose the entire dam schedule, they would lose all advantage over the river for Christ knew how long. Thirty timely railcars of gravel, dumped on the weak side of the cracked concrete pier to temporarily shore it up, saved them from that at least for the moment. But now came the question of holding together both the bridge's underpinning and the channel shoulder of the dam until they could get the river plugged.

Owen and Sangster and everybody in the vicinity nervously sized up the Corps officers as the briefing was convened there at the river. Colonel Parmenter appeared to be wishing for the Philippines. Major Santee looked a little smirky, as he often did when things went wrong.

The colonel made short work of discussion. "What about this, Duff?"

What about what? What the floodwater did along here, so that neither I nor God Almighty can guarantee you that chunk of earthfill won't move some more, won't cave off and take the bridge with it, in the next four days or the next four minutes? That there was only, what, one chance in five that we'd get the highest water of the whole project this spring, but that's exactly the thing we did get? Or that what I most want right now, the one thing I can think of to maybe stabilize the fill that's slipped, is to have high water up against it again? What are you going to think of any of my whats, Colonel?

Owen took the deep, deep breath needed to go for broke.

Fort Peck woke up to dynamite at dawn.

The detonation, at 4:20 A.M. sharp, breached the dike which had been holding back the riverwater above the tunnel portals. That quick, with one *ka*-BOOM and a dirt geyser of blown dike, the map of the Missouri River changed. Now the river forked at the dam, the main flow still tumbling through the channel but an easternly eddy swirling its way into the tunnel inlets. It was a bit past dawn when the first riverwater made its passage through the tunnels and surged into the outlet channel below the dam, frothing white against the confining concrete.

At the main channel, at the truss bridge, four years of calm planning and temperate engineering about how to most handily close off the Missouri River had to be fed into the meatgrinder of the next twelve hours. Improvising every inch of the way, they were going to make the river into the counterweight proposed by Owen Duff, by backing the water up against the sloughed section of fill like a liquid retaining wall. Which meant plugging the river here and now, at the *down*stream end of the channel, instead of upstream at the trestle the intended three days from now.

"Owen, where the hell's that dispatcher, we got to get rolling on —"

Which meant that the forty-five-car trainload of plugging boulders could not be jauntily dropped straight into the river — the side girders of the truss bridge were in the way — but needed to be unloaded at both ends of the bridge, spilled down onto gravel approaches to the river.

"I know, I know, Colonel, it's not the greatest field office there ever was, but it's all the ready-built crew could skid over here to us in a hurry. What exactly is it? Well, sir, it's a two-holer."

Which meant that the crane barge laboring in the middle of the river current had to grapple the boulders from the gravel banks one by one, to build a rough sill out into the channel.

"Okay, Max, so this is slower than the

wrath of God, but we don't have any choice but to keep that crane boat at —"

Which meant that the rail fleet of gravel cars couldn't let fly with their massive plug of gravel until the boulder sill was firmly there to keep it from washing away.

"Oh, Jesus, it won't be done until WHEN?"

To the engineers, this was like being trapped in a very long game of checkers when they had been all set to play bombs-away.

Hold, you so-and-so. There's no damn reason *for you to be falling into the river.*

Owen wasn't addressing this thought to the truss bridge although, heaven knew by the blue smoke of invective and energy he was lending in support of Sangster and it, he did not want to see the steel span hit the water either.

Either nobody savvies or nobody's saying — not even you, Max — that the truss bridge could be only the first symptom here.

Whatever else he was at, through this longest day, Owen kept the slipped section of damfill guardedly in sight, forever in mind.

Just hold. That's not asking such a hell of a lot, is it? Sit there, another few hours is all, and then I can tend to you. If he ran

645

the arithmetic of the situation through his head once this day, he ran it two hundred times. The site of the slippage, the core pool, the distance between: by every calculation he could think of the core pool sitting dumb, fat and happy up there in the east half of the dam should be safely far enough from where that odd shell of fill had given way; look, millions of other cubic yards there in the channel shoulder supporting the core pool *hadn't* given way. Result: the slippage as it now stood didn't necessarily mean that the core pool was going to start leaking out of it any minute and the leak would increase to a gush in less time than it took to tell about it and the gush would speedily grow to be a breach and the breach majestically would cave away and the entire sonofabitching core pool would rush out in a 150-foot-high avalanche of water and fill, tearing the guts out of the dam.

Owen Duff, engineer, knew the slipped spot didn't necessarily mean that.

Owen Duff, alarmed member of the human race, Fort Peck subgroup, was not so sure. This version, the one he had to traipse around in while big rocks got fumbled into place beneath the bridge, would not breathe easy until he had the plugged Missouri and a Niagara of freshly piped dredge material both at work shoring up that slipped spot.

So hold, damn it, okay?

The bridge pier needed helpings of gravel every so often, and so Sangster at least had spurts of being busy at that, having the train dispatcher roll another thirty-car cut of dumper cars in, which Owen envied him. He himself had the pipeline crew hauling and installing along the channel shoulder and had called in the bullgang to help out with the last needed section of the strutworks there, and all four of his dredges were standing ready downriver, so that as soon as the river was safely plugged they could pour material like mad into this neck of the channel and backfill the slipped slope. Begin to end the dam, as well. Oh, there'd be another full year, fifteen months maybe, of building it up and topping it off. But the vee of the river channel was the last gap, the four-mile valley between the chosen bluffs had shrunk down to it. Owen had ready or was getting ready everything he could think of to throw at the channel. But for now he was reduced to scenery inspector, standing watching the ungodly slow progress of the rock sill under the bridge.

The river boiled around the crane barge, which stood there in midstream like a patient broad-butted fisherman, its long boom swinging as it brought a ton-and-a-half boulder into the water, going back for another.

Reporting for pipeline work, the bullgang watched the scurry and commotion around the truss bridge with envy.

"Not much call for guys with hammers in that, is there?" someone asked wistfully.

"Afraid not," answered their foreman, Jepperson. "No, most of you, just whack away at setting up the next section of struts. I goddamn well know you're going to spend most of your time gawking over there, but try and look busy once in a while." Jepperson shifted his weight. "But four of you get to be gravelmasters."

A silence settled on the crew.

"What this is," Jepperson went on, "they're gonna double up on the gravel dumping. Constantly run trains until they get the river held. The four guys up there," he jerked his head in the direction of the railroad bridge, "who're used to doing it will show you how. Oh, and you'll draw an extra two bits an hour." Someone sang out "Our chance to be big rich!" and there was a little laughter.

"So, let's say —" Jepperson made a show of looking around "— Morrie . . . Livingston . . . Duff . . . ."

Not I, said the man named Me.

The expression on Darius put a sourball look on the foreman as well. "Not you, Bonny Prince Darry. Other Duff, Neil there."

Neil bit a corner of his mouth, but stepped forward.

"And . . ." Jepperson shopped through the crew for one more. He stopped as Birdie Hinch moved indicatively. The three the foreman had named so far were all much younger, fitter. "Birdie, sorry, but I'm supposed to send guys who can run like —" He broke off, then grinned. "Yeah, okay. And Birdie."

By midafternoon, officers and engineers were running on coffee and habit. They had all been up through the night, pitching in on the final readying of the inlet channels and the tunnels for the river diversion, and ever since early morning they had watched boulder by boulder as the sill gradually grew, and they were close to becoming zombies before Sangster cured them with:

"That's as much as we can do with rock. Hadn't we better go to gravel, Colonel?"

The quartet sent to be apprentice gravel-masters were at the end of the bridge, receiving the fastest education of their lives. The four men already working the gravel cars which periodically shored up the ailing bridge pier were showing them the routine. There was a catwalk between the truss girders and where the train ran. Scrambling along that, you had to keep pace with a given dumper car and when the shout of "Pull!" came, reach down and yank the big springpin which opened one of the two hopper doors beneath the railcar. Your partner on the other side of the train opened the other hopper door at the same time and the dumper car was emptied of fifty tons of gravel, falling with an appalling roar and a hellish cloud of rockdust into the river. This had to be done constantly at a trot — the trains were not to stop, not for anything — and the newcomers' respect for the gravelmasters rapidly rose by hundreds of percent.

This was Sangster's show now, the gravel plug to be dumped down through the bridge car by car and train by train, and Owen caught a fleeting look of gratitude on the bespectacled man when he told him he was clearing out of his way, going up to a perch in the bridge girders for a ringside seat.

He was startled to see Neil, below on the catwalk, then wished he'd thought of that himself, getting Neil assigned out of the

650

bullgang to perform this. With a little softsoap and pressure, he could have wangled Bruce onto the gravelmaster crew too. Wouldn't that have been something, Owen thought to himself, twin Duff brothers plugging the Missouri.

Neil developed a lope to keep up with the dumper cars, although Birdie Hinch somehow managed simply by scampering. The four pairs of men ran a strange looping race, the lead pair dumping their car of gravel and turning to run back past the other three sets of men to the fourth dumper car back in line, following beside it until the "Pull!" signal again. They finished the first train, two thousand tons of gravel gone to the river bottom, and the next train immediately came.

Suppers went uncooked. The crews were not going to be home until the river was plugged or the bridge was lost. Light lingered, this time of year, and as the blue evening came on, wives drove down from Wheeler or walked across from Officers' Row in the Corps townsite and clustered on the bluff by the Ad Building. Rosellen said something to Charlene about having to get used to being bridge widows for however long, and while Charlene didn't answer, she thought there was no getting used to anything at Fort Peck.

Proxy showed up, saying with fine disgust that taxi dancing was slow tonight anyway. All it took was a nice evening and males were occupied with softball, she said, making it sound like a social disease.

The three of them and the other women watched the activity at the truss bridge and the river gap, where tiny figures scurried and traincars marched in constant file and bulldozers lurched across slopes; from their distance, it looked like the place on an anthill where boiling water had been poured.

"Making the gravel fly pretty good, aren't they." From the sound of him, Bruce was the authority on stopping rivers. He had come up without any of the three women noticing until here he stood with his hands in his hip pockets, expert appraiser of the roiled water beneath the bridge.

"Decided to hang around the widows' club, mmm?" Charlene looked glad to have a chance to kid him as a break in the monotony. Proxy cold-shouldered him without making a big issue of it. It was Rosellen, until then absorbed in watching the drama at the truss bridge, who cut her eyes over to Bruce a couple of times and right away wanted to know:

"What'd you do with Kate? Isn't she along for this?"

"Doesn't get off until nine," he handled that in a breeze. Actually, he added, he was on his way to the Rondola to pick her up after work. "But the view is better from up here." Whereupon he grinned around at Charlene and Rosellen and Proxy in turn, although only for the barest instant at Proxy.

Rosellen caught him off guard by asking:

"Don't you kind of wish you were down there closing the river off for good?"

"There'll still be stuff to tend to, don't worry your head about that," Bruce gave her. "For a while yet I'll keep on doing the clog dance on the river bottom."

He flinched when Proxy, as if to herself, hummed a snatch of *When We Danced Close and the World Stood Still*. But then Charlene began a big conversation about Fourth of July intentions, whether Bruce and Kate would be available if everybody could get together for another Nettle Creek picnic. "That last one was a lot of fun," she smiled as if calling back a favorite dream. "Sure it was," Bruce laughed, "because you shot the pants off everybody else."

Rosellen could have slapped them both. Here the time was, the dam taking hold, the river changing forever, Fort Peck within inches, minutes, of becoming the monument they'd all spent these years making, and the two of them chose now to go coochy-coo at each other about that stupid shooting match.

Expert reader of faces that she was, Proxy kept watch on Rosellen. *Smile, chile. If Big Sis wants to get her jollies by teasing Bruce-ums, not a thing in this world we can do about it. She'd just better know when to turn it off, is all.*

"There goes the river," Hugh wanted to say in the worst way. All that prevented him was the understanding that it *would* be the worst way. Meg would lay into him like a catamount if he took a dig at Owen's triumph. He believed it constituted un-natural forbearance, but he stoppered himself while he and Meg and Jackie watched the action at the bridge from the roof of the Rondola. Customers passing beneath into the cafe joked about hoping the roof held long enough for them to get a cup of coffee, and it was true the flat tarred surface groaned a little as a dozen people at a time took short turns as spectators, but the Duffs by some unspoken consent had residence up there while the river was being pinched off between the great halves of Owen's dam. Holding Jackie, Meg was keeping him mesmerized with the tale of a selkie, a man who was also a seal — "Think of it, Jack, he could catch himself a fish anytime he felt like it and wear lovely fur trousers as well."

"Meg." Kate came climbing the ladder, careless of knees and more flashing out from under her waitress uniform. "Let me have him a minute." She took the boy and turned so that he was looking with her toward the railroad bridge and the rumbling gravel trains. Hugh distinctly heard her say, "I want him to see the river go."

In the bullgang, Darius did his work on the dredgeline supports with his hands only, his true attention on the contest between the might of the dam project and the strength of the river. Were it not for Owen and Neil, he found, he would silently cheer for the river.

Another train done, another came. Every time a carload was dumped now, some gravel was swept away in the current as if the Missouri was determined to deliver it to St. Louis, but some stayed, a loose and shifting pyramid there under the water.

Neil, sprinting and wondering along with the other seven gravelmasters how much more of this there would be, how much more they could take, glanced up at Owen whenever he could. Braced there in the girders like a spiffed-up steelworker in a

Stetson and pressed khakis, Owen looked somehow distracted, gazing off at the channel shoulder instead of watching the bombardier-bursts of gravel into the river. *What do I expect, though, that he's going to act like some kind of radio announcer up there calling a fight? "Here's a haymaker from Neil Duff . . . followed by a wallop of gravel from Birdie Hinch . . . but the Missouri is absorbing all the punishment they can throw at it, so far." Huh uh. Owen is going to go about it his own way, whatever it is.*

Catching himself at this, knowing he was going a little giddy from exertion, Neil concentrated on his running, staying exactly even with the next dumper car, the little hop-skip when "Pull!" was shouted again and the thunder of gravel.

He could feel it all, Owen could, through the bridge. The slow rumble of the train, the concussive force as each carload was dumped: the incessant rhythms came up through his shoes, and sideways out of the girders into his gripping hands. Owen knew better but he could wish, couldn't he, that he and the bridge were taking into themselves all the tremble of plugging the river, that none could reach and dislodge the slipped area of fill. So far, the wishing had worked.

In the half-dusk, the gravel dumping slowly but unstoppably gained, the hail of pebbles building up in a rough slurry which would show for an instant above the riverwater and then slip from sight.

Tired as they were, the gravelmasters worked like acrobats now, bouncing to the catwalk railing to peek down at the effect of each dumpload, then back into the rhythm of catching their next dumper car, yanking the springpin —

In the end it was a carload dumped by Birdie Hinch and a very tired Neil that brought the shout:

"That one's staying dry!"

Neil scooted to the railing beneath Owen's perch and the two of them stared down. In the vast wallow of gravel mush below, a low conelike heap — as Darius would have said, "Not two hands higher than a duck" — was a drier gray. The Missouri, by just that much, was captured now.

Part Six

THE SHERIFF
1937

The big gravy spreader himself came to
show off at the dam after they had managed to pen up the river, to the sheriff's
steaming despair. Franklin Delano Roosevelt at his rosiest, jaunty as if he'd built
Fort Peck Dam with his own pink hands,
when the fact was he couldn't even maneuver himself from his special train to
the presidential touring car without a gang
of help. Didn't seem to matter, though, to
this President's smiling repeal of the law
of averages, the disgusted sheriff thought;
three thousand counties in the United
States and here was Roosevelt majestically
roostering around in his, for the second
time in one lifetime.

Waiting, watching, the sheriff hardly
knew where to start in being nettled. GLAS-

GOW, the depot sign read as the President's entourage began to disgorge from the train, but to Carl Kinnick it might as well have announced NIGHTMARE. For the past two weeks now the Secret Service advance man, Boatwright, barging into everything as if Valley County all of a sudden belonged to him; the elaborate chain of command it took for the sheriff to get the simplest thing done, such as roping off the depot platform; the wise-ass Highway Patrol special contingent who wanted to know whether the President's motorcade was going to go for the speed record from Glasgow to Wheeler; the on-loan police from Great Falls who figured they knew everything because they were from a city; the couple of hundred of the National Guard called into uniform and deployed along the presidential route, who figured that because they were military they knew more than any cops; and all that only brought you to Roosevelt's own voluminous retinue of staff and newspaper people and the mob of politicians from far and wide, to be dealt with starting now. As a Democratic officeholder the sheriff had to be part of the political folderol, too, and it was amazing to him as he herded them through to the train, the number of delegations who on the Fort Peck example wanted to talk to the President about a water scheme for the Marias River or the Two Medicine River or whatever their closest river happened to be; you'd think, the sheriff thought, Montana could be dammed up enough to irrigate this entire side of the earth.

Something moved, whirled, at the corner of the sheriff's vision, and he twisted in that direction with his hand on his gun butt. Tornado of pigeons, scared up from the grain elevator on the other side of the railroad tracks. Nerves. The sheriff wished he didn't have any.

One more patriotic blast the Glasgow high school Kiltie band now let loose with, red-kneed in the October wind. The crowd had been gathering for hours, the street behind the depot solid with people across to the Goodkind Block and all the way down to the Coleman Hotel, and wouldn't you know there'd be at least one, some smart-aleck Caruso at the front of the throng warbling out a popular mock version:

> "My country 'tis of thee,
> Sweet land of Franklin D.,
> next thing to king!
> Won't you please run again,
> Third term for fun again . . ."

The serenade did not actually constitute

disturbance of the peace — hell, the peace was already disturbed by the President himself — so the sheriff folded his arms and turned around to reconnoiter the trackside situation again. The delegations wanting this or that had been busily trooping through the presidential Pullman, and the schedule pretty quick called for Roosevelt to emerge onto the rear platform to smile and wave at the crowd, then descend into the open touring car for the drive to the dam. *About time,* the sheriff told himself as he was given the high sign by McIntyre, the President's secretary, to step up into the Pullman with the final delegation of supplicants.

In there, the presidential parlor car was surprisingly old-fangled. Velvety. Kind of musty, to tell the truth. Not that Carl Kinnick was there to sightsee. He knew from the '34 visit that the presidential rail quarters would be chockful of important hands to be shaken, and he first of all made sure of Governor Ayers's and Senator Murray's and Congressman O'Connell's and then merely shook whosever until it came his turn at the President's. Giving the sheriff the most famous smile this side of the man in the moon, Roosevelt assured him how perfectly delightful it was to be in Glasgow once more.

Even the FDR handshake — the master

campaigner's proffer of just-enough: *this much touch of my flesh shall ye have, and not a pore more* — provoked the sheriff, as he stepped back to watch the political menagerie in here sort itself out. Conspicuous by his absence this time was Senator Wheeler, who by now was at odds with the President for the New Deal having veered so far to the left. Here and appearing thoroughly unhappy about it was Congressman O'Connell, who appeared to suspect that Roosevelt didn't know where real left was located. The thought of FDR dainty-handing his way through the whole damned national picture like this, maybe even for another term after this one, was just about more than Carl Kinnick cared to look ahead at.

Right now, though, the local officeholders were going to be accorded the privilege of following FDR out onto the train's rear platform so their constituents could view them in the presidential presence. Roosevelt had to be got onto his feet. The sheriff was determined not to miss this. He forged his way around the end of the milling group of aides and politicos in the Pullman so he would have the clearest possible shot at seeing. A Secret Service agent scrutinized him sharply, then evidently decided this was only a short man's natural behavior.

From the waist up, Roosevelt there in his chair was monumental. Even his head seemed sizes larger than anyone else's. Commensurate shoulders and chest. The sheriff knew the story, how Roosevelt swam, swam, swam after polio hit him. All that work in the water and the exertion of the wheelchair had built him a torso that would have done a lumberjack proud.

The legs, though.

Even to the unsympathetic sheriff it appeared pitiful and painful, Roosevelt's ritual of going clenched from the jaw on down, gearing himself for the lurch upward so the metal leg braces could be locked to hold him in a standing position, his son James there on his left, his weak side, to provide firm tensed biceps he could grip onto, now the President of the United States grunting himself ready, then the actual massive tottering rise like —

The sheriff didn't know like what, but it was damn sure unforgettable.

The town of Wheeler, democratic and Democratic, antic and frantic, was boiling over for Roosevelt.

Cheers sang out at the approach of the motorcade of the President who put the country back to work, who provided a wage to those whose pockets had been emptied by the Depression, and, not incidentally, who reopened the nation's saloons. Theoretically the damwork was going on uninterrupted until FDR's big speech upon leaving Fort Peck, but somehow there were crews, complete with foremen, who saw the President from vantage points such as the Wheeler Inn and the Blue Eagle as well as from the jobsite later on. Toddlers and taxi dancers and cardsharps and Corps wives in their Sunday best jammed in next to the damworkers on the board sidewalks. When at last it arrived in the procession, the open touring car gave them their money's worth, the confident presidential smile and wave as Roosevelt was borne along the main street of Wheeler until the motorcade proceeded, naturally, to Delano Heights.

Back in the jampacked Blue Eagle, a patron shouted out: "How about a free round in honor of the President?"

"How about go screw yourself," Tom Harry replied from the busy cash register.

As the motorcade wound down the ridge to the dam, the sheriff in the follow-car behind the President's brooded ahead. Not that Franklin D. himself seemed to have a care in the world, jovially letting his ear be bent by Colonel Parmenter in the jump seat or the governor or the senator alongside him on the big backseat. The man truly did possess the ultimate politician's knack of appearing interested in every gopher hole and dandelion.

All Carl Kinnick could think about was what could go wrong, here in his county, as the rajah of the Hudson River was shown the conquered Missouri, transported across the great earthfill, shown the entire sprawling dam project from the overlook on the east abutment, then driven up into the hills to the spillway and at last to the spur railroad where the special train had been brought around for the presidential speechmaking.

The sheriff's heart, or at least the place where he pinned his badge, sank as the speaking site and the winter harbor parking lot grew into view. There and waiting were thousands. Thousands of *cars,* to only start the matter off; the intermittent sun caroming off all those windshields, the dazzle of vehicles looked like the mass lot at Ford's Rouge River plant. And it didn't take much figuring of how many people would have piled into each car to come to this and then adding on, what, ten thousand damworkers already swarming around here — Sheriff Kinnick knew this was going to be even worse than his worst dream of it.

The sheriff hopped out fast when the

motorcade pulled up alongside the special train. He spotted his undersheriff Peyser, a head taller than the rest of the cordon at the back end of the train. Cussing his way through the crowd, the sheriff wriggled in to make sure Peyser was doing what he was supposed to, keep an eye on the radio guys who were putting up microphones on tall stands to catch the President's speech from the train's rear platform.

"How you doing, Carl," the undersheriff placidly greeted him.

Sheriff Kinnick scowled at the poker-faced Peyser in return, then stared up through the grillwork of the rear platform to where the hen herd of politicians was forming up around Roosevelt and his microphones.

What if somebody took a shot here at Roosevelt the way that crackpot did back East in '33?

The sheriff was no connoisseur of history, but he knew a lot about blame. Oh, sure, the gunman there in '33 potted the Chicago mayor right next to FDR instead. But people in Montana were good shots. No, if the President — particularly *this* President — was killed in Carl Kinnick's county, that would be it for his career as sheriff. He'd might as well go pick grit with the chickens, if that happened.

And unfortunately he could think of just countless ways it could happen. Somebody mad about being let go from his job at the dam. Some liquored-up bottomlander who was sore about losing his land to the dam. Some Republican driven nuts by the New Deal. Some Communist; you never knew what that bughouse bunch was up to, but the report was that they hated FDR for keeping the country from going far enough to the left; incredible to the sheriff.

Or some woman. So far as he knew, women hadn't taken their turn yet at assassinating. (Congressman O'Connell's young knockout of a wife, prettily stationed right up there at the presidential elbow. Beauty turned beast, bango. Wouldn't that be a setup.) God, if the women ever started cutting loose . . .

So there was every kind of possibility here in this Fort Peck crowd, and one of the uncomfortable thoughts wasn't only the danger to Roosevelt. Supposedly the Secret Service bodyguards were to shield the President from assassin peril, but where were those boys when the Chicago mayor got picked off? The sheriff knew that if it came to that, if he spotted somebody here yanking out a gun, he'd have to put himself between that gun barrel and Roosevelt. He'd take death. There wasn't any choice, sheriffing.

As the governor launched into amplified greetings to Roosevelt and his trainload, the sheriff went and claimed the roof of the cab of the truck that had been pulled up parallel to the presidential Pullman for the newspaper photographers and reporters to see over the crowd.

"Governor Ayers, and I almost said 'My old friends of Fort Peck,' because some of you were here three years ago."

The presidential voice now, and if the sheriff had been a praying man he would have asked that Roosevelt just say it was nice to be in Montana, accept a bouquet and kiss Miss 4-H Beef on the cheek, and scoot back inside the railroad car. But the sheriff knew FDR, blast his lordly guts, was not going to pass up a chance at an all-out speech.

Roosevelt looked out around the Fort Peck valley and at the dam as if making sure of something.

"The one thing that I have specialized on ever since I started collecting postage stamps at the age of ten years is geography. The geography, especially, of the United States."

The squire next door, this familiar kindly confiding tone of Roosevelt's was. The sheriff shook his head. You had to half-admire how much the man could get away with. But then after predictably wafting himself and his audience out here "beside the wide Missouri," FDR turned up the oratory:

"This great river gathers into story, the written and told tributary, out of passages cut by large desires. Beginning, so far as we know, with the first cleaving of its water, by downstream Indian adventurers whose tribal name for 'canoe' was 'missouri' — never bettered, may I say, as a beautiful name for an inspiring river. Then came Lewis and Clark's Corps of Discovery, the day-by-day eyes and inks that captured onto paper for us the two-thousand-three-hundred-mile arch of the river from St. Louis to its Three Forks headwaters. Then followed the building of forts, America coming west by military and trading post handholds along the Missouri's immense chain of drainage. From that, the axe-quick renunciation of the river's forest silence as woodhawks, perhaps within sight of here where we stand today, chopped trees into boiler-lengths to feed the steamboats. And onward, then, to the imprints of homesteaders and town-planters on the floodplain of this great river. Until now, a little more than one-third of the way through this century, the pattern is as set as cry and echo, each annal desiring a next — the human tide and the Missouri River, hungrily flowing together into storied destiny."

Roosevelt paused, to let the applause roll before he went on to the invocation of the dam and the useful work it had brought and the future in which every drop of the river's water would do its duty. The sheriff stared at him from his trucktop, finally grasping this President's bargain with danger and all else.

Surfacing. That was what it was like, the way Roosevelt rose. The sheriff himself was only a so-so swimmer, nothing like this famous habitue of therapeutically warm pools, but he suddenly savvied FDR's way of thrusting himself up out of that wheelchair. Breaking upward through the polio that had sucked him down into it; rising past the political turbulence that ought to have sunk him. And once up there, having breached crippling infirmity and gravity and whatever the hell else, the irons clamped on his more or less legs to hold him in place, the presidential sonofabitch *presided.* You couldn't not listen to him, the sheriff had to admit, even if you thought you couldn't stand any more of that voice sanded so smooth by old family money. No, you listened, to his old tricks, new tricks, whatever he brought up to the surface with him this time. When Franklin Delano Roosevelt dove up into the air, onto a political platform and on out into the ethers of radio, he took you over by all the tricks that ever swam.

The majority of the President's hearers in the crowd had seasons of Fort Peck behind them, the making of the dam the prime calendar of their lives, and like the intent little sheriff, they listened as if they were being paged, one after another. Dam-workers of every stripe, householders of Wheeler and the other shantytowns and the apple-pie Fort Peck townsite, in their thousands they took in the grand words FDR had come to give them. There were absences. Nan and J.L. Hill, with the wages of laundry and dynamite, gone back to their ranch country of English Creek. Jaarala self-vanished, of course. But others and others were here, shareholders in this day. The Birdie Hinches of this earth, by that name and many others. Tom Harry in shining fresh shirt and blackest bow tie. The crisp officers of the Corps. Years' worth of Duffs, in plentiful scattering across this Fort Peck scene. The Fort Peck they had cooked for, and notched its paydays one after another. Hairdressed. Waited on. Danced with and more. That they had cleared brush off. Built dredges for. Walked beneath in diving uniform.

Fashioned an earthfill onto. Carpentered and dug and labored for in a dozen different ways. Now they listened hard to the great voice telling them this dam was theirs as much as anybody's. A searching eye with enough patience could have picked the tribe of them out of even this crowd, family resemblance in the way they stood akimbo but attentive, like soldiers picketed, one here, another over across, pair there, the Duffs as ever unmistakably in evidence. All but two.

No one would notice, today. That much they knew about this. The rest was the treacherous part.

Where they were, the sound of Roosevelt and the crowd's roars of applause were a distant surf.

They kissed hard, as if to get past any doubts.

Holding to each other, they clung so close their heartbeats registered on each other's skin. When they broke apart for breath, her fingers walked up the cleft in the middle of his chest. She asked, "Are you thinking about suppertime?"

"No." Last thing on his mind; the way they were touching each other crowded out all else. "Why would I be?"

"That's when we have to start pretending." He knew what she meant. From here on, careful at home, careful at family get-togethers, to not say each other's name too often. Or too seldom. "I'm not going to like that," she whispered, although there was no need for whispering. "It just came to me, the feeling of dreading supper tonight. And I wondered if maybe I was picking it up from you."

His hand cupped the back of her head as if weighing its contents judiciously. "Am I getting myself in with a mind reader here?"

Her fingers went back down the dale there on his chest. Not whispering now, but softly enough, she offered: "I suppose we'll see."

"Then we had better hope it doesn't run in the family," he provided back to her.

Slowly their hands moved down on each other to where things begin.

Part Seven

SLIPPAGE

1938

Know something, Shannon? I'm hungry for mountains."

"Tom, what the sweet hell do you expect me to do about that?" Although she immediately knew.

"All I'm saying, it doesn't hurt anybody to think ahead. Fort Peck isn't going to last for —"

"Cut the guff. How quick are you pulling out?" she demanded.

"While yet. Before winter hits again." Proxy kept up her ice pick gaze at him until he had to specify. "End of October. Gonna try it over in the Two Medicine country. Pretty, around there." He folded his arms on his chest, looked at her and said as if reminding them both: "Mountains."

"Have fun." Proxy's smile was so slanted

that Tom Harry muttered about bookkeeping to tend to and strode to his back office. She watched him go, the entire length of the Blue Eagle. She would miss this place, not to mention its contribution to her stash of Durham sackfuls of dollars. Wouldn't be the first in either category, though. *Jee Zuz, though. End of October.* Next month already. Tom was playing his cards so close to his chest they had to be read through the back of his shirt. One thing sure, she was in no mood to fend with some new cherry of an owner here; didn't want the hassle of breaking a fresh one in to the way she went about things. The new stupe probably wouldn't even have a Packard. Briefly she wondered whether to ask Tom to put in a word for her with Ruby Smith. That skag Snow White was working the Wheeler Inn, though; room for two milk-blondes? Proxy decided not to ask, she didn't want to be obligated. As Tom Harry had always put it, no hobblegations.

"Funnily enough, Owen, I am for war."

They had been back at their surgery of the world, arguing through mouthfuls and dipping philosophical sustenance out of open lunchboxes, for the past week of noons during the spectacle of Munich. Darius, considerably red-eyed from sitting up nights with the radio and the Czecho-slovakia crisis, could not help but feel history was dogging him personally. *Down your tools, boys!* The cobble streets of Scotland in '15, ringing against war. *The fields of death are hungry . . .* They still were. Across them now, though, the big bugs in brown shirts, black shirts, trousseau of goose-steppers. *There's this bit, too: pick the bones of truth out of it and I myself have already employed war. Against Crawfurd.*

"What, for King and country?" Owen winged in on him as if snapping down a playing card. "Where's that in the workers' catechism all of a sudden?"

"You have to understand, Owen, this Hitler is an armed daftie."

Nineteen thirty-eight, Munich's year, spun out of the sun in days spoked with fierce light and shadow.

Marx's grave at Highgate in midnight gloom while a steel dawn slides across the eight time zones ruled by Stalin.

Hitler, howling hate in the Nuremberg torchlight.

Spain a political bed of cinders, under Franco. Italy, the dark bootprint of Mussolini.

Japan's flag of a bloodbright rising sun, catching the morning across the Greater East Asia Co-Prosperity Sphere.

The United States can quench all this at our shores, say Senator Burton K. Wheeler and Charles Lindbergh and other isolationists. Water will do it, oceans lay between America and the world.

Meanwhile, Roosevelt and his people govern on the principle that almost anything, including water, can be amended.

"They're feeding Europe to him like a tray of buns," Darius went on. He shook his head at what passed for statesmen these days. "Joe Chamberlain's chinless lad Neville. You can bet the best part of him ran down his daddy's leg."

Owen shifted a bit on the shale cutbank where he was sitting on his coat. His attention tended to drift when Darius got going on British political Pooh-Bahs. From this lunch spot on the east abutment, above the core pool, the dam lay below like a scale model on a classroom table and bone-weary as Owen was from the pace of work, he never grew tired of this instructive view. The jigsaw puzzle pieces around the edges of the project — railway spurs, haul roads, maintenance yards, the spillway three miles over the hills behind him — done now. The dam itself already functioning, the four giant steel-lined diversion tunnels taking the regulated flow of the entire fifty thousand square miles

of the river drainage. The beautiful phys-
ics of this, the matter of the water funneled to become white foaming energy, the
contained Missouri fauceting out of this
one-of-a-kind dam, he had tried and tried
to make Darius see. He was the one of the
whole damn family who ought to be able
to see it, grasp the process. But the only
physic that seemed to interest Darius was
the one he wanted to administer to the
world and make it purge its political guts.

While Darius went down his list of major
fools in charge of things, Owen contented
himself with his inventory of the dam. Oh
sure, a few items of it he happily could have
done without. This shale under the seats of
their pants, to name the foremost, with its
tendency to crumble off the abutment and
mess up the waterlevel in his core pool.
*Bearpaw, yeah, it wouldn't take much of a
bear to paw this crackerass rock apart.*

To name the other, he never had liked
the scheduling setup on the face of the
dam, where he as fillmaster was responsible for the gravel layer but not the riprap
work which was always treading on the
gravel crew's heels. *How about all or nothing for me there on the facework?* he'd tried
on Major Santee. *How about doing it the
Corps way for once?* the major put the
kibosh on his try.

Minor stuff, though, either of those,

compared with the big thing they were leaving to him, the topping-off. Twenty feet to go, on the last of the mountain of fill. *Height of a nice two-story house, is all. Okay, it'd be a two-story house four miles long, but so what.* Off in the haze along the autumn river, his dredges were flushing fill in from as much as five miles downstream and doing it smack on schedule. Darius was not a hundred percent wrong, the world was a worry, but Owen's own bit of high ground couldn't have looked better this cool September noon. He knew almost to the day, now, when Fort Peck would be topped off.

"And France." Darius was shaking his head twice as strenuously. "The French, Owen, have gone steadily downhill ever since Sorel."

"Speaking of downhill," Owen seized that opening and stood up, unaccountably intent — to Darius — on not missing any minute he could spend on the dam. "We better get back down on the job, world or no world, while we still have one."

The year was producing something like armor on the Fort Peck Dam, the riprap boulders steadily being lodged into place on the upstream side. A blanket of gravel was laid first, down the slope of the dam, so the gravel trains still ran incessantly across the ghost trestle. Bruce shook his head every time he glanced over there where the trestle had been systematically buried, footings and pilings and everything except the railroad track itself, every high-stepping inch of it now under two hundred feet of Owen's earthfill sluiced in since last spring. No sign of the river channel, either; by now the dam made a solid blunt horizon across the entire valley, and while Bruce granted that it was nice all their work, especially his, had added up to this piece of geography the world had never before seen, it left him restless and bored.

Goddamn it, though, we ought to up and leave. Going to have to pull out anyway when . . . but yeah, when is when?

Bruce didn't like being of two minds this way. Mostly he was on idle time anymore, "getting paid for drinking coffee" as he liked to boast of it, just a little. Whenever he was summoned to dive, these days it was usually to inspect the end wall of the inlet to the tunnels or to deal with something caught in the trash rack there where the river funneled through the dam. Lots of yawn time, though, as now. He wandered over to the middle of the dam, where the truck ramp came down to the snubnosed dock called Port Peck, and watched the crane barge unload base boulders for the riprap, each one a truckload in itself. When the appeal of that shortly wore off, he prowled back to where the diving barge was moored, trying to look like a contented man of leisure.

But, he couldn't help it, the not-diving made him hungry for the river. The lake, as it was awfully quickly turning into. The plugging of the river had changed the look of things there, underwater; without the channel flowing, the water had muddied up, gone filmy. Curtained. The last dive he'd done he had tried as many as three of the thousand-watt underwater lamps at once and they weren't much better than, what, candles. Far from cursing it, the new darkness of the Missouri intrigued him. Nighttime in the river, midday. It all went with what Bonestiel had told him, when he was breaking Bruce in at diving. *Watch out for the kill-line.* A kill-line, said the Louisianan, was where the tidal salt of an ocean surged up a river delta and certain freshwater fish went belly-up. *Difference is, you can't see our kill-line. Which is why you got to watch for it* — Bonestiel tapped him in the center of the forehead — *in here.* The Missouri's new dark drew a diver's kill-line a little closer, Bruce knew, but kept him on his toes more, too. And that was what Bruce wanted, that kind of edge to toe up to but no farther.

Standing on the idle diving barge, he yawned and wished a little something would go wrong, a clog in the trash rack maybe, so he could suit up and go down. It helped keep life interesting.

Hugh as dispatcher of rattlesnakes was still making the rest of the Duffs uneasy, but as Meg would have been the first to point out, when had he ever made them easy?

It's not exactly a livelihood we can take with just anywhere, though, eh, Meggie?

WHOP. Another rattler off the living list.

Not sheathing his machete yet, staying poised atop the riprap until he was sure the severed snake didn't have a companion down there in its lair, he pondered whether it was worthwhile to keep collecting the tails. The rattle trade was in decline, with the dam workforce at only about half what it was a year ago. Birdie insisted sales would take a turn up, anytime now, as soon as it dawned on everybody that now was their last chance for a Fort Peck keepsake, but Birdie was not someone you wanted to set your watch by. Although who was he, Hugh, to think that.

What am I, anymore? Graduate of Carteret, class of six hundred twenty-eight days ago. (KEEP TRACK. TAKE PRIDE IN

YOUR NEW CALENDAR OF LIFE: another Carteret golden rule.) *Dry days, every last blessed damned one of them. Now that I have the moisture out, though, I amount to — what? Farmless farmer. Damless damworker, about to be. Where our next wage is going to come from, I suppose we shall need to see, eh, Meggie? Winter in this country does have a way of concentrating the mind.*

He stepped down off his refuge of riprap and took the rattle off the snake.

I am not a forgetter, Hugh. Haven't you done well, at staying on the wagon; but there is still your large record, from before. To this day I can hear you, prating against Owen's dam. Hugh the yew hewer, you scoffed at yourself when you were put at clearing the bottomland. "Meg," you said, "this piddly work-by-the-hour, this is never us." Fort Peck has not always been my cup of tea either, but without it, where would we be? Shorn of the boys' wives, each of whom I occasionally wish I could give a good shake, but all in all, not a bad lot. Darius would be an ocean away, still, and while I cannot commend his taste for peroxide, he has stirred you to life more than once, has he not. (You are better off not knowing the stirrings he induced in me.) And we might lack Jack, companion of my unemployed days.

684

And you would be the specimen you so long were, a bottle worshipper anytime the moon changed.

So, we are past much. A corrected man, you of the Carteret cure, at least in that one habit. But there is yet old distance to be made up, between us. That, Hugh, has not changed.

She was practicing her eavesdropping. Charlene was in her hair but properly so, pushing a wave in and then making it hold with the marcelling iron, and while this was going on there was no reason not to rubber in on the A-1's other customers, one woman done under the dryer and waiting to be combed out and her permed friend waiting for her and both with tireless tongues. *Blue Eagle* and *dancing* had been uttered.

"Who's on?" the one asked.

"The Melody Mechanics," said the other.

"Oh, them. I can't stand to see that Three Finger Curly on the guitar. It gives me the willies, the way those stubs —"

Three Finger Curly! I never in a million years could get away with a name like that in a —

"I like the one who foodles around with the clarinet, though."

Rosellen could not help but despair for a moment. Try as she might to invent

685

people in her stories, in life they simply sat around and, well, foodled themselves beyond what she could think up.

Uneasily waiting to take her out for a bite at the Rondola before they went home, Neil was sitting up front by the coatrack, whizzing through magazines. The beauty shop even smelled to him like someplace a male shouldn't be. The two biddies gabbing at the back had given him an acute looking-over when he wandered in and took a seat while Rosellen was being finished up, and Charlene had not helped matters any by kidding: "Relax and enjoy it, Neil. Blessed art thou, among women."

He sneaked peeks between flipping pages, rare chance to see what went on in here. Each time the marcelling iron came out hot from its midget oven, Rosellen's hair benefited that much more. Working over her, Charlene still had on a full-front apron from putting the chemicals in on the permed pair, but being Charlene, she simply looked like a million dollars that happened to be wearing an apron. Neil had heard that a place like Chicago had lady barbers, one of the prime attractions for ranchers who rode the trains in with their cattle, and he could see the benefits over having just any old guy rubbing the hair slickum in, yes he could.

Rosellen had her eyes closed now, waiting out Charlene's ministrations to her hair. She had spent this week, which seemed like forever, typing up the Corps' history of the dam project, Colonel Parmenter having instructed Major Santee to compile it and Major Santee having delegated it to Captain Brascoe, and Captain Brascoe might as well have written with only one letter of the alphabet, zzzzzz.

Churning out the captain's version, Rosellen had wished, now that everybody's time at Fort Peck was numbered, that Charlene or Kate or Meg or even Proxy had lived somewhere else, so that she could have written letter after letter telling whichever one all the things of these years here. (Toston would have done, for Charlene. Proxy was harder to imagine a place for, she had worn out so many addresses already.) That wasn't quite it, because Charlene and any of the rest of them who had alit to Fort Peck, including Darius down from the moon, were all part of the story. There'd need to be another Charlene or whoever, the way Neil and Bruce were twins. In any case, someone out there on the other end of the words. But, lacking that correspondence in the invisible ink of wish, all she could do was keep ploughing along with Captain Brascoe's compilation. Rosellen, not much one for sighing, sighed now. Hugh and Meg and no doubt Darius had a saying for doing anything that annoyingly useless: *Pulling up nettles to clear a way into the thistles.*

"About done, hon," Charlene's voice broke in on her drifting. Alert again, Rosellen realized Neil had been watching her get the beauty treatment, and she rewarded his patience with a quick grin and wink.

On his part, Neil had been saving this for supper, but for the sake of something to do besides sitting here like a bump on a log he offered it now:

"Your hubby is landing me a new job," he said as if talking to Charlene about the weather.

"Hey, don't I get to hear this, too?" Rosellen let out, as he'd figured she would.

"You're hearing it, aren't you?" Neil grinned at her over an opened magazine.

"All right, Secretive," Charlene said. "We bite. What is it?"

"Poking traps."

When he said that, he saw eyebrows go up in an identical way on both Rosellen and Charlene behind her. After a moment, it was Charlene who giggled and said, "In the footsteps of giants," meaning Hugh and Birdie.

"Size twelves." Neil shed the magazine, onto the pile he'd been through. "I'll be working with Birdie, so it's kind of an easy-chair job, in a way."

Rosellen hoped she was looking convincingly surprised. She hoped a lot harder that her having wangled this fresh job for him would simmer Neil down on his inclination to quit Fort Peck before she was ready to. *"Keep at it," you're always telling me. You don't know the half of it.* " 'Duff, Neil Milne, dredgeline trap inspector,' " she tried out loud, just the way she had it already down on the payroll roster. "I like the sound of that, Neiliepoke."

"Yeah, well," he said, wishing she wouldn't call him that in the hearing of the biddies at the back, "it was Owen's doing."

"Too bad this didn't work out so that we could all get together tonight," Rosellen said on impulse, as much to Charlene as to Neil. The three couples of them, supper at the Rondola and then the movie and afterward maybe seeing what those Melody Mechanics amounted to, would have been fun; but Bruce and Kate anymore could only afford a night out on payday, a full week from now, and Owen was working late on paperwork he'd been putting off. "How about coming with for supper?" she tried for Charlene at least, make some kind of occasion out of this. "Birdie Hinch's new right-hand man will probably even buy, hnn, Neil?"

"Likely to be chicken, real fresh," Neil got in the spirit with Rosellen.

"Just because you're beautified and ready to paint the town," Charlene said to the back of Rosellen's head. "Some of us know the meaning of work." Addressing the intent two customers at the back of the shop: "Mrs. Foraker is going to have my scalp if I don't get to hers right after this, isn't that right, Mrs. Foraker?" The two tittered, and went back to an uneasy low conversation.

"It sounds like you're stuck with only one of the famous Tebbet sisters for dining companionship," Rosellen informed Neil in a kidding la-di-dah voice.

"Aw," he registered disappointment. "Too bad you weren't quints, my odds would be better."

Just listen to them, Charlene thought as she manipulated the marcelling iron. A lot more than Rosellen, Charlene wished she and Owen had the night off, could go out with others and frolic. They both could stand that kind of a change. Nights lately, he had been giving her a hard time about life after Fort Peck. Or pretending to.

The Corps has levees on the Mississippi up the gigi, Charlalene, he teased. *I could latch on there and build forty-foot versions of Fort Peck the rest of my life, how about.*

Or worse yet:

They're already talking about another big Missouri dam, over in North Dakota. Who knows, if they think this one is a sweet enough example they may go for dirt on that one, too.

She wasn't sure how much of it was teasing. She figured Owen was not any too sure, either. What she had managed to pin him down on was leaving Fort Peck.

Around the time we put the dredges in winter harbor — he caught himself, and laughed with what sounded to her like rue. *Okay, we'll be quits with the dam around the first of November, does that suit you better? No winter harbor, this year.*

It gets to be a lot, Kate thought. The waitressing hours she could handle, Jackie as a wildcat three-year-old she could more or less handle, the complicated raft of Duff in-laws she could handle, even Bruce in his less sterling husbandly moments — well, handle was too strong a word there; put up with was the better expression, for now. But anyway, handling them all together would test Houdini, she was beginning to believe. She felt guilty for feeling so, but take right now, when she had just rounded up Jackie from Meg and was trying to keep an eye on him and listen to him chatter about his day with Mum Mum while at the same time supper had to be figured out and an educated guess be made on Bruce, whose hours were more unpredictable than ever now that he was on idle time.

"— an' it scared me poopy, Mommy."

That nailed her attention. "Jackie, honey, let's don't be saying that, all right?" With his particular grandfather, two uncles and great-uncle added onto his father, not to mention the general run of mouths in Wheeler, Kate considered it a wonder that Jackie's language wasn't saltier than it was. "If you say that around Mum Mum, Mum Mum will have kit— Mum Mum will not be very happy." She snared the boy to her, then knelt down on one knee to be at his level. "Now then, Jackerado, what came along and scared you?"

"My nap."

The boy watched the tip of his mother's tongue peek out between her lips, and then she was making a frown at him.

"How — what scared you about that?" Kate asked, doing the best she could with her voice. Normally Jackie slept in the style of his father, like a petrified log.

"There was — there was a, a, a swimmy thing."

The tightness in her throat now threatened to shut off words there entirely. Instead they flooded to her mind. *Dreams aren't — I can't have passed it on to —* She worked her dry mouth and throat, the boy looking in her face reproachfully. "Tell Mommy" — she knew what she had to say, although not what to do if Jackie started telling her about being tied to the thing in the river — "tell Mommy all about it."

The boy lifted his shoulders nearly to his ears. "Nighthorse!"

"Night — ?" *Meg is going to have him talking in Pig Latin, if I don't watch out.* "Yes, honey, everybody gets those. But in yours, what did the swimmy thing look like?"

The boy pouted tragically. "Like a wash-claw."

Kate nearly fell forward in relief. Jackie resisted baths. She and Meg long since had enlisted Bruce to do tub combat with him, and even so it took all of Bruce's persuasive and other powers before the boy would let himself be subject to soapy water and washcloth.

"Mum Mum says don't let the old nighthorse get me. I too big to, Mum Mum says."

"That's right, Jackie. Be big." *That's what we all have to try to be, against the nightmares.*

It was tricky, finding ways to meet, be alone together. The two knew that carelessness, even once, would do them in. All it would take was some other member of the family noticing the least little thing, odd coincidence of her and him. Or picking up a bit of gossip: *I thought I just spotted your better half on (her) (his) way into* . . . Reading it back into the behavior they both tried to keep so pussyfoot. Then word would be dropped, well-intentioned and devastating: *They're not going off together to learn to play the zither, are they.*

They'd managed to meet three times before, this way, and if the third time was a charm, did the count grow better or worse from here on?

They did not absolutely have to, but they made love in whispers.

Afterward, other whispers:

"They're going to catch us yet."

"Not if we quit this now."

"If."

With so much of Fort Peck done, there was a general expectation that the last of the damwork would fly into place. Veteran and expert as they were at it by now, and with only the topping-off and the riprap left to do, virtually anybody on the workforce would brag that the dam could practically finish itself now.

Darius, however, had noticed something to the contrary.

A hiccup in the system always attracted him, and this one had locomotive proportions. What had been the regular rhythm of the gravel trains, laying the way for the riprap work, seemed to have a skip in it now. Keeping track day by day from his vantage spot in the bullgang, he found that the interruption sometimes stretched to half an hour or more, before a train would come backing onto the crest of the dam from the east — opposite of the usual rail flow — and hurriedly dump its gravel cars. The third time this happened, he also caught sight of Owen in an armwaving argument with the train dispatcher.

Interesting. Here they have this piece of work by the throat and it slips away on them that little while every day.

Owen would tell him in a trice, what the problem was. For the sake of tactics, of course, the one person Darius was not going to ask was Owen.

That night he said to Proxy, "Dust off your in-law manners, love. I want to have Hugh and Meg over for supper one night quite soon."

"My ears must be playing out," Proxy told him. "It sounded like you said have people over. Here."

"The last I knew, here is where we live," he said with what she thought was undue reasonableness.

"But look at this place!" She seemed genuinely scandalized by the muss of the houseboat, as if heaps of this and stacks of that had crept in on them during the night. "There's stuff everyfriggingwhere!"

"Paint it all gold," Darius said airily.

Proxy looked at him narrowly, but knew there was no seeing it yet. What he had up his sleeve.

Lima beans of extraordinary hardness and a meat loaf dry as Melba toast and an unfortunate brown gravy and mashed potatoes with the gravity of dumplings — Meg could not have been more pleased with the meal Proxy produced, believing as she did that food was a direct index of morals. Hugh, too, appeared to take the philosophical approach. Nothing like these tastes, he thought, since those shots of goop at the Carteret Institute.

Munching gamely, Darius kept up the conversation through the meal while the other three made pretenses with their forks. At the predictable point where Proxy scraped the leftovers into the slop pail and Meg insisted she would like to help with the dishes and Proxy sharply said never mind, they'd just put the plates outside to poison the gophers, Darius cleared his throat a trifle.

"Umm, Meg," Proxy issued. "Want to see the view from out on deck?"

Actually Meg felt quite at home in the clutter of the houseboat and had been daydreaming a bit again of Inverley and when she and Hugh and Darius were green in judgment and trying to make up for it in kisses and flirtation. But Proxy sounded as if she had something on her mind. *Such a novelty is not to be missed,* the Milne attitude toward battle formed up in Meg, and the two women went out.

"You're a man of exalted position now," Darius said genially, meaning Hugh's hopping route atop the riprap and the burrows of snakes. "You'd know this. What's the bind with that gravel crew every infernal day? We're racing past them with the rockwork."

"I do my best to be on hand up there," Hugh said like a regular at the opera, "just to hear Owen cuss a blue streak when he's short that train."

"Whyever are they running fewer gravel trains? I thought a big push was on to —"

"They're not. What they're trying to do is squeeze in an extra train, on our shift. That's their headache."

"Pull my other one, Hugh. How can they be carring in more gravel and ending up with less?"

"It takes some doing, I admit. But figuring out when to squeeze that train in, get it backed down onto the dam and so on, that's what's giving them fits. Owen no doubt can cite you chapter and verse as to how soon now they'll have it worked out and the extra train will be one more feather in —"

"No, no, I wouldn't want to take up Owen's time with such a small matter."

"An exceptional meal, Proxy," Meg was saying.

"Sure, you bet. Dessert is going to be a stomach pump."

"No, now, don't go hard on yourself," Meg said as if glad to do it for her.

Evening brings all home. From the deck of the houseboat, riding the swell of ridge above the long dam and the waterglassed valley it now stopped the way of, the two women could see the lit curving streets of Fort Peck, the dashes and dots of lantern-yellow windows in the shacks of Wheeler and Delano Heights and Park Grove and the other thrown-together towns, nocturne of the Missouri. They watched the car lights streaming out of the harbor lot as the last of the day shift went off work.

"Quite a picture, huh?" Proxy said at last.

"Quite," said Meg.

"Had an offer once from a guy to come

in with him on a photo studio up near Lake of the Woods," Proxy spoke as though this tale was being spelled out to her in the lights of the night. "I could be his darkroom assistant, he said. It all seemed kind of phony, though. I mean, here he was, lining up honeymoon couples under cardboard trees in that studio of his, and right outside there was this real woods." Proxy shook her head like an auctiongoer. "So how could I trust him on that darkroom stuff either, right?" When Meg chose not to comment, Proxy mused on. "Real picture shooting, that'd be something else. That fancypants photographer who was here, I asked her what kind of a deal she had. She said her wages were just okay, but the way that magazine paid her expenses was a dream. 'Here, hire an airplane.' I could go for that. But I've never had any too much luck, taking pictures. Not sure I've got the eye for it."

"A person can't have equal talent in all directions," Meg stated.

That got under Proxy's skin, as Proxy knew it was intended to. She turned her head enough to size up her adversary there in the dusk. Meg's composed profile, with that aggravating knack of staring off as steadily as a figurehead. On down, she was better than okay in the entire figure department, too. Meg was a beckoning woman, still. Not that there were as many years between them as Proxy wished. *Try this on for size, though, old sister — one of us used our time better on Darius, didn't I.*

"Speaking of talent," Proxy returned the needle, "you're happy putting yours into being grandma these days, hm?"

Meg now turned her head and studied Proxy a moment, then seemed to go back to counting the lights of the dam and its towns. "I am attached to Jack."

"Attachments are tough," Proxy could agree.

"I know these dammers are always pulling things out of hats," Darius was saying. "But wherever do they hide an extra train?"

Hugh, sudden dam expert, was only too glad to hold forth. "What, can't you guess? Someplace where they can tuck twenty gravel cars, then yard them down by gravity when there's a little time between other trains?"

Darius's head stayed cocked quizzically, which seemed to please Hugh. As though Clydesiders were not the only ones who knew the ins and outs of equipment, Hugh now provided:

"The spur line, up at the spillway."

"Ah," said Darius.

Mouthfilling kisses led to this. Always

had, always would. He hoped.

Honey and milk. Under the tongue. Solomon knew whereof he sung. She granted.

Almost there, both, crashing at each other, their crazy pockets of passion about to spill, she under the tent of his elbows, he on her and in, straining together in sounds that threatened the shack and could tighten throats and make lips lick among the rest of the populace of Wheeler for all they cared right then.

Duet under the covers done, she caught her breath. "That was spirited."

"Margaret, you always let your praise run away with you," Hugh said through gasps.

Meg knew she was never going to be proficient in the afterpart of this as, say, old campaigner Proxy, but she determinedly pecked a kiss onto Hugh's sharp cheekbone and let spring: "I wonder if they know what ingredients they put in at that Carteret establishment."

"Fruits of love, Miss Milne," he surprised her right back.

Combatants on the field of marriage so many years, they lay there a familiar number of inches apart, waiting for each other's speculations on houseboat matters to come to the surface.

"That brother of mine," Hugh finally mulled out loud. "He must have his eye

701

on a foreman's job."

"Darius as a gold-watch gaffer?" Meg could picture a lot about him, but not that. "What do you read that from?"

"He's keen on the dam doings, all of a sudden. Wants to know how to twitch every switch, when it comes to Owen's fancy train set."

When it comes to many things, Darius has his wants. She shifted a little on the bed. *In my experience, though, such as it is — I will spare you the details, Hugh — the pronouncements that count with him are of the all too private sort.* Her fresh furrow of wondering about Darius kept carefully within the lines of conversation, she said now: "Too true, you never quite know with him, do you. I know one job I'd see him have. Yours. Lord High Executioner of snakes. Hugh, I do worry —"

"There've been times when I'd gladly have sicced them onto him," Hugh announced in the dark beside her. "Just to nibble on him around the edges, mind you. Teach him some manners."

There's ever the question, isn't it, Meg held in private. *How teachable any of us are.*

September had come chilly, with mean early frosts and a sharpness to the air, and Charlene drove to work these mornings. Why she had let herself in for this she wasn't sure, but she swung by to give Kate a lift to work each morning now, too. *Two* lifts, as Charlene saw it: to Meg's to leave off Jackie and then on to the Rondola. Regular bus service. The Charlene Stage Line.

"Aun' Charlene! Watch!! I being a pony!!!" Jackie thundered past her when she stepped in to collect Kate and him now. Charlene thought Jackie was as spoiled as they come, and equine behavior at 8 A.M. didn't sway her opinion any.

"We're having a time of it this morning," reported Kate, still in her slip. She examined Charlene, dressed to a T, and wondered how she managed it at this hour of the day. Without a stampeding three-year-old, that's how.

"Sorry, Charlene," Kate said by rote. "We'll get ourselves lined out here, in no time. Won't we, ponyboy," she captured the scampering Jackie.

"What can I do to be vaguely helpful?" Charlene offered, to encourage matters along.

"Mmm" — Kate glanced around from putting shoes on Jackie — "my uniform still needs pressing. That fancy iron of Bruce's ran out of gas on me." Charlene firmly tucked her tongue in her cheek. *Must be the only thing about him that ever runs out of gas.*

Kate was saying, "Better let it — Jackie, honey, you are such a wiggleworm. Don't you want to go see Mum Mum?"

"I can contribute a swipe or two of ironing," Charlene offered, and unscrewed the spout cap on the gallon can of white gas.

"*Jackie,* you're going to squirm us both to death," Kate scolded. Then remembered: "That iron maybe needs another minute to cool before you —"

The WHOOSH of flame came then, over where Charlene had poured the first trickle of gas into the iron's teacup-size tank. Fire flashed up the streamlet of gas into the can, then rivered across the floor as Charlene had to drop the can. "Wouldn't you just know," she said almost conversationally. Then over her shoulder, sternly, "Get out! Take Jackie out!" Still so calm she was amazed at herself, she scanned around for something to beat at the fire with.

"Fi'e," Jackie said, sitting up and pointing at the flames.

Kate scooped him into her arms, but stood desperately hesitating, blocked by the spread of flaming gas across the floor. The dry wood of the shanty was burning like sixty.

Charlene tipped the blazing ironing board over, out of her way to get to the

704

water bucket. She grabbed the bucket and sloshed Kate and Jackie, bringing a shriek from the boy. With the rag rug from beside the bed she whapped out a spot in the fire nearest the wall, momentarily. "Now!" she directed. "Go, along the wall!"

Kate hunched over Jackie, keeping herself between him and the flames, and twisted toward the door. Beating away with the rug, Charlene could hear her gasp at the heat, but then the door was open and the woman and child were outside.

Charlene saw that she and the rug were in a losing battle against the fire, and wished she had saved a douse from that water bucket to pour on herself. She backed across the room to the window, got it unlatched and yanked it up with all her strength. It rose six inches in the windowframe and then the catchpins zinged into the casement holes. *Oh, fiddlesticks*, still calm but needing to hurry. Another twelve inches above those holding holes was another set and if she could just get the window open that wide, she could climb out. But she needed three hands to simultaneously pull up the window and manipulate the catchpins on either side of the window. She instead let the window down and grabbed the water bucket one more time. Scars are better than burning to death, she told herself, clamped her eyes shut, and with both hands swung the empty bucket to shatter the windowglass. She had no time to knock out every last shard that stayed in the frame, and felt one get her across her shin, but then she was out, free of the licking fire.

It was all over but the embers by the time Bruce arrived. The Fort Peck fire department was parsimoniously hosing down the charred heap — not that much of a heap, either; the place had gone up like a wad of paper.

All right, so it's bobbed. Maybe my customers will all want it, too — the latest style, the bobcut with a singe.
Charlene lay back in the easy chair, exhausted, although it was barely noon. Silence at last, after the doctor murmuringly patching her up where the broken glass raked her leg, and Hugh and Meg telling her over and over not to worry, they would see to Kate and Jackie until Bruce took hold, and Rosellen arriving breathless and pitching in to help her snip the fire-frizzed hair down to a presentable bob and making her comfortable here in the living room and insisting she and Neil would bring supper over tonight, and — Charlene thought there had probably been

even other chapters of commotion so far today, but she was losing track.

Her mind kept marching back to that blasted iron. *Expensive purchase, Bruce.*

Now, finally, she heard Owen's pickup door slam, and he came charging in, stopping short and blinking at the sight of her, radically barbered and with her bandaged leg up on the footstool.

He crossed the room and sat on the footstool, his hand lightly cupping her ankle, the nearest safe place to touch.

"I hear you had yourself quite a morning."

"Mmhmm. One like that will do me, for good."

Hurt no, scar yes, more of a scrape than a cut, heal up in couple of weeks, lucky it wasn't a lot worse . . . when they had done the topic of her leg, Owen said as if carefully taking stock:

"Glad you got the kid out."

"*You're* glad. That was the part that scared the pants off me, Jackie in there." Now that it was over, the boy seemed to her the best kid in the world.

Owen kept nodding. With everything going on inside of him, he knew he had to be extra careful in what he said. As utterly sympathetic as he was toward Charlene about the fire, he also was spitting mad that there would inevitably need to be another loan to Bruce and company. He knew it was the day that had him out of sorts, not to mention the shock of coming home to a shorn and wan Charlene, but he still felt entitled to be damned good and tired of having to pull strings for members of this family. *It's neverending. Wouldn't you think* somebody *could hang on to what they got, for a change?* No, now, that wasn't fair, not even toward Bruce who had never heard of a piggybank, or at least it wasn't what an attentive husband ought to be stewing about while Charlene sat here looking badly used. To buck her up, he commended:

"When that undersheriff gave me the news, he said you had to have been cool as a cucumber, staying in there and trying to tackle that fire the way you did."

"What about dumber than a truckload of them, too, for trying to fill a hot iron." As Owen opened his mouth to loyally knock that down, she said in quickstep: "No, I didn't know it was hot, it was not my fault, nobody's fault, it could have happened to Eenie, Meenie, Minie or Moe." She stopped, to put together the next. "But something about it was dumb, Owen. The, I don't know, the *situation* was dumb, if nothing else."

"It must be catching," he surprised her with. She saw that he suddenly looked as tired as she felt. "Lot of dumb situation going around," he went on, absently stroking her ankle. "I got greeted with a gravel train that broke loose last night. A cut of twenty cars. They're scrap iron now." He brought his attention up from the ankle and white-wrapped shin to her face. "That's why they couldn't track me down for you sooner. I was up there at the spillway, trying to get somebody to tell me how long that siding will be out of commission."

Charlene quickly put a hand to her leg so he might think her wince came from there. "That's dreadful, Ownie. Is it . . . going to put you off schedule?"

"It doesn't make a fillmaster's life one goddamn bit easier, that's for sure. Now I have to tackle the colonel and Santee on squeezing in a few more gravel cars per train until —" he broke off the work talk, a little guiltily. "Well. I'm glad you're in one piece."

"Mmhmm. Pretty much."

Rat-a-tat-ta — Knuckles on the front door seemed to spring it open, and Bruce was standing there.

"Came to see the firebug."

Before Owen could launch up from the footstool, Charlene started trying to fend: "Sorry about how that ironing job turned out, Bruce. Really, I —"

"Hey, never mind."

Plainly Bruce was in an ashen state of mind. *Who wouldn't be?* Owen had to admit, still tensed to head him off. But Bruce didn't seem to need any heading off. "I hate it that you got banged up yourself," he told Charlene, giving her the most solemn expression she'd ever seen from him. She looked grateful beyond measure.

Big of the kid, thought Owen, amazed. *If somebody had just burned up everything I owned, I'm not sure I'd —*

Turning to Owen, Bruce kept his face arranged to hide what he felt. Christ Jesus, this was hard. He'd still rather take a beating than to have to deal with Owen. But he managed to say the rest of what he intended. "Mother's got matters under control — Kate and Jackie are getting her royal treatment. I seem to have a housing situation to talk to you about, though, Ownie."

Owen swallowed, and nodded.

They lived with Mum Mum and Gramp now. Daddy, Mommy, him.

"For good?" he asked Mommy.

She told him, "For worse, seems like, Jackiebox."

Daddy heard and gave her a frown and him a tickle and told him they were going to live in a tailor house soon.

Every morning now Darius stepped out onto the deck of the houseboat feeling the world had gone farther downhill.

The minuet of the cowards, London and Paris to Munich and Berchtesgaden, played night after night from the pitiless radio. Proxy would arrive home in the small hours and find him hunched, captive to listening, mind on the Czechs and the Sudetenland Germans and the frantic diplomats and Hitler's troop movements. The first few times, she came over to where he sat, and did things to him until Europe couldn't compete. But when this kept on, the choir of woe from the radio holding him there each night, it irritated her to have to draw his attention that way — *it used to be, he was all volunteer* — and she took to stepping past him, turning the radio down low, and with her fingers making a mocking walkie-walkie exit up his sleeve and over his back and away, she drifted to bed alone.

He knew he could not get by with being automatic toward Proxy. Not for long. Part of him knew too that hypnotic flames such as Munich were the oldest hopelessness, man fated to be more savage than any creature the world had seen yet. It would have settled everything, the corner of dour logic in Darius Duff said, if the first human looking into a fire had gone blind from it. Cats or ravens could have evolved into the arbiters of life. But no, the human species had learned to peek, and then to eye each other across the dancing blaze and argue the distribution of firepits. Politics, the answering corners of Darius said, were a necessary madness. If the argument with our own natures did not go on, why exist? And so, all apologies to Proxy and her wares, but these nights he was away to that other desire.

"Rough luck about Bruce and Kate and the lad."

"Yeah," Owen ground out around the sandwich he was wolfing into, "you bet." Darius was right on that score at least. Bruce seemed to take it as a matter of course when Owen came through with not only a transfusion of money but the idea of his and Charlene's old trailer house, now sitting surplus in Park Grove, which was taking some real finagling with the Corps. Not the easiest item to fit through channels, a kid brother with pernicious anemia of the wallet. Acting as if his household burned down every day, Bruce merely had said "Getting us a ringside seat for your dredging, huh, Ownie?" And it was true, the *Gallatin* held sway in that vicinity, slurping away at a neighborhood of abandoned shanties, and its giant pipeline and all three from the other dredges snaked right through town — life in Park Grove, down from the dam, had the reputation of being like living under a sink. Owen felt sorry for Kate, reduced to those circumstances, but for Bruce, not noticeably.

"Is that to be the story of what you in this country call 'the American century,' do you think?" Darius was suddenly at. These noon jousts of theirs often took sharp turns, and this one caught Owen mired in a mouthful of sandwich. Chewing fast to catch up, he stared inquisitively at Darius.

"Bruce and company hiphopping from handout to handout, make-work to make-work," Darius inclined his head to the half-dredged sprawl of Park Grove below the dam. "While Owen and company" — here he mimicked doffing his cap to the dam and the Corps townsite beyond — "are the masters with the blueprints."

Owen swallowed furiously. "You've been here since I forget when and you still don't savvy thing one about Fort Peck."

"I 'savvy,' as you say, that it has paid off handsomely for you. A good house for you and the lovely Charlene, a fancy wage, doubtless your pick of a next job as Roosevelt doles out these projects. While the rest of —"

"Is that what you think I'm at, here? Jesus aching Christ, Darius. You make me tired. I'm at this job to do it up royally, build this dam the best way I know how. *That's* the point, to any of this."

"Ah, but is it. Isn't it more the point to keep society lulled with a bit of work, a bit of wage, while there's no real solving of anything?"

"Lull— ? Where's anybody who's lulled, around here? These guys are going to go around saying until their dying breath, 'I worked on Fort Peck.' "

"But you'll always sing the lead, won't you."

"What the hell is it you think, that a mob of people can just fling themselves at something and it'll be built? You can't get away with that. They couldn't even at Dnieperstroy. The Sovietskis had Cooper and Company in there as engineers, somebody's got to be answerable when you're build—"

" 'Knowhow, the American language,' I'm sure."

"In *any* language! Even in Red!" Owen was up and standing over him. Now he shouted over the top of Darius's head. "Max!" Sangster, middistance figure overseeing an extension of the dredgeline strutwork, turned and waved. "Cover until I get back, okay?" Owen called to him through cupped hands. "And ring up Jepperson, would you, and tell him I'm detaching this one" — he jerked a quick thumb at Darius — "for a little while." Then he spun around to his uncle, frowning intently at him and then down the abutment slope to the motor pool vehicles. "Get in the pickup."

Darius cocked his head warily. "What would be the reason for that?"

"There's something I want to show you at the spillway."

"Hold on, Owen — I've had the ha'penny tour of the spillway once already, you know."

"Get in the goddamn pickup before I stuff you in it!"

Darius closeted his anger in the face of Owen's worse case of it, and climbed in the government pickup. Owen veered over to the nearest ransack shack where tools and supplies were kept, grabbed a sizable empty box and flung it in the back of the pickup. Then, mystifying Darius, he drove without a word across the dam, the opposite direction from the spillway, and up into the Fort Peck townsite. At the bowling alley, he jammed to a halt. Darius could not resist asking:

"Are we going to settle this with a duel of skittles?"

Still wordless, Owen slammed out of the

715

pickup and into the bowling alley and soon came back with the box full, heaving it with a grunt into the back of the pickup. He glowered at Darius for a moment through the back window of the cab, then jumped in again and drove across the dam, this time unmistakably into the maze of humpy little hills that would bring them out beside the spillway, and its rail spur.

Darius appraised Owen, stonily driving, and felt a sense of arguer's stimulation along with his apprehension. He had missed Jaarala something fierce; someone who grasped by habit, almost by blood-right, the need to chew at the heels of the powers that be. He even pined a bit for Mott, bent trumpet though he had turned out to be.

Darius tensed as the pickup barreled down a hill to where acetylene flickers threw light and shadow over an iron valley of wreckage, the cutting torches at work on railcars crumpled and tangled like a kicked set of toys.

Sabot, Owen. A wooden shoe — French, as it happens. The word is from that, sabotage is. But I suppose you know so, educated fool that you are.

The first time, the wrench into the gearteeth, was mad fury; Darius himself would not have called it anything other.

716

Tactics, however, were fury pounded cold and snippered into actions, were they not.

The movement, you see, Owen. You think you know by book what it is about, what I am about. And you can't, poor learned mealmate. "In the mind of every man, hidden under the ashes, a quickening fire" — biblical to me as your blueprints are to you. Tactic by tactic, "compatible with the minimum of brutality": my gospel, old Sorel's as far as he went, you would pry at instantly, ask "Who gets to set the minimum?" I could tell you — but must never — that it sometimes sets itself; that a George Crawfurd and I blunder it back and forth between us until, bad surprise, one of us exists no more. But here within our family enterprise, as you regard Fort Peck, metal is the minimum.

The machine-breakers. Did you ever read up on them, in your earnest engineering courses? Not a man at this dam, except perhaps you, would know the name "Ned Ludd" if it floated in his breakfast bowl. But what a bogeyman old Ned was, set loose by laborers when they burned hayricks and clothiers' mills, broke up knitting looms and wrecked the winding gears at mine pits. You're a man of numbers, you'll appreciate this: before the Luddites were done making their point riot, London had to put them down with an army the size of those it was sending against Napoleon. But even that didn't put paid to the tactic itself. Were Jaarala here, he could tell you of the IWW's knack of slowing a sawmill with but one spike driven into a log.

And here we're all at making this one great machine of yours, this dam, are we not. And why? To take everyone's mind off any cause except perfecting the gadget, a thing that turns running water into standing water. Cleverest sink plug in the world, this Fort Peck machine.

So what I have done to machinery in a few nights of slipping sabots into the works, Owen, dear, is to make the kings of things know. Your Corps. Your construction companies. Your dolemaster Roosevelt. For that matter, you, who have no quarrel with the order of things so long as it meets schedules and sets records. But those who put their hands to the work ought to own that work, Owen. That's flat basic. That's the meaning of the movement, poor battered bastard piece of history that it is. Of myself, we may as well say. As long as there is one spoor of the movement — I somehow seem to have become that minimum, here — the rest of you are made to know that the order of things can be turned upside down.

Mind awhirl, Darius cut glances from the smashed gravel cars just ahead to the

718

unreadable profile of Owen. As they pulled even with the railroad spur, Owen swept a tallying look along the wreck and the repair work.

And drove on by.

Before Darius quite caught his breath, they were alongside the huge concrete trench of the spillway, Owen jouncing them down through the hills next to the gape of it, Darius having to keep watch back and forth between his possessed nephew and the mile-long fan of spillway floor below his side of the pickup.

The pickup roared to the service ramp which angled down onto the spillway. The watchman there, appalled to have this traffic, waved them on in a hurry when Owen flashed his particular job button.

Now, by God, Darius. Push the political wool away from your eyes for once. Now you're about to see some solving.

Owen drove up the spillway, no longer the dirt canyon where Proxy gave Darius lessons in how to herd the truck but a vast inclined floor of concrete sections as neat and new as fresh linoleum. Halfway along, Owen abruptly pulled to a halt.

"Sit," he said to Darius as he would to a dog.

He himself bailed out of the pickup cab, hefted the box from the back, and over at the center seam of the concrete sections, a groove perhaps half the size of a rain gutter, he yanked bowling pins out by the neck and meticulously set them up, all ten at last standing at attention in their triangle formation. Darius watched silently.

Back into the pickup, Owen drove a ways while watching the rearview mirror. When he stopped this time, Darius knew to get out with him.

The pins were specks in the distance, against the fresh gray of the concrete. Owen hefted the bowling ball out of the box. Going over to the seam in the concrete, he put the bowling ball down onto the shallow groove and gave just enough of a push to start the black ball rolling. The two men listened to the slight rumble as the ball rolled and rolled, holding to the hairline mark of channel in the middle of the concrete expanse, until it looked the size of a BB demolishing the formation of the pins.

"That's engineering," said Owen, after the distant clatter. " 'Know-how,' if that's the best you can stand to call it." He swept his hand around to indicate the concrete canyon they were in. "This was all hills and coulees, shalebanks until Hell wouldn't have it — you couldn't have flown pigeons through here without them getting dizzy. Now take a look. Go ahead. *Look!*"

Darius with obvious reluctance moved his eyes from Owen to the immense straight gout of the spillway, half a mile of concrete ahead of them to where it met the river below the dam and even more of it behind them where the colossal spill-gates stood.

"A mile of concrete in here," Owen resumed intensely, "laid two feet thick, down a five percent grade, and all of it so goddamn exact and smooth that ball rolled along it without ever bouncing, didn't it. Blueprints and specs and hard-ass engineers and crews who want to go about it right, this is the kind of thing we can give the world. It's what the dam is going to be, something that works like it's supposed to. We know how on this, you bet we do. Those pie in the sky politics of yours, though, they can't ever take the world in hand this same way. You can work on how to run people until you turn blue, be my guest, but I'm going to keep doing what I can see a real result on. Dams, jobs. The actual factual, Darius."

"If I ever see the light, I'm sure it'll be because you brained me with it," Darius said with surprising surrender. "Does this conclude the sermon for today?"

Owen actually had been set to argue on and on, until he had Darius's cuckoo politics backed into the corner where they belonged. He was somehow disappointed to see this expression on Darius, which looked oddly like a smile of relief.

"You know my inclination about the stoppage rate," the colonel said. "Zero would be a nice number to have."

Both supposed to be at ease in front of his desk, Major Santee and Captain Brascoe conspicuously waited for each other to respond first.

Rank always told. Giving way under the major's bland silence, Brascoe had to offer up: "We — I still think the breakdowns are nothing but carelessness."

"Sugar in gas tanks isn't careless," Santee took advantage of that.

"Someone mad at a foreman is all that one amounted to, I believe," the colonel weighed in unexpectedly. "Someone has to get the deuces and treys of life, and whoever did, that day, lost his head and went sugaring."

Santee and Brascoe waited out the colonel's pensive expression. When his eyes snapped to the captain again, Brascoe reported: "The *federales* in Butte are about done running their check on our fingerprint files, sir. Nobody matches up yet to their list of known radicals, and they're up to the *R*'s."

The colonel turned his head to the other

officer. "We know there's nothing to fear in the names starting with S, right, Joe?"

"Yes, sir," Major Santee answered by rote.

Colonel Parmenter's mouth turned down. He did not make many jokes, and wanted it acknowledged when he did. He swung back to Brascoe, who resumed:

"I've put on more watchmen. Beyond that, it's a question of taking measures that will slow up the night work and —"

"No," the colonel cut in. "I'd bet these spots of trouble are just a little run of bad luck. Keep the work at full push. Dismissed, gentlemen."

There was not a man or woman at Fort Peck who did not forever remember precisely where they were and what they were at shortly after noon on September 22nd of 1938.

Hugh was by the front door of the Blue Eagle, trying to look as if the saloon had sneaked up on him instead of vice versa. With a last bleak glance along the main street of Wheeler — after all, what could he say to Meg or any of the rest of the family if he was caught slipping in here: *Eh, have you heard there's an epidemic of amnesia?* — in he went, heart hammering.

The saloon was all but empty. Right time

of day for this, at least. Tom Harry scanned down the bar at him in sardonic surprise. "Look what the snakes chased in."

"The riprap work is shut down for a little while," Hugh defended his presence here. "They're mucking around with a walking crane that got itself stuck." Giving him just time enough for this. He hoped.

Tom Harry seemed to have heard that one and all other variations before. He added to that impression with a bartender shrug and said, "What can I get you, a glass of mother's milk or what?"

By now Hugh qualified as a connoisseur of soda pop, working his way through the flavors. His latest, Orange Crush, he considered sweetly vile.

"You can't tell me you don't miss the real stuff," Tom Harry prodded as he set the garish bottle of pop before Hugh.

"I can never touch it again, that's all," Hugh said nobly.

"Not ever, huh? That's a long dry while, Duff."

Hugh looked at him with a start of panic, as if Tom Harry somehow knew what they had all ended up confessing to each other at the Carteret Institute, outside the Amen Corner sessions, afterward when no staff were around: that, yes, if a man knew he was about to be on his deathbed; say he had only a month to live, doctor's sworn diagnosis; then, yes, every last one of them had concluded that under such circumstances they would go on a final blue-screaming walleyed delirious jag. *There I stood at the gate of God, drunk but unafraid,"* quoted one of the Southerners, who tended to be dreamy and literary. But that was wish, the fuzzwuzzyland called If. Here and now, a man honorably cured would . . .

"You heard me, you smirky bastard," Hugh said to Tom Harry. "Never." He drained the last of the Orange Crush. "Give me another of those putrid things."

Owen's mind was on shale, which still was slipping off the east bank into the core pool and messing up his water level.

How the hell am I supposed to stay on the mark if that stuff dumps itself in whenever it feels like it?

The second hell of it was, this was a perfectly nice day, for a change; the rowdy weather that moved in after Labor Day had finally petered out and now the sky chose Indian summer, chinked with a few high streaks of cloud, thin and shaped like wingspans of birds. Owen a lot rather would have been at lunch, sunning himself and making Swiss cheese of Darius's arguments, than trotting to the far end of the core pool again. Not for the first time, he wished the planet had been constructed without any Bearpaw shale.

The boss of the survey crew, Pete Blegen, hailed him before he could reach the latest slide of shale and commence swearing at the substance.

"The freeboard reading is way under," Blegen reported as if relieved to be rid of the news. "Hate to tell you, but it's at only three feet."

"Can't be," Owen said instantly, then gave Blegen a quit-kidding grin. "Better *not* be."

In spite of himself Owen spun around to shoot a glance at his dredgeline, eyeballing the cascade from its discharge pipes into the pool water beneath. The specification there he knew as well as his own name. A constant four and a half feet interval was supposed to be maintained between the water level in the core pool and the discharge emptying into it, so that the fill would drain and settle properly. The reading Blegen had given him, off the mark by, Christ, a foot and a half, meant either a mighty amount of shale had slipped into the pool and brought its water level up that much, or the dredgeline had sunk that much. Either sounded wacky, and Owen had to hope the discrepancy was in the surveyors' numbers. He carefully watched Blegen's face. "You're not fooling, huh?"

"That's the reading I got."

"Pete, go run your level on it again. The Ad Building's going to want a confirmation." *So do I, you better bet,* Owen's expression told the surveyor and sent him off at double-time.

Hard damned stuff to nurse, Hugh decided of the Orange Crush as the second bottle rapidly emptied despite his every effort at moderation. Sighing heavily, he signaled Tom Harry for another. As the barkeeper bore the next bottle to him, Hugh restlessly asked:

"What time does she come on?"

"Who?" said Proxy, from the doorway. "Mother Machree?"

I hope the rest of the day isn't going to go like this. As ever, Owen would rather have eaten toads than have to shut down his dredgeline, but he trudged over to the nearest field telephone and stood by. *Specs are specs,* another unwelcome but unavoidable thought. If the core pool water level was really as far out of whack as Blegen maintained, they shouldn't keep pouring fill in. *Can't. Don't dare. It'll mush up, if it hasn't aleady.* Any toddler making mudpies knew the right recipe: just enough water, *not too damn little, not too sonofabitching much. As we all of a sudden seem to have an extreme excess of, here in the world's biggest core pool, congratulations, Fillmaster Duff.*

He watched the survey crew, down at the edge of the pool, unanimously gave him a hateful glance over their shoulders when Blegen told them they had to rerun their reading. The astronomers, as they were known, already felt it was beneath their dignity to be squinting through their lovely transits in the muck around the core pool. Blegen's tone of voice, though, was sending them hopping to do it over.

Waiting, Owen prowled three paces back and forth, as if tethered to the field telephone post. At least misery had a lot of company this afternoon. He could see down onto the face of the dam where the riprap work was gummed up, too; halted for the past half hour or so because the walking crane had mired in a soft spot. They — when it came to snotty tasks that always meant the bullgang — were going to have to walk the huge Cat-tread crane out to firmer ground by laying big wooden mats in front of its tracks. But right now, hanging loose, smoking and joking until the trucks with the mats showed up, none among the bullgang looked looser than the rail-thin figure spectating up in Owen's direction. *Darius to the rescue,* the thought momentarily entertained Owen, *whether or not a stuck crane can be elevated according to Marx.*

Blegen was yelling for his attention.

The survey boss had his arm up, three fingers extended toward Owen, as if bidding at an auction. The freeboard reading had surveyed out at three feet again. *Damn.*

Now Blegen pointed emphatically with his other arm at the dredgeline discharge pipe. The survey crew had run a separate reading on it from a benchmark this time, and Owen Duff's core pool was not up a foot and a half; Owen Duff's dredgeline had sunk, sagged, that much.

What a horseshit turn of events this is. Owen sourly fieldphoned all four dredgemasters and told them to shut down. He hated the next step and had to keep telling himself over and over *regs are regs, too, Duff, even for you* as he picked up the phone and, like any man of regulations who had both a crane and a pipeline bogged down in inexplicable soft spots in his dam, notified the Ad Building.

The two of them, Proxy and Hugh, resorted to the backmost table at the Blue Eagle, out of the saloon traffic and Tom Harry's range of hearing.

"Odd time of day for this, I know," he stabbed at making conversation.

She wasn't sure why, but she gave him a break by not asking if he had gone to all this trouble of looking her up to tell her the time. "Different in here in broad daylight," she granted, nodding a greeting to the piano player Gert as she passed by to her keyboard with a brimming shotglass carried carefully in each hand. "A little."

Hugh watched the shotglasses go past as if they were the crown jewels on show. He turned again to Proxy with a surprisingly winning rueful smile. "Not so much temptation to expand the job, you mean?"

"Hugh, I said 'a little.' " Not that it was any of his business, but she would let him know anyway. "I go out back with somebody if and when I want. But I'm not taking on drunks and wet-eared kids and whatever else in pants that walks in here, am I. I *mostly* dance anymore, okay? Now what's on your mind besides your chapoo."

"A thing I need to know."

"Just one? Aren't you lucky."

"That brother of mine and whatever he might be getting himself into," Hugh named off. He looked Proxy over, as if sizing up a witness. Not that it was possible to be neutrally judicious in looking Proxy over. "As regards political matters,"

Hugh thought he had better specify. "If that size of words covers the matter of Darius."

She couldn't help smiling a little. One thing life with Darius had taught her was that a response didn't necessarily have to be an answer. "You've known him a real lot longer than I have," she now responded.

"I knew him when we were lads and I've known him since he showed up here cap in hand. There's damn near all of history in between." *And a bothering quantity since, such as fingerprints that want hiding and trains that become a topic of conversation one fine night and let go their brakes soon thereafter. That's what I need to know of our Darius, Proxy. If I am right. If I am not the world's leading fool, which sometimes has been the case, too.*

"Why care?" Proxy asked as if she could use the answer. "Why let yourself in for heartburn?"

"Proxy, now, that's up there with the best of them, isn't it, in the all-time questions," Hugh told her in a tone that gave no ground. "It would take somebody who can lie faster than a horse can trot to say we're always happy with the object of our interest. There are times we're simply stuck with it, aren't we." He clonked the pop bottle on the table, looked at it, picked it back up, then glanced across and held his gaze steady against hers. "I was handed Darius for a brother, and I helplessly care."

Proxy studied him. More than years, or politics either, made a difference between Hugh and Darius. Hugh had rough spots in him you couldn't iron out with a steamroller, but at least they were on the map. Watching him sit across from her and take a swig of orange pop now with repulsion and determination, she kind of liked the fact that while he had cleaned up his drinking, he hadn't gone Holy Joe in any other way.

Neil liked to know what he was doing, but working with Birdie Hinch had its mysteries.

As now, when they had just come on shift, a little late as Birdie seemed to think was their right, and were starting their patrol of the dredgeline along the crest of the dam when Birdie let out a buzzsaw whine — which Neil after a moment realized was an Oklahoma rendition of GAWWWWDDDDAMN! — and threw his hat at the first drain trap.

"Lookit that!" Birdie stomped over to the huge pocket of metal beneath the first section of pipeline and crammed his hat back on his head. "Bastards on the last shift left us a clogged trap," he complained. "That ain't fair play. They ain't supposed to hightail off before —"

"Is this what's got everything shut down?" Owen hadn't looked as if he was in his best mood when the pair of them had to go past him on their way out here, so Neil was uneasy with the idea of the entire work of the dam hung up waiting on how expeditiously he and Birdie Hinch could clean out a trap.

"Naw," Birdie answered. "Something else." Slower than molasses but without wasting an ounce of effort, Birdie began undoing the turnbuckles on his side of the pipeline trap, still voicing hurt over the unfairness of the previous shift. When the trap hinged open, though, Birdie drew in his breath sharply.

"I take it all back. Our ship just come in, Neil," he crowed. "We got ourselves a wowser of a skull, look at that sucker. Tom Harry'll pay plenty for this one."

The buffalo head, with one cavern of eye socket peering out of the muck and twin hooks of horn on guard, appeared weirdly determined to stay buried in the clot of clay. Birdie in admiration, Neil in resignation, they hunkered down to study the tub-size skull.

"Alas, poor shaggy Yorick."

"Huh?" They both jumped at the intonation from Darius, who was standing over their shoulders.

"What the dingdong hell is that supposed to mean?" Birdie demanded with a querulous squint.

Darius's hand made a wiping nevermind motion against the air. "What's the bollix that has us shut down?" He knew virtually all there was to know about work stoppages, but this standstill puzzled him.

"It ain't us," Birdie fairly spat. "The bastards before us left —"

Darius did not stay for the recitation, simply shook his head impatiently and clambered back down from the crest of the dam to where the rest of the bullgang were still lounging around, standing on one foot and then the other and wisecracking about easy money today, tourist wages.

Birdie and for that matter Neil had other things on the mind right now than Darius. They barely watched him go before the lodged skull claimed their fullest attention again. "A lot of people might call me a liar on this," Birdie said judiciously, "but I'd say this is the stud daddy of all buffalo."

"Yeah, right, it's a whopper," Neil had to agree distastefully. He didn't like the look of the thing, blind to the bone yet that socket seeming to fix an eternal stare on them. Weird business with eyes bothered him, still. If it was up to him, he would smash the staring monstrosity with a crowbar, break it out of there in pieces like a giant eggshell before the dredgeline boss or even Owen himself came and got on their backs. But one of Birdie's vocations was involved here. "Okay, what's the recipe for getting the thing out?"

"See, all's we do, Neil, is you work on that clay around it and I pry in kind of gentle behind it. I got to get a lady shovel for that. Be right back."

As Birdie scooted off along the crest of the dam, Neil shrugged out of his jacket, slung it over the nearest pipeline support, and started clearing muck away from the buffalo skull.

Darius still did not like the setup of this shift.

The big bugs — some foremen of the work gangs, and contractors' superintendents, and a clot of engineers featuring of course Owen — were clustering at the lip of the core pool where the field telephone was located. In Darius's experience, an assembly of bosses always brought trouble. He glanced along the dam for any sign of equipment breakdown or someone injured, but that did not seem to be it.

He checked again toward Neil and Birdie, Neil noggin down at work on the clogged trap and Birdie skylarking off in search of a smail-headed shovel. Nothing to be divined from that pair except the cranial measurements of a buffalo. On impulse Darius headed up the face of the dam. Whatever the war council was about, up there, he wanted to take a gander at it himself.

"Hey!" the bullgang foreman Jepperson yelled. "Where you going, Scotchman? Christ's sake, you haven't even put your gloves on yet."

"Drastic case of the drizzles," Darius called back over his shoulder and climbed faster.

He reached the crest in time to see a car rapidly coming, that of the colonel, biggest bug of the outfit. Something tickled in the back of Darius's mind and down his neck. He halted and sighted west along the top of the dam.

The steel rails of the railroad track were bending sideways, bulging like a drawn bow.

Darius turned east and ran, toward the shore, to race all the way back to Scotland if that's what it took.

To Owen, the start of the slide was like a heat shimmer, as when waves of air danced in the alfalfa field in hottest summer. Slow and hazy to the eye, distorting everything. Bringing about the unbelievable: the railroad track snapping apart sideways, as if of its own volition. Next the lightpoles swayed as they couldn't possibly, and then swooned to the upstream side of the dam. The slope there of fill and gravel and partial riprap looked out of kilter to him, oddly unmoored. *God, no! The whole thing can't* — Along the crest of the dam the dredgeline was crumpling section by section, almost orderly. *Neil! Get the hell* — Then, though, everything speeded up. Crevices cut the earthfill of the dam's upstream face, collapsing it into mush. The water in the core pool was vanishing, a wet roar was over everything, people scrambled everywhere. A damworker darted past Owen so fast he only belatedly realized it was Darius. Statuelike, Owen watched as a half-mile section hinged away from the rest of the dam and slid into the lake, taking with it the walking crane and bulldozers and trucks and the railroad track and the dredgeline and men.

Some 180 of them were at work on the east upstream section of the dam when it gave way, and the eight or ten minutes of the slide turned them into hydraulic arithmetic.

The riprap crew nearest the east bank

comprised the main number, about 125. They were waiting to start laying the next tier of rock, as soon as the crane got back into action and resumed hoisting big quarry boulders from the railcars down onto the face of the dam for them. Meanwhile they were killing time by greasing their equipment and trading insults with the bullgang, below them where the crane had sunk into unusually wet gravel. Close to the crest of the dam as they were, the riprap crew had mostly level running when someone shouted LOOK OUT, THERE SHE GOES! and the slide started. They fled, clambered, vaulted, whatever it took, in wild retreat to the east bank of the river valley, the face of the dam crumbling at their heels.

Five persons were in the colonel's car. Colonel Parmenter and Major Santee and Captain Brascoe, all in the backseat, saw the calamity past flinching heads in front of them. For Max Sangster, coming out to see if he could lend Owen a hand with the core pool puzzle and sitting across from the colonel's driver, the slide was framed in the windshield, horror focused in the panel of glass. Half a decade of engineering, millions of cubic yards of Fort Peck Dam, were melting like brown sugar in front of Sangster's eyes. He and the three officers were thrown forward as the driver hit the brakes, then the car was racing in reverse, the colonel's wordless driver turned tautly half around as he steered over his shoulder and gunned the accelerator, one crevice after another opening and folding away from where the car had just been.

Scattered across the sunlit slope of caving earth, four dozen men from the bull-gang rode the slide. A typical set of them, a pair of workers watched by Owen from his helpless distance, managed to leap across two cracks that opened in front of them, but the third took them and then closed over them. For a panicked moment both thought they would suffocate, but water gushed up below and pushed them out where they could breathe. The water tumbled them down the ooze into the lake, where they had to fight not to be sucked down by a whirlpool. There were islands of muck now, a Missouri archipelago in the lake, and they managed to pull each other onto one of these mud mounds and cling there until a motorboat crew came for them. Other escapes, out across the tide of devastation by twos and threes and other handfuls, were just as miraculous.

Those who died did so one by one.

A deckhand on the workboat at the foot

of the riprap saw the vast wall of avalanche coming, grabbed the railing, but was swept overboard and buried in the mudslide.

A young riprap worker who had been down on one knee tying a shoelace when the damslope gave way also was buried, and suffocated; hours of effort to revive him in an iron lung failed.

A bullgang laborer who seized a passing section of dredgeline strutwork was carried safely down the trajectory of the slide but jarred loose when it careened into the lake, and drowned.

Four simply vanished.

Neil was carving clay away from the buffalo skull when he felt the ground shake. He thought a bulldozer must have run into the dredgeline, and he jerked his head out of the trap of the pipe to have a look. Then he felt the general motion, the slippage, everything tipping. Around him the dredgeline crew was running, trying to run; he saw Birdie disappear in a quick-sandlike whorl of gravel. The dredgeline was starting to snake down the slope, atop the avalanche of all the fill material from the crest of the dam on down. *Jesus, this is worse than* — To get out of the gravel tearing at his feet, Neil straddled up onto the dredgeline pipe, desperately hugging down around it to grab the trap's turn-buckles to hang on to. Bareback on the Chinese dragon of pipe, he rode down the avalanche toward the waiting water.

Owen backpedaled, skittered sideways, outright ran when he had to, but always with his head turned toward the slide, staying clear of the crater in the side of the core pool as it washed out, all the while trying to register where Neil would end up.

Rosellen was making short work of next week's Corps duty roster, paying only half attention to it whipping through the type-writer, glancing up and around her for the latest on the rumor that had been bounc-ing through the Ad Building. Some sort of problem at the dam. She noticed Major Santee's secretary, Betty Jane, coming her way and she timed the last of her piece of typing, as she liked to do, so that she could rip it out of the typewriter and hand it across with a grin the instant BJ arrived for it.

Betty Jane didn't take the roster. With an odd look on her face she asked Rosel-len:

"What shift is your Neil on?"

Wanting to throw up but telling himself he didn't have time, Owen edged back out along what was left of the rim between the core pool and where the face of the dam had been, desperate to turn around and start scanning down into the soupy mess of the slide but forcing himself to watch the remainder of the dam. Here where the slippage had occurred the dam now was narrowed by half, as if a monstrous bite had been taken out of its upstream side. As best Owen could judge, the downstream crest hadn't budged, yet. *Hadn't better, either, the sonofa—* If a similar slice of it fell away, the whole dam would go, Missourians would be fishing the bodies of half of Fort Peck out at St. Louis. *The Johnstown flood, hell.* The Owentown version, if it happened, would make Johnstown look like a swimming accident. Owen Duff knew there was no reason why the downstream side of the dam would go out, too; slippage wasn't a form of epidemic. Yet why, why had any of his scrupulous earthfill slipped?

Dancing from nerves, jittering himself out along the earthfill cliff with his back turned to the gulp of slide, Owen decided if the rest of the dam was going to go, it would go; looking at it would never stop it. He whirled around to what he had to face at the slide area.

An immense raw gulch lay below him, half a mile across, where the fill had flowed out into the lake, millions of yards of carefully dredged material reverting into goo and gravel, and the dredgeline was strewn on it like sections of blown-down stovepipe.

The trap, Owen remembered. Neil had been cleaning the trap. Find that steel pelican-pouch in the dredgeline, what was left of it, and Neil ought to be with it.

Charlene set her jaw and kept on combing out old lady Abbott, one of the Cactus Flat porcupineheads, as people poured past the front window of the beauty shop. Must be a fire somewhere down the street, she figured, and she was in no mood to see another one of those. People were really on the trot, though, every time she glanced up from Mrs. Abbott's stiff obdurate hair. If she hadn't known better, she'd have thought one of those pounding past in the crowd was Hugh.

From the east shore Darius stared at the delta of destruction below. Some sections of the stone-tiered face of the dam had stayed intact as they skidded out into the lake, solid islands like chunks of a jigsaw puzzle pawed apart. A queer spur of the railroad track still was in place atop the lip of the biggest island, wavery streak of rails beginning in midair, ending in mid-

air. Between the archipelago of riprap islands and the damaged crest of the dam
was what looked like a cesspool lake,
gravel and mud and the backed-up Missouri mixed into a murky brown basin.

Already the pandemonium of the escape
was precipitating into hundreds of separate aftermaths, some of the damworkers
standing petrified, overcome with thoughts
of their close call, a legion of others racing
back toward the slide area to search for
survivors. Darius thought of Neil with a
pang. Willing cog in the machine of work,
Neil had let it cost him his life. And Owen;
Darius looked but could not spot him in
the school of dam bosses, from the colonel
on down, frantic on the far side of the
slide.

Owen. Darius jerked his bitter gaze away
from the gesticulating bosses and stared
again at the riprap islands, strewn but
solid, in the lake, suddenly knowing what
he was seeing. The face of the dam, shale-
hater Owen's crafty dam, had not merely
avalanched, had it, not plummeted apart
in a simple collapse of slope. It had slipped
on its underearth, as a ship would slide
down the greased launchway into the
Clyde.

"Jackie, no, you can't play soldiers in the
flour bin. Meg, would you —"

"Jack, my man, let's go for a promenade." Meg captured the boy out of the trailer house kitchen that Kate was trying to set to rights and whisked him past Bruce edging through the doorway with an armload of bedding. "Perhaps it already has come to your attention, Jack," the parents heard her deep instructive tone begin before she and the boy were even past the front fender of the truck, "that the municipality of Park Grove is more grove than park."

Bruce furrowed his forehead. "He's going to grow up talking like a lawyer's parrot."

But Kate was busy at sliding the trailer's kitchen window open sideways, which was going to take some getting used to. She was intent beyond that at watching the huge *Gallatin*, broadside to them in a dredged pit less than a hundred yards away, the mountain of the dam behind it. The giant dredge, a cross between a verandahed hotel and a steamshovel and painted sailor-white, was nothing like the cable ferry her grandfather and father had operated, yet she felt she had been here before. She had been like Jackie, at the rampage age, when Grandpère died and they moved in with Grandmère to take over the ferry business, and that same first day her mother had caught her dabbling in the water alongside the hull of the ferry and given her an astounding bare-butt spanking. *You are to stay away from that river,* Lucille Millay made her small daughter know between whaps with the flat side of a yardstick, *you are to stay away from that boat.* Jackie was going to need the same, the first instant he wandered toward the river. Today would not be too soon, Kate believed.

Bruce's next armload of moving stuff in, she felt his flanks brush teasingly along her fanny as he edged past. "Close quarters," he alibied.

"Everything is, with you," she said.

"Owen and Charlene made out all right in here," he said hopefully, remembering in fact how the bachelor version of himself had almost burnt up, from the inside out, watching Owen go home noons and nights to this cute trailer and cuter Charlene.

The scene out the window still had Kate abstracted. "So, what's going on? Are Mum Mum and I the only ones who aren't on idle time today?"

Bruce had been curious about that himself, the dredge shut down all this while. He came over to peer out beside her, expecting more than not to see Owen storm up the gangplank and kick things into gear again.

Instead they both saw the eruption of action spreading out from the field telephone in the lever house, commotion that spilled down the decks into men running and shouting, "DAM! . . . GONE OUT! . . ."

Kate spun, toward the door, the truck, the scream to be let out for Jackie and Meg, but Bruce caught her arm.

"I don't think so, Katy," he said with monumental calm. "Or we'd be seeing about a hundred-foot wall of water heading our way, wouldn't we."

The deep gulch of the slide had eaten westward in the dam, along the core pool. Owen knew that the core pool must have emptied into the lake like a broken flume when the slide got underway, adding a lubricant into the shifting mass of fill. *Oh God oh why* . . . He plunged down the cavity of the core pool, the wet gravel making heavy going, and wallowed his way until he could struggle up onto the far part of the dam crest. The railroad tracks resumed out of midair there; beyond it the rest of the dam face, the three and a half miles of it westward, stood unchanged, another world entirely from the blowout of mud, gravel, water and stone. Grimy and bedraggled with it, Owen read the slippage like a textbook, sick inside himself at the lesson of half a mile of engineered earth strewn out into the lake.

Men along with it. *Where's* . . . Owen leaped from boulder to boulder down the riprap until he was at lake level, the muck-flat of the slide to his left, the islands of the broken-away sections of the dam face in front of him. He took a testing step out onto the slurry; there was enough gravel in it that he could flounder toward the broken line of dredgeline pipe, pilings sprouting up from it like small bones. Portions of the slide were large enough to have dry humps of ground, which he could gain footing on and plunge across to the next. He came up over one of these to be confronted with what looked like a crazy cannon, a Big Bertha elevated to fire into the lake. It stopped him cold for a moment, until he saw that it was a thirty-foot length of discharge pipe hurled atop the tipped-over cab of the crane.

The calculations Owen could not help doing as he plunged across the slideflat were coming out worse than awful. Five or six million cubic yards, he was sure it couldn't be any less, gone in this slippage. Sections of the dredgeline had been carried at least a thousand feet by the slide, every snaking surge of the big pipe amid enough damfill to bury the whole population of Montana, let alone a single missing Duff. *Neil, damn you, where* — Neil could be anywhere out here, under any depth of muck. Yet most of the dredgeline, crippled as it was, had ridden out the slide, been ushered down into the lake still oddly intact.

Owen was at the first still-standing section of dredgeline now. He filled his lungs to shout Neil's name, looked out at the long stretch of kinked and zigzagging pipe in front of him, and held the lungful of breath. Beyond on the east shore he could see the intake-gate towers, four in a row, unscathed, people everywhere up there, and men coming down into the slide area with prodpoles. They were too distant to be of any help in his search. He was in motion now, following the pipe sections out across the muck as it still gurgled and seethed, the slide carrying on an awful conversation with itself. Owen clambered alongside the dredgeline until it occurred to him, furious with himself, to climb atop it. The footing wasn't the greatest, and every dozen feet or so he had to step over a support pole lying half over the huge pipe, but he made better time than wading down there in the mud. He watched below his feet for the collar of the trap.

When he came to it, his hopes sank. The pipeline had buckled and kinked down into a crevice of the slide, hardly any of the metal showing above the muck. He reached down to a piece of glop wedged between the pipe and a support timber. A jacket.

Now Owen let out a roar of "NEIL!" and balanced himself atop the dredgeline, trying to figure out where best to plunge down and start digging. Then, halfway along the length of pipe from the drain trap, he saw a bump in the mud, almost under the big roundness of the pipe. The bump slightly turned toward him, and eyes opened in it.

Owen in six careful steps went to a place on the pipeline just beyond the mud-globbed head, spraddled down and then slid off into the mud. The blob mired under the pipe had shoulders now.

"Neil?! Neil, don't go dying on me!"

"Get your . . . goddamn . . . dam off me then."

The mud-caked figure gave a ragged combination of gasp and giggle, head wobbling back to give Owen a full white-eyed stare, making sure he was really there. Neil was drawing in tortured breaths as deep and ragged as if he had run for miles, but at least it constituted breathing.

Frantically Owen dug barehanded at the heavy mush of earth encasing him. "Stay still," he ordered.

"Did it . . . all go?"

"Shut up. Just breathe, okay?" Owen pawed away. "No, the dam didn't all go.

Just this one — slippage." He saw the relief register in Neil's eyes, but a tight squint of concern quickly came back.

"Birdie. He . . . somewhere . . ."

Still clawing muck away from Neil, Owen shot a look around. "There isn't any sign of Birdie," he said in a guilty strangled tone.

How long he dug by hand, fingernails tearing, skin tender and hurting, Owen had no idea. Neil occasionally groaned or gasped, but otherwise lay perfectly still as Owen had ordered him to. This worried Owen.

"You doing okay?" he asked Neil, as if demanding so.

"Hurts . . . on the side."

Owen drew a hard breath. He hated what he was going to have to do, but he needed to know whether this was an internal injury or —

"Here?" He laid the palm of his hand on Neil's ribcage.

"OWWW!" Neil's eyes had opened twice as wide. "Hell, yes . . . there!" He gulped painful air into himself, and used it to say: "Ownie, you'd massacre a man . . . while you're saving his life."

Owen pursed his lips, either against a madman smile or a sob of gratitude, he wasn't sure which. "Broken ribs," he told Neil. "They'll hurt some more, but I can get you out of here now."

All that endless afternoon, at last into common dusk, Fort Peck tried to pick itself up off the floor of the big slide. Searches went on until there was deemed no chance anyone could have lasted beneath the flood of muck, the mosquito buzz of planes with newspaper photographers already overhead as rescue parties slogged and poked and slowly retreated from the slide-flat. Queasy communities downstream from the dam, Park Grove only the first of the number along the Missouri's descent toward St. Louis, had to swallow hard and decide where to sleep that night, some-where on high ground or in the valley cut by the river's eternal longing to wander.

Birdie Hinch felt all beat to hell.

Gravel had gone over him and roaring water from the core pool had surged him free and then there was a pell-mell mud-swim, half dogpaddling and half being oozed along, out into the mush at the head of the slide. His shirt had filled with so much mud it weighted him into the mess like a lead sinker on a fishing line, but he managed to tear it off and bob better. Birdie had been constantly amazed at the kaleidoscope of clear thoughts coming to him as the muck avalanche tossed him along: *Wouldn't this have to happen just when we found that nicest buffalo skull . . . I'm gonna die, out of this. Ain't yet, though . . . They just can't pay a man enough to put up with this . . .* And at last, gingerbread man of mud gasping on one of the isles of the slide, *I'll be a sonofagun, look at those guys running out* onto *this.*

Rescued, and with somebody's practically new mackinaw jacket draped over him, and deposited to the hospital where the ambulatory ones such as him had to wait while the worse injured were rushed into care, he found a corner to limply sit in and ache, watching the parade of casualties pour in. Muddied and bloodied, the thirty or so men who had undergone the slide and lived weren't much recognizable, but toward the last Birdie saw Neil, bunged up but obviously going to make it, brought in by Owen and some of the rescue workers, and was glad of that.

Right in the middle of the hospital hubbub a flustered timekeeper pressed into service by the Ad Building was running around with a clipboard, taking down names of survivors.

Birdie, one of the world's talents at overhearing, caught the timekeeper's voice when that pintsize sheriff popped in to check with him: "We're up to three known dead and five still missing."

When the sheriff whirled back out, the timekeeper scanned the hospital uproar for any fresh arrivals and lit up when he finally spotted Birdie. He hustled over, pencil and clipboard ready, to take Birdie's name.

Birdie looked him in the eye and said as if badly put upon:

"Duff. But don't you already got me down there, from when I come in the door?"

"Aw, yeah, hell, I'm sorry," the embarrassed timekeeper said, his finger finding *Duff, N.* on his hasty list. "You guys look all alike with the mud on you."

That was all it took. By nightfall the name of Birdie Hinch was everlastingly among Fort Peck's missing, and the man he had been was hopping a boxcar on a Great Northern train bound for the Pacific Coast and a next life.

They crammed into Neil's hospital room the minute the doctor would let them.

Except for the way his face drew down a little on one side in the direction of the sharp complaints from his ribs, he looked like a Neil who had been severely scrubbed, bleached and wrung dry and was happy that was over. Sitting beside his bed Rosellen, eyes wide, kept watching him as if he might go out of sight against the hospital sheets in the manner a winter-pale rabbit does against snow.

"Neil," Meg began, "that was a ride we do not want you to repeat."

"Came pretty close to the line that time, didn't you, brother," Bruce began, in what sounded oddly like envy.

A majority of the Duffs chimed in that way, Neil able to grin and kid them back between winces. But everyone uncomfortably knew that the worst casualty in the room was Owen, who looked as though he'd been hammered directly on the heart. Charlene stayed always next to him, not saying much.

Proxy, to contribute, said Owen ought to take up fortune-telling, if he was able to pick out where Neil ended up in all that crap of the slide.

"All I could see of him were eyes and teeth," Owen managed to vouch.

One saves the other, and by doing, something of himself, Meg was pursed with thinking, rue and relief and an oddly sad love mixing in her as she watched her sons. *The ladders of this family run up and down, both, don't they ever, Owen.*

"You'd grin too when you saw it wasn't some geezer with a halo and wings coming for you," Neil spoke up from the bed. Then, as if he had been giving this some thought, he said: "Unk, you must've known a short-cut off the dam."

Hugh stirred, and sensed a warning look from Proxy as he did. He too had been curious, at Darius's spotless deliverance while the rest of the bullgang and poor devil Birdie were handed a flood of mud. In no position himself to bring up precise whereabouts at the time of the slide, Hugh awaited with terrible interest Darius's answer on this.

More fool you, Neil, to be scrabbling around at that trap rather than tending to the goings-on around you, as I was. Aloud, though, Darius had ready: "Nature called at the right time and in the right way, in my fortunate case, Neil. I was on my way to visit the littlest of houses, when the dam began to shimmy."

Small Jackie, tongue-tied for once in this confusing hospital visit, was awed at Grand Unk 'Rius telling everybody about going to the little house.

Darius shook his head to show them all his wonder at his own escape.

"I gave a shout," he declared, looking to the hospital bed as though Neil had been truant.

In the starchy sheets, Neil tried to remember. The shudder of the dredgeline, the tremor he had thought was a big piece of equipment ramming the pipe, was the first thing that would come back. Then the ground under him giving way, and his instinctive scramble atop the dredgeline. Life as he now possessed it began with those.

Owen stared across him to Darius. He couldn't recall any shout from Darius either, only the wordless sprinting figure who had flown past him on the dam crest. "I didn't hear that," Owen said, "but you did whistle by me getting off the dam."

Darius locked eyes with him. "Now, Owen, I'll deny to my last breath that I was running. But I will say, I overtook a good many who were."

The assembled Duffs at last laughed, all but Owen and Hugh.

Stained with disaster but still standing, Fort Peck Dam met each morning now in the company of hollow-eyed engineers and Corps officers and construction bosses. They took turns staying up nights in the Ad Building, emerging with a fresh day's schedule for the work of repair, and then machines and crews would go warily into the half-mile gouge of the slide area.

"It went fast," Darius mused. "You wouldn't think soil could outrun a man. Eight men."

He and Proxy had formed the habit of watching out the houseboat window at this work, before time for their own. By now, pretty sure she had seen what there was to see, Proxy had gone back to favorite morning pursuits, such as propping up on the bed and studying her picture in the old copy of LIFE. Darius had sometimes warned her, humorously, that she would wear that page out with looking. But right now he was all intent himself as he watched a railroad speeder go across the dam to the slide area and stop, the section crew climb off. "Very damn nearly nine, counting our Neil," Darius said as if in afterthought.

Proxy still did not say anything.

He kept watching the railroad repair crew as he asked: "Where exactly again were you when the news came, love?"

"The usual." The sound of her turning the pages. "Yakking with Tom Harry. He was telling me again all about how he plans to pull up stakes and go off where he can see a mountain any time he feels like it, and I was saying to him gopher holes are more his style. Same old routine."

"Liar, liar," Darius crooned in schoolyard singsong, then dropped his voice harshly: "cunt on fire."

Proxy sat up rigidly on the bed and stared at his back.

"Woman, you think I don't hear? You ought to be married to yourself — you'd soon find out. Every loose mouth at Fort

Peck lets me know who you've been with. Oh, casually, of course. Merely making a bit of joke. 'Saw that goodlooking wife of yours dancing the pockets off of old Smitty, wish I had a means of support like that,' " he mimicked. He kept on looking out the window. "When the slide went, you were monkeying around with Hugh."

Proxy hurled the magazine at his back. "Whatever the hell happened to 'we don't need to oversee each other just because we're married'?"

Darius reached down, swung around and slammed the magazine back at her, pages wildly flapping. "I didn't count on caring so much about you!"

"Huh *uh*, Darius," Proxy told him tensely but levelly. "What you didn't count on is caring about any frigging thing but those politics of yours."

"And you?" he said in worse than a whisper. "You know all the ins and outs of caring about, do you, Proxy?"

He walked out onto the silent spillway, alone this time.

Why didn't I savvy . . .

In the back of his mind he was aware of the watchman's uneasiness, off behind him on the approach to the highway bridge over the spillway, where he had parked the government pickup. But Owen

Duff made a lot of people uneasy, since the slide.

Neil, in that mess . . . it would have to be . . . job I put him on . . . why'd I ever . . .

This time Owen was atop the spillway's imperial gate piers pictured by the LIFE camera, the highway bridge going across them like the lofty trough of an aqueduct. Beneath the slowly walking man and the midair highway were the sixteen great gates of the spillway, waiting to regulate overflow from the lake into the spillway channel. If the dam, his dam, would ever hold together long enough to produce an overflow.

When he reached the middle of the structure, Owen stepped up out of the road onto the walkway and halted there, hands resting on the waist-high balustrade while he stared down at the vast concrete trench below as if it mirrored everything.

The sonofabitching Bearpaw shale. Here they had known to rocksaw the exposed shale and haul it out, or to face it over with waterproof bituminous compound; known they did not dare let any scour of moisture in to crumble that shale to mud under the heavy concrete channel. *But no, Duff, you couldn't carry that idea for only three miles over those hills and . . .*

Why hadn't he demanded rockcutting the entire face of that bluff, or bitumen sealing of everything in sight, or a mammoth retaining wall, something, anything, back there at the east abutment where that bank of shale kept tormenting his core pool. Having the bluff, one whole wall of the valley, as the anchor bank of the core pool was supposed to have been an advantage; sure, bits of it might crumble, but as soon as the impervious fill built up onto it and the core pool water was drained away, there the sealed east end of the dam was supposed to be, natural and perpetual. Except that shale sidehill had its own ideas about how it was going to behave around water, didn't it, Duff. The lost face of the dam's east section — *now* he knew, *too late* he knew — had slid on a wettened underbank of that shale like a hog on ice. *Huh uh, slicker and quicker than that, even.* Owen could envision instantly the railroad tracks, like pieces of a model-train setup neatly pulled apart, out there on the several slide-islands. Couldn't have asked for smoother sledding. The geologists — *Christ, toboggan experts would've been better* — the geologists back there at the core sampling and porosity tests had missed the deep-seep process, that saturation could keep spreading down through the abutment shale like water through a monstrous sponge. The Kansas City blueprinters of the dam had missed it. And he himself had missed it, in worrying about what the shale was doing to his core pool instead of what his core pool was doing to the Bearpaw shale.

The board of inquiry wasn't going to miss it.

Owen leaned into the balustrade, elbows on it now, still seeming to contemplate the mile-long concrete floor down there. Corps scuttlebutt had it that Quigley, the Harvard brain on the investigating board, was saying the dam was not worth finishing. Its other eight engineering whizzes, though, were not likely to conclude that a slide of 3 percent of its total earthfill was anywhere near fatal to Fort Peck Dam. No, they were going to want the slide fixed, weren't they, and by whatever prescription needed to make certain it did not happen again.

Engineering truly was a clever whore, Owen Duff at this moment would have told you in something like wonder and nausea: no sooner did it allure a person into committing a phenomenal disaster than it came flirting back with the exact cure. He had seen the fix to be made there in the dusk of slide day, after he had Neil to the hospital and found his dazed way back to the edge of the gouge in the dam. Piledrive a secondary cutoff wall, cover it with a fifty-foot core of impervious fill, then replace the dredged material in a gentler slope; with that kind of barrier and a dry and compacted mass over it, the shale would have no way to pull the rug out from under four million yards of earthfill again. That was all that was necessary on fixing the slide.

On himself, Owen was not at all sure what was needed. Over the side here, off this bridge onto that expanse of concrete, would do it quick enough. Be like dropping an egg off a cliff. He knew to the specified inch the height of this spillway gate structure; plus a three-foot balustrade to climb up onto and drop from. The equivalent of a six-story building, down to death. Not a record, but far enough.

Or stay. Stay in life. Face down the board of inquiry — *I followed every spec, on the core pool, the fill, everything; the core of the dam never budged, did it; the dam didn't go out, did it* — and make the case for fixing the slide area as he knew how. Fixing it might take a year, time enough to get himself back to normal. Whatever the hell normal was, anymore.

Like a man dizzy, Owen backed away from the balustrade.

Kate was doing battle with the ready-counter of the Rondola, asking whether her orders of ham and eggs were past the oink and cluck stage yet, when in Mr. Important walked and marched right past the counterful of customers. He turned her around to him, lifted her off the floor in a full-length bear hug, and carted her like that through the swinging door into the kitchen.

Dola and Ron and the dishwasher swiveled to the arrival of the enwrapped pair, then looked studiously elsewhere.

It was only inches worth, but Kate stared worlds into Bruce's face until he set her down.

"All the fixing up after the slide? — they've decided they have to bring in a dozen divers for it," he told her, grinning a mile. "The inside skinny is that we'll be diving here all next year, maybe more. And guess who's being made the lead guy."

Kate's dazed expression failing to change, he spelled it out for her.

"I've got all the seniority, hon. Crew chief — that'll be me, just got told. At twice the money."

Finally out of things to reel off to her, Bruce was the one who looked dazed. "Katy, we've got it made, again."

764

Part Eight

THE SHERIFF

1991

With grunts of pain that he could barely prevent from being yelps Carl Kinnick rolled the wheelchair to his bed, reached over and yanked down hard on the emergency call cord.

The nurse was there in under a minute. She whipped into the room, white britches swishing, then stopped short at the sight of him, scrunched in his wheelchair same as ever.

"Going on the dam trip," he notified her.

"Like fuck huh uh, you are." In her surprise she forgot to professionally cushion the words with his name. "Can't, can you? The way your hip hurts you?"

"Don't care." He kept squinting at her as neutrally as he could, needing her help on this.

All she would have to do to dispose of

this situation was to ask him the four little words, "Did you sign up?" Shit no, he hadn't signed up for the outing to the dam, she knew. He hadn't done anything except sit here and be ornery for as long as she had worked here. *Why on my shift?* she reflected as she angrily stretched past him to flip the emergency call button back to OFF. *Why couldn't the old poot take it into his head to go to bingo tonight, if he finally wants to get out of his room?* She didn't even really have to think through all the kinds of trouble involved in letting him go to the dam. They would need to take the cabulance van instead of the rec bus because of him in his wheelchair, and Mosteller the driver would shit a brick about that. Doris the recreation director went miles out of her way to avoid Carl Kinnick ever since that birthday party fiasco; she'd be spooked silly to have him show up for her pittypat little visit to Fort Peck this afternoon. Howls would go up from the other residents on the excursion, too, the nurse could just about hear those already: *old devil him anyway, has to spoil it for everybody else, coming along and sitting there like death warmed over.*

On the other hand, such as it was, the Little Prick had never before shown her he really wanted anything.

"If I let you," she said in her tone that

kidded and didn't, "promise not to come back?"

Mosteller, the longhaired driver, had earphones on and wobbled his head from side to side in tune with whatever musical racket it was he was listening to. In the old days the sheriff would have slapped a reckless-driving ticket on him so fast his head would swim.

There weren't all that many on the dam trip. The bridge-club biddies from the third floor, and Theresa Machias who used to work at the courthouse and was the only one who so much as said hello to him, and old Danvers who was half ga-ga three-quarters of the time, and of course Doris, who kept slipping nervous eyecorner glances at him. He wished the dirty-mouthed young nurse was along.

He and the wheelchair were cinched in at the back of the cabulance, the others' gray heads and Danvers's empty bald one poking up in front of him from the bench seats. *Tail gunner on the hearse,* he thought of, and pursed a tiny smile to himself.

This very first part, right out of town, was the only bit of this familiar route he cared anything about. The intense green, a color almost savage (although the sheriff found it restful), of the cottonwoods concentrated along the Milk River, before the road headed over the ridge toward the Missouri. Otherwise this drive down from Glasgow still did not amount to much, by his standards of interest. The traffic deaths of speedball damworkers had all happened before white roadside crosses were put up to mark car-wreck fatalities, so the sheriff couldn't even pick out the spots where he'd had to gather up the crushed and flung bodies.

What still surprised him, as the cabulance topped the last rise before starting down to the river, was that the town of Wheeler had vanished absolutely. The hasty frame buildings had been easy pickings, torn down for salvage or hauled away to farms and ranches for use as granaries and chicken coops. The sheriff enjoyed the thought of Wheeler ending up as barnyards.

Fort Peck, the town of, still featured the big dark hotel and the Swiss gingerbread theater, and a Corps of Engineers office with a Spanishy red roof in the permanent portion of the old Ad Building. Then it thinned radically, to a couple of neighborhoods of cookie cutter houses fixed up and a luncho-gaso-laundromat. Not nearly as gone as Wheeler, New Deal, Square Deal and all the others, but plenty depleted.

As were those Army Engineer big shots

who went on into the war, the sheriff ruminated as the cabulance drove on. Parmenter, Santee, and Roscoe — no, Brascoe. Dead, dead, and dead. Santee, the story they told on him was that he'd been assigned as one of those top-secret couriers sent places with a briefcase handcuffed to his wrist, and that he'd somehow lost one of those courier cases. Killed himself, over it. Huh. Those pretty-pants Corps boys all gone and here he still had breath in him.

Suddenly, the dam.

You were on the thing before you could ever recognize it as such. It had never seemed right to the sheriff that the down-stream slope of the dam had grassed over, looking like a sidehill hayfield that had been there forever. Overall, the dam now resembled a narrow-topped and particularly flat benchland which somehow happened to stand in the way of a body of water backed up across the curvature of the earth. (Out there on the water was another thing the sheriff was never going to grow used to, the everyday sight here of boaters and fishermen. *Tourists* even, a few anyway.) You had to study this view inordinately to realize the scale of the dam, the immensity of fill that was diked across here. And over near the dam's east side there was not even a trace of where the big slide had happened, they had riprapped over that so it looked as innocent as virgin scenery, too.

The cabulance's destination, site of the tour that Doris was hugely determined to herd them through, could be seen poking up down by the outlet channel where the river came out of the tunnels: the pair of powerhouses that had been added after the dam was done. Twin concrete skyscrapers amid the gopher holes. More federal money, in the sheriff's estimation, typically pushed up into the air instead of just let slide down those gopher holes. He shifted in his wheelchair, so as not to solidify in one position, and was careful to gasp behind the clench of his mouth so the others could not hear the pain.

Slowly the cabulance drove and drove across the dam, west to east, one full mile, two, three. Far down the slope now, at the toe of the dam, the river tore out of the diversion tunnels in a narrow white gush. On the dam's other side, upstream, across that entire half of the horizon the lake lapped against the midriffs of hills. Outdoing the original intentions of the engineers, Fort Peck Dam backed up the waters of the Missouri for 135 miles from here. The sheriff read somewhere once that this lake's load of standing water affected the rotation of the earth, and he didn't doubt it a bit.

"Almost there," Doris sang out.

The lake steadily slapped at the riprap below the road, coloration on the boulders marking how much higher the waterlevel had been during runoff, late last spring. Just ahead now, at the east abutment of the dam, an overlook ringed with small boulders jutted up, wayside signs there telling the history and vital statistics of the dam.

"This'll do," he pronounced. "Pull over, in there."

The recreation director badly wanted the voice to be that of poor old Mr. Danvers, who harmlessly piped up at odd moments. But, whittled down and propped in a wheelchair though he was, Carl Kinnick vocally still had an unmistakable edge, about like a police siren's.

She turned to him with the best smile she could manage and said, "Now then, Mr. Kinnick, if you need to . . . go, in just a minute now there'll be restrooms at the powerh—"

"Not a matter of me going. Staying put suits me."

Even the bridge-club bunch, normally Doris's most durable allies, tittered at that. And Mosteller the driver, who had heard Carl Kinnick's tone over the din in his headphones, was already pulling over into the outlook parking area, stopping to see what was the matter.

Doris unbuckled her seatbelt and went to the back of the cabulance, to the sheriff situation.

"Just leave me off here," he ordered, if she was hearing properly. "Pick me up on your way back."

"But what . . ." The reasoning against that was automatic, it was as plain as the wrinkles on his face. "Mr. Kinnick, we can't just go — drive off and leave you here all alone."

He stared back at her as if giving her a minute to learn common sense.

"Don't you see?" she said against that stare. She was also aware that the whole contingent in the cabulance, from Mosteller on back, was watching intently, sopping this in. "We simply can't . . . the responsibility . . ."

"Any responsibility for me is mine."

". . . is a big one and . . ."

"I'll stay and keep the sheriff company," Theresa Machias spoke up from one of the front seats. "I've seen that powerhouse nine Septembers in a row."

Doris turned in the direction of Theresa and said that was certainly nice of her but was she sure, and Theresa said of course she was sure or she wouldn't have opened her mouth in the first place.

Then Doris was hovering over the sheriff again, asking whether it suited him to have Theresa stay with him, which he thought he concurred with civilly enough, considering.

Even so the recreation director hesitated, hanging on in his vicinity but staying a little away from him, too. She evidently couldn't make up her mind whether he was more likely to pitch over and die, or reach up under and snap her garter. After another uncertain hover, Doris backed off and asked him:

"Will this be all right for you, are you sure? It's so windy here."

He couldn't help looking at her as if she was a complete fool. "There's always wind in this country."

"Yes, well —" She bit her lip and told Mosteller, "All right then, Jerry," and the driver operated the cabulance's lift platform and indifferently wheeled the sheriff off and over to the lake end of the overlook.

Theresa Machias sensibly had a coat with her and her donut cushion to sit on, Doris was a little relieved to see as she trailed after to supervise getting the two of them settled. Already the sheriff was ignoring her, refusing to swerve his gaze from one particular promontory of the river bluffs, across there to the west, even when Doris's hand darted in and tucked his jacket collar closed around his neck. She heard him say:

"It was up there."

The recreation director tried to follow the line of his gaze, across the lake to the high blunt bluffs. "What, Mr. Kinnick. What was?"

Didn't she wish she knew. The sheriff shook his head, holding in the tiny smile until he was sure she had turned away.

After giving the pair of them one last assurance that she would be back before they knew it, Doris climbed into the cabulance and the vehicle trundled down the slope out of sight behind a powerhouse.

Theresa had parked herself on a sittable rock a decent distance from the sheriff's wheelchair. She dug a pack of cigarettes and her silver-plated retirement lighter from her coat pocket. After lighting up, and then letting out a crashing cough which somehow seemed to satisfy her, she offered the pack in the general direction of the sheriff for politeness's sake. "But you never used these, did you."

"Hmm-nn. They stunt your growth, Therese."

Snorty chuckle from her, something equivalent silently from him. Then, shriveled up there in his wheelchair, he turned his head from her, back toward the bluff across the dam.

Theresa periodically emitted smoke and checked up on Carl Kinnick with a glance. What a little sonofabitch on six wheels he had been, when he was sheriff all those years. Bite your head off if you couldn't put your finger immediately on whatever piece of court paper he was after. She timed another casual glance at him. Two-wheeled now, though.

It was up there, that he had gone through it that other time.

Procedure took him to the point, back there in 1938 in that aftermath of the truck, where he had questioned the remaining Duffs until the questions wore out. Their answers, though, showed no wear at all. *I was at home.* Or: *Working my shift.* Or: *We went to the show together that night.* Their chain of alibi, always somebody handy to vouch for this or that in their stories, except on the central matter of the pair in the truck cab.

No idea he was up to anything like that, the widow of the drowned unclothed man maintained.

Never knew there was anything going on between them, the husband of the dead and unclad woman swore.

Then the sheriff would have to backtrack, go through the questions again, trying to weave a case that would catch one or another or, for all he cared, five or six or all eight of the damned surviving Duffs.

At last, he gave in and borrowed the truck.

More like confiscated it, if you want the truth. Well aware that his undersheriff would blab something like this all over Fort Peck, the sheriff went by himself to Moore Motors in Glasgow and informed Ted Moore he was taking that reconstituted Ford Triple A for a couple of hours, making sure to mention to Ted that he'd be piloting the truck to the dam project to check out a circumstance. But halfway down the highway to Fort Peck, the sheriff veered off, west, along an old section-line road, no more than a set of ruts grooved alongside a stretch of barbwire fence. The truck jolted across the prairie on the twin wheeltracks, the sheriff perched on the edge of the wide-bodied seat, up close over the sizable steering wheel, grimly absorbing the bumps.

After a matter of more miles than he had remembered on this route, the sheriff came out above the Missouri, on a high bluff some ways upstream from the dam. Below, at the turn of the bluff, a little treed-over stream called Nettle Creek used to empty into the river, but the lake had filled back this far by now. What little of the bottomland that was left to view looked eaten into, a dredge's trademark bites with huge scalloped edges. At the dam, a fleet of barges and workboats had been pulled in to work on repairing the slide; the sheriff could see their boxy forms against the scar of the slide, but at such a distance no one could see what he was up to in the truck.

Here the slope to the water was quite sharp, higher and steeper than the ramp the truck had freewheeled down at the dam site to its plunge into the lake, so Kinnick took care in nosing the truck to a stop, facing down to the valley of the Missouri. Wasn't sure why he needed the actual water below him for this; knew it was basically a dangerous idea, if the truck should happen to get away from him. And wouldn't that be one sweet hell of a way to go: the whole county talking about him drowning, too, same as that Duff affair, and not even a woman keeping him company. He wished there had been a way to bring a woman along for this, make it considerably more real; but if word about something like this escaped, he'd be laughed out of office. Drowning would be simpler.

So he sat alone and thought through the onset of this maddening case.

The truck parked as it was, barely over

the brow of this big ridge, enough tilt for an absolute panorama of the river but not enough for much sliding forward if you lay down across the seat: somebody trying to use a moonlight view of the river to encourage the clothes off somebody else might find this the best angle, he figured.

The sheriff took off his hat and hesitantly placed it on top of the back of the seat against the rear window, couldn't see what else to do with it in the circumstances.

Even though he had examined this vehicle to the point of eyestrain before the remaining Duffs turned it back over to Moore Motors, now he made himself systematically scan the inside of the truck cab one more time, starting at the steering wheel and then the emergency brake, defunct, of course, and sideways and down to the gearstick angling up from the transmission housing in the floorboards, and across the wide seat to the passenger-side door, and on up and around to the rear window where that cloud of their clothing had damply clung. Only to divine the same thing again, nothing.

Maybe he was carrying the experiment kind of far with this next maneuver, but he unscrewed the standard black knob of the gearshift, tossed it in the glove compartment, and screwed on the fancy amber whorly one that had been there when the truck went into the river.

Nothing more to do but do it.

The sheriff licked his lips. Lips and licking were pertinent to what he was attempting to emulate, sure, but he wasn't employing them out of pleasure.

Staying as studious as he could, he lay down, extending himself across the seat to the passenger side, belly down in the male position.

The seat felt a little cool, ungiving, against his freshly shaved cheek. Not like the woman's skin would be, there, but he couldn't help that. He checked over his left shoulder to the knob of the gearstick. It was within range of his hip, but not nearly touching. The sheriff was sure as anything that the truck had been left in low gear, the night of the deaths; that's what people do, after all, when they park a vehicle anywhere that it might roll, jam it into grandma-gear.

Drawing a deep breath, feeling foolish but impelled at the same time, he nudged his hip against the gearshift knob, as might happen if a man went a little sideways in excitement.

Nothing. His hip twinged, but the gearshift stayed steadily in place.

The sheriff swore quietly at the gaudy knob, then tensed himself and battered it as hard as he could with his hip. Still nothing, except the major bruise he knew he was going to have there. The sheriff could not believe the woman's hip would have been more lethal, but in the interest of research he turned over onto his back as he imagined she would have been, knees somewhat sticking up, and banged against the gearshift with his other hip, hard and harder. Next he flung out an arm sharply against the gearknob. Then he tried a tumble against it, half-falling off the seat so that all his sideward weight went against the taut metal rod. He thought for a moment, then scrambled behind the steering wheel, and careful not to let the truck start rolling, jammed a foot on the brake while he shifted gears into reverse, toward the dashboard. His personal theory was that the couple would have been so involved they wouldn't have bothered with getting the gearshift a little more out of their way, but okay, say they did. With the truck now in reverse, the sheriff lay back down to see if he could bounce the shiftstick out of this gear, either, with his hip.

In any combination of positions that Sheriff Carl Kinnick could think of, any semblance of accidental bump or shove or knock or thrust or lunge during the blind concentrations of lovemaking, the gearshift would not pop out of gear.

And so the truck at the dam site had to have had help in starting to roll, coasting down the slope of the ramp in its deathride to the floor of the river. Back then, more than half a century ago, the sheriff despised the feeling of frustration after his failed reenactment, and it still got him worked up, just thinking about it.

Accident, the answer that would have closed the case then and there, simply did not fit the picture.

From his solo session there in the truck cab the sheriff was positive there was no inadvertent way to depress a clutch pedal while having sex, either, and even if something that weird had managed to happen and some way there was the shift of gear out of low or reverse into neutral, why couldn't the man or even the woman have tromped on the brake pedal, or flung a door open, or swerved the steering wheel, or anything like that to save themselves? Okay, say they were going at each other to the point of oblivion. The sheriff still found it very hard to believe that the jolt of the truck starting into motion down that rough planked slideway wouldn't have interrupted even 101 percent passion.

Murder, then?

Both of them knocked over the head and sent rolling into the river? The two bodies were a bit banged up, but that dodo of a coroner had not been able to single out any contusions that the plunge in the truck wouldn't itself have caused. In his own mind the sheriff could come up with a way for it to happen at gunpoint: somebody following them to their tryst on the damslope ramp, surprising them there naked in the middle of the action, shoving a gun in their faces and forcing them to start the truck rolling, the gunhandler riding the running board until the last moment, leaping off as the truck sailed into the Missouri. But that scenario was a stretch, several ways. And how come the pair still couldn't have bailed out as soon as the truck hit the water?

Two lives gone. And others thrown into a hell of a tangle. That fed the sheriff's fury, too. Anyone who encountered Carl Kinnick at, say, a car wreck would remember forever his snappishness, his coil of what seemed to be affronted anger. Which is absolutely what it was. The waste of lives drove him wild: how dare they? how could they throw away, through too much speed or booze or showing off, the sum-result of themselves? Sheriffing could not control everybody's behavior, he had concluded with reluctance, but that did not alter the fact that it needed some controlling.

And so, the final *so* he always came to,

the Duff case always had been doubly perturbing to him because the deaths in the truck stacked up as a deliberate forfeit of life. Not just the foolishness of making seatsprings sing in the night, although there plainly was some of that involved in this episode. But beyond that, what had happened was done intentionally. What people were capable of thinking up. That was the lasting perplexity, wasn't it. Carl Kinnick supposed it had better be, or he might as well be wadded up and tossed in this lake instead of still pursuing thoughts along that line.

"— move around some, so I don't stiffen up like a rock," he heard Theresa Machias say, in the tuned-up tone people use when they're saying something a second time. "Anything you want done, Carl, first?"

He moved his head enough to see her, on her feet now but still a healthy distance from him. "Doing okay the way I am, Therese," he told her, and as she went off on a short walk to the other end of the outlook, he turned his attention back to the bluff across the water.

He sat there, hunched, confined, older than the hill of manufactured earth beneath the wheels of his chair; sat and with all the ardor left to him kept at it. Kept furious at the Duffs for the mystery they lived with and two of them died by, and just as helplessly loving them for this last slick stone of sheriffing to gnaw on, this case of theirs that would not let itself be solved.

Part Nine

TRUCK AND RIVER

1938

You wait in the weeds long enough and sometimes something tasty will come along. He almost couldn't believe the luck of this, this midnight chance at her.

Here where they were parked, the light-poles along the dam showed the spew of the dredgeline, small silver waterfall in the torn canyon left by the slide. On out into the lake, the temporary lights of the slide-islands were as pretty and crooked as star formations, clusters strung wherever the crews were at work salvaging the drowned machines or scavenging the riprap boulders onto barges for use again when the face of the dam was fixed.

"Going day and night, patching the roof of the Missouri River," he said to break the hard little distance of silence between them there in the cab of the truck.

She did not say anything. Day, night, still not enough to fix how wrong this had all gone.

He looked across at her. It was going to be like this, was it. Mood, when he'd prefer her nude.

All right, she had reason to be upset. She was not the only one.

"Proxy —" he began in a blurt that even surprised himself, and broke off huskily.

In the dark of the cab of the truck, she could just see his profile. They all looked inescapably alike, the Duff men, as though traced on paper several times over. Although she was finding out their differences.

"Proxy is climbing Hugh's leg," the words came bitterly out of him, "good Lord, woman, haven't you seen that?" She watched him take off the cap, run a hand through his hair, hesitate for a place to set the cap. *You came saying you tip your cap only to yourself, didn't you, Darius. Here you are, still at it.* Looking across at her again, he put the cap up on the back of the seat behind him. "Proxy hot to trot, time for a new Duff, a little taste of brotherly love direct from my brother? Hasn't everyone seen that?"

She didn't answer.

The truck stayed silent except for the hum of the heater, and as if all at once deciding the cab was warm enough, she felt down to the ignition key and turned it off. Darius waited for her move toward him, but none came.

He put a hand over to her, to see what it might bring.

"Does that engineer even do this by blueprint?" he asked, touching her skillfully enough to change her breathing.

"No." She swallowed, but then got the words out. "At least not with me."

More of Darius's hand. She concentrated past it to the note of mockery in his chuckle, kept herself tensed toward the hateful sentence she knew was coming. "But with Charlene," he was saying it, "it must have got that way for our man Owen, why else."

There in the dark, small tight fists resting on the steering wheel, Rosellen hated him all the way back to first principles. Bone, blood, breath, everything of Darius Duff she hated. The force of this was beyond anything she had ever imagined, it was as if there were suddenly several of her, furious cast of characters all of them her, packed into everything she felt against him. She hated him on behalf of Neil, Charlene, Owen, herself, any and all who would have their lives come apart if he told what he knew.

He had been looking high and low for Owen, core pool to the toe of the dam, as the crowd poured to the Fort Peck railroad siding and the presidential train, waiting for Roosevelt. In their tournament of argument, noontimes, FDR was ever there like the mercury in a thermometer, register of what Owen believed was politically far enough and Darius believed was doctrinally never enough, and Darius could hardly wait now to keep company during the speech and then argue it degree by degree with Owen. A chance to see America's royal trickster in action, it would be a treat for any thinking man, as they both were. Word had reached the crowd that the President's motorcade was on its way, down through the hills from the spillway, and Darius was as keen for the coming performance as any. He lacked only Owen.

Tracking down the engineer Sangster and wife in a good spot at the end of the roped-off area for Corps officers and their families and dignitaries not quite entitled to the presidential train's rear platform, Darius found out the most recent sighting of Owen. "Left a little bit ago. Had to go pick up Charlene."

Darius opened his mouth to set Sangster straight, then instinct snapped it shut for him. He moved off quickly into the crowd, thoughts weaving as he went.

Charlene had already been picked up and delivered here. By Proxy and Tom Harry in the Packard. By plan of Owen.

"Favor to ask you, Proxy — I'm going to be snowed under by Corps rigamarole on Franklin D. day," Darius could hear again Owen of a few nights ago, at one of those encouragement suppers at Hugh and Meg's. "Can you give this working wife of mine a lift out to the shindig?" Proxy had said sure, why not, somewhat unnecessarily adding that the Packard always had plenty of room, and then Charlene had joked about finally riding in style at Fort Peck. And just now, in this prowl for Owen, Darius had spotted the three of them, bartender and hairdresser and taxi dancer, perched like nabobs on the Packard roof where they could see to FDR's train.

And Sangster, spectating in a coveted spot with his arm around his wife, did not much look as though rigamarole was overburdening the engineers this day, did he.

His brow knit, Darius searched higher, heading up the bluff toward the Ad Building. This is not like our Owen, to miss out on a Roosevelt holy day. *Latecomers from Glasgow and beyond were hurrying onto the bluff's slope here between the Y of the road to the Ad Building and the dredgeline* road down past the winter harbor. The side-hill gave a clear view out over the gathering, FDR's motorcade in sight alongside the train down there now. Darius hesitated, lingered, then decided this onlooking site was as good as any, Owen or no Owen.

The preliminaries gradually came and went and then all at once the lordly Roosevelt cadences, of politics and the river, and of the river and politics, were rolling out over the thousands of cars and more thousands of listeners, including the impressed skeptic Darius. Voice like God's town crier, *he was thinking to himself,* no wonder the man can get away with —

Then he saw the truck.

The Model Triple A, unmistakable with its little cap-peak outside visor, was on its way from the river, the oxbow section down-stream from the dam where the dredges were working. Working, that is, except during this Roosevelt event, when all crews were given time off. Watching in the Triple A's direction, Darius could not help but wonder why Neil would be trucking anything at this hour, this day. The truck pulled in at the back edge of the winter harbor lot solid with vehicles, a scrawny deputy sheriff pointing to a parking spot. And out hopped Rosellen, walking swiftly, head down, around the parked mob. She looked for all the world like someone hastening back now from a quick errand, something tended to at home or the office, taken care of by dashing off in the truck. Except she had been on the fork of the road that went only to the dredges.

After a moment's incredulity, Darius laughed, knowing.

And in minutes here the other one came, in the familiar beat-up government pickup. Around to the motor pool lot, and then Darius could make him out on foot, Owen in long strides cutting across to see the presidential train pull away. Owen the fillmaster, from the dredge Gallatin *where the fillmaster had quarters.*

After that, Darius believed he could even tell the times when they were slipping off together, to whatever hideyhole. Whenever Owen edgily excused himself out of a noon, it had been all Darius could do not to give him the oldest mocking smile there was and pipe out, "Have you tried a pantry yet?"

Rosellen wished she and Darius had this over with. The ending, the going. Primed as she was for this, she found it hard to make happen. Rage of this depth was a new story to her. She felt half-dizzy between it and the despondency; the same kind of desperate batty intensity she'd had after Neil looked into the eclipse and there was nothing she could do for him, and when stories she'd written her heart out on were mailed back to her with editors' polite scorn. Clenched all over; that was how she —

"Rosellen, love, how long do we have?" Darius asked urgently.

"Enough." Honey it as he would, love had nothing to do with tonight's deal.

She had come for him at the houseboat. "Not here," she had said. "Not under Proxy's roof." He had chuckled, dry sound. Then followed her out and into the truck.

As she drove to the dam, he'd started to ask: "Where's —"

"At the show." Neil, Charlene and Owen, Kate and Bruce, all five of them in the midnight dark of the movie theater, the newsreel coming on now; more Europe. They'd been determined, the three couples, to try to make a night of this, supper together as they used to and then the usual few beers and music at the Blue Eagle, Neil was recuperated enough to dance gingerly. Everybody needed this Saturday night out, they said as if it was a chorus, Owen the only one overly quiet but not the only one deep in worry. Rosellen had pleaded a splitting headache when the movie came up, but insisted Neil go with the others, he needed some fun. The headache was close to the truth, although the sensation reached all the way down through her, the harrowed feeling and the taut determination.

Darius had left the choice of site to her, she was the expert at slipping around to such places, wasn't she. She had driven with him, curious passenger in America, to the quiet end of the dam where the riprap work stood stalled until the slide section was rebuilt. Deserted this time of night, the little dock called Port Peck was a dark stub into the water at the base of the dam. Where the planked ramp angled down to the dock and the lake, Rosellen parked carefully, on enough of the incline that they could see out to the temporary lights on the slide-islands, and killed the engine. "Scenic," Darius had commended then. "If it's the sort of thing you're here to see," she had said back, trying to sound composed.

Now his words broke in on her, the string of lights still constellated across the truck's windshield. "I'll tell you a thing that board of inquiry ought to interest itself in, there. Why a man who knew shale could go slick as lard didn't call everyone off the dam, when we were all standing around flummoxed just before the slide. It'd have saved your Neil some woe."

All the long thoughts that led her here crisscrossed now. Neil would have to take the hurt of this, but less than if he had been hit with the news of her and Owen. Owen, Owen and Charlene, this was a way to make up for the trespass there, wipe away his escapade. Proxy? Proxy knew about stories and consequences, she would grit and bear this and go on. The others, they would close ranks against whatever the world said about this, as Duffs always did when they had to. Rosellen only regretted this wasn't the kind of thing she could run by her debating partner Kate.

"That board yet could, you know," Darius's voice a goad in the dark. "If someone were to put a word in their ear."

She didn't believe what he said about Owen and the slide. Or about Proxy and Hugh, for that matter. Liar as well as everything else he was. Next on that list would be snitch.

" 'Tell us, Jealous,' " Rosellen said.

He cocked a look at her. Sounding suddenly cautious, he asked: "Whyever do you say that?"

"It's what came. Words have that habit."

She remembered to the word how it started, it could have been a farther cry from what she was trying for on paper.

Seeing she finally could get rid of the dredging report she'd typed up for him, that April noon, she took it to Owen's office right away after Sangster emerged from their session of dam talk and whistled off to lunch. When she stepped in, Owen was turned in his chair, facing the window where he could see the river and the dam, the eraser on his pencil bouncing brup brup brup on his desktop as he sat there mulling. At first she wasn't sure he even knew she had come in, but then he said: "Thanks. More paper ammo for the battle of Fort Peck."

Curious, she said: "You look like you're in danger of thinking yourself inside out. What about?"

"Winter harbor." The wide line of his mouth tucked down at its corners, his sign of joshing at himself. "It's only six months from now, so I figured I'd get a little head-start on the worrying."

"That's funny." The cute serious concentration marks showed up between her eyebrows. "The sun must be doing different things to us. I just looked up the opposite of hibernation."

Quick as presto, Owen gave her an appreciative look and was hooting with laughter about getting his seasons crossed, next thing he knew he'd be outside on Christmas trying to aestivate with the snow snakes. And after a surprised moment at all that, Rosellen laughed because she was glad the two of them chimed this way.

Is there such a thing as inadvertent flirting? Unintended mad pash? She came to wonder after that noon and others, as the two of them paid attention to each other, new ways, little ways, ways that did not necessarily have to lead dangerously far but could, could.

After they took the plunge, dazed and giddy and guilty and stimulated there in the tight shiplike quarters while everyone else was off seeing Roosevelt, she tried to sort out what was happening. Juanita and Gilbert chasing through the grass with her typewriter keys after them, chickenfeed. What she and Owen were drawn into was as complicated as a family album, it seemed to her. The best way she could put it was that they each wanted something like a portion of a person more, another helping, in their marriages. Not the first pair ever to catch catnip on the breeze at the same time, they both knew; plural of spouse is spice, *but that oldest of jokes on humans is always freshly played. Slipping off to meet, their not many times — Rosellen's educated guess on Owen was that he tiredly wanted back his dating days of Bozeman, someone warm and willing and without Charlene's grudge against his work. Someone, instead, who prized Fort Peck as he did. Go for broke, the part of him beyond blueprint had chosen when the chance with Rosellen surfaced. Her diag-nosis on herself didn't take much: a little starved, that was all, for somebody who when you asked what was on his mind, told you. And getting back at Charlene, of course that figured in, too — all the big sistering, any Bluebird Girl could spell that out in macaroni letters. Charlene and her prettiness, her fanciness, her little flirts traded with Bruce. Sisters paired like ark animals that didn't quite match, she and Charlene. On his side of things, Owen had to flinch past the fact of Neil; but brothers fork apart where a woman is concerned, ask anywhere in history.*

So, neither of them meant anything last-ing by their handful of times together. Rosellen pretty much knew what she was having with Owen wasn't actual love, al-though there were things about him she wished she could take home and put under the sheets. She didn't even think she was out of love with Neil, although as Proxy advised they did seem to need a fresh shot of each other. What Rosellen, pressed to it, would have said she loved was the expe-rience itself; the experiencing of their tryst. The story, secret, then would just be there, put away in herself — and of course Owen — when they all left Fort Peck. Except that Darius had pushed himself into the picture. After the slide, the first time they'd man-

aged a minute to be alone to talk in the back hallway of the Ad Building, she had taken a look at Owen's painfully peaked expression and said, "Don't blame yourself to death. You went out there and saved Neil's skin."

"It's nothing as simple as a few million yards of mud," he responded. Darius had been at him about the two of them, he told her rapidly. Like a beak into a wound.

"Mad as hell about something, everything — I can't get him simmered down." Hollow-eyed, Owen shook his head as if finally having met the impossible. "Maybe having it to hold over us will be enough for him. Maybe he'll never say anything." Rosellen watched him, feeling it begin to burn at her, as Owen finished: "Except to me. And I hope not to you."

"What's this 'Tell us, Jealous'?" Darius's mimicking voice rose in the truck cab. "Is there more where that's from? Because —"

"Because nothing. Forget I said anything." Rosellen gazed steadily across at him as if convincing herself of something. Then said: "I told you I'd make you a deal." She reached down and took her shoes and socks off. She began to unbutton her dress, turning toward him enough to make sure he could watch her at it. But before scooting over to the middle of the seat to finish undressing, she dropped her hand to the gearstick. "Better get this out of our way first." Stepping hard on the brake to keep the truck from moving at all, Rosellen pumped the clutch in with her other foot and moved the gearstick up into reverse, farthest away from the truck seat.

"Barefoot driving," Darius said of her quick exploit. "I am all admiration."

"Barefoot all over, next," Rosellen said, that saying of Proxy's making him blink in the darkness. Then he felt the drift of her fingers onto the buttonline of his shirt. "You, too," Rosellen stipulated.

Darius complied, he would have taken his clothes off at high noon in Picadilly for this.

All garments at last tucked up onto the back of the seat with his cap, the two of them made what position they could on the long narrow truck seat, and it began. *Never pass it up,* ran in Darius's mind, not that he ever had or intended to, especially now. The world was a goner, since the festering cowards' peace at Munich, and a man may as well lose himself in his favorite hiding place of pleasure while he could. These otter-smooth maneuvers of woman, white magic of their thighs and their moon-touched breasts, the hidden delta where the loins meet, this and then this and yes this —

"Wait." She wriggled, out from under and up onto her side, breathing openmouthed. "Let's . . . trade places."

Bare and bright-eyed, Rosellen moved partway over him, hands kneading the strategic hollows between his collarbones and the root of his throat. He couldn't help but wonder whether she was taking tips from Proxy, where else did she learn spice such as this? Rosellen was surprisingly instructive, what a bonus, coaxing him to lay his head back, kissing her way down him, *wait,* she said again, and he did, letting her shift around to where she wanted, murmuring something tersely to him about not wanting to bump into the steering wheel, until he could feel her finding a position over his lower thighs. His head turned a little, he could see up at the windshield which had grayed over, steamed up from their breath and body heat. Darius would have chuckled at that if his throat had not been too tight with wanting. He shut his eyes a moment, all the desires humming in his head, *Fiona, temporary Proxy, missed-chance Meg,* as he waited for this next.

Rosellen paused in midmotion there low on him. She had to slip behind the steering wheel, a bit sideways, for this. There was just room. She kept as much of herself applied to him as she could while her left leg angled down and her left foot just touched the clutch. This ending she had found in herself. Employ the eraser. On him, on the mess made of her own story and three others', on the way life was ambushing all hopes. *Over with.* Rosellen pushed her foot down on the clutch and palmed the gearstick knob to her, out of reverse, out of gear.

"Wh— ? We're going!" he let out, struggling to rise in the darkness.

Rosellen answered for everything with herself, flinging for all she was worth onto his neck, shoulders, any of him she could fight as he tried to get out from under, adding her weight and terrible determination as the truck tipping forward on the ramp started him sliding off the seat, Darius borne under her as the truck kept picking up momentum, coasting faithfully until it glided from the dam, into the gather of the water.

ACKNOWLEDGMENTS

Engineering News-Record for its coverage of the Fort Peck Dam project, 1933–39; the Fort Peck Lake Manager's Office for use of the basement files, with particular gratitude for the help of JoAnn Solem and Stacy Braaten; the Montana Historical Society and staff members Brian Shovers, Dave Walter, Marcella Sherfy, Bob Clark, Lorie Morrow and Becca Kohl, and particular kudos to the 1987 Fort Peck Dam oral history project and the oral historians who achieved fifty interviews in three days — Mary Murphy, Laurie Mercier, Rick Duncan and Diane Sands; my own interviewees of Fort Peck life and times, Harold and Edie Aus, Jerold B. Van Faasen, Mary Smith Krefi, Frank Henderson and Sylva Noel; Ron Haaland for showing me the works on the Missouri River ferry at Carter; the libraries of the University of Washington; Shoreline Community College Library; Special Collections of the Montana State University Library, and particularly Elaine Peterson, Kim Allen Scott and

Nathan Bender, for providing Montana Writers' Project files on Valley, McCone and Sheridan counties, and county extension agents' reports on alfalfa seed production; the Oasis Bordello Museum of Wallace, Idaho; Plentywood native Verlaine Stoner McDonald for use of her doctoral dissertation, "Red Waves of Grain: An Analysis of Radical Farm Movement Rhetoric in Montana, 1918–1937" (University of Southern California, 1994) and for advising me on Sheridan County politics of the 1930s; Myrtle Waller, for a courthouse-eye view of those same politics; Fred Quivik's "Historic American Buildings Survey" of the Fort Peck townsite, provided me by the Montana Historical Society; Vicki Goldberg's biography of photographer Margaret Bourke-White; M.R. Montgomery's memoir *Saying Goodbye* for his account of his father's years as a Fort Peck engineer; Mary Clearman Blew's *All But the Waltz* for her chapter on the Fort Peck experience of her uncle and aunt, Ervin and Sylva Noel; Robert V. Hine for his provocative characterization in *California's Utopian Colonies*, "a locomotive's machinery on a bicycle"; Jean Roden for springing to my aid in the American library network; Tom Moran for Internetting to the Mitchell Library in Glasgow, Scotland; Liz Babbitt for all her research

803

delving; Mark Damborg, Ann McCartney, Ann Nelson and Lee Rolfe for their keen-eyed manuscript reading; choker-setter and scholar William G. Robbins; Nancy Reeburgh for expert advice on riflery; Marshall J. Nelson for being Marshall J. Nelson one more time; Liz Darhansoff and Rebecca Saletan for bookmaking; Gary Luke; Zoë Kharpertian; Denise Roy; Janet Kreft; Marilou Parker; John Roden; Katharina Maloof; Gloria Swisher; Eric Nalder; Ben and Jeanne Baldwin; Dan Weidenbach; Jo Ann Hoven; Marcus Matovich; Merrill Burlingame; Joan C. Ullman; Louise Curtis Cline; William L. Lang; and Carol Doig for her photos of the Missouri River country from its Three Forks headwaters to the bridge south of Culbertson, and for her love and tolerance while I went away for three years into the 1930s.

3/11